DEATHBRINGER

*To my husband,
who believed in me long
before I believed in myself.*

The Ten Provinces of Draterra
Sea of the Gods
Sea of the Dead
Isles of Carac
The Rotting Sea
Osneau
Wanora
Aurignan
Holm
Imglen
The Dry Sea
Riverview
Old Iserine
The Narrows
Farbon Desert
Bale
Iserine
Gorhail
Albion
The Whispering Sea
House Arcane
House Death
House Poison
Gorhail Woods
Gorhail Institute of Magic
Gorhail Academy
Gorhail

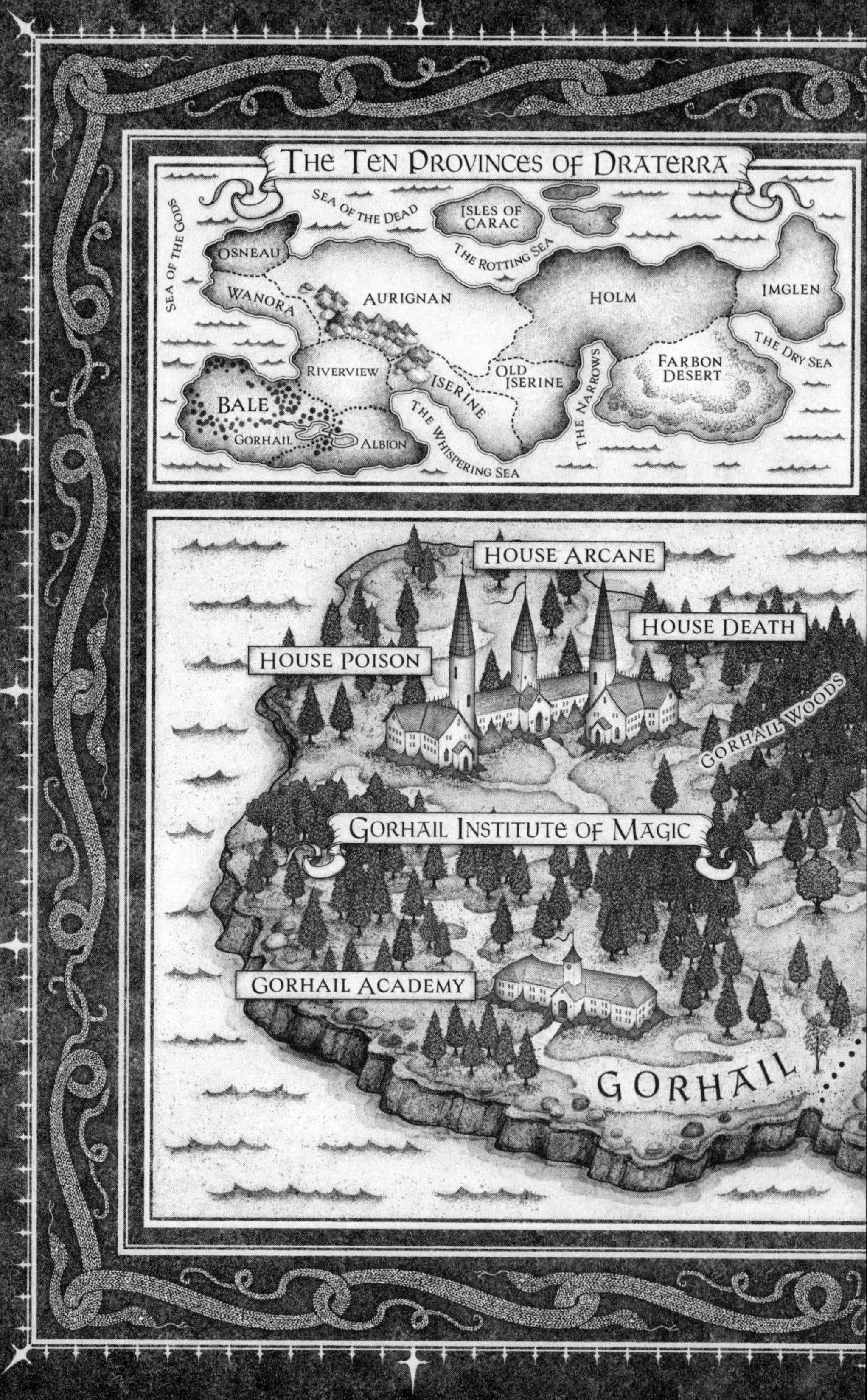

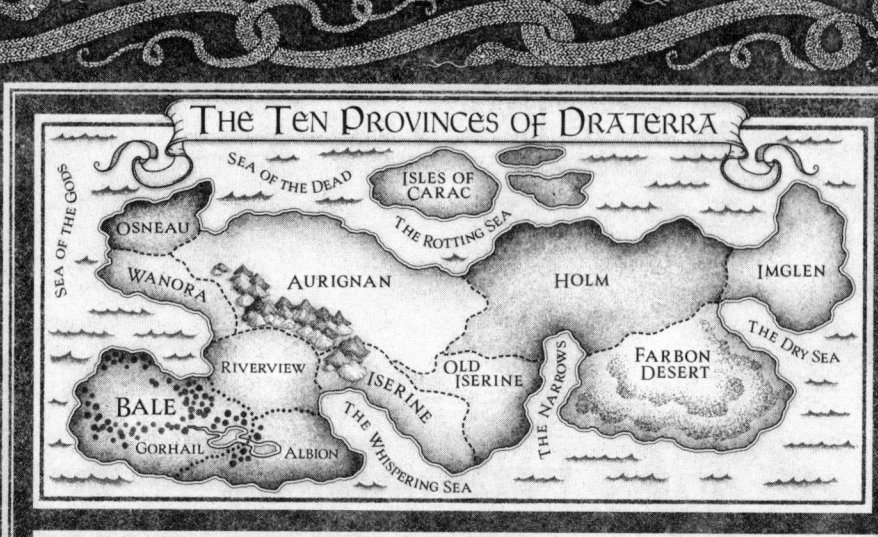

DEATHBRINGER

SONIA TAGLIARENI

London · New York · Amsterdam/Antwerp · Sydney/Melbourne · Toronto · New Delhi

First published in Great Britain by Solstice Books, an imprint of Simon & Schuster UK Ltd, 2026
First published in the United States by Atria Books, an imprint of Simon & Schuster, LLC, 2026

Copyright © Sonia Tagliareni, 2026

The right of Sonia Tagliareni to be identified as author
of this work has been asserted in accordance with the
Copyright, Designs and Patents Act, 1988.

1 3 5 7 9 10 8 6 4 2

Simon & Schuster UK Ltd
1st Floor
222 Gray's Inn Road
London WC1X 8HB

For more than 100 years, Simon & Schuster has championed authors and the stories they create. By respecting the copyright of an author's intellectual property, you enable Simon & Schuster and the author to continue publishing exceptional books for years to come. We thank you for supporting the author's copyright by purchasing an authorised edition of this book.

No amount of this book may be reproduced or stored in any format, nor may it be uploaded to any website, database, language-learning model, or other repository, retrieval, or artificial intelligence system without express permission. All rights reserved. Enquiries may be directed to Simon & Schuster, 222 Gray's Inn Road, London WC1X 8HB or RightsMailbox@simonandschuster.co.uk

Simon & Schuster Australia, Sydney
Simon & Schuster India, New Delhi

www.simonandschuster.co.uk
www.simonandschuster.com.au
www.simonandschuster.co.in

The authorised representative in the EEA is Simon & Schuster Netherlands BV, Herculesplein 96, 3584 AA Utrecht, Netherlands. info@simonandschuster.nl

Simon & Schuster strongly believes in freedom of expression and stands against censorship in all its forms. For more information, visit BooksBelong.com

A CIP catalogue record for this book
is available from the British Library

Hardback ISBN: 978-1-3985-4750-6
Trade Paperback ISBN: 978-1-3985-4752-0
eBook ISBN: 978-1-3985-4753-7
Audio ISBN: 978-1-3985-4754-4

This book is a work of fiction. Names, characters, places and incidents are either a product of the author's imagination or are used fictitiously. Any resemblance to actual people living or dead, events or locales is entirely coincidental.

Interior design Kyoko Watanabe
Cover design Micaela Alcaino
Map by Virginia Allyn

Printed and Bound in the UK using 100% Renewable Electricity
at CPI Group (UK) Ltd

HOUSES OF GORHAIL

House of Arcane
UNITY ABOVE CONQUEST

Mages: Arkani

Dustmaker
Illusionist
Manipulator
Reader

House of Poison
BOUND BY LOYALTY

Mages: Aspieri

Killer
Healer

House of Death
SACRIFICE AND SERVITUDE

Mages: Mortemagi

Whisperer
Conduit

RANKS OF GORHAIL

Magus
Study of inherited class of magic at Gorhail Academy

High Magus
Mastery of inherited class of magic at Gorhail Institute

Grand Magus
Mastery of two classes of magic at Gorhail Institute

Magus Principalis
Mastery of three classes of magic at Gorhail Institute

Note that further studies beyond a student's inherited class of magic is purely theoretical. Interclass research and collaboration are allowed only after earning the Grand Magus rank.

FOUNDERS OF GORHAIL

The First Founder—**Sileas Ronin**—Poison
The Second Founder—**Helna Azgar**—Illusion
The Third Founder—**Kali Telam**—Metal
The Fourth Founder—**Nel Penbryn**—Dust
The Fifth Founder—**Fabian Lussier**—Secrets
The Sixth Founder—**Ysenia Faro**—Death

Houses of Illusion, Metal, Dust, and Secrets merged into the House of Arcane in 1566

DEATHBRINGER

> **Mortemagi (n)**—Death magic practitioner.
> Death magic is intuitive, but it takes more than it gives.
> **YSENIA FARO, *DEATH MAGIC FOR BEGINNERS*, CHAPTER 1**

one | viola

MAY 2, 1927

I was ten the first time I touched a corpse.

Nan died in her sleep a day before her seventieth birthday. When I went to pay respects by her casket, she grabbed my wrist and whispered, *The last words of the dead are sacred. Speak them, and you'll meet your end.*

Of course I screamed. The softness of her hand, which used to stroke my hair as I fell asleep, was now a stiff palm with icicles that dug into my tender skin, and her mouth, which used to tell me stories, had doomed me with my worst nightmare: magic.

Mother pinched her lips, her reprimand only a breath away, but my younger sister, Olivia, clutched her throat with feigned disgust. "There's a roach in Nan's casket."

It didn't work.

Mother knew us too well, and she knew that at least one of us had inherited Nan's peculiar affinity for the dead. Later that evening, as we sat around a lukewarm casserole of macaroni and cheese, she asked Olivia and me if one of us had the *gift*. I stuffed my mouth with food. *Gift*. What a cruel way to describe the magic that killed our father and left her without a husband.

Olivia set her fork down and gave me a look that was halfway between "forgive me" and "don't stop me." Then she wore her brightest smile, held her head high, and said, "It's me. I have magic."

The moment I realized what she was doing, the half-chewed dough in my mouth became like glue. Years of late-night talks under the single ceiling light of our bedroom, telling Olivia how much I hated magic because it killed our father, culminated in this moment: my sister, the light of my life, was going to lift that burden off my shoulders. I didn't need to forgive her, and I was never going to stop her. It was selfish, but I would never lean into the magic that destroyed our family. Mother was a nonmagi; no one would question that magic passed to only one daughter.

At her declaration, Mother shot out of her chair, hand on her heart. She looked at Olivia like she had won a prize, made a fuss about how she was destined for greatness. "A mage in *my* family," Mother squealed, fawning over my sister.

It was no secret that Nan could see the dead. Rhea Corvi was revered around Albion. The townspeople often came to her to confirm their loved ones had moved on, and now that she was dead, they would come see . . . us. We'd probably inherited Father's magic after he passed, but Nan was the first dead body we witnessed. And if I could *hear* the dead, it probably meant Olivia could *see* Nan's ghost. Was this why she was fixating on me with furrowed brows, her throat bobbing every time Mother exclaimed she was a mage? Could she see Nan next to me?

But when my sister reached to hug our mother, the angry red skin around her fingernails brought me pause. She only picked at her fingers when she was lying. That's when I knew that Olivia didn't possess an ounce of magic.

"We're enrolling you at Gorhail Academy tomorrow. My beautiful girl is going to the most prestigious secondary school." Mother cupped Olivia's cheeks with tears streaming down her face. My sister's smile froze on her lips; her eyes wouldn't leave mine.

Gorhail Academy stood tall on the cliffs of Gorhail, the town west of Albion. Set in a separate building on the same premises, it was the younger arm of Gorhail Institute, a university where Nan had been the dean until her death. Both were magic schools, where mages traded their lives to further their magic. The academy taught the fundamentals, their curriculum overlapping much of what we learn in nonmagi schools. The institute was a different story; Nan used to say it forged the best and the worst of mages.

Lying about magic was one thing. Mother knew the basic rules of magical birthright. She wouldn't give up until one of us admitted we inherited Father's magic, and I was never going to. But willingly walking into a school of mages when she wasn't one was reckless. Surely Olivia would tell Mother that she was joking, that she didn't have any magic, that she wasn't going to break the promise we'd made when she'd turned five. I had held myself back a grade so we could start secondary school together next year. I didn't want us to be separated, didn't want to grow up without my sister.

"Don't leave me," I whispered as we lay in my bed that night, watching the Albion sky twinkle. She knew I would've followed her anywhere but there. She knew what magic meant to me. She knew what it did to our father.

Olivia reached for my hand, squeezed it, and promised, "I will never leave you, Vi."

Then she did.

MONDAY, NOVEMBER 15, 1939

Twelve years later, I know more than I care to about Gorhail Institute of Magic, the mages who go there, and the dangers lurking on the outside. I loathe it for taking away my sister, but if I'm honest, I'm jealous that she chose Gorhail over me.

The dead still talk to me in riddles that I spend too much time deciphering. Sometimes, their last words are as simple as a confession. Other times, they have me run errands across town. As I stand before this old lady's open casket in a stiff dining room, I know today's an errands day.

The dead woman's white hair is meticulously combed. Sapphires in her earrings, necklace, and ring tell me that this family is superstitious, probably devout followers of the God of Death. It's ironic to me that nonmagi uphold mage traditions when their spirits go to Orga—the afterlife for the nonmagical among us. It doesn't matter how much jewelry they bury with their dead. The God of Death will never let a nonmagi cross into the Underworld.

My hand hovers over hers. It reminds me of Nan's, frail and wrinkled from decades of years well lived. I don't know why I hesitate—maybe because this is a private viewing at someone's home or maybe seeing all the love poured into preparing her body for burial makes me feel like a predator. It would have been a different story had they sent her to Dearly Departed, the funeral home where I work; I would've felt less guilty about encroaching on a family's grief. But death magic cares little about privacy. It rings in my ears, demanding to be quelled—and I, an unwilling servant of Death, like my sanity intact.

Ten minutes have passed since I walked through this small house. Instead of hurrying, I am questioning my morals. The quiet chatter of mourners drones in the adjacent room; they're gathered around the kitchen island, most of them holding steaming cups of tea that they'll drink to honor the deceased, a typical funeral custom in Albion. I hope I'm not expected to join them after I pay my respects.

My pulse rises. I've been here too long.

Someone will question my presence, and I will have to leave without releasing my magic. But this woman deserves to have her last words heard, her final wishes fulfilled. And I suppose that's how I manage to live with this despicable magic: I tell myself I am helping.

Blowing out a breath, I close my fingers around her cold, stiff hand. The chill creeps along my arm and crawls around my throat until I stop breathing. Stop and listen, the magic always seems to say. The old lady's eyes open to cloudy white irises. I look at her dry, pale lips. They never move. Instead, a sweet, old, textured voice speaks, *Where the sun meets the moon, the cat sleeps.*

"Bloody saints," I mutter, pulling my hand away. Another ridiculous riddle, and if I don't solve it, the incessant ringing in my ear will erode every corner of my brain. My stomach growls; I skipped lunch to be here, and right now, I have very little regard for where the sun and the moon meet.

Behind me, gentle footsteps click on the floorboard. My breath catches into my breastbone. Leaving now would be suspicious. If they ask why I'm here, I'll tell them I've occasionally helped the lady with her garden. "The lady." I don't even know her name.

"Subtlety is still not your forte, I see," a musical voice whispers next to me. "This is the second time this year I find you at a random person's funeral."

My lungs relax. Olivia stands to my right, decked out in a light pink sweater and a long white pleated skirt. She looks like a pink peony against the somber room. Now they're *definitely* going to know we don't belong here.

"I don't work on weekends, and there were no new bodies this morning. I need to expel the magic somehow." I hook my arm through hers, hurrying us to the door before we run into the family. "You didn't tell me you were visiting today," I say. She usually visits twice a year, once during the Pine Festival and the second time during the Midsummer Festival, neither of which is today. When she was at the academy, I used to see her every month, but the institute heavily controls the movement of their mages, so my sister's visits have become my personal favorite holidays.

"Surprise." Her lips curve up in a mischievous smile. Then she nods at a picture of the dead woman on the wall in the sitting room. "A riddle, I imagine."

"How did you know?"

"You cursed." She lifts her eyebrows. "You never curse." She pauses, then asks, "What did she say?"

The last words of the dead are sacred. Speak them, and you'll meet your end. Nan's warning rings in my head, but I don't keep secrets from my sister. It's been twelve years, and I've shared the last words of the dead with Olivia more times than I can count. Sometimes, out of necessity; other times, to help me solve riddles. And we're both still alive. "Where the sun meets the moon, the cat sleeps," I whisper, my eyes darting to the three people glaring at us from the living room as we walk by.

We're almost to the entryway when a woman in her late fifties stops us. She looks like a younger version of the deceased. "Thank you for coming," she croaks. "How did you know my mother?"

"I..." I didn't.

Olivia lets go of my hand. In two steps, she's hugging the woman. "We are so sorry about your mother," she says. Then she quietly adds, "Where the sun meets the moon, the cat sleeps."

The woman's eyes widen as Olivia lets go of her. The pause between them gnaws at my insides. I bite my lips, waiting. This can go one of two ways—Albion's general sentiment around mages is either overt enthusiasm or downright fear. As much as I tell myself I don't care, it always hurts to see that flicker of terror across their eyes when they meet a mage. It may not be directed at me, but it crushes me all the same. I am not like the other mages, I always want to say. I try to use my magic to help. Still, I cannot blame their sentiment. I do not fear mages. I *hate* them.

"He's in the treehouse. My granddaughter's cat. Someone left the door open yesterday and Buttons ran out. We thought we'd never see him again." The woman's eyes brim with tears. She takes Olivia's hands between hers. "Thank you," she says. Of course she would be grateful; their family worships the God of Death. It's ironic, how much Olivia fits into a world that isn't her own; she carries magic with pride while I carry it as a burden.

"May Death light her way," Olivia whispers, and I give the woman a quick nod, my cheeks warm with the thought of a child reunited with her cat. I don't even notice the lull in my ears until Olivia and I walk out of the house.

"You're welcome," Olivia teases as we begin our fifteen-minute walk home. She enjoys everything that comes with being a mage, loves everything I despise. How wicked are the Gods? They gave magic to the wrong sister.

Our house sits at the end of a cul-de-sac, with Nan's rose garden spanning the front and back. After Nan died and Olivia left, tending to the roses became my only comfort. At first, they were dying, but over time, I've managed to grow thirty-three different varieties.

"Olivia," Mother calls out from the front porch. She runs down the wobbly wooden stairs, down the pathway, her dress brushing along the fresh blooms of a rare hybrid I've been nurturing for the last three years. The petals fall to the ground, and my breath hitches.

Mother pushes me aside, taking Olivia in her arms. "What a lovely surprise—I didn't think I'd see you so soon."

"Mama, I've missed you so." Olivia kisses her cheeks. "I wish I could stay longer, but I'm only here to get a book to study for my promotional exam this week."

"I can't believe you'll be promoted to High Magus soon," our mother says, holding Olivia's face. "I am so proud of you."

I share both her pride and her disbelief, albeit for different reasons. I don't need any reason to be proud of Olivia, but I cannot believe she's lasted four years at the institute without being caught. When she passes her promotional exam, she'll be the first nonmagi with a High Magus rank. More importantly, she'll finally be free to leave Gorhail. After earning my mastery in botany last November, I've been counting the days until her graduation.

Leaving me behind, Mother walks Olivia to the house, trampling over the pink petals from my roses. It's always disconcerting seeing them together. We may be sisters, but Olivia is a mirror of our mother. They both look like they belong here in Albion, with their green eyes, mildly tan skin, and dark brown hair. They even style it the same, loose curls falling mid-back. I share Nan's golden-brown skin, dark eyes, and black hair. With her gone, I feel like the roses, scattered on the ground, crushed by the boots of a woman who should have nurtured them.

When I walk through the front door, Mother is already pouring two cups of tea. I take off my shoes and dart across the kitchen, squeezing myself between the sideboard and the backs of the dining chairs, and make a beeline for the stairs. Early this morning, the mailman brought two letters bearing the golden seal of DOTS, the Department of the Supernatural, for Olivia.

"Viola, do you not care that your sister is home?" Mother asks quietly. The silent threat between her words dares me to take the first step up the stairs. For a split second, I consider it, but her sharp inhale pulls me back.

"Of course I do." My feet drag to the wooden kitchen table covered in a gaudy pumpkin-patterned tablecloth, where she placed two steaming cups of tea next to each other at the head of the table. I settle in the seat farthest from them, although it makes no difference because any room with my mother in it feels small. Even smaller when Olivia is here.

"How is work?" Olivia's eyes wince in apology. She slides her cup toward me even though I'm too far to reach it, but I shake my head. Mother's tea is as bitter as her tongue.

"Good," I reply. I know Olivia's trying to include me, but the less I say, the fewer opportunities Mother has to ridicule me.

"You've been at that funeral home for four years now." Mother takes a sip. There we go. "It's not a forever job."

"It pays." I sigh. "I'm saving for a postgrad botany program in Osneau."

"Osneau." She lifts a brow. If I didn't know better, I would think she was taking interest in my future. She crushes that thought immediately. "Pity you cannot join your sister. Gorhail takes care of all expenses."

"It's a pity indeed," I mutter.

After a tense silence, Olivia taps her watch and gets up. "Mama, I am so sorry, I don't have much time before curfew. I'll get my book while the tea cools. Vi, will you help me?"

She doesn't have to ask twice. I'm already out of my seat and climbing the stairs, grateful for any excuse to get out of there.

The attic door opens with a familiar creak that doubles as an alarm on the rare times Mother comes up here. Despite it being the middle of the day, the single round window toward the back of the room only lights up a few feet. I flip on the switch to the right of the entrance, and Nan's favorite old chandelier that she picked up from a local thrift store illuminates the room, giving life to the rows of books on the walls. It may be old and stuffy up here, but it wraps me with the same comfort as Nan's embrace.

After Olivia left for Gorhail, I spent most of my days reading the stories in Nan's journals, glossing over intricate drawings of skeletons straight out of a horror movie. I perused thousands of handwritten notes about Gorhail's Houses, classes, relics, and poachers who hunt mages that only strengthened my desire to stay away from that place. The only silver lining was helping my sister with her death magic homework when she was at the academy.

"They don't have wares like Nan's chandelier at Gorhail," she muses, studying the ceiling. "Sometimes, I miss the mundane."

Before I'm able to reply, she skips her way to the wall of dusty books in the far left of the room. I recently unpacked them from one of Nan's old crates and haven't gotten around to dusting them. I'd wanted to sell Nan's collection to the local bookshop to save for my move. Their fascination with mage history would see them spend a hefty sum on these ancient tomes.

"Did you know Gorhail still doesn't run on electricity?" she asks.

I have half a mind to veer the conversation back to her missing the mundane. It's a good sign that she does; it means she's ready to come home. But I know my sister. If I bring it up, she will avoid the discussion until she leaves.

"How many candles do they burn through in a year?" I join her, coughing as her pink sleeve turns brown from wiping the cover of a worn-out book. She frowns at it, then puts it back.

"You're funny," she deadpans. "They use lamps powered with magic dust," she says, her eyes slightly widening in wonder like they do every time she talks about Gorhail.

"That sounds innovative. Unnecessary, but innovative. Do they hate nonmagi so much that they created their own form of electricity?" I jest. She once told me about Gorhail's attempt to use more nonmagi technology, which was cut short when a fire broke out in one of their Magisters' offices. Perhaps it's best they keep to magic.

She laughs. "When I was at the academy, I remember learning that they were fed up with the constant power cuts."

I can't blame them. Albion has at least two power cuts a week, more when it rains.

Olivia reaches for a book on the top shelf, and her sweater catches on her armcuff. Muttering a curse, she unclasps it and slides the polished brass relic out of her sleeve. It looks nothing like the intricate one she wore the last time I saw her, one that looked identical to Nan's cuff.

"Is this a new cuff?"

"It is." My sister's eyes snap up at me, a devious grin playing on her lips. "A real one this time—my friend broke through the magic that prevented nonmagi from wearing relics. It does nothing for me, of course. Do you want to try it on?" She hands me her cuff, but I recoil.

"If you wore yours, you'd be able to speak to ghosts instead of only hearing the dead when you touch them." She feigns a shudder, then bursts into laughter.

"Not funny." I frown. I am terrified of ghosts, and I have no desire to explore this curse that flows through my veins. I'm glad she doesn't have to experience the harrowing sound in my ears if I don't use my magic for a while, or if I take too long to solve a riddle. "It's easy to jest when you don't have to carry the weight of the unfulfilled dead."

Her laugh falters, an uncomfortable yet familiar silence settling between us—whenever we talk about my magic or about Olivia leaving Gorhail.

"I asked my friend about the constant noise in a whisperer's ears. Wearing Nan's cuff will contain the magic so the ringing stops." She regards me with concern. "I fear it will only worsen as you age. Mages aren't supposed to be without their relics, Vi. At some point, the dead bodies won't be enough."

I shake my head. I'm *thriving* without the relic, and I refuse to let a piece of metal dictate my life. Once I'm up in Osneau, I will find a Sealer—exiled mages who can rid any person of their magic. And I'll finally be normal.

"And what did your friend say about nonmagi with fake relics?" I give her a pointed look, my lips tugging upward. I hope she follows my lead. "It's been twelve years, and they still haven't caught you. I'm impressed."

"Why the sudden suspicion?" She clips her cuff back on, then snorts. "Do you think the relic gave me magic overnight?"

I roll my eyes. Relics store magic. The older the relic, the more magic it stores. It doesn't grant magic, although for Olivia's sake, I wish it did. And if it did, I'd run to my room to retrieve Nan's cuff and give it to her.

She's so happy at Gorhail, so I hate myself for what I'm about to say.

"Two mages turned up dead at work last week." I hesitate. "Maybe it's time to come home."

The uncomfortable silence is back, but this time, I'm not letting up.

"Vi," she finally sighs, pushing in the book she was about to retrieve. "They both knew the risk of leaving school grounds after curfew. Even nonmagi know not to venture into Gorhail Woods after sundown, and they're not even the target of poachers."

"Please, Ole." I hold her gaze. The slight twitch in her bottom lip gives me hope, but then she breaks our stare and continues to peruse Nan's bookshelves, crushing my sliver of optimism. Still, I have to keep trying.

"Why did you go?" The last time I asked was during her first Midsummer break from the academy. She hadn't replied and had begun distancing herself from me, so I never asked again.

At first, I thought she would come home after the academy, but when she willingly enrolled at Gorhail Institute, I felt a betrayal so deep I didn't reply to any of her letters for a month. Then I saw how happy she was, how she spoke of her friends with so much love. I realized I was selfish to want her to come home. But that was then. Mages weren't turning up dead every other week.

Olivia clears her throat. She turns to me, her face solemn. "Do you think Gorhail would've believed that Rhea Corvi died without leaving a legacy? Father died before her, so it was only logical that her cuff was passed to one of us." She gives me a weak smile, and guilt knots my throat. She knew I didn't want to go; I spent years telling her how much I hated magic, how much I hated Gorhail. She went because of *me*.

Deep down, I had known the reason, but I needed Olivia to *tell* me.

"DOTS has relic trackers," she continues. "Every time a relicsmith crafts a relic, they make a tracker that tells DOTS whether the relic is dead, dormant, or alive. They would've broken into our house to find the famed Corvi relic." She breathes out, and her eyes twinkle with tears. All these years, she took my place so I wouldn't be somewhere I hated, so Gorhail would think they have eyes on Nan's cuff, so they would leave me alone. And I had the audacity to be angry when she chose to stay. Of course, she'd stay. Gorhail was all she'd known growing up, and I expected her to leave that comfort and reassimilate into a world she was no longer a part of.

I pull my sister into a tight hug, and she wraps her arms around me, occasionally patting me on the back. It's all I can muster to thank her for saving me years of a life I didn't want. My beautiful sister was only nine then and so clever. But now, it's my turn to save her.

Too soon, she begins to pull away. "I love you, too, Vi, but I have to hurry. You don't want me to end up like those mages who missed curfew, do you?"

"Olivia," I exclaim, stepping back. "Don't joke about that."

Olivia bites her laugh and goes back to looking for her book. Her fingers land on an old leatherbound tome. The spine is a stunning weave of red, blue, and silver. It's one of the books I shelved last week. Olivia grabs it, wipes off the front, and smiles with satisfaction.

"I've been accepted to Osneau's Postgraduate School of Botany," I blurt out, and her eyebrows shoot up. She *has to* leave Gorhail with me. I will make sure of it.

"Vi," Olivia exclaims. "That's incredible. They only take fifty students a year."

I nod, looking down. "Come with me to Osneau. I'll wait until your promotional exam is over. I— I saved enough for a place." I haven't. In fact, I will have to use the tuition money I saved to afford a room for the two of us, but I would give up on my dreams if it meant that I could keep my sister safe.

"Viola—" It's never a good thing when she uses my full name.

"Think about it," I implore. "Plenty of mages stop at High Magus. You don't need to sink four more years into Gorhail for Grand Magus. And it'll become harder and harder to hide. The other classes of magic aren't as theoretical as death magic."

"I . . ." She hesitates. "I've built a life there, Vi. I have friends and people I care so much about. Leaving would be selfish."

Don't you care about me, I want to scream. *Is it selfish to want to keep you safe?* Maybe she's blinded by the glamours of the magic world. "You've been gone over a decade, Ole. I want my sister back. I *need* you back. Please."

Her eyes soften, and she sucks in her lips. We fall back into our usual discomfort around this subject, and the growing silence between us dashes any hope for an answer. With a long sigh, she leads me to the door, and I follow her down the stairs.

We reach the kitchen, and Mother pushes herself out of her chair with a screech that makes me want to claw my ears out. "Don't drink too fast." She rubs Olivia's back as she chugs the tea.

"Sorry, Mama, I have to run. Thanks for the tea."

"Ole," I stop her. "Letters from DOTS came in the mail this morning. They're in my room. Should I get them?"

She shakes her head while carefully placing the book in her canvas bag. "I'll grab them when I come back after my promotional exam." She pauses, then looks at Mother. "Mama, my exam is on Friday. Then some friends and I are going on a trip to Wanora over the weekend."

"Oh," Mother utters, hiding her disappointment with a grimace of a smile. "Perhaps I could join you toward the end of the trip and we can spend some time at the beach?"

Olivia hugs Mother tight. "I would love that. See you next Monday at the Salt Rock Inn? Join us if you're free, Vi."

Mother's nose is already flaring, her ears red as a tomato. "Sure," I reply, "I'll take the week off and we can travel up the coast to Osneau."

As she's about to walk out, she turns to me with a sigh. Then I hear them: the words that will haunt me forever. Olivia's voice, small, tender, and full of promise. "Let's talk on Monday."

> **Aspier (n)**—Poison magic relic. Snakelike.
> Aspiers are the only living relics.
> All magic comes at a cost except poison magic.
> It's a privilege to belong to the House of the Chosen.
>
> *JOURNAL OF SILEAS RONIN*, **THE FIRST FOUNDER**

two | sylas

TUESDAY, NOVEMBER 16, 1939

I do not fear death. Not when it stares me in the face, not when it draws its blade, and not when it plunges straight into my heart. I do not fear death because I cannot die.

"Your recklessness will cost us one of these days," Gryff snaps as he pulls his dagger from the poacher's neck. The same poacher who, moments ago, stabbed me with glee. My best friend wipes his blade on his black combat trousers, sighing at the man's dead body. This morning's Firstline recruitment trial in Gorhail Woods ended face-to-face with the worst kind of poacher, one who kills mages for our relics.

"If you fail recruitment . . ." Gryff lowers his voice so the other two Firstline hopefuls don't hear. We've all traded our free time for Secondline uniforms, toiling every weekend and university holiday on patrol units around Gorhail Woods, training to become *worthy* Firstline field agents, so the idea of any of us failing recruitment is sickening.

This year, Firstline—DOTS's law enforcement division—insisted on setting their biannual recruitment trial right outside of Gorhail Institute. Usually, potential recruits are sent directly to the field, without a care about whether they make it back alive or dead. With registration at an all-time low for the second year in a row, suddenly, we—Secondliners—have gone from disposable to valuable.

"I'm not worried. Firstline won't pass up a healing aspier who doesn't need recovery." I gesture to my left forearm, where Railesza's fangs are still in my veins. Her emerald scales glisten under the shy glow of the sun behind the pillow of clouds.

"You may be immortal, but the rest of us aren't." Gryff's voice pulls me back to the poacher at our feet, whose blood is staining the pristine, fresh snow crimson. Scum. I would've kicked his body if the recruitment officer wasn't hovering around.

"It was not by choice," I snap, clawing at the golden aspier around my neck. Another futile attempt.

Overseer Paltro, our acting recruitment officer, looks at me like I've suddenly grown three heads. His graying hair, sunken eyes, and wrinkled skin make him look like the human version of a gargoyle.

"Mr. Archyr, it is the greatest honor to wield the Imortalis." He swats my hand away from my neck. "Don't throw away your father's sacrifice."

Ah, there it is. The constant reminder that I am the reason my father is dead. That I should be thankful to inherit these relics that were never supposed to be mine.

The golden aspier, the Imortalis—or, simply, Raiek—sits cold against my skin. To nonmagi, he looks like a necklace of woven gold. To everyone else, he earns wide eyes and silent gasps. Raiek once belonged to the founder of the House of Poison, my ancestor and namesake, Sileas Ronin. Together with Faro's Cuff from the House of Death, and the Arkani Coin from the House of Arcane, it completes the Founders' Trinity—the three relics of immortality used to build Gorhail. Now, two of them are locked up in Gorhail's vaults and one chokes me with responsibility that I do not want.

My mother used to wear the Imortalis. Right before she died, she gave him to my father. Over two decades later, as I watched a poacher kill Dad, both Raiek and Railesza—his own healing aspier—passed to me.

As if she can hear my thoughts, Railesza unhooks her fangs and gives me a sad look before coiling around my left forearm. She and Raiek are permanent reminders of the parents I no longer have. Then my own relic warms against my right wrist, to tell me that he is here, and we have each other, like we've had since I was five. A year after Mom died, Dad brought him to me. A small, black killer aspier I named Raiku because I saw the name scribbled in one of her notebooks.

Aspieri aren't supposed to have more than one relic. DOTS—the Department of the Supernatural—advises us to lock our heirloom aspiers in our family vaults in case our own aspiers are stolen or killed by poachers. Most Aspieri abide by the advice, although a few bolder ones wield multiples. Often, they're the ones poachers track and kill. But Raiek cannot be taken off, and I don't have the heart to part from Railesza. She lost Dad, too.

"Why is everyone acting like I wanted to be immortal?" I shift my glare from Gryff to Paltro.

"I didn't mean . . ." Paltro places a hand on my shoulder. "The Imortalis chose you, Sylas. Like it did your father before you, and your mother before him."

Chose. What a funny word. If Raiek had to choose, he would've let me die, I'm certain. "It doesn't matter what you meant. They're both dead." I look at Gryff, hoping he'll get me out of this conversation. My father was Paltro's second on the field for decades; he was to Dad what Gryff is to me, a shadow, a confidant, a sworn ally. Sometimes, I forget that Paltro took the job as head of the House of Poison only because Dad entrusted my siblings and me to his guardianship. He didn't have to abandon his position as Chief of Firstline, but he did. For us. And now, my ingratitude nooses around my neck.

Paltro considers me for a moment. Then he sighs, and ushers the four of us toward the northern entrance. The silhouette of Gorhail Institute rises above the fog—three black spires, evenly spaced, for each of the three Houses: the tallest one for the House of Poison; the middle one, with four smaller spires around the roof, signifying the merging of four disciplines to form the House of Arcane; and finally, the ugliest of the three, a partially rusted turret that looks like the House it represents, the House of Death.

"What's that?" I ask, my eyes trailing uphill. Not far from the northern gates of Gorhail, a thick brown covering drapes over a mound of snow that wasn't there when we left this morning. I lower my arm, and Railesza slithers off first. We trudge behind her, steps cautious, daggers out. For all we know, this could be a poacher's trap. Unlikely, given the proximity to Gorhail, but caution is never excessive with poachers.

"Halt," Paltro orders. He kneels, pulling the covering up.

A body lies in front of him. Underneath, the snow is brown. Gods, did poachers do this?

Next to me, the shorter Firstline hopeful gags. If I were him, I'd have held it until after Paltro left. "Dismissed. Retrials in six months," Paltro says without looking at him.

"You can't—" the second one protests. Paltro stops her with a hand, his eyes still locked on the body. "Dismissed. Retrials in a year. Anyone else?"

The two Aspieri walk away with muttered curses. Bold. Even I wouldn't dare curse in the vicinity of Paltro. Under normal circumstances, he would've demoted them by one rank, but he is too preoccupied. "Approach," he tells Gryff and me, and we do.

A young man, a year above me, stares into nothingness. I recognize him. Victor Carver, a Grand Magus, from the House of Arcane. We've trained with him on the field before and even shared a few patrol rounds last year, then he abruptly left Secondline. He was brilliant, albeit sometimes distracted. But he wasn't careless.

"Poachers. An unfortunate incident," Paltro says. "How would you proceed from here?"

"Take the body to Gorhail," Gryff replies methodically. "Call in the report to Firstline, and send a unit from Secondline to investigate."

I don't answer. The corpse of a Grand Magus lies cold in the snow, two steps from Gorhail, and Paltro chooses to use it as a teaching moment? He didn't even check for a pulse.

"Archyr?" Paltro looks at me.

I gulp. "I . . . uh . . ."

Paltro's shoulders fall. He gently covers the body back up, then rises to his feet, facing Gryff and me. "Darro, you've been an asset to Secondline for the last four years. It has been an honor watching you evolve as a patrol leader. Congratulations, you've been drafted to Firstline with my highest recommendation as field leader." Paltro pats him on the shoulder. "Report to DOTS by noon."

A dead mage is at our feet, and Paltro's assigning promotions. Does he not care because Victor's from a different House? I don't know him to be this . . . cold, like the rest of our institution, thinking of mages as disposable, their deaths inconsequential.

Paltro adjusts his silver, round glasses and clears his throat. "Archyr, like

Darro, you've served as an excellent patrol leader. You are undoubtedly your mother's son. Brilliant and resourceful, but also reckless, stubborn, overconfident, and far too emotional. While these qualities served her as the Deathbringer's second, Darro has better to do than to babysit you on duty."

"I don't need babysitting." I frown. "A mage was killed, Uncle—"

He raises his eyebrows. A mage was killed; there's nothing I can do other than follow protocol. If I want my place on Firstline, I cannot question leadership. "It won't happen again." I lower my head.

"And yet, it has been *happening again* for four months, since your father's death." Paltro scribbles on his notepad. I stare at him with bated breath. He can't be considering dismissal.

"Overseer—" Gryff interjects, but Paltro raises his palm. I realize that he's already made his decision, even before we set foot in Gorhail Woods this morning. This is ludicrous; I belong in Firstline.

"On the other hand," Paltro begins. "Railesza is a necessary addition to Firstline, especially with poacher activity increasing in all Ten Provinces . . ." He glances at Victor's body. "And mages turning up dead right outside of Gorhail's walls."

At the mention of her name, Railesza takes a weary look at Paltro and then slithers back to my arm and coils herself to sleep.

"Uncle, Dad wanted me to join Firstline . . . to follow in his footsteps," I try, hoping the mention of my father sways him. He knows I've been itching to track down and kill the poachers who stole him away from us. That he doesn't want to do the same angers me. If poachers murdered Gryff, I wouldn't rest a day until I bled them dry.

Paltro hums, giving me one final nod. "Retrials in six months. Dismissed."

Retrials? I am the best Aspieri in Secondline, after Gryff. They *need* me. They *need* Railesza. He knows what this means to me. How could he do this?

"Leave the body untouched, and not a mention of this to anyone. We don't need Aspieri associated with the death of an Arkani." His loose black coat billows in the wind as he walks across to the gates of Gorhail, his boots crushing away my life's purpose.

This isn't how I thought my Tuesday would go. A dead mage at our doorstep, Paltro shrugging it off as a random poacher kill, and my failing recruitment.

I crouch next to Victor's body, lifting the brown coat that covers him. His wounds are long, deep cuts that run across his chest. They look more like the work of an animal than a poacher's dagger. As I notice the distinct claw marks at the base of his neck, a chill runs down my arms. Not an animal. A Mortemagi versed in blood magic. The covering makes sense now—only they go out of their way to cover the dead, as if this modicum of respect absolves them of being cold-blooded murderers.

"Sy," Gryff says. "Don't touch the body."

I glower up at him. "Victor Carver was a stellar illusionist. This doesn't make sense."

Grand Magus Carver was one of the youngest mages about to acquire his last rank—Magus Principalis—from the House of Poison. With his Secondline training and extensive knowledge of death magic, he should have known how to fight a Mortemagi poacher.

"Firstline will investigate." Gryff gestures to the gate. "Let's go."

What Firstline will do is toss his body to the nearest morgue and write off his death as an accident. That's what they did to Dad. They didn't care to investigate how the poachers knew where we would be. Didn't care about his decades of service as one of their best investigators.

"You are such a stickler for the rules. This administration wouldn't even think twice before executing you," I mutter, but as soon as the words leave my mouth, I regret them.

My eyes lower to Freya, his teal aspier, slithering around his hand, a flash of silver catching the light of the sun. Everyone thinks it's endearing that he gave his aspier a necklace; it's common for Aspieri from the province of Wanora, Gryff's birthplace. No one sees it for what it is—a curled manipulator Arkani relic. No one would question it either. Aspieri crossmages are rare because aspiers are notorious for rejecting secondary relics.

"I have to be, Sylas." He kicks the fresh snow.

"I know . . ." I trail. "Sorry, I . . ." I'm apologizing for more than my statement. By failing recruitment, I let him down.

"Who will cover for me on the field?" His voice breaks. I already know where this is going. We were supposed to join Firstline together. Him as a field leader, and me as his second. "If they find out I'm a crossmage, you know they'll take Freya and seal my Arkani magic. That's only if they're lenient."

Crossmages are shunned in most magical communities, supposedly because of the dangers of practicing more than one class of magic. But we all know the real reason. Purists make the rules, and anything that veers away from the ordinary needs to be controlled. DOTS's anti-crossmage laws began soon after Gorhail was founded in the 1500s because of Rafael Grimm, a Mortemagi and Arkani crossmage they couldn't control. Because of that one dangerous rogue, they punish generations and generations of crossmages for something they cannot change about themselves. As always, Mortemagi are at the source of every problem.

"You don't think of anyone but yourself." He holds my stare for a second, then walks away. "People like me . . . we don't have a choice, Sylas. Our only hope is to join the ranks to try to change the system from within."

With one last look at Victor, I fall into step with him, mumbling another quiet apology, but it's useless. I let us *both* down. My recklessness on patrol is only possible because of the steadiness of Gryff's dagger. And now, I'm leaving him alone, where DOTS risks finding out he's a crossmage.

A rush of ice-cold air cuts my face as we march through the gates and uphill toward the institute. Our combat jackets aren't nearly warm enough for the harsh winters of this town.

The black spires of the House of Poison welcome us into their shadows, towering over the rest of Gorhail. An intentional design, I'm sure, given that our House is the reason this institute even stands. We deserve no less; Aspieri are the only ones with living relics. We make up the majority of Firstliners, the law enforcement officials who keep the Ten Provinces safe from poachers and magical criminals, and we bring in the most research funds to Gorhail. However, I will never understand who put forth the idea that we only thrive in darkness. We enjoy the sun just as much as the House of Arcane and their three solariums.

We walk the length of a sheltered stone hallway, grateful for the brief reprieve from the slight drizzle of rain, and step onto the wet grass outside of Overseer Paltro's office, a tiny wooden house with a chimney to the left of a statue. Our footsteps are loud against the silence between us.

"Youngest field leader is a fine title. Do you think it'll fit on your uniform?" My poor attempt to lighten the mood earns a grunt. This is the first time in nineteen years that we'll be separated. A knot forms in my stomach. Our paths have always been predictable, a constant in my life despite all the chaos. I would be lying if I said it didn't scare me a little. He finally shakes his head. "Second to the Deathbringer."

The Deathbringer was a legendary Aspieri. Mom used to tell us stories of when she worked alongside her in Firstline. She dismantled several poacher camps, brought some of the most dangerous criminals in, and she was the reason poachers were afraid to set foot in the province of Bale. Now that she's gone, they've been back with a vengeance.

"The Deathbringer has been missing for twenty-three years. I doubt she'll come back for her title."

Gryff snorts, "If you ask Lyria, she'll tell you that even missing, the Deathbringer's legacy shadows us all."

At the mention of my younger sister, my smile falters. "Don't tell Lyria about my dismissal," I warn quietly, pushing open the oak doors of the great hall of the House of Poison, Fang's Nest.

"Congratulations!" A small voice carries over from the fireplace. Hunched over a notebook and a scatter of books, pens, and paper, Lyria doesn't spare us a glance as she scratches something off her notes. Instead of sitting on any of the three sofas around her, she is on the floor, her bag spilling half its contents next to her legs.

"Do you have something against chairs?" I jest.

"I think better on the—" She lifts her head at us. "Haal, why do you look like death?"

I give Gryff a pointed look and settle in the armchair next to Lyria. The great hall is quiet at this time of day. A few Aspieri gather for tea on the deep green sofas in the middle of the hall. Fang's Nest is designed like a flower, with coffee tables and plush velvet chairs in the center, doubling as our dining room in the morning, surrounded by different lounge sections. Lyria is by the fireplace so often that they should consider adding a plaque with her name on the mantel.

"Did you fail recruitment?" Lyria's face falls as she looks between me and Gryff.

"No." Gryff answers with a grimace.

My sister's head snaps toward me. She clutches her heart, feigning outrage. "Sylas Archyr, you're a disgrace to our name," she says, unable to contain her smile. If it were up to Lyria, Gryff and I would've remained at Gorhail as long as she was there.

But instead of laughing at her quip, I wince. I *am* a disgrace to everyone.

Gryff's farewell was filled with tears—mostly Lyria's, who made him promise to write to her every week. She spent the whole rest of the morning lamenting about how far away DOTS stationed him. In the afternoon, as I'm trying to find peace in a cup of tea in the middle of Fang's Nest, the laments continue.

"Couldn't they have stationed him in Gorhail Woods?" Lyria sets her fork next to her untouched eggs.

"Secondline oversees Gorhail Woods, Lyr." I sigh into my cup, but she already knows that. *Maybe you should consider telling Gryff how you feel about him* is what I really want to tell her. They both insist they are friends, yet they've *both* been acting like the other is going to war, never to be seen again.

"He's *one* town over," I deadpan. Gryff is stationed at DOTS headquarters in Riverview, only a half hour drive away. For reasons that do not concern me, my sister acts like they sent him across the country.

"Aren't you late for class?" I ask. With Paltro dismissing me, I had to sign up for a few Grand Magus classes at the House of Arcane. Given that the ranks of Grand Magus and Magus Principalis do not have time off, I am looking at six excruciating months of back-to-back classes.

"I'm a Grand Magus, Sylas. I—" She sets down a stack of paper, and the nauseating royal-blue crest of the House of Death assaults me.

"Why do you have Death's letterhead?" I interrupt her.

Lyria purses her lips, looking toward the lunch buffet behind me. Then she takes a deep breath. "Beau and I have requested to continue Mom's lifedrain research at the House of Death."

I stare at her blankly. Mom's lifedrain theory is an extension of Grimm's own theory, where he discovered how to transfer lifeblood—years of a mage's life—from one mage to another. Of course, our mother's research was not this sinister; she was trying to help Mortemagi heal instead of draining their years for blood magic. And they rewarded her by killing her.

Why would my siblings willingly go to the House of the Forsaken? Nothing good comes out of that place, only manipulation, murder, and betrayal. Their history is rooted in bloodshed; their mages rooted in death. Literally.

"Why?" My shoulders stiffen. "That wretched House killed Mom."

"One bad Mortemagi, Sylas." Lyria draws her notebook from her bag and shoves it under my nose, and all I can make out are sketches of dead flowers, aspiers, living flowers, and a series of complex equations that fly over my head.

"I think Beau and I solved her theory," she exclaims, eyes wide. She looks so much like our mother. She has the same long black hair, the same big brown eyes that sparkle every time she gets excited, the same tawny-brown skin, the same button nose, but her smile is Dad's. Mine is Mom's.

Memories of us all together flood my mind. My chest tightens, and I inhale, tucking away my grief as I've done the past four months. It's not coming out today, not in front of Lyria. I slip my mask on, looking straight at her. How could she even consider this? "Mom was killed in the middle of her research, the same research you and Beau want to pursue."

"Sylas . . ." Lyria hesitates for a moment. "I'm going to finish what she started." She raises her chin. Gods, she looks so much like Mom, my chest aches. "I owe it to her."

My sister is the model student Overseer Paltro dreams about every time he sees me. Gorhail's golden child, only twenty-two and already a Grand Magus. I'm sure everyone curses the rule of heirloom relics passing onto the firstborn child. I don't deserve the Imortalis or Railesza.

"House of Death." I fake a shudder. "They drag their feet around like the wraiths they bargain with." The House of Death is notorious for rejecting Aspieri applications, and the House of Poison returns the favor. This is why there are so few Aspieri or Mortemagi Magus Principalis; the animosity between Houses prevents mages from earning their last rank. One can only hope they will reject both my siblings out of spite.

Lyria glares at me. "Whisperers are the only ones who bargain with ghosts. The rest are just like you and me."

"Until they kill you," I reply, and she rolls her eyes. But I am not letting this go. "If you don't want me to lobby Paltro to deny your application, help me take Raiek off."

A sore subject with my sister. Now she'll understand how I feel about her walking into a death trap.

"The Imortalis cannot be taken, only given in a time of need," she recites from one of our textbooks. "Absolutely not."

"Lyr—" I start, but her glare pins my lips shut.

"You know, I'm the only one who could bypass the magic because we share the same blood." She places her notebook in her backpack, pushes her plate aside, and folds her arms on the table. "But I'm not an idiot, Sy. The second Raiek is off, you're going to do something stupid and get yourself killed. Gryff told me about your recklessness on duty since Dad's death. You can't let your unfounded guilt dictate your will to live."

Is friendship no longer sacred? Besides, what was I thinking bringing this up again, when she's already refused twice?

Lyria meets my eyes with tears, and the hairline crack in my heart grows bigger. "You're all Beau and I have left," she mumbles.

I reach over the table and gather her small hands in mine. "I'm sorry, Lyr. I shouldn't . . . I *don't* want you and Beau to study at the House of Death."

But it's too late. My apologies mean nothing now. I shouldn't have gone there. "Dad saved you because he wanted you to live, Sy." A tear rolls down her cheek. I stare at it, contemplating my selfishness. "Don't leave us, too."

I squeeze her hands and promise her I won't go anywhere. But inside me, a fight is brewing. How do I live with the guilt that my father died because of me? How do I tell Lyria that if it weren't for my brazen foolishness, Dad would still be alive? For that alone, I deserve the worst fate. Perhaps one day, she will understand.

"Sylas, why are you always making our sister cry?" Beau sighs as he walks toward us and sets a stack of books on the plush chair between Lyria and me. A few months after Mom died, Dad adopted Beau after his own parents were killed on assignment. We grew up together, and in more ways than one, he was everything Lyria and I needed after losing our mother.

"The House of Death hates us." I cut to the chase. I refuse to let either of them suffer the same fate as Mom.

"They are misunderstood." Beau shakes his head. Of course he'd agree with Lyria. They are like twins—they're the same age, and they do everything together. "It's been a while since they've done anything out of line."

A while? Has the House of Death poisoned their minds? I frown. "Do you forget that Mortemagi are the reason poachers even exist?"

Four hundred years ago, Rafael Grimm started a cult of mages without limits. He openly defied the founders' principles of using magic only for communal progress. He taught his followers forbidden lifeblood magic, and when he died, his legacy lived on through the criminals he trained. And because they'd never be able to go to a relicsmith for new relics, they became poachers—harvesting dead relics so they can be reforged into ones they can use.

"And you"—I turn to Lyria—"Gryff's right to practice magic is constantly threatened *because* of them."

Lyria looks at Beau, chewing her lips. She always does this when I remind her of the harm Mortemagi have caused everyone.

"Even Gryff doesn't hate them, though." Beau speaks in her place. "Does your prejudice toward Mortemagi make you forget that there *are* Arkani poachers and maybe even Aspieri ones?"

Before I can answer, Fang's Nest's massive front doors slam open, shaking the ground. Every mage present looks up, their aspiers' heads turned toward the entrance as Overseer Paltro storms in. The last time we had this much commotion was only ten days ago when two Year Eights died near Albion Creek. Gryff and I were a part of the Secondline unit who investigated their deaths, and we ruled it as yet another poacher attack.

Paltro strides straight toward us and pauses in front of my brother. His eyes are as sharp as his killer aspier's. Both are locked on Beau. "Is there any reason your aspier's venom would be in Victor Carver's blood?"

I slowly get up, and my sister does, too. We exchange a brief glance, both confused. Paltro's making a mistake. Why would Silver's venom be in Victor Carver's blood? From the claw marks, it was clear a rogue Mortemagi killed him. Beau stares at Paltro, face as pale as a ghost. For a moment, I fear that my brother has died from our guardian's question.

Lyria slips her cold hands through mine. "Who died?"

Paltro's frown shifts to her. "Victor Carver from the House of Arcane was killed. We found Silver's venom in his blood."

"How?" Lyria gasps, but no one answers her.

"Beau didn't even know Victor," I argue, before Beau has a chance to respond. "You saw the claw marks, Uncle. Aspieri don't have claws . . ."

Why isn't Paltro questioning that Mortemagi who'd latched on to Victor recently? Every time I saw them together, he seemed desperate to get away from her.

"I—" Beau chews his bottom lip, and my stomach drops. Haal, what isn't he telling us?

"What were you thinking?" Paltro raises his voice. "Unless you have a credible alibi, you'll be sentenced to death without trial."

Beau gulps, taking in slow, labored breaths. "I didn't kill him," he chokes as he turns to Lyria and me. "I didn't, Sylas, you have to believe me. I didn't."

Of course I believe him.

"Uncle—" I don't finish my thought, because the room darkens, a heaviness settling among us. All the air has been sucked from it along with any modicum of happiness. Even the aspiers coil into submission.

I don't need to look to know who it is. Magus Principalis Matilda Rhodes, the dean of Gorhail, stands by the oak doors, casting a shadow over Fang's Nest. She is impossibly tall; her black hair sticks to her skull like a second skin. Her lips are as red as her dress, and she glides toward us like an octopus. In my six years at Gorhail Institute, she's never set foot in the House of Poison. The dean doesn't leave her den often, and when she does, she's out for blood.

"Mr. Cardot, my office, immediately," she hisses.

> Mortemagi are divided in two subclasses: whisperers and conduits.
> Conduits can see ghosts but cannot hear them.
> Whisperers can hear ghosts but cannot see them.
>
> **DAVIN GAREY**, *A SHORT STORY OF THE HOUSE OF DEATH*, CHAPTER 3

three | viola

TUESDAY, NOVEMBER 16, 1939

The funeral home is always quiet on Tuesday mornings. The familiar earthy musk of the place is muddled with the lingering scent of roses, lilies, and carnations from one of last week's funerals. All the decorative art is gone, and the old brass candleholders along the walls are empty again. Without them, the main room is barren of any personality—at least when we host funerals and memorials, the place comes . . . alive.

Mara, the mortician, isn't here yet. For the last four years, I've been stealing these brief moments of solitude to visit the departed. Mara thinks my interest in the dead is bizarre at this age, but she's never questioned me. Instead, she welcomed me with a job and the longest friendship I've had in Albion.

I slip my key in the front door, and it opens with a soft click. After dropping my bag behind the empty front desk, I pick up the broom and head to the cold room. No new bodies—great. I still have a few more hours before the ringing in my ears starts, a few more hours to hope for someone's death. Do I hear myself? This magic is abhorrent. Maybe Olivia is right. I *should* wear the cuff so I can stop chasing after the dead. But that would mean trading my momentary peace for an open line with ghosts, and I'll never be ready for that. Despite what Mother says, this is the perfect job: I'm helping people while saving enough money for Olivia and me to leave.

The front door clicks open, and I scurry out, leaving the sterile metal lockers of the cold room for the warmth of the wooden preparation room. My job is to make sure the right papers are filed and the right calls are placed, and occasionally, Mara will let me help prepare the dead for burial. When I get in earlier than her, I sweep the floors—always the best excuse should she catch me somewhere I'm not supposed to be.

"You're here early." Mara pokes her head through the door, her curly brown hair bouncing on her shoulders. Even in the dim light of the preparation room, I can see that she's tired. "Viola, I've told you many times before. You don't *have* to sweep the floors."

"When I leave, you'll miss my sweeping." I bite down a smile as I set the broom against the wall and walk toward her. Sometimes, it's hard to remember that she's the funeral director of Dearly Departed, the only funeral home in the province of Bale. She acts less like a boss and more like a mentor to everyone who's worked here.

"I will miss you." She sighs, then leads us to the front desk. Now that we're in front of the tall windows of the main room, I can see exactly how exhausted she looks. Dark circles line her eyes, and her shoulders sag as she reaches for her bag next to mine.

"You look tired," I note. I want to tell her to take the day off to rest, but I don't want to overstep. We may be friends, but I still work for her.

"Exhausting night." She half smiles, pulling a wrapped sandwich from her bag. "Join me by the lake?"

"We can't leave the place unattended." I protest, but I'm already following her with my own breakfast. No one would rob a funeral home.

Mara and I met four years ago at the local bakery. She overheard when the baker sent me away as I was looking for a job and offered me a position as her administrative assistant. Thanks to her, I managed to save enough to move to Osneau, albeit with a slight change of plan now that I'm taking Olivia with me.

"When do you leave?" Mara asks.

"After my sister's promotional exam, so in about a week." I settle next to her on the cold bench and look out at the water as I peel my sandwich wrapper. Out here, the trees sway with the breeze, carrying some of their dark green leaves over the quiet ripples of the lake. The air is crisp but not unwelcome. The frost creeps under the sleeves of my sweater like a sharp caress. If I were superstitious, I would think this to be an omen. "I'm hoping she'll come with me."

"Viola." Mara reaches for my arm, gently rubbing it. "Sometimes, it's okay to go our separate ways. What is good for you may not be good for her."

Mara doesn't understand what's at stake. Mages are dying, and Olivia could be next, for all I know. "True," I reply quietly as I throw some of my bread to a couple of ducks paddling closer to us. I no longer have an appetite, neither for the food nor to continue the conversation about how I should leave Olivia behind.

"I know it's not what you want to hear." She sighs. "But you need to focus on your own future instead of trying to save everyone else. I've noticed how involved you are with our clients and it's sweet, but the dead are dead, and you don't owe them anything."

I don't know what to reply, so I settle on a smile. If I don't help the dead, I will lose my mind. And if anything happens to Olivia at that wretched institute, I will never forgive myself.

When I reach home that evening, Mother stands in front of the stove, her hair pulled into a ponytail. If she hears me walk across the kitchen, she doesn't acknowledge me. After Olivia left yesterday, I locked myself in my room to avoid her. Then, this morning, I left before she was even awake.

"Why do you always steal Olivia from me when she visits?"

Not this again. If I ignore her, she'll follow me to my room, so I breathe in, willing myself to calm down. "Olivia is my sister."

"She's my daughter first."

And what am I in this family? I clench my fists so hard my nails cut into my skin. I don't remember a time when I talked back to my mother, so it comes as a surprise to us both when I say, "You need to stop acting like you only have one child."

The metal spoon clangs on the floor, and she whirls around, eyes lit like the heart of a volcano about to erupt. She approaches. For a second, I think she's going to hit me, but instead of backing off and apologizing, I take a step forward with my head held high.

Mother's ears flush. She purses her lips, eyes twitching, her breath calculated. "Viola," she says with a calm that crawls under my skin. My momentary boldness leaves me then, and I am ten years old again hiding in my room, waiting for her anger to dissipate.

"I miss her more than you do," she says. It's not a competition. I don't complain when she hogs Olivia's free time when she's home from Gorhail on Midsummer break. I didn't even say a word when they took a two-week trip to the province of Holm over the last Pine Festival break.

"I'm sorry," I mumble. I'm not sure why I'm asking for forgiveness. With her, it always feels like I'm apologizing for existing. We stand in this awkward space, the same one in which we've found ourselves repeatedly since Olivia went to Gorhail. Me, apologizing for Mother's shortcomings, and her, never admitting her faults. None of this would have happened if I had never found out I was a mage. Olivia would never have left, and Mother wouldn't have grown resentful because of her absence.

I don't wait for her to respond. Reality finally sinks into my bones: I have no choice but to leave Albion. This house, this town, this province, they're all too crowded with metaphorical ghosts I will never be able to outrun Nan and Father's death, Mother's hatred, and the constant reminder that I threw my sister to the wolves.

I run up the stairs to the room Olivia and I used to share. Her side has been frozen in time, and above her bed is a string of glittery butterflies and twinkling lights that I still light up every night. I sit on her bed and let the smell of white roses on a rainy morning wrap around me. It takes me to a simpler time when our biggest worry was hiding from Nan after picking her precious roses from the garden. My side of the room is drab in comparison. Bare walls, a desk filled with empty pots, and books stacked to the ceiling. Most of them come from Nan's library in the attic—it's the only reason I know as much as I do about Gorhail and my whisperer magic, and the only reason I've managed to keep myself sane without a relic.

In the corner, two suitcases stare at me like old friends. I've packed and unpacked them countless times over the years, but I could never bring myself to leave Olivia. Deep down, I know Mara is right. I can't force her to move with me, but what kind of sister would I be if I didn't try? I sigh, looking out the window over my rose garden. Nan would've wanted me to protect her.

My peace doesn't last long. The door creaks open, and Mother stands in the doorway. Under the faint glow of Olivia's lights, she looks like she stepped out of a dark fairy tale.

"You look so much like her."

I don't need to ask. She means that I look like Nan. Would she have loved me if I looked more like *her*? Like Olivia does? Does she hate me because I remind her of Nan? Of Dad?

She strolls into the room and picks up one of Olivia's old pictures of us. "The old crone always favored you."

Now that's a lie. Nan loved Olivia and me equally. She would sneak us treats from the candy shop, bring us new books to read, and listen to us ramble about stories we made up. Nan's love for us lives in every corner of this house, and sometimes, I think it's the only thing that gave me strength to stay.

Mother scoffs at my silence. "Do you think she knows *my* Olivia inherited her precious magic? Your sister saved this family's reputation; she saved your grandmother's family line after your father got himself killed."

The only memories I have of my father are the ones I make up in my head from the only two pictures of him on the wall by the stairs. One with Mother on their wedding day, where he looks like he is attending a funeral. The second one a school portrait from the time he was at Gorhail. Every time I walk by it, I wonder if he would be disappointed in me for running away from the burden that he passed on to me. He died shortly after Olivia was born. Nan told us he miscalculated a spell, and it killed him. Ever since she told us that story, I've hated magic. I don't want to die like him and leave my sister alone. This curse pulsing under my skin took so much from us. Maybe if Dad were still here, things would have been different. Olivia would never have gone to Gorhail, Mother would never have been so bitter, and maybe he could have helped me understand why he loved magic so much he died for it.

"Good night, Mother," I reply, before crawling under the covers. I refuse to tangle myself in her fight of the week. When I open my eyes again, she's gone.

Anxiety and anticipation don't mix well, I learn every time I close my eyes, but soon enough, sleep envelops me, and I dream of her again.

It always starts with a woman with bangs and beautiful straight black hair that falls to her waist. She reads me a story about a girl who defied the odds. She strokes my hair with such gentleness. Everything about it is so vivid, but when she smiles at me, I always wake up.

When I close my eyes this time, I dream of falling into nothingness.

> **Crossmage (n)**—A mage with parents from different Houses, with the ability to wield magic from both Houses.
>
> **DOTS Decree**: Crossmages are required to choose a single class of magic. Unregistered crossmages are to have both their classes of magic sealed upon capture.
>
> **Addendum**: All children entering Gorhail Academy are to be tested.
>
> *DAILY MAGE*, ISSUE 1525.89

four | sylas

TUESDAY, NOVEMBER 16, 1939

Dean Rhodes's office is where happiness comes to die. It reeks of sterile surfaces and the faint smell of tulips.

"Mr. Archyr," she says. "Are you Mr. Cardot's keeper?"

"No, but—" I didn't want Beau to come here alone, now that I know someone's framing him for murder.

She ignores me and takes a seat behind her desk. "Victor Carver is dead."

Beau doesn't answer. This is exactly why I'm here. Because Beau would choose to walk to the execution block instead of explaining himself. "We've only heard it ten times in the last five minutes." I roll my eyes. Next to me, Beau rubs his thumbs together, his eyes fixated on his hands.

"Victor's relic is missing," she continues. How is this news when relic poachers exist? They must have stolen it to be reforged. The market for counterfeit relics is huge. Although, the poachers risking capture so close to Gorhail only to get Victor's relic doesn't sit right with me. Relics are worthless once the mage is dead, and reforging doesn't warrant the proximity to Gorhail. So it could have been anyone. Did he have enemies?

"Don't you have those creepy eyes all over our House? Can't you read them to see where Beau was when Victor died?" I snap. Rhodes is an accomplished Arkani Magus Principalis. Before taking on the position of dean at Gorhail, she used to be one of DOTS's leading inventors. She largely contributed to the creation of dustmaker-powered cars.

At the request of the Grand House, many years ago, Rhodes enchanted a dozen glass eyeballs and had them placed in every corner of the House of Poison's study hall and great hall. Serpent's Den and Fang's Nest are the only halls she watches. As if we're some unruly degenerates, plotting the downfall of the institute. Yet, she won't watch the real threats: the ones who've proven over and over that they don't deserve our trust. The Mortemagi.

"I did," she says. "And I saw nothing. Someone has tampered with my watchers."

"Isn't that proof enough? Beau could never do that!" I slam my hands on her desk. Rhodes's face falls, and I find worry in her gaze. She wouldn't have called Beau here if she didn't believe in his innocence. "How much time can you buy us?"

"The Grand House has agreed to grant one day for us to conclude internal investigations." Rhodes pulls open her drawer, retrieving a blank Gorhail letterhead.

When I don't reply, she adds, "If there isn't concrete evidence of his innocence by tomorrow, Beau will be executed without trial." The Grand House—the governing power of all mages across the Ten Provinces of Draterra—would find the littlest excuse to condemn an Aspieri. They claim that we have too little regard for our fellow mages, that they often end up dead when paired with us on the field. As if it's our fault they don't know the limits of their own relics.

"I'll see to it that we have concrete evidence." I close my fists. Only Haal knows how we'll prove his innocence.

Before dismissing us, Rhodes looks at Beau. "I would hate to lose one of my most brilliant students."

And I would hate to lose my brother.

We walk out of Rhodes's office, and I nearly bump into a small woman rushing in. It's her—the Mortemagi who latches on to Victor like a leech. Why is she here? Does she know something about Victor's murder?

"Go ahead," I tell Beau. "I'll meet you in our rooms."

I retrace my steps until I'm out of sight but within earshot.

"Dean Rhodes, would you sign off on my exemption for practicals? I'm afraid I've lost the sight. I must be too stressed about my promotional exam." The panic in her voice tells me there's more to her request.

The door closes, and I realize why this Mortemagi has been sticking to Victor so closely. Victor, illusionist extraordinaire from the House of Arcane, dies, and this woman suddenly "loses" her sight. Even without their relics, conduits never lose their sight.

Haal, she's a nonmagi.

Over the years, we've had a few nonmagi pretending to be mages—illusionists charge an outrageous amount of money for their trouble, although none have lasted as long as this one, as far as I'm aware. Unless Rhodes is too preoccupied with Victor's murder to connect the dots, today is the day her carefully crafted facade will shatter.

"You have five minutes to tell me why Silver's venom is in Victor's blood," I say the moment I step into our rooms. Lyria, Beau, and I share the House of Poison's Founder's Room. Every House has one and every descendant of a founder is privy to these large living spaces—three bedrooms, one kitchen, one living room, a study area, and an expansive personal vault downstairs. Is it unfair? Yes. But I'm never going to complain about not having to share a bathroom with four other mages in the common rooms.

Beau's face is sullen. He sits on the navy velvet couch by the fireplace, fiddling with his aspier. Silver coils and uncoils around his arm, restless. When an Aspieri is executed, their aspiers are executed, too. After a long pause, my brother turns his attention to the crackling fire, and I take the seat opposite him. "Three minutes."

"Can you stop?" Lyria emerges from her bedroom, a scowl on her face. "He's already on death row."

"If he doesn't tell me why his aspier's venom is in the blood of someone he doesn't know, Death won't have to wait until tomorrow to welcome him. One minute, Beau."

His eyes snap toward me, narrowing when our gazes meet. "I'm not a child."

"Clearly." I lean back into the sofa. "Since you will not speak, I'll get Paltro . . ."

"You're insufferable." He glares at me, then mumbles, "I sold a few vials of venom to Victor a couple of weeks ago."

Lyria gasps, rolling over the back of the sofa into the empty seat next to me.

"Stop looking at me like that," Beau exclaims. "Both of you!"

"I'm... surprised," Lyria says with an eerie calm. "I didn't think you to be a venom seller. Do you need money, Beau?"

Beau glowers at her, then the edges of his face melt into sympathy. "I didn't know he was going to inject himself with the venom. He said he needed frost venom for his mother, to help with her seizures. Did you know his mother was at Riverview Ward?"

How would we know that? I press my lips together so I don't yell at my brother, because, compassionate or not, he's broken at least four laws by selling aspier venom. If the Grand House finds out, death would be a merciful fate.

"If it was for his mother, why was it in his blood?" Lyria asks.

"He could've changed his mind." Beau shrugs. "Maybe he wanted to stay pretty forever."

Lyria gags. Even though its primary use is to soothe seizures, frost aspier venom is sought after on the black market to preserve eternal beauty after death.

"Some people are weird, Lyr. I hear Delaney's late husband is displayed on her living room couch."

"That's simply untrue. Overseer Delaney is one of the most righteous Mortemagi at Gorhail. She knows the importance of mage burials."

Beau's laughing at his own quip, and Lyria's grimacing as if we have all the time in the world and he's not going to die tomorrow. Neither of them understands the gravity of the situation. Killing a mage is one of the most serious offenses in the provinces. Maybe they think Paltro will swoop in and save Beau. How will anyone defend against the cold, hard proof that Beau's aspier venom was in Victor's blood? The Grand House doesn't care about reasons why, only facts. But I cannot fail my brother like I failed Dad. I will not lose him, even if I have to lose myself proving his innocence.

The hallway to Hollow Tree isn't as long as it is winding. When I step in, two Magus are fighting over the last slice of honeyfig bread, oblivious to the dangers that hide in every crevice. On a normal day, the main floor buzzes with the latest gossip, but tonight, it's a collection of worried faces, nervous chatter, and awkward laughs. They all know something is deeply wrong, yet they'll do nothing about it. Today, it's *my* brother on death row. Tomorrow, it could be *theirs*.

I pause, taking in the place. I've been here six years, and I'm still in awe of the architecture. Hollow Tree is the empty base of a gigantic tree primarily serving as our dining hall. It joins the three Houses on the base level via hallways that act like branches of the tree. The Poison hallway is winding like a serpent, the Arcane hallway's ceiling has an illusion of the twinkling night sky, and the House of Death's hallway probably looks and smells like death. I'll never know, because I never intend to set foot in that torture chamber.

I search the crowd for a head of shiny brown hair. Standing by the entrance of the House of Arcane, she is the only one in a cornflower-blue shirt amid a sea of black.

"Sier." I touch her elbow as I approach, and she steps aside. Sierra Ducas is a longtime family friend, but more importantly, she is the most gifted reader of her generation, who also happens to be best friends with the Mortemagi who stuck to Victor like glue.

"Sylas." She looks over both shoulders. "You've heard about Victor, I'm sure." It takes me a second to catch what she means. Her pronunciation leans more toward her native Rignan than Balish when she's stressed.

"Yes, and I need your help." I'm about to ask her to break the rules for me, and she knows it. Her clear blue eyes narrow, her nostrils flare, and she steps back, shaking her head. "Not after what happened . . ."

Not after what happened with my father. Not after she helped Gryff and me get out of Gorhail without approval, and Dad was killed saving us that very night. I don't blame her reluctance, but I *need* her help.

I lower my voice. "They found Silver's poison in Victor's blood."

She says nothing. Instead, she grabs my hand, and her eyes darken like an angry ocean waiting to swallow whoever dares cross her. Below her collarbone, her relic, a small silver key pendant, faintly glows.

Sierra is a reader Arkani. Their magic lets them read people's memories, coercing even the darkest secrets. After Gorhail, they're stationed outside of government buildings, so they can screen anyone who meets with the Grand Masters. They are so crucial to security that even nonmagi officials fight to recruit them.

"How is this possible?" She releases my hand abruptly, wiping her palm, as if this would somehow alter the memory.

"I don't know, Sier." I plead. "Beau doesn't deserve this. It will crush Lyria." It will crush me.

The moment she hears Lyria's name, her eyes soften. After Dad died, Sierra took Lyria to our family home in Iserine and spent weeks helping her through her grief. I owe her more than I will ever be able to repay, yet here I am, asking even more of her.

"What do you need?"

"Read Victor's memories."

"Sylas." Her face twists in horror. Reading a dead person's memory requires lifeblood.

"I know what I'm asking of you." I hold her stare. "The Grand House will call for Beau's execution without trial."

She pauses at my words, but her frown worries me. I'm asking too much. She looks around and lowers her voice. "I know another way, but it will cost you."

"Anything," I say.

"A trade for a trade." Her eyes darken, and her pendant glows again. She's asking for a secret in exchange for one of her own—readers use secrets as currency; they cannot share a secret without receiving one. Lucky for me, Victor's little follower gave me everything I needed earlier. Sierra would want to know that her best friend is a liar.

"A trade for a trade," I agree.

"Your Mortemagi friend has no magic," I say.

She considers my answer.

"Olivia?" Sierra struggles to quell a laugh. When I don't react, she reaches for my hand. Her amusement dies, her eyes prying into mine, searching for a sliver of a lie. Of course, she finds nothing. I would never trade a lie to a reader. I almost feel guilty making her doubt her own magic, wondering if she glazed over her best friend's secrets. And I hate that I feel nothing selling out a nonmagi.

"Well then, I am surrounded by liars." She clears her throat. "Fable Rowan is seeing Lorne, behind Olivia's back."

I frown. Sierra and Olivia's friend, Fable, is seeing Olivia's boyfriend. How does that serve me? The secret is as empty as Fable's brain.

"Stop looking at me like I tricked you. Fable can erase Silver's venom from Victor's blood," Sierra clarifies. "Before the execution order is set, they'll retest Victor's blood . . ." She pauses at the confusion on my face, then explains further, "It's procedure: they always retest twice to reduce the likelihood of a false outcome."

"Will this work?" I ask, my jaw tense.

"I'm not known to fail." She gives me a hopeful smile. "Meet me in the infirmary courtyard at midnight. And be nice when you ask Fable for blood-cleansing dust."

Now I understand why she told me it would cost me. I hate Fable Rowan.

My heart beats to the tick of my watch—Dad's watch. The reflection of the half-moon stings me with memories of the night Dad died. It took me three weeks to bring myself to clean off the blood that splattered on the face of his watch. As I stand in the infirmary courtyard, I pray to Haal that I will not have to bury another member of my family.

Lyria and Beau insisted on following me to the meeting because they do not trust Fable. Rightfully so, since she's been holding a vendetta against our family ever since her mother was killed on a mission Dad assigned.

A bob of yellow hair scurries out of the southern hallway, tugging her tan coat to her neck. The three of us look up to see Fable speeding toward us. She moves like a fugitive, even though curfew doesn't apply to school grounds. Behind her, Sierra walks with purpose, a notebook in her hand.

"Fable." I give her a curt nod in greeting, but she ignores me.

"I thought you needed to go to the infirmary," she snaps at Sierra, her sharp nose lifting in disdain. "Why did you lure me to this pit of vipers?"

Pit of vipers. I stifle a laugh, even though I'm sure Fable meant it as an insult. It's no surprise coming from a dustmaker Arkani. They walk around thinking that all magic would cease without them and their little ground-up plants. To be fair, there is merit to their arrogance. Our world *would* cease to function without Arkani; they are the backbone of our technology. Their inventions allow us to further research, find cures for illnesses. It's a pity Fable is the worst of them, selfish to the core—she only looks out for herself. I don't say any of that, because right now, her magic is Beau's lifeline.

"I need blood-cleansing dust," I say. "Name your price."

Blood-cleansing dust is a family recipe belonging to the Rowans, as are the majority of the complex dust recipes. Rumor has it Fable's family has spilled a lot of blood over the years to grow their collection. Judging by her predatory smile, I believe the rumors.

"Why should I help you?" she scoffs. "Your father killed my mother."

"Dying on assignment is a risk of the job." I measure my tone, not wanting to jeopardize my only chance to save my brother. "Your mother knew this just as we all do."

"I'm leaving." Fable whirls, walking toward the infirmary.

"I'm sure Olivia would love to know that you're excellent company to her boyfriend," I call out.

Fable freezes.

I don't even know Olivia. Before this afternoon, I didn't even know her name. But she is the ticket to Beau's freedom.

At my side, Lyria shifts her weight with discomfort. She disapproves, I'm sure, but our brother's life hinges on how well I play my cards. I can see Fable's brain whirring through my threat, weighing the consequences, and finally, she sighs. "Olivia can never know."

I've won.

"I'll make your stupid dust if all of you take a vow of silence." She crosses her arms. "It would ruin what I have with Lorne."

Pathetic. She doesn't care about her friend at all. "We'll take the vow when you hand us the dust," I reply.

Fable straightens her narrow shoulders, bobbing her head like a porcelain doll. "You'll have to get me the substitute ingredients. Two, you'll find in Gorhail Woods, and the third, you'll find where River Grand meets Albion Creek. Bring them before dawn. My classes begin at eight."

"What are the ingredients?" Beau asks before I can.

A sinister smile pulls at the corner of Fable's lips. "Chasmore, Afa's Bloom, and Purple Bittercress."

Absolute silence follows her words. I don't know how long it lasts, but my sister's sharp inhale snaps us back to reality. Beau shifts uncomfortably, and Sierra gapes at Fable in horror.

Fable has no intention of helping us at all. Chasmore is in the Eastern Forest, nearly impossible to find at night because the flowers blend with its surroundings. Afa's Bloom is locked in the Northern Greenhouse, deep in the Northern Forest—only the overseer of the House of Arcane has a key. And Purple Bittercress only grows at the junction of two rivers, under Junction Bridge.

This is a death sentence.

"Poachers," I manage to say, repressing memories of the last time I was by that junction. Dad was killed on that bridge, and she *knows* that. "Substitute the bittercress," I snap.

"I assure you I'm not being malicious." Fable's smile says otherwise. "Devil's Wort is the only substitute, and it only grows in the Farbon Desert. I suppose you could wait a week, and I'll have someone send it from Imglen."

We don't have a week. We don't even have half a day.

"If you leave now, perhaps you'll make it back in time," Fable sneers, as if I needed another reminder of why people hate the Rowans. They're cruel.

"You haven't changed at all, Fable. Your selfishness will catch up to you one day." Sierra shakes her head.

"Yet you need me to save your little friend." Her high-pitched voice rings against the quiet of the night. "Bring me the ingredients no later than five. I'll need at least two hours to make the dust." Then she leaves.

"That bitch," Lyria curses. "Chasmore? At this hour? That plant is virtually invisible in the dark." Not only invisible but also protected. Even to pluck it for classes, we need special permission from DOTS.

"The three things we need are in opposite directions. There is no way you'll make it back on time," Beau points out.

He's right. It will take me hours to get to all three locations, not counting the time it'll take to search for the Chasmore and dive for the Purple Bittercress. But I have Raiku and Railesza—maybe they'll help me go faster.

"You know nothing about plants, so I'll find the Chasmore," Lyria volunteers. The words hurt my ears like nails on a chalkboard. Lyria isn't field certified; no matter how I try to spin this into my going on an impromptu Secondline patrol, I will be severely reprimanded if Paltro finds out I took my sister with me. Besides, how will she fare if she comes face-to-face with poachers when a Secondline-trained mage like Victor succumbed to them?

"I'll get the Afa's Bloom. Silver can freeze the lock on the greenhouse," Beau adds. Are both my siblings out to antagonize me tonight? Beau, too, is not field certified, but to his credit, he's not a stranger to sneaking out into the woods past curfew.

"Fantastic," I grunt. One wrong turn, and their fate is sealed to the God of Death.

"It's either this, or I die tomorrow anyway." Beau shrugs with a nonchalance that grinds my teeth. "We have a better chance of succeeding if we split up."

"True, but . . ." My protest dies immediately. He's right.

"I can do this. Trust me?" He looks at me with clear blue eyes that take me back to the first day Dad brought him home. He was so small, only two then, but his eyes have always been so profound. Perhaps he is right, perhaps I should trust him. Would things have been different if Dad had trusted me that night? Would the poachers have found us if he hadn't come looking for me?

"That leaves you with the Purple Bittercress." Lyria winces in apology.

"I'll be fine," I lie, running a hand over Railesza. Sooner or later, I'll have to face my fears. "Set your watches. If you're not finished in an hour, come back and we'll find another way."

What I don't tell them is that there *is no* other way. If we fail, I'll take responsibility for killing Victor Carver.

> Arkani need relics to practice their magic.
>
> Mortemagi need relics to channel their magic.
>
> Aspieri need relics to exist.
>
> **YSENIA FARO**, *THE FOUNDER'S BOOK OF RELICS*, **CHAPTER 2**

five | viola

WEDNESDAY, NOVEMBER 17, 1939

Four loud bangs jolt me awake.

When no one answers, it quiets into a string of incessant knocks until Mother turns on the hallway light. Her dainty footsteps pace down the stairs between grunts and muttered curses. I sigh at the clock, open my bedroom door, and follow her in silence, curious about why someone raps at our door at four in the morning.

My eyes take a minute to adjust. The faint rays of the rising sun break through the kitchen window, and it smells of morning dew. With the calm, the ringing in my ear buzzes, reminding me that I only have hours before it corrodes my brain.

Mother bumps into a dining chair on her way to the foyer. She pulls a thick blanket from the lone fabric seat and drapes it around herself as she drags her feet forward. Inch by inch, she pulls the door open.

"May I help you?" she rasps.

From where I stand between the base of the stairs and the stove, I cannot see who she's talking to, but at once, Mother's body goes rigid. An arm reaches out to steady her, and her fingers dig into the stranger's coat. She shakes her head like a madwoman, choking on words as she tries to speak.

"Ava," says the voice. It's the sheriff.

There's a brief pause, a short moment of hesitation, where they both hang on to the hope that if it's not said aloud, it didn't happen.

"We found a body at the lake."

It doesn't matter where the words come from, nor the avalanche of questions about to sweep away the sheriff standing in front of my mother.

I already know, so I'm already turning away from them.

The thin fabric of my pajamas clings to my skin when I step through the kitchen door, the frigid Albion winter punishing me for not grabbing a coat or boots. Still, I march on, the slight breeze scraping my face. I have to see for myself.

By the time I reach the lake, I no longer feel my toes, and my fingertips are about to fall off.

A small crowd gathers past the bench where Mara and I had breakfast only yesterday. The gray sky dulls the dark green branches of the trees. They look like they're weeping. With every step, my stomach knots and my limbs stiffen. They beg me to slow down, to stop.

When the onlookers notice me, they lower their eyes and part to let me through. Someone offers me their coat, but I brush past them. My mind is ensnared by the girl lying where the water meets the stones.

I kneel next to her, or maybe I fall because two red splotches form at my knees. The cold numbs the pain from the sharp rocks digging into my bare skin. I wish it numbed the pain of my heart ripping apart.

Olivia's face is as gray as the skies. Her eyes are closed, her lips blue. She looks like she's made of glass—or maybe that's all I see through the tears that cloud my eyes. I've worked with the dead long enough to know this isn't an illusion, that her chest won't move from my staring, hoping, or praying to all the Gods. She looks so peaceful I am afraid to touch her, afraid to wake her from her slumber.

A stray strand of brown hair urges my hand forward, and I tuck it neatly behind her right ear. She deserves to look like she always was—perfect. At least, one last time.

When I pull my hand away, she grabs it.

Her eyes open, but they are no longer the green of the early summer days in Nan's rose garden. They are ice white, like Albion's late winter snow. I don't move. My breathing stops, and my heart slows. "Tell me who did this to you," I beg silently. "Tell me, and I promise I won't let them rest a day in their lives."

Beware the serpent with one green eye.

Her lips don't move, no matter how much I want them to. My shaky hand slips out of her grasp, and I choke back a sob at the realization that my own sister's words stopped the ringing in my ears. She's supposed to help me *solve* riddles . . . Olivia wouldn't use her last words on a complex riddle, especially when she knew I struggled with them. Serpent could mean anything . . .

No. There has to be more.

I'm about to reach for my sister again, when someone throws a heavy blanket over me. A rush of warmth takes over. The feeling is an itch I want to claw out of my skin. How wrong it is to be warm while my sister lies cold and lifeless.

"Let's go, Viola." Mara wraps her strong hands around my shoulders, pulling me up. I don't know if she has been here all along or if she's just arrived, but I can't leave now. I can't leave Olivia here. I can't leave her alone. Not again.

I fight against Mara. I need to hold my sister again. What if she has more to say?

Mara's arms wrap me in a tight hug, despite my attempts to push her away. I don't need comfort, I need answers. Will I ever be able to breathe again without my sister's death weighing on my chest, crushing my insides?

"The sheriff will move her to Dearly Departed, and I promise I will take care of her. Let's go." Mara's grip is firm. It forces me to move.

I take one last look at my Olivia. She looks like a beacon of light against the black rocks. Her billowy, white nightgown, muddied and soaked—why would Olivia wear a nightgown out in winter? By a lake, of all places, when she didn't know how to swim? Why would she be out of Gorhail in the middle of the night, past curfew? My eyes snap to her arm. Her cuff is gone, and her arm is covered in claw marks and cuts.

"They took—" I don't finish my sentence, because Mara pulls me away.

"Let's go, Viola." Her voice is sharp, colder than it's ever been, as she maneuvers me toward the crowd.

After a few more unsuccessful attempts, my fight dwindles. I glance at Olivia over my shoulder. This is my fault. I should never have let her go to a school full of mages, knowing she didn't belong there. I should have fought harder, spoken louder. I should have told someone, anyone, that the cursed one with magic was me. And now, she is dead because of a cuff she was never supposed to wear. My silence killed Olivia.

The crowd has quadrupled, and it takes us a while to push through the wall of sympathy. I try my best to return the teary nods, but my heart sears with anger. Everyone loved Olivia. How could someone do this to her?

Our last conversation replays in my head. From her joke about curfew to her insistence that I wear my relic to help quell my magic. It was almost like Olivia was warning me, preparing me for her inevitable fate. I let her down too many times before. I can't let her down again. Even if it means betraying myself, I will wear Nan's cuff.

For Olivia, I will stop at nothing until I find her killer.

Mara walks with me until we reach our gate. She promises to take care of Olivia two more times before she leaves, and I don't even thank her. Instead of stepping into our house, I head straight into the back garden and sit on the dirt. I don't know how long I stay here, only that I fall asleep.

When I wake up, it's well into the afternoon and my clothes are wet. Cursing myself for wasting precious time that I could've used to speak to my sister's ghost, I drag myself to the house and head straight to my bathroom. Mother is not here, although I wish she was. Right now, I want to be around someone who knew and loved my sister.

I tear off my wet clothes and step into the shower. The water scalds my hands as I wash the mud off them. I scrub my skin until it's raw, but nothing will scrub away the guilt that's eating me from the inside.

After getting dressed in a sweater and jogger pants, I pull my mattress up, sliding it out of the frame. In the center lies a small, wooden box with a bronze latch. I haven't touched it since Olivia gave it to me a week after she started at Gorhail. She said Nan's cuff wouldn't open for her, and she'd managed to get a counterfeit relic from someone at school. For the longest time, she spoke about wanting to wear a real relic, wanting to *feel* magical. I hate the Gods, for they grant wishes with poisoned gifts. If Olivia hadn't insisted on getting a real relic, would someone have killed her? *Killed*. That word feels so wrong.

My hands shake as I flip open the bronze latch. I've had twelve years to bring Olivia back from Gorhail, and I did nothing. Pushing the box open with my thumbs, I hold my breath. On a bed of folded black silk cloth lies a single brass cuff. Nan's cuff. And behind it, a yellowing note from Olivia: "Tell me if ghosts are real when you put it on."

My eyes sting, and I blink away the tears. I have to speak to my sister's ghost, beg for her forgiveness, and hope she remembers enough from her final moments to tell me who killed her.

I gingerly pick up the cuff, feeling the weight of the cool metal. Letting out a quick exhale, I slide the relic underneath my sweater. In one motion, it snaps around my arm. I flinch, anticipating it to be as cold as snow, but it molds to my arm, soft and warm, sitting comfortably against my skin like it had been waiting for me all these years.

"Olivia," I try.

Nothing.

"Ole," I try again.

The chirp of birds grows louder outside my window, but I still don't hear her. Is my magic gone when I need it the most? I begin to panic. But then I remember reading that ghosts tend to linger around their bodies for a while. By now, the sheriff's office should've moved her to Dearly Departed, so I turn on my heels, ready to find my sister.

"I should've known." Mother stands in the doorway, face puffy, eyes bloodshot. She looks wild. "Why did you lie?" The usual dismissal in her eyes has morphed into loathing. She knows. She knows Olivia doesn't . . . didn't have magic.

"I didn't," I mumble. But by not correcting Olivia, I was complicit in the lie.

"It all makes sense now, you working at that funeral home." She laughs without moving her mouth, but her eyes aren't on me. They're on the box that held Nan's cuff. *My* cuff.

"What did she say?" Mother asks, approaching me like she's gone mad. "What were Olivia's last words?"

"Nothing." I blink at her.

"Don't lie to me again, Viola." She grips my arm, and it hurts. "I know how your wretched magic works. What were her last words?"

Tears brim my eyes. The only person whom I shared the last words of the dead with is now dead. "She said nothing." I double down. Nothing I want to share with Mother anyway.

Mother releases my hand, and I hold my breath, waiting for the slap to come. Instead, she backs off. "Olivia is dead," she spits. "Her blood is on your hands."

My head lowers at my upturned palms. Her blood *is* on my hands.

Mother has a way of pulling to the surface everything that's wrong with me, every flaw, every misstep. Looking at her, standing like a shell two steps away from me, I realize that she is but a mother who's lost a child. Selfishly, a part of me wonders if she'd be as distressed if I were the one killed. I shake my head. Why am I so desperate for a love that will never come?

"I'm going to the funeral home," I say, pausing at the door, expecting more vitriol. But she doesn't say anything, and she doesn't stop me as I walk down the stairs.

The kitchen feels bigger than usual, as if it knows Olivia is no longer here. I linger behind the chair she sat in on Monday, hot tears prickling my eyes again. I reach to wipe them away. We never even had one last cup of tea together. I never even gave her the letters from DOTS. Now, none of it matters.

The light dims and I glance outside, through the small kitchen window. Daylight is nearly gone, and with it, my sister will have been dead for more than half a day. Not dead, killed. I have to force myself to be acquainted with the word, no matter how much it churns my stomach. Killed. Suddenly, my throat is closing, and my body sweats despite the cold. I need to get out of here.

I run toward the front door, desperate for fresh air. As I'm about to reach for the knob, it turns. My gaze shoots up, limbs frozen. The door creaks open slowly, and between the outstretched seconds, I realize for the first time that Olivia may have been killed by mistake. That they could have been after Nan's cuff. And now, they're after me.

> The first aspiers were sacred, a gift from Haal, the God of War, to mages who were brave enough to stand by his side during the Battle of the Gods. Now, relicsmiths from the province of Iserine forge them with a single hair from the family line. When a mage line dies, an aspier is free to choose a new Aspieri.
>
> **ROME RONIN,** *A BRIEF HISTORY OF THE HOUSE OF POISON*, PAGE 23

six | sylas

WEDNESDAY, NOVEMBER 17, 1939

Overseer Paltro's office hides one of the oldest passageways from Gorhail Institute into Gorhail Woods. When Beau, Lyria, and I mapped out the closest starting point for all three of us, we landed on the moss-covered trapdoor to the right of Paltro's office. Six years ago, just weeks after we'd joined the institute, Gryff and I tried to use these passageways to sneak out after curfew, but we ran straight into the previous overseer of the House of Poison, and he suspended us from Secondline for a fortnight. Lucky for us, Paltro values his sleep and won't be in until dawn.

The sky is still dark, covered with disapproving clouds whose warning we should heed. The slippery grass doesn't inspire confidence as I search for the circular latch, knees in the mud and my hand mostly digging through dirt. Raiku could help, but he's slithered from my wrist to my forearm.

"I thought you knew where it was," hisses Beau.

"By all means, I'd like to see you digging your pristine nails into the soil," I retort just as my hand brushes over cold, hard metal. I jerk the door open with a crack.

One after the other, my siblings and I squeeze down the narrow steps in front of the ridiculous statue of Sileas Ronin. His marble face looks down on us, glasses resting on his nose, judging us for bringing shame to the Ronin line.

"It reeks down here." Lyria turns up her nose and halts.

Beau grimaces. "Lyr, did you expect Gorhail to maintain its hidden passageways?"

I run a hand over my face. At this pace, we'll be lucky if we make it out of *here* by dawn. "We don't have all the time in the world. Move along."

With a grumble, my sister continues on.

The moment I step into the tunnel after Beau, the pungent odor of death and mildew assaults my senses. Lyria wasn't exaggerating. It reeks, but thank Haal, the walk is short.

"If either of you even have a sense that poachers are around, promise you'll run back right away," I tell them as we emerge from the tunnel into a small clearing bordered by redbushes. We should be about fifteen minutes from Beau's and Lyria's tasks and about twenty minutes from mine.

"We will," Beau promises, readjusting Silver around his left hand, but my nerves coil tighter in my throat.

"Nothing bad will happen, Sy," Lyria reassures me, twirling a dagger between her fingers. Sometimes I forget that she's trained with Gryff for most of her life. Our parents were friends, and after Mom died, the Darros were frequent visitors. Over the years, Lyria joined him, Beau, and me as we began combat training. And Gryff took it upon himself to make sure Lyria had the proper techniques in case she ever needed them. Beau and I think it's because he secretly wanted her to join Firstline with him, but he'll never admit to it.

"Chasmore isn't far from here. If I finish early, I'll come help or send Nyx." She glances down at her black aspier, whose venom kills within seconds.

Haal, she's already deviating from the plan, and we haven't even started. "Stick to directions, Lyr. You may have the deadliest aspier *after* the Deathbringer's, but you have no field experience."

"Neither does Beau," Lyria retorts. "And the Deathbringer is gone, so I *do* have the deadliest aspier."

"I do have field experience," Beau adds nonchalantly, while adjusting two daggers on each of the thigh holders of his combat pants. "It's not entirely legal, but it's still experience." He winks at Lyria, and she rolls her eyes. Before disappearing into the woods, he looks over his shoulder and yells, "Last one back cooks dinner for a week."

"Sylas doesn't know how to cook." Lyria chuckles. She sets off, Nyx slithering ahead of her.

If their quips are supposed to reassure me, they don't. As I watch the silhouettes of my siblings fade in the shadow of the trees, the reality of what awaits sinks into the pit of my stomach. If we fail, this ends in a prison sentence and a funeral.

The quiet of the woods is unsettling. Even the dead leaves have silenced their crunch with the drizzle of an unusual nightly rain. Gorhail Woods is known as the Talking Woods, where the trees hum the songs of the night and the flowers echo the morning chirp of the birds. Where owls hoot at foxes trotting from cave to cave, and wild cats hunt for mice in redbushes.

Tonight, it sleeps.

And that only means one thing: poachers.

Raiku slithers to my index finger, and Railesza stretches the length of my forearm. Both aspiers are well acquainted with the dangers lurking in every crevice.

I trudge deeper into the woods, where the massive trees hug each other so tightly they block out the light of the moon. Something shifts ahead, and I press my back to the nearest trunk, my finger nudging Raiku forward. He slithers off, his bright onyx scales dulling to blend with the shadows. There's a brief pause, a cry of pain, then a muted thump.

My ears reach for the rustle of leaves, the cautious clap of a poacher's boot, the slash of a knife, but nothing comes. In three strides, I'm kneeling next to the body of a middle-aged man. His eyes are empty, his breath gone. Raiku doesn't usually kill without command. But then I see it. A single arrow tattooed behind the poacher's neck that marks him as a poacher of magical animals. I nod at Raiku; I would've killed him, too. Animal poachers are cruel, hunting for sport rather than necessity. But their hunting grounds are up north in the provinces of Aurignan and sometimes Holm. Not in Gorhail Woods. Haal, I'm a fool for leaving my siblings alone.

Raiku hisses hesitantly before slithering back onto my wrist. His neck veers north, in Beau's direction, then he looks back at me expectantly. I shake my head. I have to trust that my brother can handle himself. Besides, he and Lyria should already be on their way back to Paltro's garden by now.

I pause, studying the silence before I move again. The rest of the walk to the Twin Lakes is uneventful, and it worries me. Poachers never travel alone. I shouldn't have long until his unit realizes he is missing. How many more poachers crawl these woods?

I reach the divide between Lake Glass and Lake Stone, the two bodies of water that make up the Twin Lakes of Gorhail. From above, they look like lungs, fed by two rivers meeting in the middle: Albion Creek and River Grand.

Junction Bridge is straight ahead.

My throat knots in anguish. I only need to walk to the middle and dive. I take the first step on the wooden bridge, but my legs are stiff. I draw a sharp breath. It's been four months; I can do this.

For Beau.

The second step is heavier than the first, and my ears grow warm, a bead of sweat trickling down my temple. I can still see Dad ahead, taking a poacher's blow in my place. I run my hand over the Imortalis, and Raiek is still as always.

"It's been four months," I say out loud.

Not long enough, a voice inside me whispers back.

Without being prompted, Raiku and Railesza slither to the ground, hissing between me and the water. They pause, exchange a look, then they both slither off the side of the bridge into the lake. Relief floods me. If Damas, the God of Luck and Treachery, will have it, my aspiers will come back with the bittercress.

I retrace my steps and sit on the bed of pebbles closest to the bridge. I understand now why Paltro failed me during Firstline recruitment. If I can't even handle *seeing* the bridge where my father was killed, what will I do when I come face-to-face with the poachers who killed him?

A few ripples in the water drive me to my feet. Are my aspiers back already? Finding the bittercress must have been easier than I thought.

My answer comes as my shoulders slam against the ground and a hand pulls my leg, dragging me to the water. Instinct takes over, and I kick with my free leg. The hand disappears. And that's when I hear them.

The sharpening of the knives and the quiet snickering betray their position behind me. I scramble to my feet, my hand reaching for the dagger at my thigh.

"What have we here?" A familiar crooked voice asks. Suddenly, I'm stuck between three poachers, two in front of me, one emerging from the water behind me. My limbs freeze, the same way they did four months ago, except this time, no one's coming to save me.

Sylas, you must fight. My father's voice plays in my head. That's the last thing he said to me before they killed him.

I zero in on the poacher who spoke. A man in his thirties, his hair in a buzz cut with his poacher's mark tattooed on the left of his skull. One line with four arrows. A mage poacher.

"Little birdie shouldn't be flying alone in the forest," he taunts. The others laugh, and it sends me into a blind rage. Gripping my dagger, I ready my stance. I know I cannot take all three of them, but I'm hoping to buy enough time for Raiku and Railesza to come back.

The man on the right lunges first, and I sidestep him, swiping his face with the blade. He staggers to his feet, hand on his cheek, shock flashing across his face.

"Little birdie has claws," spits the poacher behind me.

I scoff, "I don't need claws to deal with scum like you."

Speaking was a big mistake, because Crooked Voice uses my distraction to throw a punch at my side, sending me flying into the second poacher. This one wastes no time, kicking me in the shins. I keel over, holding my side. The one behind me kicks me with the strength of two hammers. If Railesza doesn't come back soon, I won't be able to move. Raiek will keep me alive, but he doesn't heal injuries.

Crooked Voice laughs. "Did daddy dearest take away your fight when he died?"

My rage simmers; it studies my enemies, bides its time. Crooked Voice was part of the unit who killed Dad. I have a chance to avenge my father, and I will not miss.

I reach for another dagger from my right boot and stab into the second poacher's leg. He wails, falling backward. I seize the first dagger, flip around on my stomach, throw it straight at the third poacher. It sinks into his chest, and the man falls into the water with a splash.

Crooked Voice's eyes widen.

"If you don't pull him out, he'll drown," I say, as I pull myself up.

He bares his teeth. "He's just some low rank." He throws his knife in the water without looking away from me, his relic earring glowing as his blade finds its mark. Unlike us, poachers have no qualms sacrificing their underlings to fuel their magic.

He draws another knife and dives straight at me. It happens so fast I pull him down with me in my tumble. Somewhere along the scuffle, he drops his weapon, and his hands reach for my neck, trying to pry open the Imortalis. He's distracted. Seizing the moment, I knee him in the stomach. He recoils. I throw a punch, and it lands on his jaw. He returns two blows to my abdomen, and my vision blurs. I see the silhouette of another knife. The world darkens, and I only feel the rip across my shoulder.

Fight, Sylas. My father's voice echoes again. But I have no fight left. The poacher drives his fist into the cut, and I scream. He pins me down with his knee, and I look around desperately. A glint of the moon on metal catches my eyes. I stretch my hand as far as I can, until my fingers feel the cold of the blade. Once I have a firm grip on the hilt, I drive the knife straight into Crooked Voice's back. He howls. I gather whatever strength I can and kick him off.

At the same time, Railesza slithers up my arms, fangs sinking into my veins. Cool relief washes over me, and I welcome it like a traveler tasting his first drop of water after an endless trek in the Farbon Desert. My vision sharpens; my limbs regain feeling. Railesza's venom eases my pain until it stops.

"Thank you," I rasp.

My green aspier hisses, before coiling herself around my arm.

I push myself up. Crooked Voice lies in front of me, groaning in pain as Raiku unhooks his fangs from his arm—the poison will take its sweet time. Then my aspier slithers to the other poacher curled in a fetal position, moaning while holding his leg. Raiku hovers around his neck, and a single bite later, the moan stops, and the man goes limp.

I crouch next to Crooked Voice's face. "Who do you work for?"

More groans of agony, but no reply.

"Why did you ambush me four months ago?" I ask.

He struggles to speak. "Kill me."

He would rather die than betray his kind; I respect the loyalty, but I don't forgive it.

"Kill me," he rasps again, coughing up blood.

"No," I say. "I'm not going to kill you. You don't deserve a quick death."

He mumbles something I don't care to decode.

"You deserve worse," I say as I walk away, leaving him to simmer with Raiku's venom. He'll die, unless someone comes for him. And even if he survives, he will never speak again, never move again, never kill anyone again.

Raiku crawls to a small bunch of purple leaves farther from us. The Purple Bittercress. I snap it up, and offer my wrist to my black aspier, but he stills, his tongue flicking, his head reaching for something east of us.

The scream comes seconds after.

My legs move before my mind processes what I've heard. Lyria's voice. Then complete silence.

Raiku glides across the dirt, guiding me to her. I don't know how fast I'm running, but my lungs burn, and pain blooms in my legs. Yet there's no sign of my sister.

It smells like burned skin, salt and cedar, and my stomach churns half in horror half in panic. I follow the scent, pausing to let Raiku slither around my ankle. The closer I approach, the tighter my insides twist.

The trees start humming again, a somber song of death.

Not Lyria. No, not Lyria. Please.

In the crook of a large trunk, my sister kneels, her arms around her middle. She's crying, hurt maybe, but she's alive. I breathe out. She's alive.

Railesza slides off me, but she stops shy of Lyria. I look down, and I can't breathe. My body is a shell, no longer my own, and my mind races in a million directions.

Beau lies in front of her, his clothes torn and soaked in blood.

I kneel beside him, feel for a pulse, find nothing, and start pumping his chest. Railesza moves around his wounds, biting several places along his veins, and I ease on the compressions. She will save him, like she saved me.

I don't know how long I stay there doing compressions, but eventually, Lyria's delicate hands grab mine, lifting them from Beau. I look at her puffy, red eyes and her mud-stained face. Fresh blood cakes the side of her neck, her clothes, and the arm where her aspier sits. Her head shakes so gently as she squeezes my palms.

I try to jerk my hands away, but she holds them still. Does she not understand that I have to continue the compressions? Beau will die if I don't.

"Sylas," my sister croaks. Her words die on her lips, because she starts sobbing the moment her eyes fall on Beau. My chest constricts again, and breathing becomes unbearable. It's impossible. Railesza's healing is unparalleled; she draws magic from the Imortalis. Beau will wake up soon, and we'll laugh about it at dinner tonight.

"Sylas." Again, her small voice cuts through the string of hope I refuse to let go.

"No." I shake my head. "No."

I run my fingers across Beau's neck, feeling for any sign of life. Nothing. Railesza switches veins three more times, trying to heal the open wounds, but it doesn't work. There's nothing to be healed.

The trees have moved, seemingly to give Beau one last look at the moon. But even the glow of the moon cannot hide the dulling of his bright blue eyes—eyes that will never blink at me in surprise again. I rest my hand on his clenched fists on his abdomen, and something soft brushes against my skin. Clutched in his hand is a single white flower, sprayed with red.

Then the grief I've so carefully tucked away for the past months swallows me whole.

> Dear Olivia, I wish we were celebrating my birthday together. My magic is weird. I have to be near a dead body to hear the last words of the dead. It's nothing like in Nan's books. I'm scared.
>
> **LETTER FROM VIOLA CORVI TO OLIVIA CORVI, JULY 11, 1927**

seven | viola

WEDNESDAY, NOVEMBER 17, 1939

The door creaks open, and a woman stands a few inches from me. Her straight brown hair is neatly tucked behind her ears, and her hands mindlessly adjust her long black coat as if she's waiting for me to invite her in. I notice a muted navy crest embroidered on its left pocket, the profile of a raven with a golden eye: the symbol of the House of Death.

Her expectant gaze lands on me, and I take a few steps back, putting enough distance between us. In all the years Olivia has attended Gorhail, no one from that forsaken place has ever set foot in our house.

"Madame Corvi," she greets, shifting her look behind me. Mother must have heard the door and come downstairs. "May I come in?"

I'm surprised she's asking, given she had no trouble turning the doorknob earlier.

Mother takes measured steps until she's standing next to me. Her face is blank, and her lips are drawn in a thin line. "I would prefer we speak on the front porch," she says, and the woman immediately turns on her heels.

I frown, following Mother out. Nightfall is nearly upon us; a flock of birds flies to the north toward Gorhail Woods, and if I listen closer, I hear the clatter of shoes on the pavement—people rushing home in time for dinner. A slight breeze carries the sweet scent of purple roses to where Mother and I hug the door, facing the woman's back. Mother flips the switch, and the single lightbulb hanging off the wooden beam lights up.

"I am Overseer Delaney, the head of the House of Death at Gorhail Institute. Olivia—" she begins, but Mother interrupts her.

"You killed Olivia."

The woman's lip twitches at the accusation. She clasps her hands as if, were she to unclasp them, she would do terrible things to my mother. Her lips stretch into a forced smile. "Olivia left school grounds after curfew. She was well aware of the dangers."

Olivia would never break that rule. Just two days ago, she was joking about that very scenario. She *knew* not to leave that wretched place after curfew. My heart races, rage flowing into my veins. Did this woman come here to tell us that Olivia died because she broke the rules? Died. Again, the word leaves a sour taste on my tongue. Olivia didn't die, I remind myself. She was killed.

"It is under investigation both by the Bureau of Magus Nonmagi Alliance and DOTS." She relaxes her smile. "Early reports say that it was an accident. Little Lake Albion's boardwalk is slippery from all the rain and melted snow this time of year."

An accident? Olivia's arm was butchered with claw marks, and they stole her relic. I move, but Mother's bony fingers clasp my arm, holding me in place. "My daughter was terrified of water," she says calmly.

"I'm sorry." The woman lowers her head. "Olivia excelled at school," she offers, as if this would erase her blasphemous statement. When she lifts her eyes at us again, the slight annoyance is gone, replaced by regret. "She was brilliant. In fact, I personally recommended her for a junior magister position at the academy."

This is why Olivia wanted to stay at Gorhail. They sold her dreams of a future that was never written for her.

"Oh." Mother lets out a small gasp. Don't fall into her trap, I want to tell her. Olivia was killed and they are trying to blind you with posthumous accolades while dismissing her death as an accident. They don't care.

"I'm here to let you know that Gorhail will be taking care of all funeral expenses," she says matter-of-factly. I hate how she speaks of Olivia's murder as an afterthought, as a formality to file away. I hate how my sister died thinking they wanted her among them.

"We appreciate it," Mother replies.

I step away from her. The ease with which she accepts Delaney's offer repulses me. Only moments ago, she was holding me responsible for my sister's death, and now that we have someone concrete to blame, she folds.

"Very well." The woman gives her a curt smile, as if Mother's answer has checked another box on her list. See Olivia's mother. Check. Offer to pay for funeral expenses. Check.

Then she turns her gaze to me, studying me like I'm an exhibit at the museum, as if she can't decide what to make of me yet.

"What is your name?" she asks, moving into the light. Her face is worn, threads of a sad life woven in every crease around her eyes and mouth. Her thin rose lips twitch with impatience the longer I look at her.

"I don't owe you a name," I finally reply.

She laughs. "Rhea taught you well."

"You knew Nan?" My curiosity gets the best of me. This woman is baiting me, and I am taking it like a starved fish.

"Rhea was my dearest friend." Her gaze is distant at first, then it locks on me. "DOTS has informed me that Olivia was a nonmagi."

Next to me, a strangled sound escapes Mother's throat. Did she think the three of us would carry the secret to the grave? That DOTS, the governing department of magic in Draterra, wouldn't realize Olivia didn't have magic when they examined her body?

"How could *you* not know?" Mother asks instead, to my surprise.

"Did you?" Delaney's voice is chilling behind her smile. "Because if you did, it would be a grave offense, and I would have to report you to the local sheriff for allowing your daughter to impersonate a mage."

I feel Mother's glare burning into me. I want more than anything for her to shut her mouth. Now is not the time to be vindictive. The moment Delaney finds out I am a mage *and* I've lied, I doubt she'll afford me the courtesy of the local sheriff. Mages in violation of any rules go straight to the Grand House at DOTS for judgment. I don't have *time* to rot in jail, not while Olivia's killer walks around Gorhail free.

"I didn't know," she replies. "Thank you for your visit, Madame Delaney, but it's been a long and difficult day. We appreciate your financial help." With that, she leaves me alone with this stranger.

"How long have you had your magic?" she pries.

I return a blank stare. She's fishing for confirmation.

"Oh my dear," she coos, her eyebrows knotting together. "If Olivia was a nonmagi, it only means that you are the Mortemagi in the family. Magic never skips a generation." She offers me a sympathetic smile before turning to face the garden again. Now that it's dark, a few lightflies buzz around the flowers; Olivia used to love watching them from our bedroom window. Usually, there's a cluster of them, but tonight, they all seem to be mourning my sister.

"I don't know," I answer truthfully. She probably thinks I'm lying, but I don't know how long I've had my magic. Nan was the first dead person I was around, the first one to share her last words with me. After that, I had to sneak into every funeral I came across so my ears wouldn't ring into oblivion.

"Olivia never mentioned a sister," she muses. "I could report you to DOTS. It's illegal for mages to not register themselves."

A knot forms in my throat, and it becomes clear that she's not here for Olivia at all. "My sister was murdered this morning, and you've come here to make threats?"

"It was an accident, Miss Corvi," she states, turning to me. "Poachers aren't idiots. They wouldn't murder a mage when Secondline patrols the area every hour."

Her insistence makes me sick, but it also reminds me that the authorities will likely brush Olivia's murder under the rug. By Friday, my sister will be nothing but a statistic, her senseless murder not even worthy of a headline. I refuse to let this be Olivia's legacy.

"What do you want?" I ask through clenched teeth. She clearly has something in mind. Why else would she drive to Albion to threaten me when she could've reported me to DOTS the moment she found out Olivia was a nonmagi?

"For you to attend Gorhail."

A laugh bubbles at my throat. No. I did not spend the last twelve years staying away to cave in to threats now. But then, this woman's words spark an idea. What if attending Gorhail could help me prove that Olivia was murdered? I think back on Olivia's riddle, and Gorhail is filled with mages with serpentlike relics. Still, I ask, "Why?"

"The Grand Master of the House of Death wishes for you to enroll at the institute," she replies.

Delaney is giving me the chance to investigate Olivia's murder on a silver platter, yet something gnaws at the back of my head. The Grand Master doesn't grant leniency out of the goodness of her heart. What *else* do they want?

At my hesitation, Delaney's gaze flicks to my arm. "You may not realize it yet, but your cuff holds centuries of cultivated magic. It would be a waste for DOTS to seal it all away."

Of course, it's the magic. In the end, mage or nonmagi, they're all the same—it's always about what they can get from you and never about you as a person. I haven't even begun to grieve my dead sister, and these people already see me as a commodity to add to their circus of monsters.

"I . . ." I begin, but I don't know what to say. No matter how much I hate magic and Gorhail, my investigation into Olivia's murder has to start there. "I'll need some time . . . please."

"Of course." She holds my gaze for a moment, then turns away. "I suppose you will be busy with funeral rites, so I will await your answer by Friday morning." She climbs down the steps, stopping at the barren rosebush that Mother ruined two days ago. "You know, Miss Corvi, even a trivial lie festers like a wound."

As Delaney drives away into the night, her words linger.

What I thought was a harmless secret ended up killing my sister, and in the end, that same lie is taking me to the place I was so desperate to escape.

Founder's relic: One of three relics of immortality belonging to the founders of Gorhail Institute of Magic. Founder's relics include Ysenia Faro's Cuff, Sileas Ronin's Imortalis, and the Arkani Coin from the four founders who joined the Houses of Illusion, Metal, Dust, and Secrets to form the House of Arcane.

YSENIA FARO, *THE FOUNDER'S BOOK OF RELICS*, **CHAPTER 7**

Private Note: Faro's Cuff missing since Willow's death.
—**HANSEL, 1925**

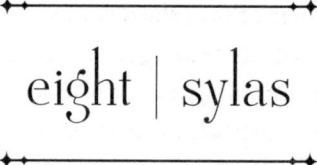

eight | sylas

WEDNESDAY, NOVEMBER 17, 1939

Beau is dead.

My shoulders ache from the number of people who squeezed them, offering condolences. By now, they must be familiar with the routine. They all look at me with pity in their eyes when they should be wishing death upon me. Dad and Beau were both killed because of me.

We've been back from the woods for hours, and I haven't moved from the front steps of Overseer Paltro's office, unable to go anywhere near the institute. The cold early afternoon air bites at my exposed skin. Still, I don't move because I deserve every ounce of pain the weather chooses to inflict.

Paltro was in his office when I walked out of the passageway, my dead brother in my arms and my sister at my heels. He'd considered me for a moment, wondering if this was yet another of my antics gone wrong. But when my tears started flowing, and Lyria wouldn't stop crying, he took Beau's body from me without a word and carried him away, with Lyria following closely behind.

My fists unclench, and the stupid Afa's Bloom stares at me—white petals splattered with Beau's blood. Damas wears his name well as the God of Luck and Treachery. We came back with all the ingredients and my brother's corpse. Then again, why do we pray to the Gods for a gamble?

I squeeze my fist, rub the flowers together, and toss them to the side. It's all useless now. Beau is dead. And nothing can bring him back.

Around my wrist, Raiku coils and uncoils himself, occasionally slithering to my hand, and then back. Railesza hisses, her sharp eyes studying my face, then she wraps around my forearm. I run my knuckles against the soft scales of her head. She tried so hard, harder than she did with Dad, but like before, even she can't bring back the dead.

"Sylas." A labored voice calls in the distance. I lift my head, and Paltro walks toward me with an unsteady gait. As he gets closer, I notice his bloodshot eyes and the quiet sniffles.

"Let's go inside, son." He pats me on the shoulder, his face somber. He looks like a decade swallowed him today. I probably look worse, with my torn clothes and maroon-crusted nails.

I drag myself into his office, the rust stink of blood trailing after me, taking over the room's usual scent of pine and wood. Paltro gathers a couple of books from his desk and neatly shelves them on the wall behind him. When he turns around, his face looks gaunt. He clicks his tongue, lets out a long sigh, then takes a seat, beckoning me to do the same.

The brown leather armchair squeaks when I slump in it. If Paltro expects me to talk, he'll wait a long time. I already know what he's going to tell me: I'll have to answer to the Grand House for Beau's death. They've probably already decided to throw me in prison. I've broken too many rules to ask for leniency—endangering the lives of two uncertified mages, one of whom was killed under my watch; breaking curfew with a mage who was accused of murder; stealing Afa's Bloom from the Northern Greenhouse; and retrieving Chasmore without prior authorization. Even if I didn't *kill* Beau, he was killed on an unauthorized field assignment led by *me*.

Besides, what would be the point of fighting their sentence? Going through life with Dad's death weighing on my every thought is agonizing, but even the mundane task of breathing feels impossible when I think of Beau. How will I carry on for Lyria if I can't hold myself together?

In silence, I watch Paltro drop two heaping teaspoons of tea leaves in the black iron kettle to his right. Beau used to be fascinated with these kettles when he was younger—Arkani made, forged by manipulators and powered by dustmaker dust, they heat up the moment water is poured in.

"Silver's missing." Paltro catches me off guard. I was expecting him to chastise me, not go straight to investigating. Perhaps it's how he copes. He lost himself in work after Dad died.

Beau's aspier, Silver, was given to him a few years after his mother's death, while his father's aspier rests in his family vault in Riverview. Normally, a young Aspieri goes to a relicsmith to have their own aspier forged with a hair from their bloodline—usually their own—but Beau's parents died when he was only two. They didn't even have the chance to take him to the relicsmith.

Now the Cardot line is dead, and Silver is free to bond with another Aspieri.

"Rhodes mentioned that Victor's relic was also taken," I reply with a frown. I want there to be a connection, want a reason for the poachers to have murdered my brother, because I refuse to think Damas was this cruel. We've all gone into the woods countless times past curfew. Why did it have to be Beau?

Paltro hums while he retrieves a small towel soaked in alcohol and hands it to me. I hesitate. Washing Beau's blood off my hands feels like I'm already moving on. He died mere hours ago.

"Son." Paltro looks at me like I'm broken, and maybe I am. "Grief will swallow you whole if you don't forgive yourself," he says, edging the towel in my direction.

My hands wrap around the wet cloth. With each scrub, I hold back my tears. How could I let this happen?

"Sylas, I understand what you're going through, but you need to pull yourself together," Paltro says softly, plucking the towel out of my hands. Then he pulls two cups from his drawer. He reaches for the kettle through the mess on his desk and pours us each a cup. The earthy smell of his special blend of mint, vanilla, and black tea from Old Iserine calms me a little. I take a sip.

"Olivia Corvi also died this morning," he says.

"How?" I nearly spit out my tea. Now, he has my attention.

"Drowned in Little Lake Albion. A gruesome sight." He recoils, setting his empty cup aside. "Claws ripped through her arm. I'll spare you the details. Her relic is also gone."

Three relics stolen in three days. It can't be a coincidence. "That doesn't make sense, Uncle. Olivia Corvi was a nonmagi, wasn't she? Nonmagi can't wear relics, and poachers can track them."

"A nonmagi who hid so well that no one found her until her death." He nods. "Per the Firstline investigator assigned to her case, someone fashioned a *real* relic for her at some point. She was going to be offered a teaching position at the academy, and they needed to test her relic for modifications, as per protocol."

I have a hard time believing that the nonmagi wanted to stay at Gorhail for a teaching position. Magisters—mage teachers—are somehow paid even less than their nonmagi counterparts. Her motivations for staying aren't convincing . . . and now she's dead.

"Do you have the preliminary report?" I lean forward. This nonmagi may be key to figuring what happened to Beau.

"Firstline hasn't released one yet, but the Albion sheriff says she tripped on the boardwalk and fell into the lake." Paltro gives me a knowing look. "It's certainly not a coincidence that Victor was found dead yesterday morning, and Olivia and Beau died around the same time this morning."

He doesn't have to say more. This isn't the work of random poachers if they were unafraid to murder them in Gorhail and Albion, where Secondline patrols night and day. There's a link between the three of them, and I have to find it. I need to know why my brother was killed. Only then will I allow myself to grieve him. "Who's Firstline assigning to their case?" I ask.

Paltro nods. "Darro's first case."

At the mention of Gryff's name, I look away. As much as I am comforted that Gryff has been assigned to the case, I hate that this is probably how he and his brother, Grayson, found out about Beau's death.

"Poacher activity is rampant across the Ten Provinces." Paltro pulls down the map of the country from a shelf behind him. With a long pen, he taps on the border where Aurignan and Holm meet Old Iserine. "Reports of settlement expansion across the country came in."

I squint for a better view of the map. It's filled with red crosses. "It seems like they're preparing for something."

Paltro rises from his seat, walks around his desk to the low table encased by a warm brown sofa behind me. I stand and watch him pick up a copy of *The Daily Mage*, a national newspaper spreading propaganda like it's their only purpose. He raises it up so I can see the headline: "Rafael Grimm: Monster or Misunderstood?"

The increase in poacher settlements makes sense now. For centuries, *The Daily Mage* has been rewriting history about Grimm, making him out to be some sort of hero and dismissing his crimes. As a result, his followers have been growing in number and becoming bolder. But he is dead, his soul bound for eternity in a Mortemagi relic in our ancestor's personal vault, which only Lyria and I can access. It's ironic how Mortemagi don't even trust themselves to contain a monster they forged.

"Why doesn't DOTS put a stop to *The Daily Mage*'s Grimm propaganda?"

"Money," Paltro says as he puts on his coat. "*The Daily Mage* pays a hefty sum to DOTS every year to be able to operate in the Ten Provinces. Walk with me." Paltro holds his office door open, and I follow him outside. Without the distraction of the map and the newspaper, my thoughts drift to Beau again.

"The Grand House has yet to deliver your sentence, Sylas," he says. We cross the grass and take a left past the empty fountain of a snake with three heads, until we're under the sheltered walkway that leads to Hollow Tree.

Haal, I had momentarily forgotten about the Grand House.

"Raiek does complicate things," he adds when I don't reply. Of course the Imortalis *complicates* things. If the Grand House could sentence me to death like they did Beau, I would've already been dead. It's almost comedic how poachers are now emboldened to murder mages right outside of Gorhail walls, and the Grand House's priority is to discuss me.

"When's my hearing?"

"Tonight in Riverview," he says. "They've agreed to let you see your brother one last time, because you won't be allowed to attend his funeral."

I halt, clenching my fists at my sides. They know how important burial rites are to mages, and yet they won't let me bury my brother. Instead, my sister will have to stand alone as her aspier's venom locks our brother's casket and his body is lowered into the ground.

"Lyria . . ." I choke up.

". . . will be fine," he reassures me. "A Firstline investigator questioned her, and she was cleared immediately. Not that she didn't try to take the blame. I've sent her home to Iserine for a few days until we settle your case."

Guilt punches me in the gut. I took so much from my sister, and she's still trying to defend me.

Hollow Tree is quiet when we walk in. It's suspicious for this time of day, when mages should be having their afternoon tea. As Paltro and I walk across the expansive circular room, the few people there avert their eyes. Out of fear? Out of shame? I'm unsure. I follow Paltro up the stairs in silence, every step steeling myself to see Beau's body again.

We take the narrow hallway opposite Dean Rhodes's office and pass by three portraits of the Deathbringer, her golden eyes looking down on me. Why do we still celebrate her? What does she know of duty? If she hadn't abandoned all of us, poachers wouldn't have returned to Bale and killed my father, or my brother.

Our steps slow down. The chapel is on the other side of the large opening overlooking Hollow Tree's dining hall. I glance down, and the mages below scramble to resume their meals.

When we round the corner to the chapel, four High Guards block the entrance. Paltro holds his hand across my chest, barring me from taking a step forward. Two of the High Guards hurry toward us, black masks covering half their faces. They are high-ranked Firstline mages, tasked with the most dangerous cases. By the way they're acting, one would think I'm the leader of the poachers.

As they come to a stop in front of me, I peek around them into the chapel.

Beau's and Victor's bodies are gone.

My head snaps toward Paltro, but he's also in shock. Did someone move their bodies? I step around the guards to inquire, but one of them grabs me by the arm. "High Magus Sylas Archyr, you are under arrest for the murders of Beau Cardot and Victor Carver, as well as the abduction of their bodies. You will be tried for coconspiring with poachers."

My hands begin to sweat, and my muscles stiffen. Beau's *and* Victor's murders? How did the Grand House come to this absurd conclusion? At the commotion, both Raiku and Railesza awaken, their eyes shifting between me and the guards. But there is nothing I can do. Conspiring with poachers means high treason.

And high treason means they will kill me and my aspiers.

> Cultivating the blood arts bears the penalty of execution. Only Firstline Mortemagi are allowed to practice thread magic. Firstline Arkani are allowed the use of blood arts under extreme circumstances.
>
> **DOTS DECREE, 1503**

nine | viola

THURSDAY, NOVEMBER 18, 1939

Dearly Departed looks haunted from across the street. The shadows of the surrounding trees brush along the side of the single-story white building. Chills trace a line down my arms as I cross over, and I convince myself it's the frosty air, and not at all because I am terrified of the dark and the ghosts that roam. When I was younger, I read in one of Nan's journals that wandering ghosts—those that haven't crossed over to the Underworld—gather by the church at night, pleading with the God of Death to grant them safe passage. I know now how futile it is. Without proper burial rites, mages never cross into the Underworld.

I try the main door, but it's locked. It's also five in the morning, and in my haste to leave the house before Mother awoke, I forgot my key. After Delaney's visit yesterday, her parting words swirled in my mind, their poison slowly taking root until it was impossible for me to sleep. Even a trivial lie festers like a wound, she'd said. And yet she was happy to get behind the lie that Olivia *fell* into the water.

Delaney's ultimatum comes barreling in my head. Gorhail or DOTS.

I'd choose neither, but this isn't about me. Olivia deserves justice, and I won't find it by running away.

I take stock on the front porch, sighing when I count sixteen owl planters. Mara keeps a spare key to the back-office door in one of them, and they all look identical. Bloody saints, I just want to get in, talk to my sister, and leave before Mara comes in.

The low chirp of birds urges me forward. Soon, the sun will rise, and the ghosts will leave the church. As much as I want to believe it's a myth, I don't want to be caught in the middle of a gaggle of ghosts while wearing my relic.

After three wrong pots, a silver key shines up at me, buried behind a succulent. I pluck the key, studying the rust on the biting before walking around the corner. The back door unlocks with ease, and I slip inside.

The air feels wrong.

It smells of blood, salt, and something sharp. It smells of death. Were it the middle of a busy day, I wouldn't question it. But we always leave the place spotless before we close for the night, out of respect for the dead.

I weigh my first step. Complete silence. My shoulders relax a little. I continue down the hallway, past the preparation room until I'm in front of the cold room. Olivia's body should be here, and I pray to the Gods that her ghost lingered around long enough for me to speak to her.

When I reach for the door, my cuff sears against my arm. I flinch, releasing the handle, but the burning doesn't stop. I step away, and the pain deepens. It gnaws at my flesh until I press down on the handle, pushing open the cold metal door. I wonder if this could be Olivia's ghost, guiding me.

Two bodies lie side by side on cold steel tables. Neither of them is my sister's. I look around, but no one's here. Mara would never leave bodies unattended. She'd promised Olivia would be here, so where is my sister? Where is Mara?

The air shifts again, and I whirl, but I'm alone in here. It's nothing... Maybe Mara had to rush out to get Olivia's body from the sheriff's office. There's a reasonable explanation, I'm sure.

My gaze returns to the bodies in front of me. The first one is a young man a couple of years older than me—black hair, angular face, bruises along his jaw, his cheekbones, and three deep clawlike cuts on the side of his neck, stretching to his collarbone. The second man is around my age. His light brown hair is stained crimson with blood, his features more boyish. Underneath his left ear is a birthmark shaped like a broken heart. His face as pallid as the first man. And yet, even in death, his lips quirk with a slight smile.

Something's off. They're unlike the dead I've worked with before, or maybe it's my cuff misleading me, but they look like they're frozen in time.

I lean over the dark-haired man, studying his clothes for any identification. He wears a long-sleeved black shirt with a detailed silver crest—divided in four quarters, one knife, one pen, one laurel, and one key—embroidered on the left pocket. The crest of Gorhail's House of Arcane. The second body wears a similar shirt, but the fabric is torn where his House crest would be—ripped by claw marks.

My skin prickles. It can't be a coincidence that three Gorhail students were killed on the same day. Olivia's arm was riddled with claw marks. The clues are in plain sight, and with this, the authorities won't be able to argue that her death was a mere accident. I swallow, the reality of it all sinking into my gut. Someone is murdering students.

A cold hand snatches my wrist. I yelp, but no sound comes out. The frozen tendrils of death crawl along my veins until I *feel* my bones turning to frost. With the cuff, the magic is relentless. It holds my breath, locks me in my own body, reminds me that right now, it has total control.

The black-haired man opens his eyes. White irises stare at me. I expect his dry, flaky lips to move, but they don't. They never do. *He whom you seek lies in the catacombs.*

The chill dissipates, and I snatch my wrist away, rubbing the invisible imprints of his cold, dead fingers off my skin. Another complex riddle. Olivia and this stranger chose the most inconvenient time to be cryptic, but I know one thing for certain: Gorhail houses both serpents and catacombs that stretch all the way through Bale to the holy grounds of Old Iserine.

Behind me, the door squeaks. I whip around, bracing myself on a table for balance. I don't know who I was expecting, but it was definitely not Mara. Relief floods me—she must have come back to handle these bodies.

"Viola." She leans against the doorframe, amused. I don't know why I don't greet her back. "You're here . . . early," she observes.

"I . . ." I pause. "I thought Olivia would be here."

"She was, but a Firstline officer from DOTS headquarters came in late last night and requested her body for further investigation," she says.

I lift my eyebrows. Did they make the same connection about the three murders? Thank the Gods. If DOTS made the request, it means that they're finally taking Olivia's death seriously. If Firstline finds her killer, I won't have to set foot at Gorhail. And if DOTS wants to seal my magic as punishment for my and Olivia's deceit, I'll gladly turn myself in.

"Oh..." My response is delayed, the words not quite coming together.

"How are you holding up?" Mara's eyes soften. I hate that she regards me with such pity. Until now, I kept my sorrow at bay with the promise of speaking to my sister's ghost. But she's not here, and slowly, my grief is creeping back, sinking its claws into my heart. This time, I'm afraid it won't stop until her death is imprinted on my soul.

I shake my head, biting back sobs that threaten to spill any second.

"You're allowed to grieve." The softness of her voice wraps me with the comfort I needed yesterday, one that my own mother couldn't provide. Mara's warmth beckons me to tell her everything that's on my mind. How I'm hoping that Firstline rules Olivia's death a murder, so I don't have to go to the institute. How I loathe myself for being so selfish—Olivia didn't hesitate a second before she took my place, and here I am still trying to find ways to stay away from that wretched school.

But I cannot bring myself to speak about her. "Did they just come in?" I ask instead, my head bobbing toward the bodies.

After a long sigh, Mara nods, her smile fading into a thin line. "Can you get started on cleaning both of them and wheel them to storage, please? I'll be right back."

When I don't answer, she adds, "If it's too soon—"

"No," I stop her. "No, I can do it."

Mara excuses herself, and I turn my attention back to the second body. Stepping in between the tables, I wait. But nothing happens. He doesn't grab my wrist. So I reach for his hand. Nothing again. How is that possible? I've never come across a dead person who didn't have last words to share. I lean over, studying his face, wondering if he's in fact not dead, because there's no other explanation for him to be quiet.

As I look him over, my eyes catch on the tiniest red embroidery on the side pocket of his thick combat pants. I squint, trying to make sense of the pattern.

A red serpent.

Olivia's warning hits me again, and I stagger backward. At the same time, I hear a voice. Young, male, layered with a slight resonance. *Run*, he says as my cuff sears against my skin.

A ghost. I feel it in my gut.

Footsteps echo, and with each one, my breath shallows. The dead have never spoken to me without a touch before. Why did the voice tell me to run? Run where? Run from what?

"They are far too young to be dead," Mara mutters as she walks back in, putting on a pair of gloves.

My shoulders relax. It's only Mara.

"Your sister didn't deserve this either," she continues.

I murmur my agreement. "You don't think she fell?"

She gives me a pointed look, and I could cry in relief. She shares my suspicion. Maybe she can help me investigate Olivia's murder.

"What's under your shirt?" She motions to the silhouette of the cuff under my sleeve. Bloody saints, I should have worn a sweater. I don't want Mara to know I have magic, don't want her to see me differently.

"A gift from my mother," I lie with unease.

"Is it like the one your sister wore?" she asks.

Her question brings me pause. How does she know Olivia wore a cuff? Yesterday was the first time Mara saw my sister. And her relic had already been stolen then. Maybe Mara assumed Olivia wore a cuff because she was a mage—

Run, please run. The voice echoes in my head again, his tone a raw despair.

"Family jewelry from the Isles of Carac," I lie. Nan was from Carac; I doubt Mara will question it. Panic courses through my veins. "Actually, I'm not feeling well. I think I'll head home . . . You're right, it's too soon . . ."

"Of course, Viola. Take all the time you need." She smiles, but her face is void of her usual warmth. Even her blue-green eyes look greener, sharper now. Or maybe my mind is playing tricks again. Mara's my safe person; I've known her for four years.

Run, now, Viola. The ominous feeling deep in my belly takes root. It tells me to listen. It tells me that the dead never lie. So I make a beeline for the back door.

"Viola," Mara calls out. I don't look back, terrified of what I might find. I hurry my pace, keeping her in my peripherals. As I move, she speeds toward me like a lioness chasing her first dinner after hibernation. I push through the door, trip over the steps, catch myself, and keep running.

In a blink, she's standing in front of me. Her eyes are an icy green now, unrecognizable, framed by dark veins that remind me of something I've only read about in Nan's books: puppets—bodies controlled by death magic. Mara lunges for me, and by some divine intervention I sidestep, and she falls.

I bolt across the street, toward the lake and away from the town into Albion Forest, running as fast as my legs will go. My chest tightens, my lungs threaten to give up any minute, and my thighs burn to the bone. Still, I push through until I no longer recognize the path ahead.

I pause, heaving, begging my lungs to calm down. The tallest trees I've ever seen shroud me from the light of the full moon. In the stillness, I only hear the falter of my breath and the thumping of my heart.

Then the sound of crushed leaves steals my next breath. I don't know where it's coming from, only that it grows closer. I don't wait for it to catch up to me. I take off deeper into the woods, but now the once slender trees are thicker, humming a low tone I'm unfamiliar with. And if I listen closer, I hear the song of death. I am no longer in Albion Forest. I am now in Gorhail Woods.

My shins are on the brink of shattering, my lungs are trying so hard, but they squeeze within my chest. My body can't keep up with my will to survive. Finally, I halt, finding the nearest shelter in the hollow of a tree trunk. I gulp in desperate breaths, looking to the skies, praying to any God that will hear my plea. The momentary silence fools me into believing that I am safe, but I fail to see it for what it is: the calm before everything goes wrong.

The steps are back. More of them; some walking, some running. I don't dare look. I don't dare move. I don't dare breathe. It's dark, and my only hope is that I'm small enough to go unnoticed.

At the first break in the footsteps, my ears strain toward the sound of voices. The whispers grow more and more distant. Now is my chance. I run.

My pace has slowed to half of what it was before, but I can't stop moving. I follow the trail ahead, rounding five quick bends, and drag my feet along the only broken-stone path north. My mouth is dry, and my stomach caves in on itself. I want to go home, lock myself in my room, and never come out. In truth, I'll be lucky to survive the night. If the puppet that was once Mara doesn't kill me, the sheer pain and exhaustion will.

I round another corner with white flowers. This is the third time I'm seeing these within the last ten minutes. Gods, I'm going in circles. My legs retract, walking in the opposite direction, and I smack face-first into someone.

Mara stares at me for a beat. My naivete thinks she will rescue me, but the second her hands move, I curse myself for hoping. Her fingers morph into thin, sharp claws. In one sweep, she scratches my cheek, and something warm trickles down my neck. I bring my hand to the cut. By Death, it stings.

"Please, Mara." I back off. "Please let me go."

She cocks her head, examining my face. Is she considering my request? Is Mara even in there? Her eyebrows twitch, and her claws retract. Gods, let Mara be back. Bring her to her senses. Free me of this madness.

Right as I allow myself a breath, her knifelike claws slash across my chest. The shock dulls the pain that blooms beneath my skin.

I'm on the ground. She boxes me in, readying herself to strike again.

I cannot die tonight. If I die, Olivia's death will be yet another headline. She'll be forgotten, left to rot while her murderer runs free. I kick Mara as hard as I can. For Olivia. She stumbles backward, and I scramble to my feet.

Then I run.

I run until my lungs are on fire. I run until my breath starts to falter. I run until my legs slam against the cold soil. I run until darkness is all I can see. And when it swallows me, I tell myself at least I tried.

> A mage bond is sacred, a promise to value the other mage's life above one's own.
>
> Double bonds remain until both mages die.
>
> Mages who share a class of magic can only double bond. Double bonds between different classes are only allowed among Firstline mages.
>
> **Note**: In order to heal a mage from a different class of magic, an Aspieri is required to bond with them through a single or double bond. Aspieri are allowed to single bond only under dire circumstances.
>
> **KALI TELAM, THIRD FOUNDER OF GORHAIL,**
> *ON BONDS AND SACRIFICE*

ten | sylas

THURSDAY, NOVEMBER 18, 1939

Excessive. The Grand House's display of power is excessive.

After my second hearing this morning, they shoved me into a car flanked by two High Guards, each holding an Arkani-made box, one with Railesza and one with Raiku. Had they asked nicely, Raiku wouldn't have sent two guards to the hospital and Railesza wouldn't have choked a third one to sleep.

I suppose this is what they mean when they say Aspieri are volatile. They want to be able to control us without consequences.

For these minor inconveniences, I was sent to the Riverview Correctional Facility for Wayward Mages, and Raiku and Railesza were taken away in boxes. Judging by how yesterday went, I might as well make myself at home. After the High Guards tried to take me away by force, we ended up sitting in Rhodes's office with Paltro, arguing about the incredulity of the accusation. Normally, high treason bears the death penalty, but with the Imortalis around my neck, the Grand House took a whole night to decide that they needed more time to deliver an appropriate punishment. As of this morning, they *still* needed more time.

As I sit on the floor, staring at the bare white walls, I wonder who has enough pull with DOTS to accuse me of crimes I haven't even committed. Save for the metal bars, I would've thought this to be an asylum. Prison would've been better.

This place is supposed to rehabilitate "misguided" mages, but the truth is more sinister. It houses the worst of the Mortemagi, mostly summoners and puppeteers, well versed in the arts of blood magic. The former raise the dead, and the latter become the dead. The majority worship Grimm, furthering his cause of what he called "magical freedom," at the expense of those unlucky enough to be their sacrifice. Rogue Mortemagi used to be executed before, but the Grand House's most recent ruling offered them a chance at rehabilitation. Pity they don't afford unregistered crossmages the same understanding. In this world, a proven murderer is less dangerous than a mage who can dual wield.

Beau's been dead for more than a day now, and instead of pooling resources to find his body, they've assigned six Firstline officers to guard me as I "rehabilitate." To top it off, they went out of their way to assign me Firstline Arkani and Mortemagi.

"Archyr," one of them calls out, his hands working open the lock. Earlier this morning, he threw a platter of food at me like I was some animal. I want more than anything to slam my fist into his jaw. "Someone's here to see you."

"I didn't know I was allowed visitors." I smile, but the Mortemagi isn't amused. I'm hoping it's Lyria or Gryff so I can ask them about my aspiers. Maybe the Grand House has a heart after all and will spare them.

"Probably allowing you a last goodbye with your disgusting snakes," spits the Mortemagi. Haal, grant me freedom so I can send him to the seventh circle of the Underworld.

Paltro appears in the doorway then, his usual black coat traded for a gray one. He wears a plaid flat cap and round, black sunglasses. "Mr. Archyr, please come with me," he says.

Immediately, the Mortemagi stops him. "We have orders to keep the criminal in this ward."

Paltro lowers his glasses and looks the young man up and down. "Percy," he reads off the Mortemagi's name tag. "The Principal Grand Master has ordered his immediate release."

The Mortemagi scoffs. "PGM Parrish would never sign off on an Aspieri's release."

PGM Parrish's sister was the Deathbringer, I want to remind him. But due to pressure from purists around the Ten Provinces, she *has* been harsher toward Aspieri lately.

Paltro pulls a rolled parchment from his pocket, and I recognize DOTS's official red seal. The Mortemagi—Percy—snatches the letter from his hands, tearing the seal off. His eyes scan the page, every line deepening the scowl on his face. He calls a second Firstline mage and shoves the parchment under her nose. She takes one look at the bottom and nods. "Patient nine three zero four, you may leave."

I suppose I am Parrish's exception.

On my way out, I glance at the Mortemagi. "Do your fellow Aspieri officers know how you feel about their . . . disgusting snakes?"

"Less theatrics, more urgency." Paltro practically pushes me through the building.

"Who has enough pull to accuse me of both Beau's and Victor's murders?" I ask Paltro right before we exit the facility.

"Who do you think?" Paltro sounds irritated. "Viv Rowan." Fable's aunt, one of the four Grand Masters of the House of Arcane. Together with the Grand Master of Death and the Grand Master of Poison, they make up the six Grand Masters of the Grand House. My case probably went to a vote, and she likely blackmailed the three other Grand Masters of Arcane to vote against me. The Rowans' grudge against my family clearly knows no limits.

I'm about to ask him how he convinced Parrish to release me, but he motions me to the passenger's seat of his car. In silence, he climbs in the driver's seat and starts the engine. My stomach drops when I realize that Paltro does not have my aspiers.

"I hope one day you'll forgive what I'm about to ask of you," he says as we drive toward Gorhail.

By late afternoon, we've arrived at the House of Poison. Paltro doesn't wait for me as he rushes down the winding hallway to Hollow Tree. Instead of taking the stairs to Rhodes's office, we cross the dining hall, walk past the entrance to the House of Arcane, and go down another long hallway—this one dark and morbid, with dustmaker-powered red candles staggered on the right side of the wall. They look like blood dripping down the wall. Two right turns later, we are in front of double oak doors with a royal-blue raven crest in the middle.

I stop.

The overseer and I are standing outside of the House of Death. A line I refuse to cross. I've spent all my years at Gorhail avoiding that forsaken House and their mages that reek of despair. They deal with obscure magic, trading lifeblood and their sanity in the process.

"Sylas." Paltro beckons me forward.

I don't move.

Mom's smile flashes across my mind. The last time she read Lyria and me a story before bed, she had promised us a trip to Osneau to see the wild redbird. A promise she died with because of the Mortemagi who ripped her away from us.

"At the request of PGM Parrish, the Grand House has agreed to return your relics and drop all charges against you." Paltro's words weigh heavy with hope. My aspiers are fine. But I know this institution too well to celebrate. The Grand House doesn't grant favors without asking for twice as much.

The door opens.

Priya Parrish, the Grand Master of Death—who also serves as Principal Grand Master—steps out, her shoulders dropping the moment her eyes land on me. Beads of sweat dot her forehead. She is far from the pristine woman who's often on the front page of *The Daily Mage*. Her red-stained lips are now a shadow of pink, and her painted face is gone, revealing dark circles and creases between her eyebrows. She looks taller than her sister, the Deathbringer, with a narrower face and a sharp nose.

In her hands are two boxes. Without a second thought, I reach for them, but she pulls them out of my reach. "Does our agreement stand?" she asks Paltro.

"He *will* need his aspiers to heal her." Paltro's reply is short.

"Heal who?" I ask quietly.

"She's barely holding on. Are you certain this will work?" She ignores me, directing her question at Paltro again.

"Priya, his healing aspier draws on the magic of Raiek, the Imortalis. Railesza is your *only* option."

"*Who* is barely holding on?" I inquire. For a moment I worry about Lyria, but it can't be my sister. She wouldn't be at the House of Death.

Parrish's gaze lingers on me, then one after the other, she opens the boxes. Raiku springs out first, and I catch him with both hands. When he realizes it's me, he hisses and coils around my wrist, resting against my skin like a long-lost friend. Railesza yawns like she's awoken from the longest slumber. She takes her time slithering to my left forearm, going back to sleep the moment she settles.

"I'll be inside when you're ready. Please hurry," she says.

The moment she walks through the double doors, I glare at Paltro. But he doesn't look at me. "They need you to heal . . ." His throat bobs with discomfort. "A Mortemagi."

"No." I turn, then stop halfway. "Do you realize what you're asking of me?"

Paltro still doesn't meet my eyes. How could he do this? Heal a Mortemagi? He knew Mom. He was her friend.

"Sylas, you don't have a choice." He sighs.

I do have a choice. I can—my thought dies immediately. Paltro's right. I *don't* have a choice. But if I do what he asks of me, I would be betraying myself. Worse, I'd be betraying Mom.

"You know I cannot heal another class of mage without bonding to them. Our bonds are sacred, Uncle." Bonds are more than a promise. They are a commitment to value the other person's life over yours. Bonds across different Houses used to be outlawed but now are seen as a strategic part of Firstline. With the proper ranks, mages from different classes can double bond with each other, sharing a fraction of their magic.

"Sylas—"

"I am not throwing away my one bond," I say. Once I bond with this Mortemagi, I will never be able to bond again until they die. It's not even a double bond—I'll get nothing in return. And even if she were conscious to double bond, I would never accept her horrifying magic. "They can have the aspiers back. They can even have Raiek if they can take him off," I say. Raiku and Railesza hiss at me in disbelief.

"The Rowans have a vendetta against your family. They *will* kill your aspiers," Paltro reminds me, and I feel like an arse for even suggesting sending them back. "And they *will* find a way to take Raiek. He has been in your mother's family for centuries, Sylas. The thought of any other bloodline wielding him is revolting."

My head lowers to face Raiku and Railesza wrapped around my forearms, both staring at me like I've deeply betrayed them. "I wasn't serious. I'll never let you die," I murmur in apology.

Is this Mortemagi royalty or a god? Because it makes no sense for the Grand House to break their own rule to save someone's life. They *never* release people accused of high treason. On top of that, if Viv Rowan learns that this was part of a personal deal between Paltro and the PGM, Parrish could lose her title.

Paltro's eyes meet mine. I hear everything he doesn't say. Think of Lyria, Sylas. Think of everything she will lose. Think of Beau, of how his killer runs free while his body lays cold somewhere unknown. Think of the looming threat of dead mages and stolen relics.

"Fine." I force out the word. With a grunt, I cross into the House of Death, and Paltro leads me through a smaller set of doors on the right.

The room is a small, hexagonal mess. The walls are lined with shelves, filled with books, flasks of potions, dried flowers, hanging bones, and jars full of... body parts that make me want to bolt out of there.

Parrish is bent over someone, wiping their face with a washcloth. The low lighting strains my vision, and I squint, noticing the silhouette of a young woman. She looks a couple of years younger than me. The moment my eyes land on the cuff around her arm, I gasp.

Olivia Corvi. Liar extraordinaire from the House of the Forsaken.

"I can't heal the dead," I say. "Is this a sick joke?"

Overseer Paltro ushers me forward. "Look closer."

My steps are careful as I approach her. This could be a trap.

The young woman is covered in blood, so much blood that my steps falter and my stomach churns. How is she alive? There are open wounds across her chest, her abdomen, her legs. Her face is a canvas of bloodied cuts, and her hair is matted with a mixture of dirt and blood. She looks so fragile I'm afraid to get closer, terrified that even the gentlest touch might break her, terrified that I will fail again. If I couldn't save my father or Beau, what makes them think I can save this person? She's lost nearly all the blood in her small body.

"This is Viola Corvi," Parrish says. "Olivia's sister."

My throat bobs. Olivia had a sister? Her eyelids flicker, as if she's trying to hold on to whatever little life she has left. Every shaky breath she takes threatens to be her last.

I blink hard. This woman looks harmless, but she's still a Mortemagi. She could kill everyone I love the same way that one of them killed Mom. Or she could become the next Rafael Grimm.

Her breathing quickens. Railesza loosens around my forearm, tightly wrapping her tail around my wrist. For reasons I will never understand, she tugs on my hand until it rests on the woman's, and she slithers along. When she gets to the tip of my finger, she pauses, as if she, too, is considering whether we should do this. Once her fangs sink into this Mortemagi's veins, I am bonded to her until I die, or she dies.

Raiku hisses at me. He thinks it's a mistake, too. He hisses again, at Raiek this time. He is right: the cost is too high. I am not just any Aspieri. I wield the most powerful aspier in history. "I cannot—"

The girl's breathing begins to drop, and Railesza is already halfway wrapped around her arm and mine. Before biting the Mortemagi, she looks at me in question, or maybe in defiance. She seems to be telling me to think about what Dad would do. Would Dad heal a Mortemagi knowing they killed Mom? *We are defined by our actions, not theirs*, he would have said.

My teeth cut into my lips. I am not Dad. I cannot bring myself to forgive so easily. But Railesza doesn't wait for my answer, and her fangs sink into the girl's wrist. My breath hitches. As much as I want to blame Railesza for making the choice for me, we both know aspiers act on their Aspieri's desires.

I won't let her die tonight, that's the only mercy I can promise, but Gods forgive me, I won't honor the bond. I will never put a Mortemagi's life above mine. Even if I have to suffer the consequence of being sent to the tenth circle of the Underworld.

My healing aspier works slowly but with precision. The Mortemagi whimpers as Railesza moves across the wounds, and I find myself holding her hand, silently speaking prayers to the same Gods who took everything from me. If she lives, I am free.

"Is she a mage?" A rhetorical question. Of course she's a mage. Aspiers can't bond with nonmagi, let alone heal them.

"Yes," Parrish croaks. "She's Rhea Corvi's legacy."

My hand pulls away, but Railesza's grip holds it in place.

Rhea Corvi was the worst of the House of Death. Her tenure as dean of Gorhail saw the highest number of unregistered crossmages sent to DOTS. She ruled with an iron fist and a heart of stone. She is also the reason why Firstline began recruiting select Mortemagi, allowing them to train in the arts of blood magic. Now they are surprised when the same Mortemagi defect to poacher camps. I can *hear* Lyria telling me not all of them are bad, but I disagree; they're all the same. Give them a taste of power, and they'll drown in it.

"What's her magic?" I ask. She's either a whisperer or a conduit. I doubt she even knows about lifeblood magic; if she did, she wouldn't have been hanging on to life.

Parrish casts the Mortemagi a sympathetic look, brushing her wet hair away from her forehead. Her empathy unsettles me. It goes against everything I've learned about Mortemagi. Why is she so invested in this woman?

"I don't know. Whatever it is, she's untrained," she answers.

This is who they bent the rules to save? Who I wasted my only bond on? An untrained Mortemagi is a dead mage. No one has to kill them; their magic does the honor.

Parrish meticulously wipes blood off the Mortemagi's body. Her touch is so gentle, as if the woman is made of glass. "She cannot die, High Magus Archyr," she says. "Rhea Corvi's bloodline cannot end here. Her relic holds centuries of magic."

I scoff. So that's why Parrish is so invested. It's always about the heirloom relic, never about the mage. If this Mortemagi dies, centuries of magic will end with her. Centuries of harmful, wicked, unnatural magic. Perhaps it's not so wrong that she dies. I can argue that I tried to save her. I even threw away my only bond to do so.

Pulling my hand away, I nudge Railesza back, but she continues healing the Mortemagi. So I gently tug my hand backward, but my aspier pins me with a glare that makes Raiku perk up. "Railesza," I call out. She ignores me again and resumes healing.

I'm about to reach out and physically remove my traitor aspier when two brown eyes snap open.

The second they lock on me, a deafening scream leaves the Mortemagi's mouth.

Raiku reacts before I'm able to catch my bearings. His fangs sink into her veins, and she passes out again. Haal, what has he done? What have I done?

Parrish grabs me by the shoulders, and it becomes clear why she has sovereignty over the Grand House. Her fingers dig into my skin, and through clenched teeth, she utters, "If she dies, I will kill everyone you love while you watch."

> Crossmages could be an asset to Firstline. I have included a twenty-page examination of their potential. Please consider reviewing the decree that one of their classes should be sealed.
>
> **LETTER FROM DEAN MATILDA RHODES, MAGUS PRINCIPALIS, TO DOTS, 1929**
>
> Case Created No. 3264
>
> DOTS Ruling on Case 3264: Rejected

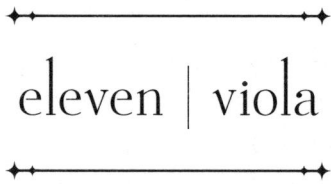

eleven | viola

FRIDAY, NOVEMBER 19, 1939

One green eye. A harrowing scream. Everything goes black.

When I come to my senses again, thin rays of sunlight caress old books and dead plants across the room. My vision blurs, and my head hurts like it's carrying the weight of a tree.

Faint voices murmur in the background, but I can't make out the words, only the unmistakable inflections of worry. I'm trying to keep my eyes open, but instead, I drift off to a perfect world. A world where Olivia is alive, and I never had magic.

After a while, they open again to flameless torches lighting the room. Faint but beautiful. My vision still struggles to adjust. A woman stands in front of me. She's my mother's age. She's striking, her black hair braided around her head in a crown, dressed in a simple black tunic. An angel of death. Has she come for me? I don't get my answer because sleep swallows me again.

The third time I open my eyes, I can *see*. The ceiling is cherrywood, with several dead plants hanging from the beams. It looks as it smells, old, morbid, and sad. At my side are several bloodied washcloths and a pile of torn pieces of cloth. When I realize these are my clothes, I panic, look down, notice that I'm in a linen robe, and calm down.

"Water," I croak. The sound coming out of my mouth is not mine.

A chair moves, and a woman approaches with a cup. It is her, the angel of death. Up close, she looks younger than my mother. But her bronze skin has dulled, her brown eyes are sunken, and her mouth is pulled in a frown.

She helps me sit up and brings the cup to my lips. The first sip doesn't make it down my throat. I cough, spraying water over myself. By the third or fourth sip, I'm fighting back tears. The liquid feels like it's peeling off the lining of my throat.

"Where am I?" I rasp, my voice still so foreign.

"You're safe," the woman says softly. "You're at the House of Death."

Gorhail. Why didn't they just let me die?

"We'll head to your room when you're ready." She brushes my hair tenderly. "The overseer has assigned you your sister's old room."

Olivia's room? Death would have been more merciful. Do they want me to drown in the memories of a sister who was killed because of me? To find pieces of my sister that I lost over the last twelve years and have to say goodbye all over again?

I've barely been conscious a minute, and the institute already feels suffocating. I stop myself. Maybe waking up here is a sign from the Gods. Maybe they spared me so I could find out what happened to Olivia.

"Miss Corvi . . . how are you feeling now?" the woman asks when I don't reply.

I open my mouth to answer, but all that comes to mind are Mara's eerie green eyes and the sharpness of her claws digging into my flesh. My throat closes, and my stomach tightens. Instinctively, my hand drags up to my chest, where I was certain she ripped out my heart. Nothing's there. I peek inside the robe. No open wound, not even a bruise, just white scars.

"What happened to me?" I finally manage to ask.

The woman gives me a tight smile. "You were attacked." She shifts her weight and looks away; she doesn't plan to elaborate.

"Who are you?" I ask.

"Priya Parrish. Call me Priya." Her smile warms, and she takes a seat on the chair near my bed. "Grand Master of Death Magic, and I also serve as

Principal Grand Master at the Department of the Supernatural. You may know it as DOTS."

DOTS. I can ask her about Olivia's murder. Firstline took her body for further investigation, and Priya has to have more information if she's in charge of DOTS.

"You have your father's eyes," she says, right as I'm about to ask her about Olivia.

I stare at her. She knew my father. Suddenly, I have a million questions. What was he like? Was he a whisperer, too?

Before I can ask, the doors creak open. Priya straightens, her eyes trained on the person walking in.

"Welcome, Miss Corvi." A familiar voice fills the space. "Good to see you alive."

Delaney's heels click against the wooden floorboard, and it's so . . . loud. How ironic that just two days ago, she gave me until Friday to make a decision, and here I am at the very place I spent my life avoiding.

"When is my sister's funeral?" I ask no one in particular. With Olivia's body moved to DOTS, funeral plans had to have changed.

"Monday," Delaney answers. "We will arrange for transport to Albion, of course." Monday seems soon yet so far. I am torn between wanting to see my sister again and not wanting to say goodbye. I imagine that's how my life will be now; a constant push and pull; anger that she was ripped away from me too soon and regret over everything I could've done to prevent that.

"Will I be able to see her before then?" I try, looking from one to the other, before lingering on Priya. She is the Principal Grand Master; she *is* the authority.

"I'm afraid this will not be possible," says Priya. "Rest assured, her body is being well cared for. It's just . . . the full extent of magic doesn't work on nonmagi, so we've had to call in a regular medical examiner."

Magic doesn't work on nonmagi. Her words sink like an anchor, dragging down my hopes of ever speaking to my sister. I knew this. I've always known this. Only two types of magic work on nonmagi. An Arkani reader's touch to read their memories, and a Mortemagi whisperer's touch to hear their last words. How could I have forgotten? I was never going to be able to speak to Olivia's ghost. It was never going to be more than her last words at the lake, and I didn't even let her finish speaking.

"I promise, we're working as fast as we can," Priya reassures me, but it doesn't matter anymore. "Sorry, Miss Corvi, I—"

"I don't think there's a need to apologize for formalities, Principal Grand Master Parrish." Delaney clears her throat. "If one of our Secondline mages hadn't run into you, you would have been dead, too, Miss Corvi."

Of course she has to remind me that I am alive because of them. I glare at her insensitivity, but she's right. I was dying, so how am I alive? "What did you do to me?"

Delaney's head tilts to the side, her lips pulling into a proud smile. "We healed you."

"At what cost?"

"We protect our own." She meets my eyes with a silent understanding that I owe them the same. My anger boils at my throat. Why didn't they *protect* Olivia?

At my side, Priya rises from her seat, her eyes on Delaney.

"What do you know of your magic, Miss Corvi?" Delaney looks at my cuff.

A lot. "Nothing."

"Your grandmother was one of the greatest Mortemagi of her generation. The reason Mortemagi are able to serve as Firstline mages is thanks to her," Priya speaks at last. If she was hoping to offer support, she's only twisting the knife in my heart. Of course, Nan changed lives. She changed mine in the short years I spent with her. I wish she were still around. Olivia wouldn't be dead, and I wouldn't be here.

"I'd like to think you've inherited her greatness," Delaney says, her lips twitching ever so slightly.

How much further could I have fallen? All I know of my magic is from books. Before yesterday, I was only half a whisperer, Death's errand girl. I didn't even know there was a difference between ghosts and the dead I used to listen to. And now, I will walk through the same halls Nan did, disappointing her with every step I take.

"What makes you think I want anything to do with this magic?"

Delaney and Priya exchange a glance, and for the first time since the overseer walked in, I get the sense that one's trying to scare me into attending Gorhail, while the other is enticing me with kindness. That their tension is manufactured, only there to manipulate me.

"Due to this week's unfortunate events, classes have been suspended until next week." Is Delaney addressing the murders of three students as "unfortunate events"? I shake my head in disbelief. "Formalities demand we test you on practical, theory, and physical to rank you appropriately," she adds.

Why is she speaking like I've already agreed to attend this horrible place? She has so little regard for me that she doesn't even care to ask. Then again, I don't know what I was expecting from someone who essentially refers to murder as an inconvenience.

She continues her one-sided conversation. "I'm inclined to think that you are not clueless about our world and your magic, given you had free access to Rhea's personal library."

I've read nearly every book in Nan's library, some multiple times. I know what my magic can do, and more importantly, I know what it cannot do. It cannot bring my sister back. It won't even let me speak to her ghost. So why would I want to explore it further? "I couldn't make sense of most of the books," I lie.

"May I give you some advice then, Miss Corvi?" Parrish says.

"Sure."

"Gorhail has two principal rules for Mortemagi: If you are a whisperer, stay out of the Poisoned Stairwell unless you want to lose your mind. Ghosts cannot roam the halls of Gorhail because conduits will take them to the Underiver, but they flock to the Poisoned Stairwell."

"And if I am a conduit?" I am not, but I'd still like to know.

"Then stay far away from the catacombs. A conduit's cuff locks ghosts, leading them into the Underiver so they can then cross into the Underworld. The catacombs are filled with tens of thousands of ghosts—they all flock to the cuff at once, overloading the conduit with magic, killing them in the process."

I nod, suddenly grateful I'm not a conduit. I don't intend to go anywhere near the Poisoned Stairwell or the catacombs. In fact, I don't intend to stay at Gorhail. Damn the Gods and their poisonous gifts. I will find another way to solve my sister's murder.

Delaney's eyebrow quirks. "See, Miss Corvi. We are here to help. In fact, I paired you with one of our finest Magisters to catch you up to speed." She smiles empathetically. "You'll thrive at Gorhail, Viola. It's where you belong. Now, if you'll forgive me, I have an audience to attend.

Principal Grand Master Parrish, will you be joining us, given you called this audience?"

"In a moment, Overseer Delaney." Priya's tone is short. "Allow me to walk our newest addition to her room first."

On that, Delaney retraces her steps louder than when she came in, the flasks on the shelves clinking when the double doors snap back after her.

Priya helps me up from the makeshift bed, and I stumble twice before gaining my footing. "Overseer Delaney is right about one thing. Gorhail is your rightful place."

What about Olivia's? Why are they all acting like Olivia didn't just die under their watchful eyes? Is her life worthless because she was a nonmagi?

"I'm not staying," I tell her.

"Yes, Delaney said you were meant to start at Osneau's Postgraduate School of Botany." Priya nods as she holds up most of my weight and helps me to the door. "You'll enjoy Gorhail's expansive gardens."

How can she be talking about gardens while Olivia's body rots in Albion, while the authorities write off her death as an accident, and while her murderer runs free?

I stop, and she halts with me. "Have you no regard for my wishes? Do you even realize what you're forcing me into?" I raise my voice. "My sister was murdered, and you're talking about gardens."

Priya makes sure I can stand before she releases me. Then she lets out a long sigh. "Miss Corvi," she says, looking straight into my eyes, "I understand the rage, but I can assure you that should you choose—and despite what Delaney infers, it remains your choice—to walk out of this institute, you'll be dead before you bury your sister."

I stare at her in shock.

"We have not ruled Olivia's death as an accident or a murder yet, but the violent attack on *you*, Miss Corvi, should be indication enough that a killer is after you."

"Why are you telling me all this?"

"I am plainly stating facts." She holds the door open, and for a moment, I just stare at her. Her calm is terrifying, her threats not empty. She's right. If I leave Gorhail, I doubt the killer will miss twice. And if I'm dead, I won't be able to prove that someone murdered my sister.

"All right. But I'm only going to stay until I find out what happened to Olivia." The words are dry, because I'm trying to convince myself that

I can live with the magic I abhor, among the people who forgot about my sister the minute they learned she was a nonmagi.

She gives me a curt nod, ushering me out of the room.

We don't speak for much of the walk. She is patient, matching my slow steps and offering to help me up the stairs as we walk deeper into what I realize is the House of Death.

"You knew my father?" I ask as the silence stretches.

"He was in the same year as my older sister." She goes quiet for a moment. I glance at her and notice her eyes are teary. I don't dare ask what happened, afraid that I might crack open a vault of familiar feelings I am not ready to face.

"My sister." She sighs. "My sister disappeared a long time ago. I know what you're going through, Viola. The grief never quite leaves, but you learn to grow new memories around it."

A million questions dance on the tip of my tongue, but I go with the most selfish one. "Why did you save me?"

Priya stops walking and stares at me for a beat. She takes a deep breath before answering. "The Corvi relic is centuries old, and your affinity will be an asset once trained." She gestures at my cuff.

Of course, it's because of the relic. I curse the brief moment I thought she valued my life. But I'm not at Gorhail to find love or acceptance, I am here to find my sister's killer.

Olivia's room is dark, barren, and void of any personality. Nothing she would pick. No, she loved colors; she was vibrant; she was life itself. What did this place do to her?

Black jackets and wool sweaters pack the small oak wardrobe tucked in a corner of the room. No intricate designs, no beautiful patterns, only flat cuts of dark stained wood—it feels more like a ward than a dormitory. At the bottom of the wardrobe, four pairs of black boots neatly sit in a row. To my side, a chest of four drawers, an equally plain affair, is stacked with black and navy shirts with the embroidered royal-blue crest of the House of Death, along with skirts, pants, and leggings. If not for the distinct smell of new clothes, I would've thought they left all of Olivia's uniforms intact. They've already cleared the room, and Olivia hasn't even been dead two days—or is it three? Time no longer makes sense; I feel like I'm trapped in a nightmare and I'm constantly trying to wake up.

Next to the chest of drawers is a lightly stained double pedestal study desk that doesn't match the rest of the room; it's the only piece of furniture with a personality. Three drawers frame the desk on each side, and I mechanically open all of them. All empty.

Someone knocks on the door, and I seize. I have yet to change out of this filthy linen robe, and I don't wish to speak to anyone from this murderous place. There's a brief pause, and I hold my breath, hoping the person will leave, but then the knocks are back, this time more persistent.

"Miss Corvi." A silvery voice comes through. "I won't take much of your time."

Whoever is on the other side knows I'm in here. It's useless to pretend otherwise. I fling the door open, and it slams into the wall.

A young man in his midtwenties stops his fist halfway through another knock. He has soft blond hair and moss-green eyes, and he wears a blue shirt and yellow pants. He's about the most colourful person I've seen since I set foot at Gorhail. He reminds me of what my sister used to be.

The man looks at me like he's seen a ghost. His eyes flare, his breathing shallows, his mouth slightly opens. I clear my throat.

"Sorry." He blinks a few times. "Lorne Lawton. Magister. I've been assigned to y— I mean, you've been assigned to me."

"Magister?" I ask. He looks too young to be a Magister.

"I am here on behalf of Overseer Delaney to give you a brief tour of Gorhail."

"At this hour?" It's pitch-black outside. I still have days-old blood glued to my skin, and I am too exhausted to go traipsing around Gorhail with a stranger. Clearly, Delaney has no regard for my recovery.

"I-I," he stammers, taking in my bloodied robe, then sighs. "I can wait for you to change."

I return a blank stare, my hand on the door. I hope he takes the hint and leaves.

"Tomorrow then." He steps backward, considering me a second too long.

Right when I think I'm rid of him, his hand stops the door from closing. "Overseer Delaney said you need food," he says in one breath.

Food is the last thing on my mind right now. I need to scrub the filth of death from my skin. I need to peruse the room for anything that will clue me in on Olivia's secrets. And I need to sleep.

"Look." I tip my head backward to meet his eyes. "I appreciate your concern, but I'm exhausted from almost dying. I'll be ready at eight tomorrow."

"Oli—" He stops himself immediately. His cheeks flush, and he backs away. He reminds me of the townspeople in Albion, always saying we looked alike when the only thing we had in common was our height.

"You knew my sister?" I walk out after him, barefoot and bloodied, but he's already hurrying away down the hall.

"Eight sharp," I call out. "I'll wait here."

If Olivia is a puzzle, then Lorne is the first piece.

SATURDAY, NOVEMBER 20, 1939

My nightmares are a tapestry of Olivia's last moments. In every single one of them, I am the one pushing her off the boardwalk.

I wake up before the sun rises, sit with my thoughts, decide they are too much, and go back to sleep. When I wake up again, the clock reads half-past seven. I speed through the bathroom, grateful that I took an hour-long shower the night before. I refuse to be late. Today begins my foray into Olivia's secret life at Gorhail.

At exactly eight o'clock, there is a knock at the door.

Lorne is wearing a black sweater that matches mine, a royal-blue raven embroidered on the left pocket, and straight black pants. He clutches a folded newspaper under one arm. *The Daily Mage* sits at the top in bold letters. This newspaper has been around since the dawn of time. Nan had a collection of yellowing ones we had to throw out shortly after her death. Right below the title are three pictures: Olivia's smiling face, and the two boys who were at Dearly Departed. Olivia did make the headlines, after all, even though it appears that *The Daily Mage* replaced her Magus title with nonmagi. Because in death, all the years she toiled earning her ranks don't matter—they only care about her magical pedigree. At least, I hope the front page means they are taking her death seriously.

"Pants." He raises an eyebrow. "Interesting choice. It's not a common sight around here."

Did he expect me to wear a skirt in this frigid building? "It should be," I reply.

"The House colors look good on you." He hands me his free arm.

Black is hardly a House color. The two dead boys wore the same clothes with different color crests. It's like saying ice is cold. The statement is as empty as his failed attempt at a compliment.

His suspended arm lingers between us, awkwardly. I shift my gaze upward, and Olivia's final words rush to me. Now that I'm not dying of exhaustion, I scrutinize Lorne's green eyes. He could have killed my sister.

"Very well." His smile is tight as his hand falls to his side. "Let's go."

We walk for half an hour, maybe longer. I'm still not used to the complete silence the cuff affords me; the absence of the gnawing ring in my ears is almost unsettling. Listening to the last words of the dead was a constant in my life for twelve years, and every so often, I reach into the silence, looking for the familiarity of my discomfort. But everything's changed. *I* have changed.

". . . majestic of all the towers." Lorne speaking about architecture brings me back to the present, and I nod mindlessly.

Gorhail Institute has to be bigger than the whole town of Albion, because we've only been through the House of Death and the common areas. Lorne sprinkles in the rules about different parts of the institute as we come across them. About how it is of the utmost importance to acquire rank before joining Firstline or even collaborating with other Houses—High Magus to join Firstline, Grand Magus if mages want to work with a different House from their own, and Magus Principalis if they want to work with two foreign Houses. About the three types of magic Gorhail studies, and how the House of Arcane used to be four different Houses before they merged into one. Nothing I do not already know from reading Nan's books and listening to Olivia talk about school, but I nod along and remain quiet as he talks.

As we walk through a long, dark hallway with red flameless candles, a girl with beautiful brown hair bumps into me. Lorne scowls at her, as if she's committed a grave offense. She reaches for me, steadies me, and apologizes a few times before rushing away. The way she darts off reminds me of Olivia, or perhaps it is her shiny brown hair and my foolish heart wishing for my sister to walk these halls again.

"This is Hollow Tree." Lorne's voice drags me back to the present. "First floor is the dining hall; second floor houses the dean's office, the chapel, the Magisters' room, and the overseers' offices. Well, except for the House of Poison's office, which is separate because of their superiority complex . . ."

I don't hear the rest, because I'm mesmerized by this room: when I look up, walls the color of bark rise a few stories high until they meet a domed glass roof. When she'd first started at the institute, Olivia told me about this place, and I thought she was exaggerating, but it's every bit as beautiful as she said. My gaze shifts to the long tables, where students gobble up their breakfast. Four of them nearby are digging into large plates of sausage, eggs, mushrooms, and beans. "What was her favorite food?" I ask mindlessly.

Lorne follows my gaze, then looks down. "I . . . I don't know. I didn't know her, I'm sorry."

He's lying. I know it in my bones. How can he be a Magister and not know one of his students? Why did he almost call me by her name last night?

"I'm sure we can arrange for a reader to refresh your memory, Lawton." A low, threatening voice crawls up my spine. My skin prickles. It tells me that danger looms over my head.

Lorne's eyes twitch at the person walking up behind me. He reaches for my arm, but I step out of the way, angling myself to see whom the voice belongs to.

The mage glowering at Lorne is terrifying. He can't be more than a couple of years older than me, yet the depth of his eyes mirrors a thousand years.

"I do recall your eating every single meal with . . ." He pauses, a sliver of amusement in his voice. "What was her name . . . the nonmagi?"

"Ol . . ." I hesitate. "Olivia."

"Olivia," he drawls. "Still not familiar, Lorne?"

Lorne's ears turn so red I worry they will burn. He clenches his fists, and for a second, I think he's going to hit the other mage. But he grabs my wrist instead, pulling me forward. "Miss Corvi, your tour is over. Let's go."

The mage lets out a laugh. "Did you *ask* her if she wanted to go?"

"Sorry," Lorne whispers as he drags me away. "You need to stay away from that House and the scum who live within it."

"Let go of my wrist," I say. It hurts, the way he presses his fingers into my skin. He considers my request, but his grip only tightens when he notices the man following us.

The mage lifts his hand, and a black bracelet starts moving. It uncoils, and I realize it's not a bracelet at all. It's a serpent, black as night, its eyes locking on Lorne. He's an Aspieri from the House of Poison. Nan had very few books about them, and most of the ones that referred to the Aspieri had their pages torn out. When I asked Olivia about it, she'd said they weren't real mages because they had no magic without their aspiers. The prejudice in her voice had bothered me then. It was a reminder of how Gorhail was changing my sister.

"Raiku feels strongly about your choices," the Aspieri says. I stand still, mesmerized by his right eye turning black the moment his aspier moved. For a moment, I question whether he was the one Olivia warned me about, but her final words were clear: *one green eye*.

"Archyr, there are consequences for using magic against a Magister." He loosens his grip on me.

"But no consequences for dragging a mage away against their will?" The Aspieri raises an eyebrow.

Lorne's jaw clenches so hard I'm afraid it will never move again. His nostrils flare, and his eyes are fighting a silent losing battle. He releases my wrist abruptly and shakes his head at me. "I'll be in Circle Three, our study hall. I strongly suggest you follow me."

He huffs as he hurries away, bumping into two young mages and sending one of their trays flying without an apology.

I turn my attention back to the Aspieri. His face looks like it's been sculpted by the Gods: warm tawny skin, a strong jaw, high cheekbones, and yet he wears a permanent scowl, as if he's angry with the world. The Gods may have blessed him with impossible beauty, but what is beauty if you are rotten inside?

"Did you know my sister?" *I am not afraid of him*, I repeat in my head. I am not afraid of how his gaze scrutinizes me from head to toe. I am not afraid of the sneer curving his lips, as if my question disrupted his day.

"No," he speaks, and I lower my head, my cheeks warm, suddenly ashamed of my brazenness.

His hand reaches up and pauses right below my chin. "Don't look down." His soft, long fingers lift my face, so I *have* to look at him. Both his eyes are back to gray, dark like the clouds hovering before a rainstorm, threatening to spill chaos over anything he regards. My heart thrums against my chest, in fear, in anticipation, in agony of something I don't dare lean in to. He lowers his head to my ear, and the warmth of his breath brushes against my skin.

"Fear makes you prey," he scoffs, dropping my face. I snap out of my reverie, my body alert at his veiled threat. Before I can even react, the green aspier I hadn't noticed around his left forearm moves. It stretches to my wrist, its cold scales rubbing against my skin. I should be afraid, but the aspier is alluring, the way it slithers forward, its scales glistening every time it catches the light. The mage's right eye turns green, and the pain in my wrist from Lorne's hold vanishes.

Alarm rings through my bones.

Beware the serpent with one green eye.

> Dear Uncle Rodric, if you figure out how I can break this bond with the Mortemagi, I will never break a single rule again.
>
> **LETTER FROM HIGH MAGUS SYLAS ARCHYR TO OVERSEER PALTRO, NOVEMBER 1939**

twelve | sylas

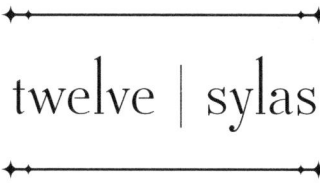

SUNDAY, NOVEMBER 21, 1939

Corvi smells like roses. I hate roses. They remind me of the sickly sweet innocence of nonmagi, always so curious, always so careless, and they die just as quick. Or maybe they remind me of Mom's funeral, where all I remember is the nauseating smell of the flowers.

As I lean over the balustrade on the first story of Hollow Tree, I wonder why mages flock to the dining hall instead of eating in their respective Houses—it's always so . . . crowded. Railesza sits at my wrist, her head resting between my thumb and index finger. Her eyes follow Corvi's every step until she sits at the long dining table, mindlessly tearing apart a fresh loaf of honeyfig bread—an odd choice for dinner. My aspier has no business being this invested in a Mortemagi, just like I had no business intervening into Mortemagi matters yesterday morning.

"You're back." My sister tackles me with a side hug. I wrap my arms around her, grateful to Paltro for getting me out of the correctional facility. I thought I'd never see Lyria again.

"I've been back for a couple of days now." I give her a pointed look.

"Paltro sent me home," she reminds me. My smile falters. Paltro did mention sending her to Iserine, but if he was with me the whole time, *who* went with my sister?

"Alone? With poachers in every corner?"

"Gryff was with me." She sighs.

I frown. Even with him, it's risky traveling to a different province with poacher camps along the borders.

"I thought Gryff was in the middle of an investigation," I say.

"He was, I mean, he is. He had to go to Iserine anyway, to retrieve Beau's birth certificate and adoption papers."

I don't press further. "How is he? And did someone tell Grayson?" Gryff's brother, Grayson, and Beau were close.

"Angry, sad. In a way, he lost a brother, too. And Gray is on assignment in Imglen. He doesn't know yet." She pokes her cheek with her tongue and looks up with tears in her eyes. "Sometimes I forget he's gone, you know? How are you holding up?"

I shake my head. I don't want to talk about my feelings right now. I'll grieve when we find Beau's body. She nods, giving me a small smile. Then she narrows her eyes at my black aspier. "Why did Raiku try to kill the Mortemagi?"

Raiku remains still at my wrist. He was almost sent back to death row after he bit Corvi. I had to convince PGM Parrish that he was only putting her back to sleep so she could heal. An obvious lie. I briefly flirted with the idea of letting her die, and Raiku acted on it. "Uncle Rodric told me to keep you in line," she says lightheartedly.

"Did he also tell you that they forced me to bond with *her*?" I scoff. "A Mortemagi."

"Sylas." Her tone drops in a long sigh, as if she's speaking to a child. I prepare myself for the same old lecture. "The House of Death didn't kill Mom. *She* didn't kill Mom."

"Death magic killed Mom, Lyria," I correct her. "Perhaps it wasn't Corvi magic, but it's all the same."

My sister huffs, but she knows I'm right. Dad told us the story countless times. How Mom was surrounded by the undead—bony creatures, oozing darkness, with the sickly sharp stench of death, the ones Mortemagi summon. How he tried to help her, but she died saving him with Raiek. Our entire world upended in one moment.

"*This* girl didn't kill Mom." She locks me in a death stare. "Your prejudice can't play the God of Death."

"If I wanted her dead, she'd already be dead," I say. What I do not say is that I lost control. After Raiku's biting incident, Paltro threatened to send me back to the correctional facility if I so much as touch a single hair of the Mortemagi. "You don't want to know what Parrish is capable of," he'd said. If she's even half as deadly as her sister, the Deathbringer, no, I don't want to know.

My answer weighs between us, then her lips pull into a smirk. "You threatened Lorne. It was all everyone was talking about yesterday."

For half a breath, I see Beau beside her, his boyish grin adding to her teasing. Grief hits in stages. Sometimes, it forgets and goes quiet for hours, days. And sometimes, it comes barreling into your chest, punches through your heart, and knots your throat. It must show on my face.

"Don't," Lyria says. "Don't, or I'll start crying."

I blow out a breath, looking away. That we even have to mourn our brother mere months after our father's murder is cruel. Somehow, we have to stay afloat in a sea of grief that's constantly trying to drown us. I shake my head, turning my gaze back to my sister. I need to be strong. For her.

"Lorne told the Mortemagi that he didn't know Olivia." I make a poor attempt at a conversation change.

She throws her head back, laughing. "Lorne? Didn't know Olivia? *Lorne?*"

"Railesza wouldn't stop hissing until I intervened." It's only been a few days, and this bond is insufferable. Railesza makes it her duty to watch over the Mortemagi, and Raiku hisses at me every time I glance her way.

"Did you tell her Olivia was Lorne's girlfriend?"

"Lorne is grieving." Sierra sighs as she joins us in the nook overlooking the dining hall. She traded her usual cornflower-blue shirts for our standard black ones today. The bags under her eyes betray the quick smile she flashes. "It's hard for us to see *her* around."

I forget that Sierra lost her best friend, that she, too, is grieving. But it's unfair to blame Corvi for kindling their pain. I look down at the Mortemagi. She looks nothing like her sister: other than their shared height, they could be strangers. Her eyes are brown to Olivia's green, her nose smaller, her face softer, her cheekbones higher, her hair is layered black waves that fall to her midback, and her skin a golden brown that reminds me of the Wanoran sands.

Her lips are drawn in a pained expression, as if she's never smiled in her life. I catch myself wondering if she's ever had any reason to. The way she fades into the shadows when she walks; how she uses the fewest words to say anything at all; how she sits alone at the table, avoiding the world.

"Lorne shouldn't have lied." Sierra squints at the girl as she leans on the rail next to us. "But maybe he has his reasons."

Lyria snorts. "Sure."

What *reason* would Lorne have for lying? Other than his being a predator. First, it was Olivia, and now her sister. I'm about to argue, but Sierra's expression keeps me quiet.

"I have a trade." Sierra's eyes darken to deep blue, her relic glowing. "About the girl, like you asked."

Lyria gives me a scathing look. She doesn't understand the real dangers of Mortemagi, that their outer calm masks death at the tips of their fingers. The best way to guard against one is to know the root of their magic, so I asked Sierra to find out about Viola's.

"I didn't ask for a trade, I asked for a favor," I snap, but my irritation only makes me look like a fool. Sierra cannot trade a secret if one isn't traded to her in exchange. I lower my tone. "I don't have a secret, Sier. I'm sorry."

"I don't want secrets; I need help." Sierra turns her gaze to the Mortemagi again. "Olivia was my best friend, and I don't think she fell, Sy. In all her years here, she's never broken curfew, not even once. Isn't it suspicious that Olivia dies, and she shows up? Olivia never mentioned having a sister. I've known her for twelve years, Sylas, and she wouldn't have lied to me."

Railesza violently hisses at Sierra, as if insulting the new Corvi personally harmed her. Raiku shakes his head, and I stifle a laugh. First, the idea of this small woman killing Olivia to take her place is preposterous; unlike her sister, she's a mage, and Gorhail is her birthright. Second, Olivia lied her way through Gorhail; I would never say this to Sierra, but it's embarrassing for a reader to miss that Olivia was a nonmagi.

"Promise you'll help uncover Olivia's murderer, too," Sierra pleads when I don't say anything. I could use this as leverage with the Mortemagi.

"A trade is a trade," I say, scrambling for a secret I can share. "I don't think Olivia's death was an accident."

"Viola Corvi is a whisperer," she returns with a grateful nod.

A whisperer. How pathetic. Whisperers are like Death's least favorite minions. They run around like hollow fools, following ghosts that either drive them mad or lead them to their deaths. But they can also be useful, especially when they can be a direct line between Beau and me.

"No." Lyria pulls on my sleeve, but I'm already halfway down the stairs. Whisperers are rare, functioning ones at least. Most of them become trapped in their own minds from ghost paralysis. Before that can happen, the majority end up sealing their magic, choosing to live as nonmagi. That we have an untouched one wandering the halls of Gorhail is Damas smiling down on us.

Someone bumps into me on the landing between the first and second flight of stairs. I pull back and Corvi grimaces, rubbing her forehead. When she realizes it's me, she backs away, her arms folded around her middle. I saved her life. Why is she looking at me like I'm going to eat her alive?

"You're never going to survive here," I mutter with a sigh.

"Is that what you said to Olivia before you killed her?" She lifts her chin and holds my gaze with defiance. Good. She shouldn't bow for anyone, not even me. But out of everything that could come out of her mouth, I never expected those words. Bold, I'll give her that, but also foolish.

"I would never"—I lift my hand, and Raiku gladly stretches along my forefinger in a threat—"ever lay hands on a nonmagi."

"You knew . . ." She staggers backward, but she still doesn't look away. Our eyes are locked in a battle of wills. She won't back down, and neither will I. She doesn't know me, and she's already throwing around accusations.

"Why didn't you report her?" she presses. "You could've saved her life."

The audacity of this Mortemagi knows no bounds. I saved *her* life; that ought to be enough. If anything, she should be glad I didn't report Olivia—she would've been thrown in prison and a reader would've altered her memories. "Had I known she was foolish enough to run to her death, I *would've* considered reporting her."

She steps into me, poking me in the chest. "Do not call my sister foolish, and she did not *run* to her death."

"The sister who, for twelve years, told everyone she was an only child?" Taunting her comes easily. She wears her feelings on her face, and I only have to pick which to prod. If mere words bring her down, she'll be gone within the week.

I'm expecting her sharp tongue to retort, but her lips quiver, tears pool at her lower lid, and she retracts her hand. Against myself, I catch it halfway, and she tenses. What is wrong with me? I drop her hand like a hot potato. It must be that stupid bond.

Corvi's shoulders fall. She draws a slow breath and turns on her heels, but I can't let her leave now. I need her to speak to Beau's ghost, so he can tell us who killed him.

"My brother was killed the same night as your sister," I blurt out, settling for honesty.

She whirls around, narrowing her eyes. "Was your brother also foolish enough to run to his death?"

Her words sting unexpectedly. I look away, blinking hard. Beau was only foolish enough to trust me. But I can't break down now. Not in front of a Mortemagi.

"I need your help," I say, hoping she sympathizes with me. "Can you speak to his ghost?" I know my brother better than I know myself, in life as in death. I know his ghost would stop at nothing to try to reach us.

Her gaze softens at the mention of Beau. In this quiet moment, grief recognizes itself. But just as quickly, her expression changes. "Why should I help you, when you wouldn't help my sister?" she scoffs.

Because I am the reason you're still alive, I want to say. Instead, I click my tongue. If I want her help, I have to offer something. "Three people died within two days, their relics taken," I say, making sure not to single out her sister as a nonmagi. I don't need her angry right now.

"What type?" Her eyebrows shift to a calculating frown. When I don't answer, she asks again, "What type of relics?"

"Er— Victor's was a laurel . . ."

"Heirloom or new?" she asks, with an edge, and I pause, considering her question. She's not clueless at all. In fact, she's brilliant. I hadn't thought about this in connection to Olivia. But what if it wasn't Olivia they were after? My gaze drops to her arm—she wears the famed Corvi relic, an heirloom.

"Heirlooms," I say. "Both of them."

Her face relaxes, and it seems like we both come to the same conclusion. "Someone's after heirloom relics," she confirms my thoughts. "But why? If the family line is dead, the relic's worthless."

"If I knew that, I wouldn't be asking an untrained Mortemagi for help," I think aloud.

"You know what..." She shakes her head in disbelief. "I'm not helping you. I'm only here to prove that my sister was murdered."

I huff out a frustrated breath. Haal, why must *she* be the only whisperer I have leverage over? Now, because of Beau, I will have to play nice. "Well," I begin, pausing to collect myself. One wrong word, and I lose my only link to my brother. "I can help you find your sister's murderer."

She stares at me, incredulous.

I'm certain she's thinking I'm tricking her, but is it a trick if it's the truth? Our siblings were likely killed by the same person. It's in our best interest to work together while Firstline sends its officers to collect paperwork. But I don't try to convince her further. I want *her* to decide to help me.

"High Magus." She glances at the patch below my shirt's House crest to confirm.

"Archyr." I stop her. "Call me Archyr."

"Archyr." My name rolls off her lips effortlessly, and my gaze lingers on them a second too long. Her eyes search mine for that treacherous emotion, the same one that urges me to listen to her, to tell her what she wants to hear, because I know it all too well. The despair, the hunger, the sliver of hope that the answers to their deaths will come.

"Can I trust you?" she asks. I hate how she looks at me in earnest, because I'm probably the only person who's even acknowledged that her sister was murdered. More than that, I hate how I can't tell her that she *can* trust me. Because she can't. Once she speaks to Beau's ghost, she'll be of no use to me.

"For now," I offer, then share what Sierra told me. "Your sister never broke curfew once in her life at Gorhail. I don't think she fell. In fact, I believe Olivia, Beau, and Victor were killed by the same person."

Corvi pauses at my revelation, relief relaxing her eyebrows and her jaw, as if my persistent acknowledgment of her sister's murder just lifted a burden off her shoulders. Then she nods to herself, chewing on her lower lip as she measures her next words. "I know where your brother's body is—" Her words falter as her gaze stretches past me.

Haal, I must have played my cards right because she's solving all my problems. I want to pry, but in my periphery, Overseer Delaney, the House of Death's personal wraith, climbs down the stairs. I glance at her over my shoulder. "High Magus Archyr, curfew began five minutes ago.

You should know a thing or two about violating curfew." Her disapproving stare accompanies her usual sneer.

She means that the last time I did, my brother was killed. I roll my eyes, more annoyed than hurt by her mention of Beau. Expecting sympathy from Delaney is akin to waiting for a poacher to offer mercy. The worst she could do to me is a day's suspension, and Paltro will simply revoke it. "The chapel is exempt from curfew." I give her my best smile as Raiku slithers around my wrist. "Unless worship is also forbidden."

Her mouth curves downward at my answer, her gaze lingering on my killer aspier. Then she shifts her eyes to her mage. "Miss Corvi, Magister Lawton is waiting for you at Circle Three."

Corvi nods hesitantly. My annoyance only grows. I want her to stand up to Delaney, to tell her she doesn't want to be anywhere near that creep, to break free from the cage the House of Death built for her. But I realize it's only the bond's magic reminding me of its vow to put her life above mine.

"You are new here, Miss Corvi, but I personally wouldn't associate with a criminal accused of high treason and murder." Does she hear herself? First, the charges were dropped, and second, I *saved* one of her mages—what an ingrate.

"Perhaps we can walk together, Miss Corvi." The crone leads the way down the stairs.

Delaney embodies everything I despise about Mortemagi. When she was still a Magister, she would go out of her way to fail everyone from the House of Poison. Dad told me she lobbied the Grand House to dissolve our House because she deemed us too unstable to wield killing aspiers. Meanwhile, she keeps advocating for rogue Mortemagi reform instead of execution.

Corvi glances at me, her eyebrows knitted in concern.

"I'll find you," I mouth, before she falls into step with Delaney. But first, I head straight to Overseer Paltro's office. This bond needs to go.

> An untrained Mortemagi is a dead Mortemagi.
>
> LUCIA KAN, *UNDERSTANDING DEATH MAGIC*, CHAPTER 1

thirteen | viola

SUNDAY, NOVEMBER 21, 1939

Archyr didn't kill my sister. Of this I am certain. He seems like he would take pride in that. Instead, I see a mage torn between wanting closure and wanting to burn down the world.

I am also certain that the boy who told me to run at Dearly Departed was his brother. His picture was on the newspaper Lorne was holding. *Beau.* The name is fitting: he was beautiful, and he saved my life.

"What did High Magus Archyr want?" Overseer Delaney asks as we walk into the study hall—it was closed while Lorne took me on the tour yesterday morning. Paneled glass lines the domed roof. The faint light of the moon shines through the glass, and the sky is peppered with diamonds. We may have the same sky in Albion, but here, it's mesmerizing. Rows of packed shelves line the walls, and freestanding curved bookshelves frame sofa nooks. In the middle, three long tables are littered with open books and stacks of parchment, with students scattered across the benches.

"I was lost and asking for directions." A lie.

"Magister Lawton left in the middle of his tour yesterday." A truth.

Like a shadow whose name has been spoken into existence, Lorne peels his tall frame from a nearby bookcase. When his eyes land on me, he frowns. "Miss Corvi, I'm so sorry for leaving you in the middle of Hollow Tree yesterday. I had to attend to urgent House matters."

My shoulders relax. I don't care if he's lying to save himself; his half lie confirms my statement and eases Delaney's suspicions.

"Good evening, Overseer Delaney." He bows his head in a way I've only seen subjects do to their kings in the staged plays I used to watch in Albion.

She doesn't acknowledge his greeting. "Miss Corvi needs rest. Will you walk her to her room?"

I don't need rest. I need answers. But I am not foolish enough to protest, so I thank her, fake a yawn, and turn to Lorne. "Shall we?"

His eyes beam in answer. They light in the same way my heart leaps in the stolen seconds I forget Olivia is no longer here. Lorne didn't only know my sister; he was close to her, which makes his earlier lie even more suspicious.

We walk the length of a corridor with the same dark walls and red candles that seem to be a recurring theme for the House of Death, take a narrow stairwell that looks like it hasn't been renovated since the 1500s, and finally walk down a short hallway where the carpet changes from black to a black-and-white diamond pattern. We've reached the sleeping quarters, and we turn one more corner before we arrive at Olivia's room... *my* room.

If Lorne has been saying anything, I've heard nothing. I am too busy looking for hidden doors, side rooms, or back stairwells I can use to slip out unnoticed. But these quarters are a fort—the only way in or out is through the main entrance. Olivia couldn't have gotten out of here unseen.

I waste no time getting into my room, eager to be rid of Lorne.

"Wait." He runs a hand across his face. I wonder what Olivia saw in him. He's so... unmemorable. "I'm sorry for being an idiot in Hollow Tree."

A real apology. It comes unexpected, to both of us, judging by the way he glances to the side. "She loved rolled toast with strawberry jam and fresh cream in the morning." He blinks a few times, then looks up, huffing out a long breath.

My heart tugs. That is my favorite breakfast. Olivia loved an egg, sausage, and spinach casserole that Mother makes so well. The first year she left for Gorhail Academy, Mother drove all the way from Albion to drop weekly servings of her favorite meal. It comforts me to know that she carried a part of me with her through my favorite food.

"She would never pass up a roast. And she loved helping people—" He lets out a muffled laugh, and I realize he's crying.

"I'm sorry." I'm more uncomfortable than apologetic. I understand his grief, but I don't see why he is crying about her when he could be helping me find her killer. Or does he, too, believe it was an accident?

My answer comes at once.

"I don't understand how this could have happened to her. She knew the boardwalk was slippery from all the rain," he sobs. "I loved her."

My hands ball into fists. Liar, I want to shout, all sympathy for him gone in an instant. If he *loved* her, it wouldn't have been a question at all. My sister was terrified of water; she wouldn't even go near a shallow pond. And if he *knew* her, he would've known she would've never strolled along the boardwalk after curfew in her nightgown in the middle of winter.

"It's impossible not to see her in you." His tears won't stop. "I never even knew she was a nonmagi. She was so bright..."

"I'm sorry," I say again. I don't know what I am apologizing for. His foolishness for thinking he was in love with her or his delusion for thinking we look alike.

After a back-and-forth that lasts longer than I have the patience for, I close the door, pressing my back against the cold metal. This will be harder than I thought. My only hope lies in the hands of someone who could kill me in a second, someone who I'm sure will drop me the moment I help him find his brother. Archyr couldn't care less about Olivia, but he does care about Beau.

Someone knocks again. Once, twice.

Does this man have no friends? No duties to attend?

Flinging the door open, I groan. "I'm tired, Lo—"

I swallow my words.

Archyr stands across from the door, one leg propped against the wall, a playful smirk in place of the earlier scowl. The soft reflection of the moon in the skylight kisses his black hair with a faint silver glow. He doesn't look real at all.

"I thought he would never leave." He pushes off the wall, dusting his hands on his black pants. My eyes linger on his short-sleeved shirt. Isn't he cold? Immediately, I shake my head. It is none of my concern.

I step outside, look left and right. "How did you get in here?"

On our walk, Lorne drilled into my head that other Houses aren't allowed through the main entrance, which only means that there are hidden passageways into the House of Death. That must be how Olivia got out.

"I told you I'd find you, so I did." He holds my gaze like he's fulfilled a sacred promise. "Besides, I am the master of stealth."

I wouldn't call him the master of stealth when he commands the attention of every person around. If the walls could speak, they would only speak of him.

"Your brother—" I clear my throat, trying to refocus the conversation. His eyes light up, and guilt eats at me. The moment I made the connection between Archyr and Beau earlier, I realized I could use the latter's whereabouts as leverage. I hate it, especially when Beau saved me from Mara. I also hate it because Gorhail is already changing me; I'm justifying emotional manipulation as a means to solve my sister's murder, using someone's despair to help myself. Maybe Delaney and Parrish were right. I belong here because, deep down, I'm just like them.

"Erm— Should we speak somewhere else?" I need to know how Archyr can move around Gorhail unnoticed so I can continue my investigation past curfew.

He rubs his chin, considering my request, then beckons me to follow him in the opposite direction Lorne and I came from earlier. A dead end, but not for long because Archyr runs his hands over the wall, pushes in a small rectangular brick, and a panel slides open to a steep spiral staircase.

"Another Arkani invention," he explains. "They may seem boring, but we wouldn't have Gorhail without their advancements."

I wouldn't call Arkani boring. I spent months reading every book I could find about their inventions and innovations. And now, being at Gorhail and witnessing their magic in every crack of every stone is fascinating. Why couldn't I have inherited useful magic like theirs?

"After you." He gestures to the darkness, and I step inside.

Behind us, the door slides shut, and I gasp as I look up and down to find an expansive stairway that seems to never end. The same candles that light the hallways of the House of Death hug the stone walls, except these are white and hang from an intricate gold laurel candleholder. They don't offer nearly as much light as we need to navigate this place, but it's better than nothing. Right as this thought crosses my mind, the candles glow a little brighter. I frown, but Archyr looks at me with amusement. "They only light up when they see fit."

Suddenly, the temperature drops, and I wrap my arms around my middle, trying to quell the sense of foreboding crawling through me. Archyr starts climbing down the steps, and I follow closely. I take the first step, immediately grabbing on to the freezing railing for dear life. It's slippery, steep, and I make the mistake of peeking down to see more never-ending stairs that wrap around like a serpent. The ominous feeling surges through me. What if Archyr did kill Olivia and he wants to make my death look like an accident, too?

Archyr stops, throwing me a glance over his shoulder. "Do you need help?"

"No," I retort, taking the stiffest second step. A murderer wouldn't offer to help me, would he?

We take a while to climb down, and I'm surprised he says nothing about my tortoise steps. When we reach another platform, he motions me forward. I follow him down an all-white hallway, then take a turn into an all-black one, and finally we arrive in one with wooden flooring. After two more turns, I no longer know where we are. I realize that if he wants to kill me, he could do it right here and now, and no one would even know what happened to me. "I'm not going to kill you," he says nonchalantly.

"Do you read minds?"

"No." He laughs. By Death, it's beautiful. "The look on your face was telling enough. Since we stepped into the Poisoned Stairwell, you've gone from curious to determined to panicked to fearful to panicked again."

The Poisoned Stairwell. I freeze. Priya told me to stay away from this place because of the ghosts, but I haven't heard a single voice since we stepped in. Was my cuff damaged during Mara's attack? But then, I would be hearing the nagging ring of death.

Archyr doesn't wait for me to reply, and he pushes open a black door. I follow him into someone's personal living quarters. The walls are tall, dark teal paired with ebony wood for the doorframes, baseboards, and the mantelpiece. The furniture looks expensive, like what you'd see in the home of a government official—nothing like the bland furniture in my room at the House of Death. Above the fire is a majestic sculpture of a golden serpent with a bleeding red crown. I can't peel my eyes away from the intricate details, the golden scales laid with precision, the black gemstones cut to perfection to fit the eyes.

"Beau made it." A small voice draws my attention.

A young woman around my age stands up from her seat on the couch. Her black hair sits at her waist like a curtain of silk, and her skin is a shade darker than Archyr's, with warm undertones that remind me of honey. She is probably the most beautiful person I've seen at Gorhail, but her eyes are red, swollen. She's been crying. I'm not the only one who notices because Archyr is in front of her in a blink.

"Lyria." He holds her face so tenderly. He can't be the same person who threatened me on the stairs in Hollow Tree earlier.

She leans against him. "We can't even have a funeral. You know how important burials are, Sylas. Will he go down to his family crypt or be buried next to Mom and Dad in Iserine?"

Archyr sighs, resting his chin on her head. "I never asked him."

Funerals are perhaps one of the most important rites for mages. Without burials, the ghosts are lost in the Underiver forever and if they do escape, they become wandering ghosts with nowhere to go. They can't cross into the Underworld. It's why Nan made a fuss about Dad's burial when Mother wanted to have him cremated. For someone who lauded Olivia for being a mage, she never really respected mage customs.

A fist of envy knots in my throat. They are all mages; in death, they will have one another. But for Olivia and me, her funeral tomorrow will be our last goodbye. I am a mage, and she is a nonmagi. Even after I die, we'll never be reunited.

"I'm sorry," the young woman says as she notices me. "It's . . . it comes in waves, as you probably know. I'm sorry about your sister." She pulls away from Archyr, wipes her eyes, walks from the seating area to where I stand by the door to the Poisoned Stairwell. "I'm Lyria, Beau and Sylas's sister." She reaches for my hand.

Sylas. What a beautiful name, although it stops at that. Lyria radiates the warmth of a spring morning by the sea, and Archyr might as well be a lake frozen twice over.

"Viola," I say, gently shaking her hand.

"Please, you'll help us speak to Beau, won't you?" She still holds my hand between hers, and I stare at them awkwardly. Is her friendliness a trick of some sort? But her eyes are so earnest, her words so sincere. As much as I want to help her, my inexperience is catching up to me, and I don't know how. Before Beau at the funeral home, I had never spoken to a ghost. Only corpses, and only when I touched them.

"I'd never seen one up close before Gorhail." I gesture to the black serpent around her wrist, desperate to veer the conversation away from my magic. More than anything, I don't want to disappoint her.

"Our aspiers?" Lyria beams, lifting her arm. I don't know much about aspiers, other than that they are a form of living relic.

"This is Nyx." The black snake uncoils from around her forearm, revealing a soft gold underbelly, and stretches the length of her arm. Its red eyes lock on me, and I don't move, afraid it will attack if I do. But no one else seems to worry. Lyria continues, "She's a killer aspier. She poisons blood."

She talks about killing with such normalcy, as if it's common to have relics that murder. Then again, with the arts of blood, any mage becomes a weapon. I think of Mara, of how she was being controlled by a puppeteer—a blood Mortemagi. And my throat closes again, my chest tightening. Maybe one day I'll revisit that night without feeling the sharp claws digging through my flesh. For now, I press my eyes together, thinking about Nan, about Olivia, about the books we used to read.

Lyria lowers her arm with an apologetic frown, and my breath evens out. Between the harrowing memory of that night and the aspiers, my heart feels like it will give out.

"Railesza, you already know." Archyr takes over as he joins us, lifting his left forearm, where the green aspier watches me with interest. "She's a healer. Not as common as killers, but we have quite a few of them in Secondline." Up close, I notice the depth of her emerald scales; if I didn't know what she was, I'd have mistaken her for a jewel. Her eyes are a mesmerizing pale green, and I wonder why Olivia would tell me to be wary of a healing serpent.

Then the black serpent around Archyr's wrist slithers forth, bowing his head, his onyx eyes never leaving mine. I tell myself that I am not scared, but killer aspiers are terrifying. They can kill within seconds, should they choose. "Raiku, also a killer, like Nyx," Archyr finishes.

"Lastly, there's Raiek," Lyria gestures to Archyr's neck, where the thin, golden serpent is coiled like a necklace. "The Imortalis, a Founder's relic, as you may know. It grants immortality to the wearer and can only be given in time of need. We've had Raiek in our family since Sileas Ronin."

This explains the grand room, the lavish furniture, and the sculpture made of gold. These siblings are the descendants of the founder of the House of Poison, who was also the first founder of Gorhail.

Lyria finishes her introduction. "I have a book on it, I—"

Her brother's stare drowns her words, and her face falls.

"I would love to read about it," I tell her honestly, and her face lights up. The pang of guilt punches my gut again. Her heart is so true, and it will break the moment she realizes I am a fraud who can't help them.

"Have you heard from Beau at all?" Lyria asks. "I apologize for asking so soon, but I know my brother—he'd be trying to reach us."

Her eyes remind me so much of Olivia's. They watch me with hope, and I feel sick because I will shred every ounce of it. I haven't heard their brother speak since Dearly Departed, and as much as I want to believe his ghost is in hiding, I get the sinking feeling that he may have moved on through the Underiver.

"I . . . I don't know how to speak to ghosts." I settle for a half truth. I can't bear sharing my morbid theory.

She presses her lips together, her eyebrows scrunch into a worried knot. I want to disappear. Nothing hurts more than hope being ripped away when you need it the most. Like the hope I nurtured in the brief hours I thought Olivia was coming to Osneau with me.

Archyr frowns, because it's not something he wants to hear. "You are a whisperer, for Haal's sake."

"An untrained one, you said it yourself." My gaze cuts to him. I never once *agreed* to speak to his brother. Suddenly, the space feels so small. I'm trapped between them and the door to the stairwell behind me.

"Maybe I was wrong." Lyria reaches for her brother's arm and whispers, "Sy, I don't think Beau's ghost would be around Gorhail, given how many conduits there are." She says something else, but I can't make it out because Archyr pins me with a distracting glare.

"Don't waste our time, Corvi."

"Viola." Lyria's voice is soft in contrast to her brother's hostile tone. "Maybe you've heard him and haven't quite realized it was the voice of a ghost . . ."

I *have* heard him, but I'm not telling them that yet. Firstly, I could use this in exchange for more information about Olivia, and secondly, I don't want them to draw the same morbid conclusion as I did. Maybe Lyria is right, and I haven't heard Beau again because he's avoiding Gorhail. For her sake, I hope that's true.

"Fine. Even if you can't speak to him, where's his body?" Archyr interrupts her. "Because you claimed to know where he was."

I don't say a word, refusing to waste my leverage. We *should* be working together to find our siblings' killer, but there he stands, making demands. This only confirms that Archyr never had any intention of helping me. He only wanted information before kicking me aside.

"Or maybe . . . you don't know, and you're a fraud, like your sister," he taunts, taking a step forward. Like a fool, I take the bait.

"I'm not lying," I spit out. "Your brother has a broken-heart-shaped birthmark behind his left ear." I give him the single detail I couldn't possibly have picked up from the newspaper.

Archyr's eyes darken, and his nostrils flare. "You can tell us where he is right now, or I'll have a reader get it out of you." He steps so close to me, his lips flattening into a sneer. "Your choice, Corvi."

His threat ignites something within me. My skin feels warm, my cheeks burn, and my eyes sting. I square my shoulders and plant my feet on the ground. Somewhere between his false acts of compassion and now, I forgot that I am only a tool to the people of this world. Parrish needs me because of the relic; Delaney needs me because of my magic; and Archyr now needs me to find his brother's body *and* his ghost. Sooner or later, I'll find other people to give me more information about Olivia. So right now, Archyr needs me more than I need him.

"Is that a threat, Archyr?" I hold my head high, tangling myself into his dangerous game. If this is how he wants to play, I have nothing to lose.

"I don't make threats, Corvi." Sylas's every word punctuates my heartbeat. "I am merely giving you options." His black aspier unravels as he moves his hand inches away from my face. The aspier cocks his head, black eyes locking on me, and the fear that had previously left creeps up my spine and crawls down my arms.

My tongue is slow to catch up. "Why the aspier, Archyr? Is your desire to kill me stronger than your desire to find your brother?"

"Do you *want* me to kill you?" His head tilts toward me, and poison drips from his words. They don't sound like threats; they sound like a possibility. My mouth goes dry, and my breathing quickens. I willingly stepped into unknown waters, and now I am drowning.

"You've been wondering whether I'm going to kill you since we met." A smirk grazes his lips, the aspier slithering between his knuckles. The backs of his fingers skims along my cheek, and he drags them up, brushing my hair behind my ear, and I let him. His aspier is so close to my neck it takes everything in me not to look away from his eyes. My limbs tense, my skin grows cold, and I don't breathe. "Should I end the suspense?" he asks so softly, his fingers flexing against my head.

A resounding slap breaks me from his spell. He flinches, blinking several times to make sense of what happened. At his side, Lyria wears a scowl, her hand still hovering next to his reddening arm. "Why—" His attention turns to her, and now is my chance. I slip out of the secret door.

Lorne and Delaney are right about one thing: I need to stay away from this wicked, murderous Aspieri.

The moment I step into the darkness, my senses fail me. The hallways all look the same, and the stairs are treacherous. I don't relent, crossing through more hallways than I did when Archyr was with me—if I continue walking, I will eventually stumble upon an exit. My only solace is the deafening silence. No one seems to be here.

That's when I hear the voice, clear as day, right beside me. *He whom you seek lies in the catacombs.*

> Fueled by the magic of the catacombs, the Poisoned Stairwell has a mind of its own. Wandering the passageway without an aspier is strongly discouraged. Aspiers keep ghosts at bay.
>
> **Note:** Whisperers should avoid the Poisoned Stairwell. Ghost paralysis is the leading cause of death of whisperers at Gorhail.
>
> **ROME RONIN,** *A BRIEF HISTORY OF THE HOUSE OF POISON,* **PAGE 56**

fourteen | sylas

SUNDAY, NOVEMBER 21, 1939

"Sylas!" Lyria exclaims as the door closes behind the Mortemagi. "A whisperer cannot navigate the Poisoned Stairwell alone."

"She'll learn." I shrug.

What Viola Corvi does or doesn't do no longer concerns me. I tried to be nice. If she upheld her end of the bargain, I was prepared to help her find her sister's killer. More because of my promise to Sierra than to her and my own interest in avenging Beau's death, but the sentiment is somewhere in there. Instead of exuding gratitude, she had to give me lip. I tried to forgive her incompetence, but she kept dangling the location of Beau's body over my head, with no intention of helping. I don't know why I expected any different from a Mortemagi; they're all self-serving.

"She doesn't have an aspier to guide her and ward her from the ghosts." Lyria throws her hands in the air. "She'll be dead within the hour. You *know* how dangerous these passages are for whisperers, let alone an untrained one."

I'm not the one who told her to skip mage school for twelve years. "Excellent." I clasp my fingers together. "She'll be dead in time for her sister's funeral tomorrow. Perhaps they'll consider burying a mage in the nonmagi cemetery."

If she dies, the bond will break, and I will be free of this gnawing need to protect her. Paltro never mentioned any of this before strong-arming me into bonding with her.

Lyria curses at me as she stalks to the black door. Her bleeding heart will be her downfall. Corvi is a Mortemagi. All of them are the same. Children of Grimm. Murderers.

Forget Mom, Lyria acts as if Mortemagi don't have the highest number of rogue mages becoming poachers. The same poachers Gryff risks his life fighting every day. The same poachers that killed our father and probably our brother, too.

"I need Railesza." Lyria extends her arm. "In case Viola is hurt and needs healing."

"No."

"You are ridiculous."

"Mom was—"

"Enough! Mom this, Mom that! How long will you use her death to justify your hatred? You're about to let an innocent woman die," she seethes. I've never seen my sister this angry before. She glares at me, then lets out a heavy sigh. "We honor our parents through our choices, Sylas. And right now, Mom would be *so* disappointed in you."

I flinch, swallowing my retort. Lyria shakes her head, looking away. We've never argued like this before, and I don't know how to react. I should be angry, but at the same time, she's right. Both our parents would be ashamed of my actions.

"Sylas." She levels my stare, lowering her shaky voice. "If anything, do it for Beau. Viola is now our only hope at giving him a proper burial. The longer his body is gone . . . Sylas, I don't want him to be lost in the Underiver. He deserves to join our family in the Underworld."

My teeth grind at the quiver in her voice as she mentions Beau. I am a selfish idiot. Beau's body has been gone for a few days. If I recall Delaney's class in Year One at the academy, if we can't bury him before his body starts to decompose, he will be lost between the realms of life and death forever, without an identity. Thankfully, unlike nonmagi, mage bodies start to decompose after a week—or, if we're lucky and Silver injected him with frost venom, we'll find him intact. Unless another whisperer appears on our doorstep, Corvi is far too valuable, at least until she leads us to Beau's body and figures out how to speak to his ghost.

"Don't you want to find his killer, Sylas?" Lyria sighs. "You know that no other whisperer will work with you."

We could always bribe a random whisperer with a hefty sum, but we don't have much time, and Corvi already knows where Beau's body is. But it's not the reason I'll go find the Mortemagi. Lyria didn't even need to bring up Beau to convince me; she hit a sore spot when she brought up our parents.

"I'll go." Sighing, I drag my feet to the Poisoned Stairwell. It's so dark I can only make out the silhouette of my hands. I stare at the candles, but they don't adjust their brightness. What a great day for the stairwell to be moody! This passageway spans around the whole institute—she could be anywhere.

Right then, Railesza wakes up, her yellow-green eyes sharp. She takes in her surroundings, before hissing to the right. "We'll talk about your shifting loyalty later." I glare at my aspier. "But thank you."

She guides me down several flights of stairs. My skin prickles from the sharp drop in the temperature, and the sudden pitch-blackness slows my steps. We must be close to the catacombs or the Underiver—it's still odd to me that the gates to the Underworld are below Gorhail, at the very end of a river.

Something brushes against me. My breath hitches, the hairs on the nape of my neck stand. Raiku awakens and slithers down my leg to the floor.

When I was a boy and still scared of the dark, Dad used to tell us our aspiers could see ghosts and ward us against them. The tale was probably to quell our fears. I chose to believe the story then, but now, I know it rings true.

Raiku leads me down a narrow hallway I've never seen before, and the darkness lets up; the floor is covered in moss, the walls paneled with decaying wood. I look up, and gulp. The ceiling looks like it's coated in a thick liquid that never stops moving, but it's still so dark I can't make out the color. Railesza slithers to my hand, her head moving left and right. The closer we approach, the frames of three doors come into view. All three are plain mahogany, with red, silver, and navy handles. The three House colors of Gorhail.

Raiku paces in front of the middle door with the silver handle. I knock. Nothing. I knock on the left one, then the right one. Still nothing. Railesza hisses, and Raiku responds with a harsher hiss. What is this place?

"Sylas Archyr, son of the House of Poison." A silky voice echoes. "Behind these doors are three things you desire."

I step back.

The Poisoned Stairwell has a mind of its own, echoing the mind of its designer, the Second Founder of Gorhail, also one of the four founders of the House of Arcane. Helna Azgar was the master of trickery; everything she worked on was a puzzle, a riddle, a game. She designed and built the Poisoned Stairwell for Arkani and Aspieri to navigate through Gorhail during the age of Grimm, and it saved so many mages from capture, while keeping Grimm's army of Mortemagi away. While it meant that the *good* Mortemagi couldn't use the passageway on their own, Aspieri and Arkani banded together to help them. This was the last time in history that all three Houses worked so closely together.

Suddenly, it clicks. I remember an Arkani Magister talking about it sometime in Year Two. I stand in front of Helna Azgar's Doors of Desire.

"One door holds your parents," the voice sings. "One door holds your brother."

A trick. Mom and Dad are dead. I saw both their bodies, bawled as their coffins were lowered into the ground, mourned them for days that blurred into nights. And Beau... Beau died in my arms.

"One door holds the woman you seek."

Curiosity holds my tongue. I know my parents and brother are dead, but I would give anything to see even an illusion of them... to hear Mom laugh again after twenty years chipped away the memory of her voice.

A faint, sinister laugh takes over the void. I jerk around, but there's no one here except me. Something moves under my feet, and I look down at the moss crawling around my boots. At the same time, a drop of liquid lands on my arm, right next to Raiku's nose. He hisses. I wipe it and bring my hand closer to my face. Blood. I stagger backward. The door has a ticking clock, it seems, and I don't have long to make a decision. Three of them are already dead, but one is alive.

"Where is the Mortemagi?" My shoulders tense, ready for another trick, but the middle door opens, and I walk in.

Nothing could have prepared me for what is in front of me.

Corvi stands in the middle of a clearing I don't recognize, in conversation with a woman with a large tattoo on her arm. One arrow, four lines. A mage poacher.

In here, it's midafternoon, and the sun bounces off the large leaves of a few dwarf trees by a pond, the habitual noise of the forest whistling with the wind. I take two steps forward, both my aspiers on alert, but Corvi and the poacher don't seem to notice me. The foul woman says something, and Corvi pulls a piece of paper out of her pocket and hands it to the poacher.

Railesza hisses, and I glare at her. I move closer, behind one of the tall trees, my arm brushing against the smooth bark. Where did the door take me? The bark of this tree is thin and black—trees like these don't grow in Bale.

"We need more relics," whispers the woman.

"I need more time," Corvi answers, shifting her weight. I move. Railesza hisses again, and this time Raiku joins her. Could Sierra have been right? What if Corvi is a fraud? What if Olivia never had a sister, and this stranger is the one behind the three deaths? It would make sense, especially that she refused to give me information about Beau. She claims to be a whisperer, but she's not spoken to a single ghost when the Poisoned Stairwell crawls with them.

Raiku hisses, and this time, the sound fills the area. The poacher lifts her head straight at me. My hand reaches for the dagger strapped to my boot. She's not getting out of here alive. In fact, neither of them is. The poacher steps forward, baring her teeth. Her hands are no longer hands, but claws.

I don't think. I throw.

Between my blinks, the trees are gone, the clearing nonexistent. I stand in a vacant room with no windows and a single door.

"Bloody saints, Archyr. You're an idiot." Corvi's voice brings me back. She lies on the floor, hands pressed to her abdomen, around my dagger. Blood trickles from her side to the tile.

I shake my head, pressing my eyelids together. I threw my dagger at the poacher. Did Corvi step in front of her?

As if she can hear my brain struggle to piece together what happened, she interrupts my thoughts. "I can't believe this," she grunts as she tries to move. Railesza hisses at me. She's right, she shouldn't move with a dagger in her abdomen. "Why are you standing there like a statue? Help me."

Railesza springs off my arm before my legs move. Perched on my finger, Raiku watches as she wraps herself around Corvi's arm, then he glances at me, shaking his head before coiling around my wrist.

My steps are measured as I approach her. Railesza's healing won't help until the dagger is pulled out. I kneel next to her, and my green aspier glares at me. "You were speaking to a poacher... I didn't mean—"

"Swallow your excuses," she snaps, but her words are pained. The copper scent of blood mars the faint smell of roses on a rainy morning. If I don't heal her soon, she will pass out, and I don't want to deal with the wrath of Parrish when she learns I stabbed her new protégé. "You're a Gorhail-trained mage, for Death's sake. What happens behind the Doors of Desire isn't real..." Her words falter, and her breath slows.

Realization smacks me in the face. It was all an illusion: the door showed me what I wanted to see. This is why my aspiers were hissing; they can't break through illusions. I should've known something was off, should've paid attention to the details, to the smooth tree bark, to the forest humming the song of the wind when a poacher is around. But instead, I stabbed her.

"You might not care if I live or die, Archyr, but..." She pauses, catching her breath. "Olivia... I can't miss her funeral. It's the last time I'll see her."

I swallow, my thoughts empty. Pull the dagger out, I tell myself. Then Railesza will heal the wound. Without a second thought, my hand hovers over her abdomen, but her groan stops me.

"I will bleed out if you..." she manages to say. "Take me to a healer."

I frown. I *am* a healer, but she wouldn't know that, would she? Of course they didn't tell her who healed her; it would go against every single lie Mortemagi love to spread about Aspieri.

"Trust me," I try, realizing how ridiculous I sound. Why should she trust me after I just threw a dagger at her?

"Just let... me... die," she breathes out, before her eyes close. Even on the brink of death, her wounded pride takes over her reason. Or perhaps it's the delusion from losing so much blood. Railesza hisses, and I come to my senses. She cannot die—we won't find Beau's body nor his killer without her.

My left hand lightly presses on her abdomen, and my right hand wraps around the hilt of my dagger. Once I pull it out, Railesza will have minutes to save her. My aspier's fangs hover over the veins of her arm. I blow out a breath; I've done this on the field before, so why am I hesitating? Railesza hisses at me once more.

In a single motion, I pull out the dagger, and her fangs sink into Corvi's veins.

My hand slides over the wound, and I gently press on it, her blood coating my fingers. My aspier is calm, her breathing in sync with Corvi's. "What am I to do with you?" I whisper as my right hand reaches to stroke Railesza's head. They say aspiers mirror their mage, but Railesza isn't me at all. She has Dad's golden heart.

My aspier will heal her, but I doubt she'll want to help us after this.

Moments later, Corvi stirs, and her blood dries underneath my hand. Her eyes slowly peel open. The moment she sees me, her pupils widen. "Stay the fuck away from me."

Railesza unhooks her fangs from Viola's arm, slithers back to mine, and coils herself back to sleep. "A thank-you would suffice," I mutter, pulling away from her. Corvi's gaze lingers on Railesza for a moment.

"It was *you*," she trails. "You healed me that first night." She pushes up on her elbows and winces in pain. I don't think, and my arm reaches behind her back to help her up. Her face is inches away, her eyes locked on mine, her breath frozen.

She wasn't expecting this.

Neither was I.

"It was me." I don't look away. I can't. This bond has me under a spell that will get me killed if I don't break it.

Her eyebrows twitch, and her lips part in a gasp. "Why?"

"It wasn't by choice." I roll my eyes as I straighten up. It doesn't matter why I healed her the first night. What matters is that I healed her today, and no one was threatening me with prison or my aspiers' death. I could've walked away, found a different whisperer, but I didn't. Of course, I'm not about to tell her that. I will not give a Mortemagi even the slightest power over me.

She sucks in her cheeks and looks down. Was she expecting a different answer? Some terribly broken part of me picks up on the fragments of disappointment within her, and I want to take back what I said.

"You stabbed me," she reminds me calmly. The coldness of her words sobers me up; I rise to my feet, extending my hand out to her. She considers it for a moment, but then she pushes herself up, shakily. "You are even more despicable than I thought you were. You are so desperate to pin the blame on a Mortemagi, you wouldn't see the truth even if someone painted it for you."

Without looking at me, she stalks to the door.

"Viola, wait," I call after her. I don't know if it's my use of her name for the first time or the unexpected anguish in my voice that makes her stop. Her fists clench at her sides, but she still doesn't turn around.

"She'll guide you back." I lower my hand, and Railesza slithers from my arm to her. Viola bends, and my aspier wraps around her arm. Then she walks out.

MONDAY, NOVEMBER 22, 1939

The clock ticks to five in the morning right as I step into Founder's Room in the House of Poison. The only light comes from the low crackling fire. Haal, did Lyria leave without putting out the fire again?

A huge portrait of our family hangs between Beau's room and my room. Dad had it painted by an old woman in Iserine. My mother's face on the wall looks at me with a smile. She holds baby Lyria, while I'm in my father's arms, laughing. Next to them, Beau's parents look down at him with so much love. And behind them, the Darros stand with Gryff and Grayson. We're all blissfully ignorant to all the horrors that await us—soon after, Mom and Beau's parents would be dead, and years later, Dad would join them.

What would Mom think if she knew I saved a Mortemagi *twice*?

I huff out a breath and take a few strides past the open study and Beau's room, until I'm in front of my room. To my right, someone moves, and my hand reaches for my dagger—the same dagger I almost killed Viola with.

"A second time tonight, really?" Viola deadpans as she stands. I notice Railesza still wrapped around her arm, and it stings a little.

I sheathe my dagger. "I'm sorry, I—" I really want to ask her what she's doing in Founder's Room, but I realize Railesza probably brought her here.

"You can't kill a man and apologize to his ghost," she says, and I look away. It's a common Balish expression that means that your apology means nothing.

"The night Olivia was killed." I choose my words carefully. If anything, I can offer information as a truce. I need her to find my brother's body and ghost, and she needs me to help find her sister's killer. "She found out Lorne was seeing someone else. I think that's why she walked out of Gorhail in the middle of the night."

Viola's face twists in horror. "How could he do that to her? He's the reason she . . . She would've been alive if it weren't for him." Then her shoulders sag, her eyes lost in a sea that I am too familiar with. Guilt. I know it's consuming her from the inside, but why does she feel the weight of her sister's choices? I also know that nothing will ease it until she gets answers. Only then might it sting a little less.

I nod, silently, afraid to make any sudden movements. I need her to trust me, to realize that we have to work together. "What happened in the Poisoned Stairwell?"

She wraps her arms around herself. "I don't know. I heard a voice I recognized—Victor's, the other man who was with your brother. I heard it before, but this time, it was different. The voice was textured, layered. It kept telling me his last words." She pauses, mulling over what she shared.

"His ghost then," I say quietly. Victor's body is with Beau's. This further confirms that the same person killed them and kidnapped their bodies. A strange feeling blooms in my stomach. If Victor's ghost is here, why isn't Beau's? Could he have . . . ? No, I refuse to believe that someone as astute as Beau would let a conduit drag him to the Underiver. "Could you . . . share his last words?" I ask. "Please."

"I don't know if I should say." Her eyes flick to mine, mildly panicked. But then she scoffs. "You probably think I'm selfish, but . . ." She gulps, looking over to the fireplace. "My nan's final words warned me not to share the last words of the dead. I've never been superstitious, but maybe if I had never told Olivia all these last words, she would still be alive—she was often the one speaking them aloud to people."

Haal, she continues to find every reason to take the blame for her sister's murder. "Guilt will eat you alive if you let it," I say. "Olivia was already a target . . . you couldn't have changed that." I don't know if I'm speaking to her or to myself.

She swallows, holding my gaze with sadness. In this moment, I know nothing I can say will absolve her of that guilt. She wears it like a stain on her soul. I know, because I wear mine the same.

"*He whom you seek lies in the catacombs.* I could never forget Victor's words." She looks at the fireplace again. "Then, the farther I walked, the more voices I heard, textured, layered. Ghosts. Next thing I knew, I was in front of the doors. I asked to see my sister, but I was really thinking about escaping the ghosts."

"You've really never spoken to a ghost before..." I think out loud, and after a moment of hesitation, she shakes her head.

"I've only had my cuff for a few days. Anyway, the doors locked me in an empty room until you—"

I look down, ashamed of my actions. She should thank the Gods for stumbling upon the Doors of Desire. Had she walked a few more flights down, she would've been at the entrance of the catacombs.

My mind mulls over Victor's last words. Catacombs. Why would anyone tell her, a whisperer, to go to the catacombs? The place teems with old death magic, and who knows what remnants of tortured mages. It's filled with ghosts who refuse to move on to the Underiver. The catacombs is the only place conduits cannot go, so the ghosts have turned it into their permanent domicile.

"Look, Archyr"—she frowns, meeting my eyes—"consider this payback for saving me that first night, and for your brother. I've not spoken to a ghost before, but one has spoken *to* me. Beau's ghost told me to run. Without him, I would've suffered the same fate as my sister."

Beau. My heart cinches.

"Their bodies are at Dearly Departed in Albion. I know where they keep the spare key—"

The front door opens, interrupting Viola, and Lyria walks in with a stack of books. The moment her eyes land on us, she grins. "We're getting along, excellent."

Viola reaches for her abdomen, but she doesn't say a word. Her calm is unnerving; she should be furious at me, not offering me help out of pity or because she feels indebted to my brother. Of course, Beau saved her life, and he could still be out there in Albion, hiding from conduits, or...

"Where were you?" I turn my attention to my sister before my apprehension kills my optimism.

"At the library. We need *The Founder's Book of Relics* to figure out a potential link between the relics being taken—I looked over some of Gryff's reports when we went home last Wednesday—but Victor checked it out last."

Great. What a convenient time to be dead and almost lead our only whisperer to her death.

"Victor has a peculiar message." I look at Viola for permission to share his last words. I don't know the rules of death magic, but now that I am in her debt for stabbing her, I'll ask permission to even speak.

"He whom you seek lies in the catacombs," she tells my sister.

"It's not quite a riddle, but what if..." Lyria springs. "We have to go to the catacombs."

For Haal's sake, we are not going to the catacombs with an untrained whisperer.

"I'll explain." Lyria dumps her books on the couch opposite where Viola stands and walks around. She plucks a small black one out of the lot, flips it open, and taps on the page, beckoning Viola over. "This line is part of a bigger poem by Rian Faran. It's about a mage's journey through the catacombs to find their lover, but it's tragic because the lover was still alive. So the mage was stuck in there forever."

Viola brings her hand to her mouth, and Lyria nods empathetically. It's a stupid poem, and if anything, it should warn them *not* to go to the catacombs.

"Viola told me Beau's and Victor's bodies are at Dearly Departed, the funeral home in Albion," I tell Lyria, hoping this information will shake the preposterous idea out of her head. "We should probably—"

"Sy, you're not thinking this through." My sister raises an eyebrow at me. "Victor is telling her to go to the catacombs for a *reason*. Last words are always a variation of a riddle... maybe the whole poem is a riddle."

Why is my sister so insistent on following Victor's trail? She was so worried about Beau's burial earlier, and now that we know exactly where to find his body, she's chasing someone else's ghost. "Lyr, we *know* where Beau is. The catacombs are not safe..."

I walk up to them, leaning over my sister to have a better look at the book. She closes it, then turns to face me with exasperation. "Neither is the funeral home, Sy. If Beau's and Victor's bodies were taken, don't you *think* blood Mortemagi are involved?"

"She's right." Viola glances up at me. I was hoping she'd side with me, given it's in her best interest to stay *away* from the catacombs. "A puppet tried to kill me moments after I stumbled upon Beau's and Victor's bodies."

Blood Mortemagi—puppeteers—are the only mages in existence who use dead bodies. And if they are the ones guarding Beau and Victor, we'll all be dead before we even set sights on them.

Maybe Victor is leading Viola to more clues about his murder, and we *should* go to the catacombs. Maybe we can even ask Victor about Beau, considering their bodies were together. Or maybe . . . Beau ran into a conduit and was led to the Underiver, because there's no other reason for him not to seek out Viola if he knew she was a whisperer, if only to get a message across to us. Gods, why must I be so hopeless?

"All right." I sigh, shoving my pessimism aside. "I'll inform Paltro about the bodies, and I need you to send an express courier to Gryff asking for updates," I instruct Lyria. If puppeteers are involved, the three of us are no match to retrieve Beau's and Victor's bodies. Until then, we can follow Victor's trail.

Viola glances at the clock. "My sister's funeral isn't until noon. If we leave now, we'll make it back on time." I blink at her. Even I am not reckless enough to take this on with no sleep. Before I can object, Lyria reaches for her hand, giving it a gentle squeeze. "Viola, no. You have to rest before Olivia's funeral. I *know* how important it is for you. You can't risk missing it. The catacombs will wait. We'll go tonight."

"Okay." Viola chokes up.

Lyria checks her watch as she steps away from us and toward her room. "I asked Paltro to bring me the Deathbringer's final field reports at half-past six. If he finds Viola here, he'll lose it."

Haal, if anyone hates Mortemagi more than I, it's Paltro.

Without a word, I bring my arm close to Viola, and she tilts her head up in surprise. Our eyes meet, and I look away. Railesza takes her sweet time slithering from her arm to mine, locking us into this awkward position.

"I'll go to Paltro instead," I mumble, walking away from Viola before Railesza's even finished her loop around my arm. "I need Dad's field reports, so I'll grab the ones you need as well."

"Probably a better idea." Lyria puts on a sweater and saunters back to Viola. "I'll take you back to the House of Death when you're ready." She hooks her arm through Viola's, like they've been friends for years. "They've accepted my request to continue Mom's research—I'll be the first Aspieri Magus Principalis since her posthumous award."

"Congratul—" Viola says, but I interrupt her.

"They did?"

"As long as I leave Nyx behind, I can attend classes at the House of Death," she says, her excitement dying down. "I wish . . . I wish Beau were here . . ."

"Why?" I ask, betrayal coating my tongue. "So he could watch you be killed like they killed him?"

I don't wait for her to reply, and I storm out the front door. What is my sister thinking? Viola confirms that blood Mortemagi are involved in the murders, and my sister's celebrating walking straight into the killer's lair?

I round the corner to the hallway leading to Fang's Nest and nearly crash into someone. "Watch where—" I swallow my words.

Delaney sneers at me, her glasses resting on the tip of her nose. Behind her, Paltro's face boils with anger. "Archyr, where is the Mortemagi?"

"Which Mortemagi?" I cross my arms behind my back, and Raiku slides down my leg.

"Miss Corvi, Mr. Archyr." Delaney's pointy mouth moves. She looks like a rat. "Where is she?"

"How would I know?" The last place to look for a Mortemagi would be at the House of Poison. With the exception of my terribly misguided siblings, Aspieri and Mortemagi hate each other so much they'd never be caught together.

"Search his rooms," Delaney orders, and six Mortemagi round the corner. Who allowed *them* in the House of Poison? I glare at Paltro, and he returns an exasperated sigh.

"You don't have the right to enter our private rooms," I say.

"Open the door, Archyr." Delaney's ears are as red as the crest of the House of Poison on Paltro's coat, and if she breathes any harder, she will hyperventilate. Then, quietly behind her, Rhodes approaches.

"Door's open." I raise my palms in surrender, and the Mortemagi push past me, swarming the room.

> Poacher camps are growing at an alarming rate. Firstliners have been sent to bolster the Wanoran-Aurignan border. I fear an uprising.
>
> Updates requested on your search for the Deathbringer—her aspier hasn't resurfaced in more than two decades. She must be alive.
>
> **LETTER FROM RODRIC PALTRO TO HANSEL ARCHYR, MAY 1939**

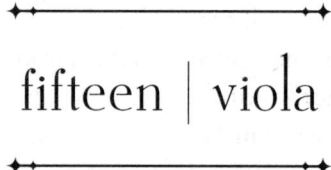

fifteen | viola

MONDAY, NOVEMBER 22, 1939

Archyr stabbed me, and I offered to help him.

Selfishly, of course. Because he and his sister seem to be the only ones who care about the murders, and I now have leverage: guilt.

Sure, DOTS says that Firstline is investigating, but it's been four days, and the fact that they haven't figured out that Beau's and Victor's bodies are at Dearly Departed is concerning. Given the caliber of Firstline recruits, I doubt they'd make such an oversight. This only tells me that the deaths of Olivia, Beau, and Victor are part of something bigger; and that it's being dismissed by the authorities.

"—so rude; I cannot believe he said that in front of you," Lyria rambles, and I feel bad for tuning her out momentarily.

"It's fine; we all process grief differently," I reassure her. Some apparently by stabbing others *accidentally*. "Congratulations again," I say, and I mean it. I find out Lyria is a month younger than me. Twenty-two and she's already a Grand Magus. It typically takes four years per rank, with mastery of Arcane taking longer because it involves different classes of magic. That she managed to do all that at such a young age ties my tongue.

"Tell me more about your research," I ask. She's so easy to talk to that I forget I need to leave.

Her face lights up. "I'm using our aspiers' venom with a Mortemagi cuff that Delaney lent to me, to see if we can reverse the Mortemagi life-drain so they can heal instead of draining their lifeblood during some spells. It was my mother's—"

Something scratches against the floor. Lyria and I glance toward the door, and Raiku slithers forward until he stops in front of Lyria. She reaches for him, and he wraps himself around her arm.

"We have to go." She glances at the clock, then she's on her feet. "Curfew doesn't lift for another fifteen minutes. They'll look for you at the House of Death. Can you run?"

Lyria's pulled eyebrows and urgent tone tear me off the sofa. She grabs my hands, and within seconds, we've crossed Founder's Room and gone through the secret door into the Poisoned Stairwell. Behind us, a door slams open. I jump, but Lyria gently squeezes my hand, tugging me forward.

The Poisoned Stairwell is as dark and unwelcoming as it was when I stepped in it alone last night. Lyria takes the first step up, and the lights on the wall come to life. I follow her as fast as I can, and after every flight, she pauses to make sure I can keep going. Her steps are sure, and her grip never falters.

Finally, we stop at a landing in front of a wall, and she lets go of my hand. She runs her fingers over the smooth stone, pauses on the right, and pushes in a small square. The wall slides open to a hallway carpeted with a familiar black-and-white diamond pattern.

"I cannot step into the House of Death with an aspier," she says. "Will you be okay on your own?"

"Why are you so kind to me?" The words escape my lips. I am not used to kindness. Not when I had to live under the roof of a woman to whom my existence was her damnation.

"The world is cruel enough as is." She glances around. "You'll need a friend around here."

Friend. I don't know what to make of that word. I don't know that I've ever had a friend, besides my sister and Mara. One of them is dead, and the other is a monster.

I blink, and Lyria's gone.

When I reach my room, my hands are shaking from the adrenaline. I will them to steady long enough for me to push the key in the door. But the keys slip and clatter onto the floor.

A hand reaches for them at the same time I do.

"Miss Corvi."

The unmistakable silvery voice ropes around my neck. My heart races in my throat, and my eyes water from the panic. What lie will I fabricate to explain why I'm outside of my room before curfew is lifted? My mind is empty, and all I want is for him to leave—he sent my sister to her death, and as much as I want to confront him about it, now isn't the time. Not when he has the power to suspend me. No. I cannot admit defeat so easily. Olivia depends on me. And now, Beau and Victor do, too.

I clench my fist, level my breathing, and blink hard, before reaching to take the keys from Lorne's hands. "Thank you," I say. But he doesn't let go.

"I came by earlier, but you didn't answer," he accuses. Why was he at my door before six in the morning?

"I was sleeping." I lift my face to him. If I'm going to lie, I might as well look him in the eye, like he did when he pretended to be devastated by my sister's death, when all this time he was the *reason* she left Gorhail.

"Curfew doesn't lift for another ten minutes. Why are you outside your room?"

"I was on my way to find you." Why did I say this?

His hand relaxes ever so slightly, and my fingers close around the keys. The lie wasn't in vain, because Lorne hangs on to my every word with bright eyes and a faint tug at his lips. With every mistruth, self-loathing boils at my throat. I am becoming everything I hate about Gorhail: manipulative and self-serving. But at the same time he deserves all the horror in the world for what he did to Olivia.

"At six in the morning?" He arches a brow.

"Is it not a good time?" I ask innocently. I don't let him answer, terrified the veil of lies will tear. "I wanted to ask you . . ."

He takes a step toward me, and my back is against the door, weighing if I should continue with the lie. "Will you . . ." I ask, and he inches forward. If he comes any closer, I will scream. "Will you come to my sister's funeral?" I ask in a breath. Olivia, please forgive me for bringing this lying, deceitful excuse of a mage to your funeral. But I cannot be caught violating curfew, not when my puzzle board has just filled with more pieces.

"Olivia," I stress on my sister's name, "would want you there."

His shoulders sag, his eyes flatten, and he vacates my personal space. I'm careful not to be obvious with my relief. Right when I think that he will agree and leave, he narrows his eyes, studying me like prey. "The funeral isn't until noon. You could've asked me at breakfast," he says suspiciously.

Oh no. He's caught my lie. He will report me to Delaney, and if she suspends me or places me under her watch, I won't be able to go to the catacombs. "Lorne..."

"I understand," he says, and another wave of panic engulfs me. What does he understand exactly? "I can't sleep either. It's not easy knowing you have to bury the person you love the most."

My skin prickles. Something about the way he speaks of Olivia twists my insides. He cheats on her, causes her to run away, lies about knowing her, then laments her death—his reaction makes no sense. Then again, I can't imagine my sister with someone like Lorne. He's too performative. What did she see in him? Or was he the one covering for her while she was here? With the rigidity of Gorhail's rules, I can't imagine Olivia's half truths sufficed as an explanation.

"Were you always at Gorhail?" I ask. "Olivia never mentioned you..."

"She didn't?" He flinches. "Are you certain?"

If she had, I would have remembered. Olivia only ever spoke of her friends Sierra and Fable. I'm glad he knows she didn't think him worthy of being introduced. He was seeing someone else. He didn't even respect her enough to break up with her.

"How long were you and Olivia together?" I ask, feeling like a parent grilling her child.

"A little under a year." He lowers his head, a shy smile playing on his lips. "I was a self-study from the province of Holm. I only joined Gorhail two years ago, and she offered to show me around. She was so kind, and when Overseer Delaney promoted me to Magister a few months ago, Olivia planned this big celebration. No one ever cared enough to do something like that for me."

She must have loved him if she was celebrating him. She loved him, and he still tossed her aside for someone else. She *loved* him, and he was the reason she ran away to her death.

I smile, but it's empty.

"Well, I'm going to get ready, and you'll pick me up?" I ask, now certain he won't say a thing about my breaking curfew.

"Of course." His eyes travel the length of my shirt, then back up, pausing at the House crest. "Is this blood?"

Archyr stabbed me a few hours ago; of course it's blood. But I frown and glance at my shirt, thanking the skies that the low morning light and the black of the fabric swallow the maroon of the dried blood. But then, I notice it. In the bottom corner of the House crest is a smidge of rust that leans to black. How did he even notice?

"Oh." I laugh, desperate to sway him away from my rocking boat of lies. The metallic tang of blood wafts through my nostrils, and I tense. "I cut myself getting the tags off my shirt earlier."

Lorne reaches for my hand, but I press it to my side. He stares at it for a moment, then nods and begins to walk away. Right as he reaches the end of the hallway, he stops and turns around. Stray rays of the rising sun soften his features, and I pity my sister for not looking past his good looks to see the rot within. "I loved Olivia. I know you don't quite believe me yet, Viola, but I really did love her."

My room is eerily still when I finally step inside. The cloudy skies framed by the window bask the room in a quiet glow, and a part of me wants to sink into my bed, hoping it'll swallow this nightmare. It's been one week since I last saw Olivia alive, and none of it feels real. Olivia's murder. Me at Gorhail. Working with Archyr.

I flip the light switch on, and a deep sense of unease curdles within my stomach. Everything is intact, down to the sweater I threw across the bed yesterday, the notebooks I neatly stacked, and the three pairs of shoes scattered across the floor. Neatly folded in a corner is a single black dress that Delaney must have had sent from the house. Olivia had the same in pink. Long sleeves, a light flare at the waist reaching just below the knees.

Grief clutches my heart. I hate how it comes in waves, at the glance of a dress, the scent of a flower, the laugh of a stranger. And yet, I still question my place in this grief.

Sighing at the dress, I turn around and head straight for the shower, desperate to scrub away the remnants of my blood and my integrity. Before magic ruined my life, I never deceived anyone. Soon, I'll start to question even myself.

My fingers unclasp the cuff. The cold metal sits in my palm. Dark red—almost brown—streaks line the filigree. It's twisted, a symbol of all the blood this magic has spilled. In a few hours, I will watch the earth swallow my sister's body as she watches me live the life she died for.

When I look at the mirror, my hand flies to my mouth. The cuff slips from the other hand, meeting the floor in a clang. The foggy mirror reads the words I've been hearing in my waking dreams. *He whom you seek lies in the catacombs.* But below it are new words I've never heard before.

I know who killed your sister.

> Aspieri need special permission from the Grand Master of Death to study at the House of Death. Unless Aspieri are pioneering revolutionary research to advance the House of Death, consider all applications rejected.
>
> Unless bonded with an Aspieri, Mortemagi aren't allowed to study poison magic. A reminder that Aspieri-Mortemagi bonding is hazardous and should be performed only in dire circumstances, such as the end of the world.
>
> **RULES AND REGULATIONS OF GORHAIL, 6TH EDITION**

sixteen | sylas

MONDAY, NOVEMBER 22, 1939

"Why would I harbor anyone from the House of Death?" I ask no one in particular as a Mortemagi turns over our sofa cushions, as if Viola would be hiding there. "In what used to be my mother's rooms?"

"Three students are dead, Overseer Delaney." Rhodes stands next to Paltro, clasping her hands together as she looks over the circus of Mortemagi pulling out chairs, looking under tables, and opening drawers. What exactly are they hoping to find? "DOTS is requesting more paperwork than can fill this room. You best have an infallible reason for bringing me here."

Paltro gives me a look. I expect him to tell me to be quiet, but his eyebrows arch ever so slightly. "Aurelia, you won't find her here. The House of Poison and the House of Death have a complicated history, as you know, and after what happened to Lilyana..."

Delaney's green eyes snap to Overseer Paltro and Rhodes, then to me. They look like an endless pit of torture. I wonder if she'll say anything about Mom, given that she was a Magister when one of her Mortemagi murdered my mother. She had profusely apologized to Dad at the time, even sanctioned the whole forsaken House, but by the time I joined Gorhail, she was a different person. Power will do that to you.

"Open this door." Delaney signals to one of her minions. She's standing right in front of Lyria's door. Why can't she open it herself?

Paltro hovers by the front door, unimpressed. He glances at his watch, sighing. He is the overseer of this House, so why isn't he overseeing Delaney *out*? And Rhodes stands next to Paltro, in her usual red garb, her lips pulled in a grimace. Delaney reports to her—why is she letting this happen?

Lyria's door opens to an empty room.

Delaney surveys the room, pausing on the large sheets of paper glued to the wall. They are filled with Mom's lifedrain theory. I've always wondered why Mom chose to pursue lifedrain—her research, albeit not nefarious, is an expansion of Rafael Grimm's own lifedrain theory with healing aspiers, enough to make our ancestors roll in their graves.

"Impressive," Delaney muses as she studies the equations.

I breathe out. Thank the Gods for Lyria's obsession with the House of the Forsaken.

"Are you satisfied now, Overseer Delaney?" Rhodes unclasps her hands. "Before I leave, I require both you and Overseer Paltro in my office. DOTS wants to know why mages are leaving Gorhail past curfew, despite your *draconian* rules."

I stifle a smile. As long as they leave the Poisoned Stairwell open, mages will never respect curfew. Preventing us from leaving Gorhail grounds is reasonable, of course. But locking us in our rooms from ten at night until six in the morning is preposterous, even for the children at the academy.

"Out," Delaney barks at the Mortemagi, as if she's not the one who told them to search our rooms in the first place. She scowls at me as she follows Rhodes out and slams the door in Paltro's face. The overseer pinches the bridge of his nose, as he often does whenever he deals with the Mortemagi ... or me.

"Where is she?" he snaps.

"Who?" Inside, I am sweating. I cannot lie to Paltro, and the more he lingers, the more I will say.

"The Mortemagi, Sylas." Paltro shakes his head.

"Uncle." I adjust the collar of my shirt. "Today is her sister's funeral. One would think she'd attend, no?"

Paltro's glare lowers to my empty wrist, where Raiku usually sits. I change the subject. "I was on my way to your office to pick up Dad's field reports and the Deathbringer reports that Lyria requested."

"I'll have them sent to your rooms." He sighs, then leaves without a word. I stand alone, like a traitor to my kin. I tell myself that I am doing this for Beau and for the greater conspiracy at play. The Mortemagi is my only ticket to the catacombs. I had no other choice.

But the truth remains, I lied to Paltro for Viola.

Olivia's funeral starts with a downpour that folds our large black umbrellas. We reach Albion's cemetery soaked, like the hundred-something other people sitting in the rain on unnaturally green grass. Most of the seats are taken, so Lyria and I stand to the side under the shelter of a willow tree. I insisted we attend in case the killer is also in attendance, although now that we're here, I doubt the murderer would risk discovery with so many readers around.

I scan the area, realize I am looking for Viola, stop looking, and then start again until I find her.

She sits in the front row next to a woman who looks like an older version of Olivia . . . and Lorne. Only two days ago, he was pretending not to know Olivia. Now look at him, cozying up to her family.

He wraps a hand around Viola's shoulders, and both Railesza and Raiku awaken with a hiss, eyes drilling into him. I *hate* this bond. Railesza, I understand, but Raiku . . . since when did he take a liking to her?

As soon as we find out what Victor wants—and hopefully he'll clue us in on Beau—I have to keep my distance. Viola might be clever, but no amount of cleverness will save her if puppeteers are involved. If they so easily clawed out Beau's and Victor's lives, she doesn't stand a chance.

While I may have wished for her death before to break this wretched bond, my sister's words now play in my mind—*We honor our parents through our choices.* They wouldn't want me knowingly risking an innocent person's life. Viola can read about her sister's murderer in *The Daily Mage* when we catch them.

"Breathe, brother." Lyria purses her lips. "Breathe."

I breathe out a curse. I don't know whether it's directed at Lorne or at Lyria.

Viola shrugs his hand off. Her face is a mask; she bites her cheeks and looks down. I *hate* that she's looking down. Her black-rimmed, round sunglasses are covered in droplets, yet she doesn't wipe them off. Her neatly tied low ponytail drips with rainwater, and her mouth is pulled in a frown.

A quick scan of the attendees brings me pause—Sierra, Fable, the three overseers, Rhodes, a lot of mages from Gorhail, and over a hundred people I don't recognize sit in silence. Not a single dry eye is in the audience. Olivia was so . . . loved, and they've all come to bid her farewell despite her lies.

The officiant says words I can barely hear, and the woman next to Viola—her mother—sobs violently. She gets up without sparing a glance to her daughter and walks to the half-open wooden coffin. She places something that looks like a necklace in the casket, then lays white tulips and lowers her head. Her lips move in what must be a prayer to the Gods to light Olivia's way to the Orga—the segregation of mage and nonmagi in the afterlife will never make sense to me. They're all dead anyway, so what difference does it make? The woman's shoulders shake as she walks back to her chair. As she sits down, not acknowledging Viola for a second time, it does something to me. What kind of mother ignores her child while burying another?

Viola gets up next. Her mid-length dress clings to her skin—it's soaked and she's not wearing a coat. Albion's warmer than Gorhail, but the occasional wind picks up, dragging the chill across the lake. How is she not freezing to death? Her steps falter the closer she gets to her sister's casket. Why isn't someone there with her? Her shoulders rise and fall, and her hand reaches for Olivia.

For a breath, she tenses. It happens in the crack of a second; her body goes rigid. It's almost like she's here but not here. I blink, and she's gently pulling her hand away, but I notice the slight shiver, the unsteady gait as she walks back to her seat. The lines of her face harden, and she looks straight ahead, not acknowledging the dozens of people who pay their respects after her. Rain continues to pour, and she remains still, unmoving, like something within her died when she said her final goodbye to her sister. Viola looks like a painting in the middle of chaos, frozen in time.

Lorne finally drags his lanky frame to the casket. His long black coat, soaked with rain, seems to weigh him down, slowing his steps. When he reaches Olivia, he lifts his hand, presumably to fix her hair. I glance at Viola, and her fist clenches. Then, Lorne does something no one else did: he leans in. He places a kiss on Olivia's forehead, then grabs her hand, slides a ring on one of her fingers, and wails. I've known Lorne for two years, and the man has never once lost his composure. He is so out of himself that the officiant has to walk him back to his seat. Did Olivia really leave after finding out about his affair with Fable? Does he blame himself for her death? Next to him, Viola's knuckles are white.

The officiant says a few words, and everyone stands. Olivia's coffin, an ornate wooden affair engraved with flowers and vines, lowers into the ground under a myriad of tears. Everyone is crying, even coldhearted Delaney. Everyone, except Viola.

Soon after, people trickle away, offering more empty words of comfort to Viola and her mother. In truth, they'll move on by tomorrow.

Lyria and I stand in the same place for half an hour, long after the other people are gone, long after Viola's mother gave her a single nod before walking away, long after Lorne tried to hug her twice, and she shoved his hands away.

Now, she kneels in the rain, her back to me, the hem of her dress drowned in mud, her hands clenching the stems of white roses at her sides. All I can think about is that I hope the stems don't have thorns.

"Sy." Lyria taps me on the arm.

"Go ahead." I'm already walking toward Viola, cursing the bond that was forced upon me.

> Dear Mr. Carver, please find enclosed the money for your illusionist services. Arrangements have been made for the next twenty years with potential for renewal. A breach in agreement will result in immediate cessation of payment.
>
> **ANONYMOUS LETTER TO VICTOR CARVER, JANUARY 1926**

seventeen | viola

MONDAY, NOVEMBER 22, 1939

"Let's go."

Archyr's low voice is barely audible against the crashing rain. I don't answer. Where would I even go after the words that trickled out of my dead sister's mouth? The very words I didn't let her finish when I saw her body at the lake.

The grass shuffles, and Archyr grunts.

"Leave me alone." My voice is hoarse from the river of tears that cascaded the moment everyone left. And they won't stop. I don't know if I'm crying because this is my final goodbye to Olivia or because this is all my fault.

"No," he answers. "Not when there's a killer looming over you for your cuff."

"Why do you care?"

"Because I—" He pauses. "Because you're my only hope to find out what happened to Beau."

"Of course." Why else would he be here? I'm an idiot. He needs me because I'm a whisperer. I cannot forget that he stabbed me behind the Doors of Desire, and I know he wouldn't have thrown the dagger unless he was suspicious I had something to do with Beau's death. I have come to realize the doors showed him exactly what he wished to see: me, responsible for his brother's death.

"What did she say to you?" he tries, after a long pause.

How does he know? No one knows when the dead speak. It's often in the blink of an eye, in the window between breaths, in the silent moment when no one is watching. I turn around and stop breathing.

Archyr kneels behind me, his black hair flat and wet on his forehead, his eyes a mirror of the angry clouds above. It takes me a moment to register that he's kneeling in a suit that looks like it could pay for a whole year of botany university. The whole thing is ruined now, soaked and painted with mud and grass. I glance up, and he's looking at me with furrowed brows, as if he's fighting against himself.

"How do you know Olivia spoke to me?" I ask, looking to the side.

"You froze," he replies. "Then, your hands were shaking, and there was a slight stumble in your steps." How did he notice that?

Why did he notice?

"I could've been cold from the rain." I drag my gaze back to him.

He lowers his head, his eyes running all over my face. "Are you?"

"Am I what?"

"Are you cold from the rain?"

Cold, no. I'm freezing, but I ignore the question. It's easier to pretend his eyes don't brim with concern than to deal with the weird feeling in the pit of my stomach. Maybe I *am* getting sick.

"*The wrong sister died at her hands. Victor Carver has the answers you seek.*" I answer his question instead. Every time I speak the last words of the dead out loud, I think of Nan. She would be so disappointed in me, yet she would still hide it with a weary smile as she always did. I hope she forgives me.

Archyr considers my words with a frown.

"Olivia must hate me." I let out a dry laugh. But I know my sister doesn't hate me. I hate myself for being so selfish. I could've lived with the magic; I'm living with it now. If I could turn back time, I would've . . . wouldn't have been such a coward.

As they lowered her body into the ground earlier, I doubled down on my promise to her. I will find her killer, and when I do, I will make sure they suffer a fate worse than Olivia's.

Archyr sighs. "Olivia was giving you a clue. Whose hands?"

"I think she means Mara, the funeral director." I meet his gaze. "Mara is a puppet. I don't know if she always was, at least I don't think so, but she nearly killed me. I suspect she may have killed Beau and Victor, too, because she brought their bodies to Dearly Departed." I pause. "It was a horrible night, and I buried it deep until Olivia triggered the memory." Even dead, Olivia still solves my riddles.

"I know," he whispers. He knows because he saved my life. Again, that treacherous feeling warms my belly, and I shove it away. It wasn't *his* choice to save me, I remind myself.

He clears his throat. "When did Olivia die?"

"Wednesday morning. The sheriff was at our door before sunrise."

"Beau was killed around four in the morning, so around the same time." He mulls over the timeline. "We were in Gorhail Woods, northwest of the Twin Lakes. Where . . . where did Olivia die?"

I inhale. The details of Olivia's death choke me up. There's still something so unnatural about it. Why would she have been on Little Lake Albion's boardwalk? Gorhail is at least an hour walk from there. The answer is stuck in my throat, and when I try to speak, my tears threaten to spill.

"Don't . . . I remember Paltro mentioned it was on the boardwalk." Archyr shakes his head, and I press my lips together, nodding. "It takes an hour to walk from where we were to Little Lake Albion, cut in half if they were running," he continues. "Still, I don't think Mara could have killed both of them."

"Maybe there's a second puppet," I offer. "Puppeteers can control multiples, can't they?"

"Only with century-old heirloom relics—puppeteering depletes magic *and* lifeblood." Sylas stands, holding out his hand. "We're getting somewhere. We know it's a puppeteer, and we know they are after heirloom relics. We just need to find the reason so we know what they'll do next."

"Stealing the heirloom relics still doesn't make sense, given they lose their magic when the wearer dies without a successor." I stare at his hand. Is this a truce or a trick to get me to trust him until he gets what he needs?

"I have nothing much . . ." he trails, hand still outstretched to me. "Except, I've been playing with the last names, and a working theory is they're all C's."

Coincidence or not, it's worth exploring. I take his hand. It's cold and clammy, but his grip is firm as he pulls me up. "Where can we find a record of all deaths over the last five years?" I ask.

"Five years?" He arches a brow.

"That's how long Mara has been in Albion."

"I have access to the records in Riverview. They're closed on Mondays, so I'll check tomorrow."

He offers me his arm. For a moment, I look at it, hung between us, then my gaze trails up to his. That odd feeling low in my abdomen is back, and I hate it so much. The only reason Archyr's affording me even an ounce of niceness is because I am the only means to his ends. *He stabbed you for a reason, Viola,* I remind myself. *And he hates Mortemagi.*

I shake my head and trudge my way to the road.

Two steps are all it takes, and my feet slip. A heavy hand braces against the small of my back. Archyr adjusts his arm behind my waist and loops the other one behind my knees. Before I realize what's happening, he's picking me up, carrying me through the muddy grass.

"Someone was in my room today," I tell him, because the awkward silence between us will bury me alive if I don't break it.

His arm tenses against my back, but he doesn't stop walking.

"Victor left a message on the mirror."

His whole body relaxes. "What did it say?"

"The same catacombs line, and 'I know who killed your sister.'"

"Do ghosts lie?" he asks.

"They aren't supposed to," I mumble.

Archyr looks down, searching my eyes for something I refuse to read into. "You need to know something about Victor." He sets me down the moment his boots clap on solid ground. "I believe he was covering for Olivia, potentially creating illusions of ghosts for her. After he died, your sister was on edge. I saw her in the dean's office the day before her death, asking Rhodes to excuse her from practicals."

"We'll find out when we go to the catacombs," I say. "Olivia said Victor has answers, and he said he knows who killed her. Besides, we can ask him about Beau's ghost. Victor's our most apparent lead right now."

"The catacombs are dangerous for whisperers, deadly for untrained ones," he mutters as he leads me to a lone black car parked a few feet away from a big willow tree. "We can't risk your sanity. Beau didn't save your life for me to waste it."

"What choice do I have?" I wince. "I don't want another death on my conscience, let alone my own, before I find out who killed my sister and why. I deserve answers, and you do too."

We lock eyes for a breath or maybe two. Time seems to slow every time Archyr looks at me, and I hate my heart for beating so fast. His jaw hardens, and he tears his gaze away. Without a word, he opens the door to the back seat, then walks around to the driver's side.

Lyria greets me with a quiet smile as she slides over, making room for me. Her cheeks are wet; at first, I think it's from the rain, but then I notice she's been crying. "They didn't deserve this," she sobs. "Olivia, Beau, Victor. They were all so young, so full of promise."

I reach for her hand, squeezing it. The lump in my throat makes it hard to speak, so I settle for a nod. In our shared grief, I feel less alone.

"Funerals are so final, and I'm not ready to bury Beau," she admits, looking down at a folded piece of parchment in her lap. "I can't even sit in the passenger seat because that's his. How will I get through life without him?"

I hold her hand tighter. "I don't know, but you're not alone."

She glances at me, steadying her breath. "We won't stop until we find who did this to them."

"What's this?" I ask, as a poor attempt to change the conversation.

She unfolds the parchment paper, and it opens to a map. "The Poisoned Stairwell leads straight to the catacombs. It's by design; Azgar wanted to discourage whisperers from going to the catacombs, so unless highly trained or paired with an Aspieri, they'd be stuck in the stairwell." She flattens the map on the empty seat between us. "The catacombs are a maze, but with your guidance, we'll be fine."

My guidance. I inhale sharply, and she immediately adds, "I know they can be deadly for untrained whisperers, but I know almost everything about death magic, and I'll never leave your side."

Her confidence helps me dismiss Parrish's warning. Deadly or not, I'll have to go there to find Victor's ghost.

Archyr clears his throat, his arms tensing as he grips the wheel. Raiku awakens with a glare, slithering from his wrist to his arm.

"No," he says with finality. "I've changed my mind about the catacombs. We know where Beau's and Victor's bodies are, and Olivia confirmed that a puppeteer is behind this." His knuckles are white on the wheel as he crosses the border between Albion and Gorhail. "We don't need to waste our time with the catacombs. I'll inform Paltro and Gryff, and they'll send a unit to retrieve the bodies. Now that we know where to find Victor, one of Firstline's whisperers will find him and they'll investigate the murders."

"But Beau . . ." Lyria protests.

"Lyria," he snaps. "You *know* our brother. I think it's time we stop pretending his ghost is still around. He would've gotten a message across somehow."

"Sylas, do you hear yourself?" Lyria's words are strangled with pain. "That would mean that he's lost in the Underiver forever . . . or worse, that he's become a wandering ghost!"

"Unfounded hope strangles you when reality pulls the strings of truth," he replies. "It's been five days, Lyria, and he hasn't attempted to speak with us *once*, while Victor has had no trouble contacting Viola."

"You're giving up on him . . ." Lyria's lower lip trembles, and I cut in.

"You don't know that. We haven't even tried . . ."

Although I initially shared his thoughts, I refuse to lose hope for Lyria. Still, the nagging feeling within me wonders whether Mara's puppeteer is a conduit who could've intentionally led Beau into the Underiver before his burial.

"Corvi, please stay out of family matters."

The abrupt dismissal pricks at my pride. I'm good enough when I give him information, but disposable when I fulfill my end of the bargain. Why did he even show up at Olivia's funeral, if he was just going to dismiss me? He even pretended to care, and like a fool, I told him everything about Mara, about Victor, about Olivia.

"I still have to speak to Victor," I maintain.

"Olivia *told* you who killed her." He huffs a frustrated sigh. "They're all dead because of their relics. Let Firstline investigate—*that's their job*." He stresses on the last three words.

"Yes, but . . ."

"Then our bargain is fulfilled," he says through gritted teeth. His words cut through my chest, their sharpness a reminder of my place in this world. Curse the moment I thought something had changed between us. These mages are all the same—they wring you dry, then toss you aside.

The car comes to a halt in front of the eastern entrance of Gorhail.

Lyria's eyebrows pinch in apology, but it's not her fault she's related to an ill-mannered baboon with the temperament of a child.

"Very well." I step out, slam the door, and then stand in the rain, watching the car speed away in the opposite direction. Once again, I am alone, a complete fool for believing they cared. Walking back into Gorhail, I strengthen my resolve. Olivia was strong enough to survive this place for twelve years.

I can, too.

I have to.

Until I know who killed her.

A few dozen pairs of eyes lock on me the moment I walk through Ghost Hall, the great hall of the House of Death. Ghost Hall is vastly different from Circle Three. Round dark mahogany tables are scattered around the perimeter, with an open kitchen spanning half the hall. The other half is bordered by low bookcases, evenly spaced to create little paths leading to private dining nooks, with the occasional hanging firepits offering warmth. From the entrance, the hall looks like a skull with a top hat.

Lorne hesitates when he sees me, then rushes to me while taking his coat off. He throws it around me, and I consider shoving him and the coat away, but I am freezing.

"Viola." He holds my face up. "You're so cold. You need to see a healer."

"I need..." I clasp his hands, dragging them off my face. "I need to go to my room."

"I'll walk you then," he offers. I don't have any more fight left in me today, so I don't argue. My limbs are shaking, my teeth are chattering, and my face feels like it's about to turn to ice. Gorhail's angry chill has turned my wet clothes into a freezer. I should never have been fooled by the warm morning sun. Bale's weather is as fickle as my mother. She gave me a single nod of acknowledgment today, which was more than I expected.

"I'm sorry about Olivia," Lorne mumbles as we climb the narrow stairwell to the student rooms. My eyes glaze over the gold-framed portraits on the wall; a few of Nan's, several of a beautiful woman with fiery red hair, some of Delaney, and some more of people I don't recognize.

"Why, Lorne?" I manage between clenched teeth. "Where were you the night she left Gorhail? Since you loved her so much. Where... were... you?"

Lorne pauses at the top of the stairs. I tip my head up, meeting his moss-green eyes. They brim with tears, while mine are filled with rage. We stand, water dripping from my dress, pooling at my feet, and him inches away from me, lips parted but unable to answer.

"I need time to grieve," I bite. "And I think you do, too." Then I walk away, his coat still wrapped around me.

Right before I take a right to my room, he says, "I'll be here whenever you're ready to talk."

"Fuck off," I bark, before hurrying to my room. I hope the message was strong enough to make him stay away. I am going to the catacombs with or without Archyr tonight, and I don't need Lorne poking around.

A quick shower later, I slip into my pajamas and climb into bed, tugging the covers to my chin. Not even the scorching heat of the water could wash away the coldness Archyr seared onto my heart. He played me like a fiddle and broke all the strings before I could learn the music.

Sleep comes at once, throwing me in the middle of my usual dream of the golden-eyed woman with long black hair. This time, she takes me foraging through the woods, telling me which fruits I can eat and which I shouldn't. She's so gentle, so calm, so happy. I wonder who she is.

Someone raps on the door, jolting me awake. I ignore the first three times, but the sound is incessant. My eyelids reluctantly pull apart. At first, I don't note anything odd, but one glance at the window and I am on my feet. The sun is long gone, and Lorne—who doesn't understand personal space—is surely wondering whether I've had dinner.

I barely turn the handle when someone pushes their way in.

Archyr presses me against the wall adjacent to the door, one hand palming my waist and the other on my mouth. He glances at the closed door, then back at me, slowly shaking his head. What is he doing here? Our bargain is over; he was crystal clear. What more does he want?

Two gentle knocks startle me. "Viola?" Lorne.

Archyr looks into my eyes, then slowly slides his hand away from my mouth. My heart pounds against my chest, the earlier frost thawing into something I have no business entertaining. He nods at the door. I think he wants me to say something, and I try to speak, but no sound comes out. I am ensnared in this moment, ensorcelled by him. My gaze trails to his mouth, and the shadow of a smirk grazes his perfect lips, telling me that he knows. His fingers close around my waist, and I can feel the warmth of his touch through the thin fabric of my pajamas. Gods, I hate him.

"Viola." Lorne's voice comes through again. "I saw the door close as I was walking past. Is someone in there with you?"

I search Archyr's face for answers, but his smirk grows into a cocky grin, followed by a lazy shrug. By one or multiple divine interventions, I snap out of my delusion.

"I'll be there in a second." I don't leave Archyr's eyes, not when they widen when he realizes Lorne may ask to come in, not when they narrow when he realizes that he'll have to hide in this tiny room, and not when they shift to something I cannot decipher. A warning, telling me that I'm starting something dangerous. And because I have nothing more to lose, I press the door handle.

> Sylas, investigations on our end are inconclusive; leadership is arguing that the deaths were random poacher attacks—they weren't. DOTS is pressuring Firstline to keep a tight lip because it doesn't want more Grimm propaganda across *The Daily Mage*. The only classes that use heirloom relics in rituals are Arkani and Mortemagi, although if bodies are involved, we already have our answer.
>
> P.S.: Tell Lyria not to slack on her training.
>
> **LETTER FROM GRYFFIN DARRO, FIELD LEADER, RIVERVIEW DIVISION, FIRSTLINE, TO HM SYLAS ARCHYR, PATROL LEADER, SECONDLINE, NOVEMBER 1939**

eighteen | sylas

MONDAY, NOVEMBER 22, 1939

Viola Corvi is playing with fire, and I have no intention of putting it out. Before that, I have to disappear. I slide into the bathroom, slip into the narrow closet on the right of the shower, and pray to the Gods that I do not suffocate to death.

"I was on my way to return your coat," Viola says as she opens the door. "Then as I was about to close the door, I realized I forgot my key."

Lorne ignores her. "I saw someone walk in here."

"Yes, me. I walked back in," she retorts. The door creaks. There's a brief pause and a shuffle of feet.

"Lorne, I'm aware of the rules. There's no one here." The slight tremor in her voice stirs an unfamiliar ache in my chest. I want to shove Lorne against a wall even more than before. I hate how he forgets his boundaries around Viola. Sure, he may be grieving, but Viola isn't her sister. Hovering over her won't erase what he did to Olivia; he should've thought twice before getting involved with Fable.

Steps echo off the bathroom walls. I hold my breath, aware that the slightest movement could give away my hideout. He stops. My mind is racing with excuses of what I am doing here. Right when I think he will open the closet door, the steps clap in the other direction.

"Random room inspections will be implemented starting tomorrow to make sure no one is in breach of Gorhail rules," he announces.

Lorne is on a power trip; he should stick to teaching classes instead of implementing nonsensical rules. For a second, I consider bursting out, dragging him to the Poisoned Stairwell, and letting the ghosts have their way with him.

"Would you like to inspect the toilet as well? How about under the bed? In the drawers? Perhaps within the fiber of our uniforms then?" Viola asks dryly. I'm fighting a smile. She *does* know how to be funny, after all.

Lorne pauses. The bastard is considering it. Then he warns, "You're new here, so you may not know that it is strictly forbidden to have guests—"

"And yet here you are," she interrupts him. I swallow a laugh.

He stammers, and I imagine Lorne's mouth is opening and closing like a fish out of water. "Viola." He lowers his tone, and I wish he would swallow his tongue. "I'm sorry. I . . . I want to make sure you're safe."

"You should've made sure Olivia was safe," she says, and I hear more steps and a door open. "Now, leave."

Lorne fumbles for a reply for a few seconds, then he sighs. "Take today and tomorrow. Overseer Delaney scheduled your aptitude testing for Wednesday." Viola's just buried her sister, and the House of Death is already back to business, eager to create more minions of Death.

The door closes, and I count a minute before joining her. She sits on her bed, gazing out the small window overlooking the expansive gardens of the House of Death—it's a surprise they can keep anything alive. A quick glance around the room brings me pause; it's small. In fact, it's not a room at all; it feels like a prison.

"You were returning his coat?" I ask, a hint of jealousy slipping through, catching me off guard. But Viola doesn't miss it. She gives me a look, then gets up, walks toward her dresser, and starts rummaging through her drawer.

"You could've pretended to be asleep when he came to your door." I even my tone, trying to sound as nonchalant as possible. But my mind is stuck on Lorne's coat, and why it was in Viola's possession. Paltro should've told me this stupid bond would come with all these unwarranted feelings and this insatiable need to be near her.

"He saw the door close. He's not that stupid." She raises an eyebrow. "I thought you were the master of stealth."

"He didn't find me, did he?" I lower my head, and she pauses, a half-folded shirt hanging over her arm. She turns around and glances up at me. Her eyes are two shades of brown, leaning toward rust at the bottom of her irises. I hate that I notice these things.

She tears her gaze away, lingering on my forearm. "Where are your aspiers?"

"Somewhere in the Poisoned Stairwell with Lyria," I tell her. The House of Death has magic preventing killer and healer aspiers from crossing into their quarters. Lyria tells me they would've blocked the Imortalis, too, but they could never get their hands on Raiek to weave into their spell.

Viola lets out a deep sigh before turning back to the dresser. She furiously pulls out a pair of training pants, stacks it over the shirt on her arm, and slams the drawer shut. Without looking at me, she heads to the bathroom. I don't move, and a moment later, the door opens, her loose sleepwear traded for her black uniform. She still doesn't spare me a glance as she walks over to the dresser and places the neatly folded pajamas on top. Finally, she turns around.

"What are you doing here, Archyr?" she asks, leaning against the furniture with her arms crossed. I let out a heavy breath; I don't remember her uniform fitting so *well* before.

"I . . ." What do I tell her? That I'm here because I was wrong, and the catacombs are unavoidable if I want to find Beau's killer? That DOTS is pressuring Firstline to bury the investigation, so our siblings will never get justice? That I will have to risk her life because it's the only choice we have?

"I need your help," I mumble, averting my gaze.

"You tell me to stay out of family matters, and now you storm into my room uninvited and drag me back into *your* problems?" Her tone gradually lowers as she glances at the door.

I sigh. I'm not above begging for her help. After profusely apologizing to my sister for my earlier outburst, we agreed to speak to Victor before damning Beau to an unimaginable fate. "Can we..."

"*What do you want?*" She stresses every word. Watching her lips move, I no longer know what I want. "My friend Gryff sent me a letter from Firstline. He was assigned to the case, and they are dismissing the murders as random poacher attacks—"

"I knew it," Viola exclaims, slamming a hand on the dresser. "So much for trusting the administration to do something right..."

"That's not all." I straighten myself. After dropping Viola at Gorhail earlier, Lyria and I argued all the way to Riverview to the Record Collector's Office. Lucky for us, she was an Arkani who knew our parents and let us in when the office was closed. We pored over records of mage deaths over the last five years, like Viola suggested, and five more before that. Nothing stood out. No gruesome deaths, only regular poacher killings on the field, some relics taken, some not, and a few accidental deaths. I briefly considered they'd been hiding reports, but these are recorded by readers and perjury bears the death penalty. "These animalistic killings haven't happened in quick succession before, and definitely not coupled with heirloom relic theft. I'm certain DOTS wants to bury the case because they don't want to fuel Grimm propaganda," I tell her.

"More reason for me to ask Victor's ghost about their killer," she says, then her eyes narrow at me. "You're here because you can't go through the catacombs without me. Pathetic."

That's not the only reason I'm here, I almost say. But like an idiot, I retort, "You won't be able to *get* to the catacombs without our help."

"So now *I* need *you*." She rolls her eyes, and I press my lips together. She heads to the door, wraps her hand around the doorknob, but doesn't pull it open. Her head drops, and very quietly, she says, "I am like a spare relic to you—something you use when you need and set aside when you don't, something you only care about when it serves you, and when it breaks, you'll just get another one."

Heat rises to the base of my neck. My mouth goes dry, my mind racing to find my words, the *right* words. I shake my head, wanting to correct her, to tell her that Aspieri don't *have* spare relics, that our relics are all we have until we die. Before I can say anything, she turns around. "Let's go, Archyr. I owe you anyway."

"You owe me nothing," I reply. In a single stride, I am in front of her.

"You saved my life. That debt can never be repaid." She meets my eyes with steel, as if it hurt her to say those words.

"I had selfish reasons." My honesty astounds me. My aspiers were being threatened.

"At least you're honest." She lowers her eyes. I hate how she folds into herself, how she puts up this armor to shield herself from the world, how she thinks she deserves nothing. How could she refer to herself as a spare anything?

I don't think, and my hand lifts her chin before I can pull it back. It's like our first exchange in Hollow Tree, except this time, I feel the softness of her skin, every smile line, and even the outline of the tiny mole on her left jaw. I want her to look at me when she hears this. "You owe nothing to anyone. In a world where people are driven by their own selfish wants, you will not give them that power over you."

She takes in a sharp breath, her gaze burning into mine. The confusion in her eyes mirrors my own as I brush my thumb over her cheekbone. I don't know what's taken over me; all I know is that I want to lose myself in the depth of her brown eyes, learn every hue of gold, red, and black, and sear it into my memory.

She blinks, and the spell breaks. I drop my hand. That stupid bond is messing with my head again, pulling me toward her.

Viola may be different, but she's still a Mortemagi. The magic that killed Mom flows in her. Like every disciple of the House of Death, she will choose that magic in the end.

I don't look at her, and I step over to the wardrobe. I flip through a few sweaters until I land on a thick wool one and push it into her hands. "It's freezing in the catacombs," I say, dragging my gaze across her body. She's wearing tight pants and a plain long-sleeved shirt, a recipe to join the residents of the catacombs by freezing to death. "Wear a warmer shirt, and please, change into combat pants and line them with tights," I instruct. Her eyebrows flinch, and she searches my eyes; I give her nothing.

"You can't tell me what—"

"I can," I interrupt her. "Patrol leader privileges, and if something happens to you while you're with me outside of curfew, Gorhail will hold me responsible."

She glares at me, huffs out a frustrated breath, and closes the bathroom door behind her.

"How will I manage the barrage of voices I escaped by slipping through the Doors of Desire?" she asks plainly as she's changing. Her mask is back. Inside me, a silent war takes root. I hate myself for slipping, for making her believe—even for a sliver of a second—that she can trust me, because I will never put a Mortemagi above anything.

"Lyria will walk you through it," I say. "She's waiting for us in the Poisoned Stairwell." My sister's obsession with this forsaken House will come in handy after all.

Viola heads to the door. "I'll go out first to make sure Lorne is gone." She leaves, and a second later, motions me to come out. She leads the way to the secret door at the end of the hallway and pushes in the notch on the wall. She doesn't look at me once, and I hate it.

Raiku and Railesza hiss as I close the passageway door behind us. I reach for them, and they both slither to my arm. Tonight, the stairwell is gracious with its wall lights; they shine so bright I can make out the divots in the stone and the aged mortar holding everything together. Maybe it knows where we are going, maybe it pities us, offering the unusual light as a parting gift.

"Give me your hand," I say as I reach for Viola.

"Why?" she asks dryly.

"Railesza will go with you, in case we are separated."

She hesitates at first, still avoiding my eyes. But then, she closes her palm around mine. I hate how the bond makes a simple touch from her ignite something within me, how I never want to let go of her hand, how I yearn for her to look at me again.

Railesza coils around her wrist, and I let go. I have no room for distractions, not when we have to brave the catacombs to speak to Victor.

Lyria meets us one flight below, her eyes immediately falling to Railesza around Viola's arm. Her eyes flick to me while she suppresses a smile. I hope she's not getting the wrong idea from this. We're only working together to uncover our siblings' murderer.

"Vi, are you ready?" My sister steps past me and hooks her arm around Viola's. *Vi.* Since when did they become so close?

"No." Viola shakes her head. "What do I do in the catacombs? I've never had an active conversation with a ghost."

Lyria tugs her forward. "The only voice you're going to listen for is

Victor's. But if the voices get too overwhelming, find a single human voice as your anchor—Sylas or I will be here to talk you out of it. If the voices try to drown you, use the magic of the catacombs and lead them into the river so they can go forth with the current."

Viola looks at my sister like she's speaking a foreign language. Because she is. How Lyria knows half the things she knows or how she finds time to learn them escapes me. I think that learning is her way of coping with all the tragedy around us.

"Ghosts from the catacombs will never give you their names," Lyria explains as we walk farther down the stairs. We're only a couple of flights from the hallway that leads to the Doors of Desire. My sister continues, "They can only have an open conversation with you if you've anchored to their voices, but be careful with this. Anchored ghosts can follow you out. The silver lining is only one ghost can anchor at a time."

"How do you know all that?" I wave my hand in the air. "You're an Aspieri, for Haal's sake."

"It's in *Understanding Death Magic* and *Death Magic for Beginners*, which we study our last year before Magus promotion." Lyria scowls. "How are you still at the institute?"

Until today, I had no use for information about death magic. Mortemagi stayed on their side of Gorhail, and I stayed on mine.

We fall silent as we climb down several flights of stairs, broken by three short hallways. I shudder as we walk by the moss-filled hallway of the Doors of Desire. The last time I was here, I stabbed Viola because of my own prejudice, and now . . . I shake my head.

Find Victor's ghost. Ask him about Beau. Get their bodies from Dearly Departed. Catch the murderer. These are the only things I should be thinking about.

"I know the way." Lyria leaves Viola behind and steps past me. She practically skips all the way down, while I measure my every step. The farther down we go, the air crawls with rancid humidity. The sharp drop in temperature means only one thing. Ghosts. We're nearing the catacombs, and down here, even the aspiers cannot ward us from them.

"Viola." I break the silence. I need to warn her about the influx of voices she'll be hearing any moment. No answer. My spine prickles with unease.

I'm too late; I know it.

"Lyria," I yell for my sister, before turning to Viola. She stands four steps behind me, frozen in place. Her glassy eyes look straight ahead, but they see nothing. Her lips are slightly parted, but no words come out.

Railesza slithers down her arm, her fangs hovering over her wrist.

"Go," I urge, and her fangs sink into Viola's veins.

Nothing happens.

Railesza lifts her head toward Raiek, but of course he doesn't budge. He's not moved since Dad's death.

Haal. Panic ripples through my limbs, but I push against it. I race back up the stairs until I'm in front of her, lacing my hands around her cheeks. Her skin is so, so cold. I slide my hand down her neck, my fingers feeling for a pulse. She has one, thank Haal.

Anchor. "Viola, listen to my voice." It cracks.

Her eyes well with tears, but she doesn't move. She's in there, somewhere. I curse myself for not paying attention in classes about death magic, curse myself for not taking an interest in Lyria's research.

"Sy, what—" Lyria rushes to us.

"Ghost paralysis," I utter. "We're not in the catacombs yet; she won't be able to use its river of magic."

"I'm an idiot," Lyria mutters. "Her cuff . . . remove her cuff."

"I can't," I reply. "She didn't bond with me; her relic won't respond." Unless she's dead or double bonded with someone, no one but she can take off her relic.

"Can you pick her up?" Lyria asks. "Hurry."

I loop my hands around Viola and lift her into my arms. She sags against my chest. "I have you," I murmur, pressing my lips to her hair.

Lyria runs a hand over mine and holds it there for a moment. "Trust me," she says as Nyx slithers from her hand to Viola's arm. Her aspier hisses at Railesza, who in turn glares at her. It's too late when I realize what my sister is doing.

"Be gentle, Nyx," she orders, and Nyx bites Viola's wrist.

Railesza hisses, but she lets Nyx continue until color drains from Viola's face and her lips tinge with the faintest shade of blue.

"She's dead," Lyria whispers. In less than two seconds, she slides her hands underneath Viola's sweater and unclips her cuff. "Now," Lyria screams, and Railesza's fangs sink in the same spot Nyx's were.

Lyria maneuvers Viola's open cuff out of her shirt and cups it with both hands, as if it were a most precious jewel. To me, this cursed relic almost killed Viola.

The seconds it takes Railesza to heal Viola freeze my lungs. What if she doesn't wake up at all? My thoughts are cut short because soon after, Viola gasps for air, and I feel my own heart come alive. She coughs in between breaths, wheezing, as if she's learning how to breathe all over again. After a moment, I set her down on the floor and step away as Lyria kneels next to her. Because I don't trust my traitor hands nor my traitor heart.

Viola reaches for her arm, frowning. "How did my cuff come off?"

"I unclasped it." Lyria grimaces and changes the subject. "What happened?"

Viola goes silent for a moment, her hand rubbing her barren arm. She takes in the emptiness around us, then shakes her head. "So many voices, so much pain, so much anger. I was drowning in all of it." She holds her hand out, and my sister gingerly hands her back the Corvi cuff. "How did you take it off?"

"Oh." Lyria gives her an awkward laugh, glancing up at me. I raise my palms, and her eyes widen in betrayal. She turns to Viola with a nervous smile. "I killed you. Revived you immediately. Is it really killing if you're not dead?"

Viola's jaw drops open.

My sister continues her justification. "I have extensive practice."

"With?" Viola asks.

Lyria murmurs, "Flowers and two mice."

Flowers and two mice? Lyria, for the love of Haal. She could have really killed Viola.

"You've never practiced on a person before?" Viola asks with an eerie calm.

"Now I have . . ." Lyria winces. My sister has lost her mind.

Viola shrieks, "I could have died."

"Well," Lyria drawls. "Technically, you did. You had to, or else I wouldn't have been able to take off your cuff and release you from ghost paralysis."

"Ghost paralysis . . . ?" Viola trails.

"You exist in a shell, trapped in your own mind, until you die and become a ghost yourself. You can never cross the Underiver. Delaney spent a whole lesson on it in year six. It only happens to whisperers."

"And you couldn't mention that detail before we went deeper down the stairwell?" Viola throws her hands in the air. "Do they kill and revive every whisperer with ghost paralysis?" Viola hisses at Lyria.

"Well, I thought the aspiers would keep the ghosts away, and I didn't think they would flood you outside of the catacombs. But it's also not often that a whisperer comes around here." My sister looks at me for support, and I shrug. Then she looks back at Viola. "I'm so sorry, Vi. I should have warned you."

A heavy silence hangs between us, and a distant sound of rolling pebbles fills the space. My sister rubs her hands together, then, as she's about to speak, Viola stops her. "You're brilliant, Lyria. I don't think anyone else would've known what to do." If by anyone else, she means me, she wouldn't be wrong. If Lyria wasn't around, Viola would have been trapped forever.

"*How* do I break out of ghost paralysis?"

"If you're in the catacombs, you can lead them into the river." Lyria and I exchange a worried glance. This is one area where Lyria's theoretical knowledge can't make up for field practice. "Out in the world, whisperers are trained to break out of paralysis," I add. "It takes years."

"It's not your fault," Lyria adds. "Cuffs attract ghosts like moths to a flame."

Viola gets to her feet. Her eyes meet mine, and guilt stirs at my neck. I can't do this to her. She's untrained. Once we go into the catacombs, it'll be worse. She'll have to wear her relic again to speak to Victor. What if the voices flood her again and she can't lead them into the river? There's only so many times we can stop and revive her heart.

"We don't have to do this," I finally say. "We don't have to go on Victor's quest."

My sister's head jerks toward me. I've already crushed her hopes once, and now I'm doing it again. I'll write to Gryff. He's a field leader; he has the authority to dispatch a Firstline whisperer to the catacombs.

"Lyr, in the off chance that Beau's ghost is still out there, we should focus on burying his body so he doesn't get lost in the Underiver." I try, running a hand over my face, a desperate attempt at swaying my sister. I can't believe I'm considering walking away from our biggest lead right now, but the last time I took it upon myself to solve a problem, Beau died, and the time before that, Dad died.

"*You* can leave, but *I* have to do this." Viola tips her chin, steeling her gaze. "For my sister, who died because of me. For your brother, who saved my life. And for Victor, because he holds the answers no one will give us."

With that, she walks off, Lyria following closely behind. The heaviness settles in again, and my heart beats at the sound of her breath. Realization crashes onto me like the freezing winter downpour: she's willingly risking death to solve the murders, and I don't want her to die.

"Viola... there is a chance you do not walk out of there alive," I remind her as we reach the iron door that leads to the catacombs. I give her one final look, one final out. But her face is blank.

Viola, an untrained Mortemagi, a novice whisperer, is about to walk into a cesspool of angry ghosts. For her, nothing good can come out of this. For Lyria and me, the only consolation is that the ghosts can't attack us.

"We don't have all night," she says, before pushing the door open and disappearing into the tunnels of death.

> **Conduit (n)**—Mortemagi whose cuff hypnotizes ghosts so they can lead them to the Underiver.
>
> Conduits are banned from the catacombs.
>
> They run the risk of death should they breach the rules.
>
> **Addendum**: Too many ghosts flocking to a conduit's cuff overloads them with magic, which in turn causes their heart to fail. A good reminder that everything should be consumed in moderation, even magic—*especially* magic.
>
> **YSENIA FARO**, *THE CATACOMBS*: VOLUME I

nineteen | viola

MONDAY, NOVEMBER 22, 1939

I stand on a slope that leads down to the entrance of a tunnel of darkness. The musty, sickly scent of decay throws me off. I thought I knew what death smelled like, but this is far worse.

Behind me, Lyria gags, slapping a hand over her mouth. I don't blame her. It's nauseating. I turn around, and Archyr stands a step behind, his brows furrowed as he stares at his sister. She looks like she's about to be sick.

"You should go back," Archyr tells her.

"No," she says with a scowl, then gulps nervously. "Have you lost your mind?"

"Lyr," Archyr says. "Victor won't lead Viola to her death because he needs her, and I have Raiek." He runs his hand over the Imortalis around his neck. "If something were to happen to you . . . please, Lyria. You're all I have left."

Lyria's chin wobbles. "You can't do this, Sy. You can't use my words against me."

"I wouldn't be able to live with myself." Archyr wraps his arm around her, and she leans into him. My stomach twists into knots. In Lyria, I see my sister. In a twisted way, the Gods are giving me a second chance to spare someone the same fate as Olivia's.

"You *need* me," Lyria tries one more time. "You don't have a clue about death magic. What if she—"

"Nothing will happen to her." He glances at me, then back at Lyria. The conviction behind his words fills me with dread. He can't look at me like *that*—like maybe I'm not just a tool to him. Not when we're about to step into the kingdom of wandering ghosts, where death magic is the only one that reigns, and my only weapon is my mind.

"I'll be fine," I promise her, snapping out of my wishful thinking. Archyr needs me to speak to Victor. Nothing more.

"All right." Lyria finally relents. Right before leaving, she turns to me. "If anything happens, anchor yourself to Sylas's voice. Nothing else."

Then she is gone.

"Ready?" Archyr asks.

I'm as ready as a bird who's not yet learned to fly.

Every step we take down the slope slaps us with sharp, frosty air. Archyr mutters a curse, tugging his coat at his neck. Before we enter the tunnel, he glances at me again. I hate that he keeps giving me so many outs. Because I want to turn around, to run back to the safety of my mundane life in Albion, back to when all I had to worry about was my mother's temper and my escape to Osneau. But Olivia, Beau, and Victor deserve justice, and my temporary discomfort is a small price to pay.

The silence of the tunnels makes me question my resolve. The same Arkani-powered lights from the stairwell glow faintly against the stone; it doesn't help because down here the darkness commands our every move. My eyes take a moment to adjust to the drop in visibility. The floor is a blur of black; it's impossible to tell where we're walking.

We use the candles and our hands on the damp limestone as a guide until we reach a split in the tunnels. "We're not splitting up," Archyr says before I'm able to suggest anything—splitting up is an absurd idea.

He doesn't protest when I turn left. The tunnels get narrower from here, the acrid smell more pronounced, and . . . *bones*. Bones protrude from the walls. We're in an endless maze of skeletons, heading straight to the depths of the Underworld. *Bones can't hurt you*, I repeat like a mantra as I find my footing on the slippery stone. I would choose falling over touching bones.

The blisters blooming on my heels tell me we've been walking for a while. We're getting nowhere, and Victor's ghost chose now of all times to take a vow of silence. He could have thrown a pebble, flickered a light, scared a rat in the proper direction. Anything to help guide us.

"I have to wear the cuff," I whisper. "We're going to die in here if we keep wandering down random tunnels."

"No." Archyr brushes past my shoulder. "Don't you feel the magic down here?"

I don't.

But I know this will change the moment my cuff clips around my arm. The magic Archyr speaks of is ancient. I remember reading in one of Nan's books that it draws on the essence of the ghosts refusing to cross the Underiver, feeding it to the cuffs. The real danger of the catacombs is that it feeds so much magic to our relics that it makes it near impossible to control.

"Viola," Archyr warns.

He doesn't understand. Without my cuff, there is no magic, no danger, and no answers. I cannot back out now. With that, I clasp the cuff around my arm.

The floodgates open to a cacophony, even louder than in the stairwell. Piercing screams, cries of terror, and wails of sadness muddle the thousands of words being thrown at me. My head will explode. Suddenly, I wish I had listened to Archyr, and I immediately reach for my cuff. My hands are right there, inches away from unclasping it, when the voices shove me out.

My fingers won't move.

"Viola." I hear Archyr say my name, but it sounds like it's coming from a great distance. "Anchor."

To what? I want to scream. The sharp sting of death takes over my senses. Like hungry wraiths, the voices flood in, eclipsing my every thought. Lyria told me to find a river, but there's none. Only a blur of red, blue, and silver threads. More cries drown out Archyr's instructions, shattering my insides. This is worse than death; this is eternal damnation.

The voices get louder, the screams more harrowing, each one threatening to split my head in five. I try to cling to one, but they are all woven together.

I am an intruder in my own mind. The voices are all over the place—blue, red, and silver in every corner. I focus, try to compartmentalize. Maybe if I can put them in boxes . . . but there are too many.

An anchor. I need an anchor; human or ghost, I don't care. I want the pain to stop.

In the narrowest corner of my mind, I am lured by the soothing voice of a girl who doesn't sound much older than I, singing the story of her death. *The climb is too high, my end is nigh. To my death I plummet, at the hands of my lover, the prophet. The tide, merciless, finally lays me to rest.*

Did she fall from Death Spire at the House of Death? That place is sectioned off with guards behind the doors. Lorne said the place is so sinister that even looking in its direction is a bad omen.

Was she a student? Why did she die? I open my mouth to ask her, and tape it shut just as fast. The texture of her voice, melodious and soothing, still has the translucent echo that I should be terrified of. But something about this ghost feels different. While the others screamed at me, she brings me peace. Maybe if I don't talk to her, she won't follow me out.

Her story sits with me long enough that my brain quiets.

"Viola, please, fight it." Archyr's urgent voice is back. He says something else, but the moment I try to focus, the angry ghosts drown him out, slowly dragging me back into the cave of insanity. I can't go back there; I can't be lost forever. But it seems impossible to resist.

Fight it, a distant voice says. I no longer know who is speaking, whether it's an echo of Archyr or the textured whisper of the girl. An explosion of colors mars my vision, and with it comes the barrage of demands. I steady my breathing. *Lean on the magic*, a distorted voice says. I close my eyes, thinking of the soft song of the girl from Death Spire.

When I open my eyes again, a river of green is ahead, faint and narrow. The voices are weak now; I hear birds and the soft ripples of water gliding on rocks. It even smells like the forest at dawn.

I reach for the nearest blue thread, twirling it around my fingers, mesmerized by the light shimmer. In my heart, I know this thread belongs to a Mortemagi who once was. Were they happy? Did they leave a family behind? I find myself hoping their end wasn't agonizing. Then I remember where I am.

The blue thread flows into the river with ease, ebbing and flowing with the smooth current. This must be what Lyria meant when she said to lead them into the river. One by one, I lead the threads into the water until I see a path ahead. The more I feed to the river, the clearer I see.

Soon, the soft forest scent is gone, replaced by the putrid smell of the catacombs. There are no birds, no water, only stones and bones.

I did it. I broke through ghost paralysis.

After some time, I snap back to reality. Archyr's hands cup my face. His eyes brim with panic as he searches mine for any sign of life. His brows furrow, and he swallows. For a foolish second, I let myself believe that he is scared for me, and not because he's scared to lose the only lead to his brother's killer.

"Do you know of a girl who fell to her death from Death Spire?" I ask without preamble.

"Did you anchor to a ghost?" he asks at the same time, drowning out my question.

"No." I shake my head. At least I hope not. I didn't speak to any ghosts. What's most important is that I broke out of ghost paralysis. "No," I whisper, with hesitation this time.

Archyr studies my face for a moment, then pulls away, giving me his back. He flexes his hands, shaking his head, as if he's trying to shake me out. I realize I want him to turn around and look at me again. And I hate it.

Our walk continues for what feels like hours. My feet are raw, and I periodically swallow my own saliva to alleviate the dryness of my mouth. Occasionally, a ghost breaks the tether, but I weave it back into the river. At first, it takes some time, but by the fourth stray ghost, I make quick work of the weave. Perhaps, the ghosts took pity on me. They saw how awful I am at magic, and they've decided to leave me alone.

Go. A voice, silver and purple—the colors of Arcane and Illusion—barrels through my calm mind palace. I'm about to lead it into the river when it speaks again. *Go.* I know this voice. I've known it since it chained me to the catacombs at Dearly Departed. Victor.

"Go where?" I ask.

Where the stone meets the sea, he answers. I echo his answer to Archyr.

"The ancient burial chamber," he explains. "It's where the... untainted lines were buried. It also houses ancestral relics, most of which are retired or only used for rituals."

My stomach flips. It makes me sick that this place even exists. Somehow, before I came to Gorhail, I convinced myself that mages were above the common prejudice of nonmagi. But they share the same ignorance and the same misguided hate. In the end, humans are all the same.

"The founders of Gorhail believed that magic lines couldn't be merged in order to maintain the potency of magic," Archyr continues. "It's nonsensical, and times have changed. No one uses these burial chambers anymore. Most mages are buried at the crypt in Riverview; some, like my parents, in their home cemeteries."

For a moment, I forget where we are, and I contemplate asking him about his parents, what they were like, what jobs they had, and other mundane questions. But small talk isn't for us.

At last, we reach a small empty chamber. "Is this it?" I ask. "They must not have had a lot of people to bury."

Archyr lets out a low chuckle, and my eyes flick to his mouth. "If I remember Lyria's map, we have one more tunnel to cross after this."

Moonlight filters through the small cracks in the stone above, illuminating the room. Other than the two doors across from each other, this room is completely empty. If I forget the smell of rot and seawater, the chamber is almost cozy. There are no bones here, only damp limestone. What more could I ask for?

Corvi. A gruff, dark voice sneaks in behind me. It doesn't sound human nor ghost; it sounds like a bit of both, grounded with a texture that's rough at the edges.

I whirl, thinking Archyr is playing a prank. When he returns a blank look, the hairs on my neck stand on end. This voice has no color.

Rhea? they ask. The voice knows Nan.

"Viola," I reply curtly. "Her gran—"

You have magic now, child? Confusion colors the voice's question. They must be thinking about Olivia. Then again, they wouldn't know Olivia unless she had been down here before. *My beautiful sister, who used to hate walking in mud, who would refuse to take out the trash. What happened to you, that you had to come through these tunnels that reek of death and decay?*

"Has she . . ." I pause, weighing my question carefully in case I get only one. "Have I been down here before?"

The voice cackles. It crawls through my bones, rooting me in place. They are dead, I tell myself. The dead can't do anything to me.

A second Corvi. It laughs again. *Oh wicked, clever Rhea.* The voice glides around me, slick in a poisonous nectar. *I'll give you this one for free.*

The veil that separates life and death holds secrets better left unsaid. Meddling with ghosts comes at too high a cost. For every ask is a price twice the worth. The voice sings in a honey-like sweetness.

I repeat the words to Archyr, and his face twists. "You shouldn't ask them questions. They'll take something from you."

I heard the words, too, but I need to know if Olivia has been down here and why. It could clue me on her death.

"Why—" I defy, looking straight at Archyr.

"Why was Olivia Corvi in the catacombs?" Archyr runs a hand over his face. "I can't hear them, so . . ."

The voice chuckles like a small child this time, yet I can tell it's the same entity. *I always thought Lyria would be the first Archyr to grace my catacombs. What a surprise.*

I repeat the words, and Archyr rolls his eyes. "Be quick about it."

Nothing like his mother, this boy, the voice scoffs.

I purse my lips to hide a smile. I imagine Mrs. Archyr would have been like Lyria: kind, funny, and good-natured—nothing like the man standing before me, pressing me for answers with a glare that threatens to slice my throat.

The moment I tell him what the voice said, his eyes darken, and he steps in front of me. "You knew Mom?" he tries.

The voice drones, *The wearer of the Imortalis gets a single question. Choose wisely.*

"They say you only get one question," I whisper. His eyebrows furrow, and he mutters a curse.

"Why was Olivia Corvi here?" His eyes don't leave mine. His jaw is tight, as if he's questioning himself for wasting his one question on me. *Why* did he? My mind starts racing, pulling me in places I cannot be.

Olivia Corvi didn't come here alone, didn't come here seeking. I may be the guardian of the catacombs, but my lips have been sealed by magic more ancient than me.

Instead of wondering whether Olivia came here with the killer, my mind is stuck on Archyr spending his only question on me. I cannot let this debt go unpaid. I won't let him have any leverage on me.

"Why was Sylas Archyr's mother in the catacombs?" I blurt, wincing when my cuff burns, the metal searing against my skin. Archyr's gaze cuts to me, his eyes narrowing in anger or confusion, I am not sure.

Lilyana Ronin came to retrieve something old and something gold, something that gives and something that lives.

Lilyana. The name catches in my throat; it's so beautiful. My gaze drifts to Archyr, who looks at me as if I hold the answer he's been waiting for all his life. Then it hits me why Nan told me that the last words of the dead were sacred. They hold the power to alter the fabric of the living. I am but a vessel, carrying messages, potentially ruining people's lives.

I repeat the words. My debt has been repaid, and he can stop being a distraction. The sooner I find Olivia's killer, the sooner I can leave.

"Mom didn't always have Raiek," he says so quietly I barely hear him. "Why would my mother trade her aspier for a Founder's relic? They were supposed to be locked away."

"Where are the other two Founder's relics?" I ask without thinking, and my cuff burns again. I didn't mean to ask the voice, I meant to ask Archyr.

Sileas Ronin's aspier is around Sylas Archyr's neck, the Arkani Coin is buried deep in Aurignan, and Faro's Cuff, it drawls. *Faro's Cuff is long gone.*

The voice is short now. Did I ask the wrong question? Something raw and cold rattles my bones, and I know we need to leave. For all I know, the guardian may decide to sandwich us between the walls of this chamber.

"Thank you for your help," I say out loud, ushering Archyr out into the tunnel. The guardian's voice grunts behind me, echoing through the emptiness ahead of us.

"Did you know that Faro's Cuff is missing?"

He halts abruptly, the chamber a few steps behind us. I wish he'd stopped farther away, in case the guardian decides to murder us.

"This makes no sense. After the founders trapped Grimm in it, the cuff was locked away under my ancestor's statue next to Paltro's office, because he argued that his bloodline would never betray him by retrieving the cuff."

"Who is Grimm?" I ask. I don't recall seeing that name in any of Nan's books.

Archyr shakes his head.

"Only the worst mage to come out of Gorhail. He was a Mortemagi who abused his power, murdering hundreds in the name of magical freedom. He wanted all mages to be able to use the blood arts—trade their lifeblood for magic—so we could progress as a society. But the blood arts are a slippery slope. Grimm is the primary reason magic is restricted, and after that purists lobbied DOTS for further restrictions, like requiring all crossmages to register with DOTS and seal half of their magic."

I know blood Mortemagi exist—I read about them through the margins of Nan's journals—but never understood how they worked, only the harm they caused. "What are the blood arts?"

Archyr recoils, looking at me like my question is sacrilegious. Then he sighs. "When you trade some of your years to live—your lifeblood—in exchange for magic from the Gods. Mortemagi can summon the undead from the ground and control corpses; that's how the puppets work. Arkani can stretch the limits of their magic, able to practice it without requiring dust." He pauses, then quietly adds, "Aspieri are the only mages who can't use lifeblood magic. It doesn't work with our aspiers."

"There's honor in not bowing to the blood arts," I say softly. His gaze lingers on me, but I cannot lose my focus, so I turn my attention forward. In these rare moments of honesty, I wonder if his hatred of Mortemagi stems from a misconception that we are all like Grimm.

The narrow tunnel in front of us drips from the roof. It's only water, I tell myself. It's . . . Gods, save us. It's seawater. We must be so deep in the catacombs that we've reached the part that stretches into the ocean, but it only means we're getting closer to the burial chamber. We're still only two steps out of the guardian's chamber, when a huge slab slides down, slamming on the ground, shutting us out. My heart leaps out of my chest. Had we not moved, it would have crushed us.

I look down the narrow tunnel again. With the chamber closed behind us, we can't go back the way we came from once we find the burial chamber. Our only way out is through. As if Archyr hears my thoughts, he reassures me, "We'll find another way out of the catacombs."

I gulp, wishing I had some of his optimism.

"I'll go first." Archyr steps sideways into the narrow passage, his arms stretched so far, his chest pushed up and his abdomen sucked in. He takes long strides, careful not to touch either side. Then he gives me the quickest nod.

I take a deep breath and, like him, angle myself sideways with my arms stretched as far as I can. Then I take the first step.

A half-split skull looks straight at me, partially buried in the wall, and I gasp, swallowing the scream that's pushing its way out of my throat. Archyr's head snaps to me, and his eyes travel down my heaving chest. He closes his eyes; takes a slow, deep breath; opens them; and gives me an encouraging nod.

I can do this. I refuse to die before I find the murderer.

Another sideways step, and I pause. My mind is stuck on the faint splat of water against the rocks. Every drip is a threat that the ocean will claim us. I will my legs to move, but they stop again after two short steps. The walls are getting narrower. Will they close on us? Will we be trapped down here for eternity and join the skeletons that leer at us from the safety of their wall?

Another step. One breath. I am safe. A second step. Two breaths. Olivia did this, and so can I. A third step. Three breaths. These walls have been here for centuries. They will not close today. Even if I cannot trust that Victor led me the right way, I have to trust that he needs me enough to want me alive.

"We're here," Archyr says. All the air empties out of my lungs, in relief that this nightmare has an end. He looks around in awe. "It's grander than in the books."

When I step out of the tunnels of death, I understand what he means. The ancient burial chamber is made up of three U-shaped rows of vaults that go up at least five stories high. The paths between them are veiny white marble, nothing like the filth we had to cross to get here.

The vaults are all black marble, with the faintest white veins. I've only seen these in photographs; marble, especially this much, is only accessible to the rich provinces like Iserine, Aurignan, and Holm.

In front of each square is a golden rectangular plaque. I feel so out of place here, and a part of me wonders if that was the purists' intent. Even in death, they wanted to divide mages. What's the point if we all go to the Underworld in the end?

Archyr walks to the second row. I follow him, until he rounds the corner and stops in the middle of the wall of vaults. He runs his fingers along the plaque, lowering his head with a sigh. I open my mouth and close it right away. His grief wraps around him the same way I carry mine: quiet and overwhelming at the same time.

"This is," Archyr says, his words muffled, "Beau's ancestral vault. His family is . . . was one of the oldest mage families, almost as old as the Founding families."

He motions me forward.

CARDOT. The engraving on the plaque is in old Serinese calligraphy—we don't see these around anymore, not even in Iserine; it's a lost art from Old Iserine. Then my eyes catch on the engraving on the next vault, this one in the bold serif letters of Holm. CARVER.

Victor. This must be why he brought us here.

I touch the plaque. *Open it.* Victor's voice is as clear as a ghost's could be.

"How do we open these?" I feel around the seams.

"Magic," Archyr replies. "They recognize bloodlines." My heart drops, but a smirk grazes his lips.

"Or . . ." He unfastens his coat, revealing an arsenal of daggers sheathed in a harness strapped around his chest. Long, short, narrow, wide, silver, gold. Everything is here. "Brute force works, too."

If I wasn't in such a hurry to find out what Victor wants, I would have had a lot more questions regarding the sixteen daggers strapped to his chest. Grabbing the shortest one, I feel the weight of it, light enough to handle and strong enough to jam in between the seams. I slide the metal tip in the top seam and push the hilt toward the upper vault.

The front square opens in a loud click.

I don't know what I expected to see. Weapons, maybe. Bones, for certain. But I wasn't expecting something as mundane as a single laurel leaf, shimmering in frosted red. Did Victor lead me down here for an ancestral relic, one that's been retired?

My fingers hover, hesitating. What if this wasn't Victor at all? What if this was a trap, and, like Olivia, I was blinded by the glamour of Gorhail? The moment I wrap my hand around the relic, I'll peel another layer of this magic, not knowing what it brings nor what it takes. Still, I cannot shake the small voice that whispers, What if this brings me closer to finding Olivia's killer?

So I close my hand.

"Hello, Miss Corvi," a very real voice says behind me.

> When a Mortemagi materializes a ghost, they become immune to conduits. Materialized ghosts walk among us—they have an uncanny habit of walking through walls and students. Even though they aren't quite human, they should be treated as such.
>
> **YSENIA FARO,** *DEATH MAGIC FOR BEGINNERS*, **CHAPTER 9**

twenty | sylas

MONDAY, NOVEMBER 22, 1939

Victor Carver stands behind us, his crow-black hair a mess, a hesitant smile on his face, and his amber eyes too alive for someone who's dead. I squint and notice the faint translucence of his skin.

Viola hasn't blinked in a few seconds. She clutches the laurel leaf so tight I worry the metal will cut into her hand. If her glare could vaporize Victor into nothingness, he'd already be gone.

"How?" she asks. "No," she replies to herself, before shoving the laurel leaf back into the vault and slamming the door shut. Then she walks into Victor, forgetting that he isn't real, and stops herself. "Why the riddles? And why did my sister tell me to find you?" Viola wastes no time.

Victor backs away. "I apologize, I . . . It's dangerous for ghosts to wander in the open because of conduits. And we don't speak in riddles; our words just come out that way when we try to communicate with the living."

"*What* are you?" I ask, instead of the ten other questions I need to ask, like who killed him, or where is Beau's ghost, or where is *The Founder's Book of Relics* he took from the library.

"Still a ghost," he says. "But now that a Mortemagi materialized me, I'm immune to conduits. They won't be able to lead me into the Underiver."

"How is this possible?" Viola asks. I would also like to know, because Victor looks more human than ghost; he even sounds human.

"We realized you were a whisperer at the funeral home. We followed you when we could. Avoiding conduits needs its own mage rank at Gorhail—it's near impossible." He laughs, then stops when he sees the look on our faces. "When a Mortemagi and a ghost touch the ghost's ancestral relic at the same time, the ghost can materialize. Now, we have perhaps one or two days to stitch my ghost with my body."

We. Who is he talking about?

"What do you mean 'stitch your ghost'?" Viola paces back and forth, her chest heaving. "Mortemagi can't bring people back from the dead. I read every book. I—"

Olivia. She doesn't have to say it out loud. I would have gone to the depths of the Underiver if it meant I could bring Beau back. Our eyes lock for a moment, hers welled with tears, mine empty. I almost reach for her—almost—but I don't. After this, we'll go our separate ways.

"Miss Corvi—" he starts.

"Viola," she cuts him off.

"Vi-Viola," he stammers. "You . . . you have a relic second only to the Founder's relic. There's little you cannot do. Besides, we're not *dead* dead."

We again.

"You've been dead for days," she argues. "Your body is in a state of decomposition by now, if they haven't already disposed of it."

"I injected myself with frost venom," he tells her. "It wasn't a lot, just enough for about a week, give or take a day, if my calculations are correct."

I clear my throat. "Beau—he sold you the frost venom . . ." My voice cracks, and I don't finish my sentence.

Victor steps back. He doesn't meet my eyes, but he nods at Viola. Her eyebrows knit together, like they always do when she's working through something. She considers me for a moment, then nods. Her shoulders relax, and she twirls my dagger in her hand. All I can think about is how perfect that dagger is for her. Then it all happens in a blur. Her prying open the Cardot vault, retrieving a red aspier, and the same light breeze that came with Victor's reappearance.

"These pesky conduits need to find a new line of work." Beau's silvery voice fills the room.

I stop breathing. My throat is thick, my tongue heavy, and my eyes blurry with tears. This cannot be real. He cannot be here. It's impossible. Yet here he stands, next to Viola, his dimpled smile so bright, his messy brown hair all over the place, and his clear blue eyes wide with wonder, oddly reminiscent of the first time Dad brought him home.

"Are you real?" I choke up tears. My hands shake as I try to reach for him.

"As real as a ghost can be," Beau jests. "Sorry I died."

"Shut up," I say, my face wet with tears. "I wish I could hug you."

Beau glances at Viola and nods. "Love you, too, Sy."

Words no longer make sense. Never in my wildest dreams did I think I would see Beau again. I had convinced myself his ghost was lost forever. Lyria will lose her mind when she sees him. I should be happy, but a faint feeling of guilt catches up with me. Viola did all of this with the magic I despise.

My eyes land on her. She's retreated to a corner, her head lowered, as if she's trying to shrink into the wall. I hate it. All of it. The way she immediately removed herself, the side glances at the door, the slight quiver of her chin. I hate that I notice everything.

"Could we . . ." She hesitates, her voice brittle. "Could we have done the same for Olivia?"

Beau's smile fades, and Victor frowns in sympathy. "I'm sorry, Viola. Death magic isn't woven for nonmagi. Their ghosts cross into the Orga," Victor says. But Viola already knew that. Hope is like a serpent; it sheds its skin with promise, while silently seeping venom into your veins.

A single tear works its way down her cheek before she brushes it off. "Olivia told me you have the answers I seek." She steels her question.

"I do." Victor nods. "I was paid to create illusions of ghosts so she could pass as a conduit."

"By whom?" Viola frowns. I glance at Beau, and we're both just as confused.

"I don't know, it was always anonymous. The bank sent yearly checks in the mail." Victor presses his lips together. "But if you help me get my body back, I can file an inquiry with the bank. The nonmagi clerks cannot see materialized ghosts."

I study Victor as he stands there, his hands wrung together, lips pursed.

"You said you knew who killed Olivia," Viola presses, but Victor looks away. I take a step forward. He doesn't know who killed them; I would surrender my aspiers on that bet.

Viola shrugs. "I'm not bringing your body back if you don't tell me."

"I meant to write, 'I know what led your sister to her death,' but the magic wrote something else." He sighs. "Fable Rowan. She didn't kill Olivia, but she threatened to tell the dean that your sister was a fraud," he says. "Olivia ran away after that. We'd spent twelve years hiding her identity, and Fable destroyed everything in a single night. I . . . I was already dead by then. I couldn't follow your sister out without being caught by conduits."

How did Fable find out about Olivia? Could Sierra have told her? That's impossible. Sierra seemed too vexed by her and Lorne.

"She never should've been here in the first place." Viola looks up, blinking away the tears that pool in her eyes. Again, with the self-loathing, and again, I have to stop myself from walking over to her.

"Do you know who killed you?" I finally speak, and then turn to Beau. "And you?" It's surreal to be speaking to my brother again.

Victor shakes his head. "I was in the woods, collecting some flowers for my mother's medicine. Then I was dead. Thankfully, I always inject myself with frost venom when I leave Gorhail, in case poachers attack." We all look at Beau.

"I was running back toward the passageway. I think poachers attacked me. Mortemagi, I'm certain, because no one forgets the coldness of the claws of the undead."

Viola winces, but she says nothing. My legs move then, and I'm standing next to her. It must be that stupid bond again—poisoning me with this uncontrollable longing to be close to her.

"Mara is a puppet," Victor offers, and Beau nods behind him.

"We are aware," I reply. Viola looks up at me, then she turns to Victor. "Who is the puppeteer?"

"We don't know, but we're fairly certain the puppeteer killed all three of us, and might kill more." Beau walks around the chamber, studying the numerous vaults. "Purists are such curious people—there are so few of them, and yet they think the masses must worship them."

Victor's eyebrows lift in surprise, as if he wasn't expecting the descendant of a purist family to forsake them. In truth, a lot of us do; their archaic rules make no sense; they're constantly lobbying DOTS to take us back to the mid-1500s when Houses were segregated, and we made next to no magical progress due to the lack of collaboration, and they've made it their life's mission to eradicate crossmages. Of course, there are still plenty of purists—like Fable—who think they're owed the world.

"We know they're after heirloom relics. Both of yours, and Viola's, but we don't know why," I muse aloud. "Do you have *The Founder's Book of Relics*, Victor? The library said you checked it out."

Victor scowls. "That's impossible. I needed the book to see if using a Founder's relic could reorganize memories. I put in a request, and they said it has been missing since 1918."

Beau's lips flatten, and I remember he told us about Victor's mother being at St. Fabian's Ward for Altered Minds in Riverview. He probably needed the book for her.

"Would that coincide with the timeline of Faro's Cuff going missing?" Viola asks. "So far, we have a missing book, a missing Founder's relic, and two stolen heirloom relics, with a third we know they want."

Haal, the way her mind works is stunning. I wasn't thinking about a coinciding timeline. I don't know how we'll find out when the cuff went missing, but at least we have another clue.

"Faro's Cuff is missing?" Beau and Victor say at the same time.

Viola nods. "It's 'long gone,' according to the guardian of the catacombs."

"That's impossible." Beau meets my eyes. "Only you and Lyria—"

Our sister always seems to know every little thing happening around Gorhail. If we are the only two with the ability to retrieve the cuff, and I didn't retrieve it . . . "We're not going to solve anything by standing here. Let's go," I say. "Lyria will know *something*."

Before we leave, Beau pauses in front of Viola. "I'm sorry we can't bring Olivia back, but I promise we'll stop at nothing until we find the killer. We owe you that at least."

"Sy, we'll meet you outside of the catacombs," Beau says. "Take the left tunnel before the guardian's chamber, and it'll lead you back."

I nod, and as I watch Beau cross through the walls behind Victor, I allow myself a smile. I owe more to Viola than she'll ever know.

"Would you like to go first?" I ask, one foot out of the chamber.

"No," she answers quietly, so I take the first step.

Now that we're leaving with my brother, the darkness is less daunting. The quiet drip of water on the rocks is music to my ears, and the faint whistle of the wind through the cracks in the stone brings me calm.

Viola follows closely this time. Every so often, our fingers brush against one another as we walk, and every time, she lets out a quiet gasp and looks straight ahead until I move again.

"I owe you," I say in a low voice.

"We're even." I hear her stifle a smile through the words.

This woman is an enigma. How can someone be from the same House as Rafael Grimm and be so . . . kind? Grimm destroyed lives, and Viola does the opposite. This is no longer about her magic or her sister. She didn't have to bring Beau back. Victor was her end goal, not Beau. She brought him back for me.

"We'll find out what happened to them, and we'll bring Olivia justice." I make her a promise, real this time.

Viola stops, turning her head toward me. Her eyes search mine for any truth to my promise. I don't know if she finds it because her gaze cuts to the floor. "It was cruel, the way she died."

After a brief pause, she continues, "Whoever killed Olivia wanted her to suffer. They knew about her fear of water, knew she didn't know how to swim. She was forced to spend her last moments with her greatest fear until it swallowed her."

I wince. I never thought of Olivia's death that way. Unlike Beau and Victor, hers feels personal.

"It's not Olivia they intended to kill." Sometimes, I wish my lips would glue themselves together. Her eyes snap toward me. Even in the dim light, I can make out the hollowness.

"Doesn't that make it worse?" She lets out a dry laugh.

"Why do you grieve someone who didn't care enough to tell the world she had a sister?" It slips out suddenly, the burning question I've wanted to ask since I met her.

Sylas, you idiot. I almost hear Lyria chastising me, telling me I don't get to police other people's grief. She would be right, but I couldn't stop the words. Viola cares too much about people, and it upsets me in ways I refuse to understand. I *want* her to be selfish for once.

"Despite everything"—she lifts her chin—"Olivia didn't deserve to die, especially not in that way. I should never have let her go to a place full of monsters—"

"Is that what you think we all are?" The hurt in my voice takes me by surprise. Her words cut me open; even the aspiers awaken. "Monsters?"

Viola looks straight ahead, her throat bobbing when she realizes her face is inches away from a bone protruding out of the wall. Muttering a curse, she casts me a furtive glare before squeezing her way in the opposite direction.

But I'm faster. I reach for her hand, and . . . she lets me hold it.

We stand side by side, in between walls of stone and bones that reek of seawater and decaying algae. The moment her eyes land on me, she tugs her hand away.

She huffs out a frustrated sigh. "Yes, monsters. Now I am stuck in a place I despise, because if I step out for even a second, someone will kill me for magic I never wanted. And who knows if we'll ever find the killer? We're powerless compared to Firstline, and they've given up."

We're not *powerless*. There's Lyria, whose brain works faster than all the Firstline officers combined; and Beau, who's resourceful, with a reach that spans the Ten Provinces; and Gryff, who'll always fight for justice; and me . . . I realize I'll do anything for her.

"Viola." I stumble on my words, swallowing them instead. I hate her magic perhaps more than she does, but she's not a monster. None of us are. We're different, but we're not all bad.

"I'm not a fool, Sylas." This is the first time she has said my name. It sounds so soft against the sharp edges of her tone. I want her to say it again and again, until it's no longer an enemy to her. "The only reason you're tolerating me right now is because I materialized Beau's ghost and might be able to stitch it back with his body."

It isn't the only reason. The words die on my tongue. I cannot go there.

Her shoulders shake. Is she crying? No, she's laughing, but it's empty. "Will I ever have a choice in this life? I didn't choose to have magic, didn't choose to be born a Corvi. Gods, I didn't choose to attend Gorhail. What is my life if I have no free will?"

"It's not the cards we've been dealt, but what we make of them," I say. "You do have a choice, Viola. You just never choose you."

My words must strike something, because she steels her shoulders, head facing the wall. "Olivia wouldn't want this for me. She'd want me to leave and start a new life. I don't want to do this anymore. Once we stitch their bodies and find the puppeteer, I'm leaving Bale."

A painful silence settles between us, weighed heavy by the finality of her decision and my unspoken feelings. "Let's not waste any more time then," I say without thinking. I take two side strides to put some distance between us. My heart races with every step away from her.

As we walk back to the stairwell, I make sure to keep my distance, while occasionally glancing at her. Railesza awakens, gently pricking my skin. Only then does my mind clear with the lone, soul-crushing realization that I don't want Viola to leave.

> **Breaking News:** DOTS offers a hefty 1,000 coins for every poacher's tracking device recovered. Rules of magic do not apply in regards to poacher hunting—use any and all means. Kill them before they kill you.
>
> *THE DAILY MAGE*, ISSUE 1910.23

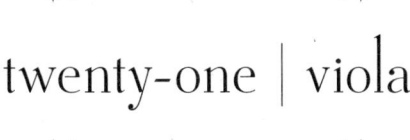

twenty-one | viola

TUESDAY, NOVEMBER 23, 1939

Everything about Sylas Archyr feels like a sin. The softness of his hands on my skin, the steady rhythm of his heart when he's next to me, and the faint scent of mint and vanilla that wraps me with warmth. Then I remember the clipped tones, the threats, Olivia's warning, and I realize that Sylas Archyr is a sin I can never indulge in.

Nearly losing my mind to the ghosts made me realize that Gorhail is not the place for me. I am fighting an uphill battle with unsharpened tools, trying to solve a murder when I can't sort out my own wants. I pray to the Gods that we catch the puppeteer when we go to Albion for Beau's and Victor's bodies. With that, I'll have avenged my sister, and Sylas will have his brother back. Then I'll seal my magic in Osneau, and this life will be a distant memory.

You just never choose you. Sylas's words simmer in my mind until they bubble over. Leaving Bale means I am choosing me.

The moment we step out of the iron doors of the catacombs, Sylas extends his hand. "Your cuff." His tone is as cold as the aspiers he wears.

"Why?" As soon as I ask, I understand. I sigh, unclasping the cuff. I don't know how to break out of ghost paralysis without relying on the magic of the catacombs. Out here, there's no river of magic, only angry ghosts yearning to be heard, and I am still a novice.

Our fingers brush when I press the cuff into his hands. "Thank you," he snaps.

We walk through the dank hallway until we reach the base of the Poisoned Stairwell. The lights cast a warm glow on the intricate designs of the railing. As we climb up, I notice that every flight has its own story, from the metal railing to the unique engraving in the wooden steps. Gorhail's history, dare I say, is beautiful. Etched in the metal are a visual of the tales Nan used to read to me when I was a child, and carved in the wood are the corresponding stories in old Balish calligraphy. After Olivia would fall asleep, I'd crawl into Nan's bed and she would pull out a big book of old tales. I remember the soft leather bookmark and the gilt edges so well. She would tell me the same stories over and over, never tiring of my asking for more. I wish she were still alive so she could see me here, in the place she loved so much.

A yelp up ahead snaps me out of my reverie, followed by sobs. We're already back at the House of Poison, the passageway door half open, spilling the faint light from Founder's Room onto the landing.

When I walk in, Lyria is kneeling on the floor, crying in front of Beau, who keeps trying to comfort her in vain. She sees me, jumps to her feet, and crashes into me with a tight hug. I glance at Beau, and he gives me a soft smile.

"There is nothing I wouldn't do for you," Lyria says between sniffles. I wear the filth of the catacombs, yet she doesn't seem to mind at all. She pulls away, thanking me at least three more times. Each time slaps me with guilt, because their reunion is eating me from within.

I am not jealous of their happiness. I am sad that I don't get to share any of this with Olivia. I wish more than anything to speak to her one last time, to hug her and tell her I love her.

The fireplace crackles every time Victor sticks his hand through it. He stands next to the fire, his shoulders slouched, his eyes blankly watching the flames dance. Like me, he probably feels out of place. I have half a mind to sit by him and ask him about my sister's days at Gorhail.

"I'm impressed." Victor looks up at me from the fireplace. "It takes years of training for a whisperer to walk through the catacombs so seamlessly."

"Or sheer luck and a good teacher," I reply nervously, glancing at Lyria.

She looks back and forth between Victor and me, then narrows her eyes. "Did you anchor to a ghost?"

"No." I roll my eyes. Why did both she and Sylas ask the same question? If I had anchored to a ghost, I would've known by now. "I only listened to Sylas's voice."

Deep down, I begin to question myself. Did I accidentally anchor to the woman's ghost by listening to her story?

Sylas clears his throat, and I'm grateful for the change of subject. "Faro's Cuff is missing." He frowns at Lyria, and her head snaps up at him, eyes flared.

"Did you take it out?" she asks.

"Of course not," Sylas answers. "Did you?"

"Sy, I don't even know how to access the Ronin vault. Paltro had the relicsmith fashion a second lock a couple of months ago," she says. "And this one opens with *his* aspier."

"Why would he do that?" Sylas's shoulders relax. "I thought . . ." He trails off.

"Paltro's so secretive when it comes to House of Poison business, I doubt we'll ever know." Lyria shakes her head, then turns her attention to Beau, a playful smile on her lips. "Did you know he had given up on you? He was convinced a conduit led you into the Underiver."

Beau raises his eyebrows at Sylas. "Despondent as always."

Sylas waves him off with a smile, and Beau walks through the sofa, crosses through the coffee table, and plops himself on the opposite sofa. "You're allowed to sit," he tells Victor.

With a quiet sigh, Victor lowers himself to the hearth, his back now facing me. Beau gazes at him as Victor sticks both hands in the fire, the bright orange flames burning through his mild translucence. Next to the warm light of the fireplace, they don't look human anymore, their bodies silhouetted with a faint silver film.

"Lyr." Beau beckons his sister over. "I need your brain. Here's all we have: Faro's Cuff is missing; *The Founder's Book of Relics* was last checked out in 1918; Mortemagi poachers killed us for heirloom relics . . ."

"One aspier, one laurel, and we know they want Viola's cuff," Sylas adds as he walks over to them, leaning his arms on the back of the sofa between Beau and Lyria. "Gryff mentioned it could be for a ritual, but that's all we have. No one else has been killed in a week."

"Could your mom have taken Faro's Cuff?" Beau hesitates.

"Are you saying..." Sylas pauses. "Could she have taken it out, and they..."

From across the room, Sylas lifts his head, and, for a fleeting moment, his eyes brush over me. They swirl with guilt, hurt, and deep sorrow. My legs take a step forward on their own, before I stop them. His sorrow isn't mine to ease.

"No. Rogue Mortemagi killed Mom," Lyria says quietly. "Dad told us the story countless times." She pauses, tilting her head toward Sylas. "I don't think... I would've known if she took out the cuff. It would be in her notes. She documented *everything*."

Rogue Mortemagi. No wonder Sylas hates death magic. No wonder he hates *me*. His hatred doesn't stem from misconception at all. A Mortemagi killed his mother. The sudden revelation garrotes me, and I want to turn around and disappear into the Poisoned Stairwell.

Lyria catches my eyes, and she worries her lips between her teeth, a frown playing at her eyebrows. "Cuff aside, a ritual is plausible if Mortemagi and heirlooms are involved, but without the *Book of Relics*, we have no way to know. Paltro sent over the reports we asked for. I'll peruse Dad's field reports; he was investigating poacher cells when he died, and they might be able to tell us something."

"Are you finished with the Deathbringer's reports?" Sylas asks.

The Deathbringer, I've learned, is a sacred name within Gorhail's walls. She's the only Aspieri lauded in Mortemagi books, also the only Aspieri Mortemagi seem to respect—Delaney admires her, and even Nan used to speak highly of her. She used to lament her and her aspier's disappearance and often blamed the rise of poachers on it.

"They're in your room," Lyria says.

As they talk, my attention sways to the dark ebony table that sits in front of the arched floor-to-ceiling windows next to the entrance to Beau's room. Four ornate wood and blue velvet chairs are half-tucked under the table, two on each side. I walk over, running my finger down the side of what seems to be the Archyrs' study desk. The wood is from the dwarf cherry trees in Gorhail Woods. Nan had one like this in her office, before Mother got rid of it.

When I look out the window, my breath catches. The cliffs of Gorhail overlook the Sea of the Gods. As the sky transitions from dark to light, the cliffs come alive, welcoming the slow crash of waves below. In the distance, the peaks of Mount Chazal shine with faint orange hues. If I lived in these rooms, I'd spend the day on the balcony, admiring the raw beauty of Bale. But I don't belong here.

On the top corner of the desk, I find a stray sheet of paper filled with a random list of chores and a pen. Moving one of the chairs to the side, I lean over, grab the pen, and, on the flip side of the page, I begin scribbling a rough sketch of the layout of Dearly Departed: where the doors are located, the planter holding the spare key, and the cold room with Beau's and Victor's bodies. This is the last thing I have to do before leaving, my last chance to bring my sister justice.

The plan is simple. I'll go in, and Lyria can help me move the bodies outside. Meanwhile, Beau's and Victor's ghosts can look for the puppeteer, and finally, Sylas can create a distraction while I work on stitching the ghosts and bodies together. But that's only if the bodies haven't been moved.

"Are we certain your bodies are still at Dearly Departed?" I interrupt the chatter across the room.

Beau looks up with a grimace. It must be strange, hearing that. "I was there yesterday, and both bodies are still in the cold room. I've been going every day, hoping to catch the puppeteer, but only Mara was in," he replies. "The puppeteer has been trying to puppet both our bodies through Mara, but until the frost venom dissipates, they're useless."

Lyria stands up. "This shouldn't be—"

"Possible, I know." Victor finishes her sentence. "It takes generations of magic to be able to cross puppet a body, not to mention the knowledge," he pauses, looking at the three siblings. "The only relics with that much magic are heirlooms dating back to the founders' time."

Gods. It all makes sense. *The Founder's Book of Relics* would have that knowledge, and Faro's Cuff would have that much magic.

"Ancient magic, a missing cuff, and a missing book . . ." Sylas straightens, and as he heads in my direction, he frowns. Our eyes meet, and an ominous feeling swirls in my stomach. Our conversation earlier barrels into my mind, and at the same time, Sylas confirms my worries. "What if *The Daily Mage* wasn't all propaganda? What if poacher activity has been increasing to prepare for Grimm's return?"

"*The Daily Mage* spreads all sorts of lies to sell copies. They thrive on sensationalism." Victor crosses the coffee table over to Beau and Lyria.

"Grimm's return is impossible," Beau adds, glancing at Lyria for confirmation. "Even with the cuff, they'd need the blood of the five founders to release him. Helna Azgar and Kali Telam have no descendants."

"I am more worried about a mage following in his footsteps. Even on the off chance they had hidden descendants, Grimm wouldn't *need The Founder's Book of Relics*," Victor says.

"But someone trying to become him would," Lyria reasons.

Sylas nods. "It would explain the heightened Firstline surveillance Gryff was talking about. Poacher cells are more active than ever."

As Beau, Lyria, and Victor talk over one another, mostly calling out the improbability of Grimm's return, Sylas's eyes study me. He walks over and stops next to the table, glances at my rough drawing, and sighs. He steps past me and pauses in front of the tall windows, looking outside, with his hands in his pockets.

"We know the puppeteer wants my relic," I say calmly, bringing them back to the plan. The sooner we stitch their bodies, the sooner I can leave. "They may have a tracker, so they'll know where I am." The moment I say this, I think of Olivia's arm, riddled with claw marks. My throat closes, thinking of stepping outside of Gorhail's walls again. The last time, Mara ripped my body to shreds.

The room falls silent, and Beau, Lyria, and Victor meet my eyes.

"Victor, how long will it take to bring you back?" I ask.

"How long does it take you to weave?" He glides back to the fireplace. I return a puzzled look. "I've never..."

"Victor," Lyria chastises, glaring at Victor as he waves his hand through the fire again, the crackling sound more of an annoyance now. "Resurrection is part of the blood arts and strictly forbidden. Besides, she isn't a Firstline Mortemagi, so she isn't even allowed to practice thread magic. I would love to have Beau back, but not at the expense of Viola's execution."

Execution. I haven't come this far to die. "Didn't I practice thread magic in the catacombs?" I ask.

Lyria sighs. "Yes, but that was nothing. You were using the magic of the catacombs; it hardly counts. Ghost materialization isn't illegal, is it?" She looks at Beau in question.

"No," he says, glowering at Victor. "But non Firstline Mortemagi shouldn't practice any form of thread magic for their own safety, let alone stitching a ghost back to their body. And if Lyria hasn't mentioned it yet, resurrection, puppeteering, and summoning the undead are all forms of the blood arts... if DOTS catches you using any of these, it will execute you upon capture."

"Stop fearmongering." Victor pulls his hands out of the fire and glances at the low wooden table separating the two sofas. "This is a simple resurrection and doesn't require the blood arts," he explains. "She already has our materialized ghosts, so she'll merely be using the magic from her cuff to stitch our bodies with our ghosts. Complex resurrections are the only ones that use the blood arts. They require raising someone from the Underworld and ancient magic that most Mortemagi don't learn."

"You never mentioned anything about resurrections or even materialized ghosts before." Beau gets up, narrowing his eyes at Victor. "*What are you plotting?*"

Victor rolls his eyes, then looks up at Beau. "We're dead, and Olivia, my longtime friend, met an atrocious end that wasn't meant for her." He pauses, glancing toward me. "Sorry."

Then he continues, "Gods forbid I'm in a hurry to get my body back so I can investigate our deaths properly, starting with whoever paid me to help Olivia keep up her facade."

Whoever was paying Victor to keep up with Olivia's lies knew she didn't have magic. I thought only she and I were in on the lie. Clearly, I was wrong, and Olivia had more secrets than she cared to share. I hope this person can shed some light on Olivia's mysterious life.

Sylas clears his throat, his back still facing me. "Enough. Are we bringing Beau's and Victor's bodies back, or are we going to sit here and bicker like children? The longer we wait, the more we risk not having bodies to return to—"

Victor nods. "I have less than a day before decomposition begins, and Beau... I don't know how much venom your aspier injected in your blood."

"About a day left for me," Beau replies. "Silver released about the same amount I sold to you."

Sylas is right. Victor has been dead a week and Beau six days. If aspier venom only lasts a week, there's a chance Victor's body has begun to decompose. We don't have any more time to waste.

I tap the pen on the rough sketch of Dearly Departed. "I'll go in as bait. Lyria can wheel the bodies out while Mara is distracted with me, and once they're out, Sylas can handle Mara while I stitch the bodies together. The puppeteer shouldn't be far, so as soon as Beau and Victor regain their bodies, we can search for them, and we'll finally find who killed you and Olivia."

"I've always wanted to visit a cold room." Lyria shoots up from her seat.

"You're not coming," Sylas clips, then turns around and stalks over to me. I straighten up, suddenly aware that we're only separated by the width of the table. "It's not up for debate." He rests his hands on the desk and tilts his head toward his siblings.

Beau clears his throat. "What he means—"

"Are you his translator?" Lyria glares at him.

"I meant what I said; out there, I'm a patrol leader, and you're not field certified, so I'm not risking your life . . . again," Sylas says, defying her. "Besides, I need you to go to Paltro's office. Inform him of everything we've found out. If Gryff noticed something was amiss within DOTS, I'm sure Paltro's already aware of what's at stake."

Lyria pauses for a second, her stare drilling into her brother. She walks around the sofa, picks up her sweater, curses the Gods, then slams the door on her way out.

"Was that really necessary?" Beau throws his hands in the air.

"You're dead." Sylas levels his brother's stare. "Need I say more?"

An awkward silence stretches between them, until I wave my makeshift map. "I'll go through the main entrance. If Mara's there, Sylas, will you—"

"No." Sylas turns his attention back to me. Without leaving my eyes, he pulls out a chair and lets himself drop in the seat, his long legs thrown over the arm, his face an endless map of frustration and exasperation. He pulls my cuff from his pocket, studying the filigree.

"No?" I return.

"No."

"Do *you* have a better idea?" I ask, crossing my arms, my eyes narrowing at him. I've run this scenario through my head at least four times while they were all talking over one another. I'm the only one familiar with Dearly Departed, and I'm certain it's our quickest option.

"I do." Sylas unfurls himself from his chair, pockets my cuff, and walks around the desk. I turn as he stops right in front of me, my heart beating in my throat. My eyes dart around for an escape, but the chairs block my way. "Well . . . then . . . ?" I utter, without looking at him.

Sylas considers me for a moment, then he leans forward, placing both hands on either side of me, caging me against the desk. I brace my palms next to his to hold myself up.

"You're a Mortemagi who doesn't know how to use her magic," he says. Raiku slithers from his wrist to mine, his cold scales rubbing against my skin as he climbs the length of my left arm.

I don't move.

"In other words." Sylas slowly drags his hand up and lifts my face with his finger. I hate that a single touch puts me at the mercy of whatever venom his mouth will spew next. "You're useless." One side of his lips curls up, and my heart is out of control. He's playing a game, but I cannot fall into his trap.

"Good luck resurrecting your brother then, Archyr." I push his hand away, but it doesn't move. I don't want to leverage Beau, but I cannot stand Sylas's arrogance. I've worked at Dearly Departed for four years; I know Mara, and I know my plan will work.

"I don't need to be resurrected." Beau shrugs, unbothered. "I was actually pretty happy being dead."

"You were?" Victor grimaces at him. "I remember you compl—"

Beau shoots him daggers, and he looks away.

"Is that a threat, Corvi?" Sylas runs his finger down the side of my neck, over my collarbone, dragging my attention back to him. Raiku slides over my shoulder, grazing the skin of my throat as he coils back around Sylas's wrist. I gulp, forgetting the world around us. My cheeks feel warm, and my breath wavers. His gaze darkens, dropping to my mouth then back to my eyes. He smirks again; this time it's triumphant. *It's just a game*, I tell myself. One that I refuse to play.

"I don't make threats, Archyr." I swat his hand away, our gazes locked on each other. Raiku flinches, his murderous eyes looking at me with curiosity. This feels like an echo of our exchange before he stabbed me behind the Doors of Desire. It's only been a few days, but it feels like ages have passed.

"I apologize for my brother," Beau says. "His manners are lacking. He's trying to tell you that he doesn't want you as bait. And neither do I."

Sylas takes a single step away from me, a scowl on his face. As my eyes shift from him to his brother, I realize once again that Sylas is offering me a way out. First, he was willing to give up on the catacombs, and now he's willing to give up on getting his brother back. And Beau . . . he's giving up a second chance at life.

"I'll be fine." I don't know if I'm reassuring him or myself. "I *want* to do this. For them. For answers. For Olivia."

Beau nods with a sigh, but Sylas won't even look my way.

"Puppets are controlled by threads of magic. Mortemagi can take over the threads. Is there any chance you . . ." Beau trails off as he walks over to us.

"No," I cut him off. I wish I understood my magic better, but since Lyria mentioned anchoring, I'm fairly certain it wasn't me at all who threaded the voices into the river—the ghost from Death Spire probably took pity on me and helped. Besides, I'm not going to become an experienced mage overnight. "Unless you have a crash course in death magic."

Beau laughs, and the world stops. His eyes crinkle, and his laugh is so pure; it's like soft classical music on a quiet morning. How could anyone kill him?

Victor joins Beau, his amber eyes full of hope. "If you do this for me . . . for us," he says, his gaze lingering on Beau, "I swear to you on my mother, I will help you find your sister's killer."

"Beau." Sylas's low voice pulls me back to him, reminding me that he's still very close to me. His lips press together, and he draws in a sharp breath. His face is unreadable. "Take Victor downstairs and choose a spare Arkani relic from the safe; Lyria has collected many from her years earning her Grand Magus rank at the House of Arcane. We'll grab it before we leave. You can have Raiku or Railesza until you get your father's aspier from the crypt."

In silence, Beau and Victor walk through the desk and head toward the small spiral staircase at the far left corner in front of the window. I hadn't even realized that staircase was there.

"Why are you such a martyr?" Sylas asks when we're finally alone. He cocks his head, a smirk grazing his lips. It's wicked, it's beautiful, and it's murderous. "You are so small, so fragile—"

"Is that how you see me?" I square my shoulders, tipping my head back. "A fragile thing?"

"All I'm saying is . . ." He rubs his chin, then his eyes briefly drop to my lips. "If you insist on going to the funeral home, just let me go in first. You're not alone anymore."

And there he is again, the man who tugs at the strings of my foolish heart. The same man will rip all the strings just as fast. "For how long? Until you get what you want, or until you decide you hate me again?" I bite my tongue for being so loose.

"I haven't decided yet." He brushes a stray strand of hair from my face, and my thumping heart betrays me once more. He studies every inch of my face, as if he's trying to unravel secrets he thinks I'm hiding.

"Why?" he asks when I don't respond, his low voice ensnaring me further into the madness of us. He doesn't have to speak anymore; I know he wants to know why I'm helping them. If I were him, I would be suspicious, too.

A flicker of concern flashes across his eyes. He loosens his back and lowers his head, his eyebrows twitching ever so slightly. My delusions would have me believe that the answer I'm about to give worries him. I loathe every second of it. Because he wraps me with this illusion of safety, this silent promise that he will catch me if I fall.

"Because for the first time, I feel that my actions, no matter how small, how *useless* . . ." I stress on the last word, and he winces.

"I feel like they matter." My heart drums against my rib cage. And for the first time since Olivia's murder, I let my fears out. "If I weren't so passive, Olivia would be alive today. She wouldn't have gone to Gorhail on my behalf, and she'd be safe at home right now. Maybe by bringing your brother and Victor back, it's my way of seeking forgiveness. Of choosing to be different. I couldn't save her, but maybe I can save them."

"Stop." He frowns, running his fingers through my hair, the softness of his palm cradling my cheek. "Your sister's death is not on you. You didn't tell her to lie her way through Gorhail."

He's right. I didn't. But even hearing it out loud does nothing to make me feel better.

Before I'm able to stop myself, my hand reaches for his. My heart is a fool. Every single touch from Sylas brings it to life. It doesn't yet understand that fools are always the first to die.

But there it is again. That look that makes my knees weak and my chest flutter. The seconds stretch into one another, and neither of us move.

Finally, Sylas whispers, "I'll wheel out the bodies. You'll go in alone, but Raiku will be with you."

"That thing tried to kill me once—" I recoil.

The black aspier's enigmatic onyx eyes bore into me. His hiss cuts between us; either he's offended that I called him a thing or reminded him that he did, in fact, try to kill me.

"Besides, how will you defend yourself without your weapon?"

A faint smile tugs at his lips, and he drops his arms. "I'm immortal, Viola. I could fight with a spoon and still live."

He's immortal. I am not. The Gods must be laughing at the impossibility of it all.

"You don't need to beguile me further, Sylas. I will bring your brother back." I break away from the invisible hold he has on me. No matter how much I've tried to reject it, I'm a Mortemagi. I will never be anything more than that to him, to any of them. It serves me to remember my place.

"Beguile you? Is that what you think I'm doing?" His voice breaks. In the same breath, the hurt across his face dissipates, giving way to the Sylas I'm familiar with. Cold and calculating. Without looking away from me, he pulls my cuff from his pocket and sets it on the table behind me.

"It's your life to bargain," he mutters before we step into the Poisoned Stairwell.

> Rodric, it is not a poacher uprising, I fear. Talks of Grimm have been prevalent in poacher communities, and I wonder if they're forging the next Grimm—I will explain in person. Searches for the Deathbringer remain inconclusive. I believe she is dead and her relic was stolen, as evidenced in my attached report.
>
> **LETTER FROM HANSEL ARCHYR TO RODRIC PALTRO, JUNE 1939**
>
> *Note:* Hansel Archyr died July 1939

twenty-two | sylas

TUESDAY, NOVEMBER 23, 1939

The sun has long set when I wake. I stare at the domed wooden ceiling, counting my breaths like Mom taught me to do when I had nightmares as a child. Something doesn't add up.

I read the Deathbringer's reports from cover to cover until I fell asleep with them on my chest. She had spies in the deepest poacher camps—no one knew more about them than her—and there were no mentions of Grimm.

Picking up Dad's reports from my nightstand, I flip through the pages and stumble upon a theory that the Deathbringer was killed and her relic stolen, stamped with the notorious red REJECTED of DOTS. But on the last page, Dad's neat handwriting underlines two paragraphs, and next to them are these words written in bold: DIFFERING PATTERN IN POACHER MOVEMENTS—ANOTHER GRIMM?

Dad's notes date from five months ago, just a month before his death. I hadn't considered that the poachers could be training someone to be the next Grimm. The endless propaganda from *The Daily Mage* must be emboldening them. But surely, if we've noticed this, DOTS and Firstline will have, too.

A timid knock breaks me out of my thoughts. I glance at the clock, and it reads ten. Haal, we were supposed to leave at nine. Am I late? I scramble to my feet and open the door to see Viola. She looks up at me, then averts her gaze almost immediately.

"I know you have a death wish since you decided to offer yourself as bait to the puppet who killed your sister and almost killed you, but please tell me you didn't just go through the Poisoned Stairwell alone?" My fingers clench the doorframe. I don't know why I bother, especially when she made it clear she doesn't want my help, and she seems to think I'm *beguiling* her to bring Beau's body back.

"Beau came to get me. We're late." She shifts her weight, still not looking at me. But I drink her in, from the black, Arkani-woven training pants that hug her curves to the long-sleeved shirt that exposes a sliver of skin. I get the training pants—the stretch allows for movement. But the training shirt? She needs a combat jacket and a protective harness underneath.

An image of her lying on that table the first time I saw her—skin torn, blood gushing out of her wounds—flashes across my mind. To this day, I don't understand how Railesza healed her completely. If things go wrong tonight, will my aspier be able to bring her back from the brink again?

Without a word, I head to the dresser and open the second drawer. For once, I'm glad Lyria uses my room as an extension of her wardrobe, because I find one of her harnesses and a combat jacket with ease.

"Turn," I order, forgetting that, in here, I am not a patrol leader.

Viola doesn't argue. She gives me her back, mumbling a quick apology about how she should've asked if I was decent before knocking on the door.

I swallow a smile. "Arms out."

Now she whirls, a scowl on her face. Her eyes drift from my bare chest to the harness I'm holding. "What is that?"

"This," I say, motioning her to turn again, "will prevent Mara from ripping your body apart like last time."

Her eyes widen, and I hold her gaze a moment longer than I should. "Okay." She doesn't protest and turns again. I thread her arms through the sleeveless harness, pulling on the strings like a corset. My fingers make quick work of the knots. Toward the end, I slip and brush against her bare skin.

She lets out a gasp, and my hand freezes. We're both quiet, save for the low hum of her quickening breath. I can't be this close to her. The bond is messing with my head again.

A few seconds later, I'm fastening the last of the knots, and she's standing two steps away from me. I throw Lyria's combat jacket, and Viola catches it against her chest.

"That thing nearly killed you, and now you're offering yourself to her on a silver platter." I lean against the doorframe, my arms crossed, watching her struggle with the zipper. "She won't miss twice."

"If I die"—she pauses, considering her next words—"promise me you'll find the puppeteer."

"You'll find them yourself," I mutter. She speaks of death so casually, as if she's at peace with dying, as if she has nothing else to live for other than finding her sister's killer. What happened to leaving Bale and starting anew?

"Take Raiku." I hold out my hand.

Her gaze flicks to my aspier, then back to me.

"No," she says, and Raiku hisses. I don't know if he's offended that she turned him down a second time, or that I suggested she take him in the first place.

"Let's hope your wretched magic cooperates then."

She scoffs. "You speak of my magic as if I don't loathe every second I have to live with it. Magic ruined my life. The day it walked in was the day my sister walked out."

How can she hate death magic more than me? Hatred aside, how can she be so blind to the raw power oozing off her? How can she hold on to a sister who took years of a life where she could've perfected her craft? It's horrifying, the things Viola could do with it. Yet she chose to live in the shadow of a sister who pretended she didn't exist.

"You're allowed to hate your magic, but when it's the only thing that can save your life, you don't have a choice but to use it." I close the door on her because I don't trust myself around her. I don't like how she makes me question something I've known my whole life. Mom was killed by a Mortemagi. Their magic of the dead feeds off their soul, chipping away years of their lives, leaving behind a shell of villainy. Once Viola tastes a drop of what her death magic can do, she will be drunk on the raw power.

Shaking away the thought, I pull a shirt from the nearby chair. Once

Beau and Victor get their bodies back, Viola needs to leave. Perhaps the distance will ease the bond's drive to keep her safe.

When I walk out of my room, Viola is gone but Lyria is sitting by the fireplace, her eyes narrowing at Beau. She notices me and waves me over. "I'm still mad at you, but I don't have a good feeling about Victor. He seemed almost too eager for Viola to resurrect him. Beau gave her a choice, but he didn't even bother."

"I don't trust him either." I sigh, dropping Dad's reports in her lap. "But maybe it's because we don't know him well yet."

Lyria scrunches her nose like she always does when she disagrees with something but doesn't want to voice it out. Then her eyebrows shoot up. "Oh, I went by Paltro's office earlier, like you asked, but he was out. So I'll try again tomorrow. Were the reports helpful at all?"

I nod. "Dad thought poachers were preparing for another Grimm."

Beau and Lyria exchange a concerned look. "So much for old purist Ronin to think his bloodline wouldn't betray him. Well, *someone* in his bloodline retrieved the cuff." Lyria rolls her eyes. It's ironic how Sileas Ronin insisted that Faro's Cuff be kept in his personal vault, and surprising how easily he managed to convince the Mortemagi that they couldn't possibly trust their kind to safeguard the cuff. As an act of goodwill, he even gave them the Imortalis to store in their catacombs.

"Did you know that Mom retrieved Raiek from the catacombs?"

"Yeah." Lyria sighs. "Her last journal entry mentioned Raiek might have been a key piece to her lifedrain theory, but she—"

Lyria doesn't need to continue. Mom never wrote another entry again, because she was ripped away from us by a Mortemagi.

"Are we really doing this?" Beau asks as he runs his hand through the coffee table. It's odd seeing him here, even odder seeing him as a ghost. "How will we explain our resurrection to DOTS?"

"I doubt DOTS will suspect a brand-new Mortemagi." Lyria shrugs. "Their arrogance won't let them admit that a self-study could perform magic most Gorhail-trained Mortemagi cannot."

"We can get around this, but I have a single condition." Viola's voice startles me. She's walking up the spiral staircase, clad in Lyria's combat jacket, which falls right above her thighs. The three dark red stripes on the left shoulder end right above our House crest—Viola wears it like it belongs to her.

"Pity she's a Mortemagi," Lyria whispers. "She wears our name well."

It takes me a second too long to register what she means. I scowl at her, but she's already across the room, hugging Viola like they're best friends.

"Get on with it, Corvi," I say while buckling my harness.

"After you regain your bodies and we catch the killer, you'll help me leave Bale and seal my magic," she demands matter-of-factly.

Her ask slaps me in the face.

Mages don't simply discard their magic, especially not when they have a relic as powerful as the Corvi cuff. Does this woman not realize the power she possesses in that piece of metal? That she's about to do the impossible *because* of the magic she despises so much?

"This life isn't for me," she says. Why does she sound so resigned?

I want to tell her that she is right, that she should seal her magic, that she should leave and go back to a mundane life. It solves two of my biggest problems. One: we are rid of one of the most powerful heirloom relics. Two: she will be safe. Somewhere deep inside my chest, it stings. I shove that odd feeling deeper within, where hopefully it'll never resurface. She can't stay, both for her safety and for my sanity.

But I can't bring myself to tell her any of that.

"We've all had to come to terms with our lives, its dangers, and its losses. You choose what you want out of this life, not the other way around," I say instead, heading to the door to the Poisoned Stairwell.

"Vi, you can't leave," Lyria drawls, wrapping her arms around Viola, who gives my sister the softest apologetic look.

"I . . ." Viola takes her hand. "I tried, I really tried for Olivia. Once we find the puppeteer and hand them over to DOTS, I'm done. I'd like to live out the rest of my life as a nonmagi."

Beau chimes in, "Viola, please don't."

I hate how my siblings have grown so attached to her. Do they forget what she is?

"It's time," I interrupt them, clicking open the door like a coward afraid to face his feelings.

"It's good that I'm staying behind in the end. In case someone has to explain your absence," Lyria offers. Thank Haal, she's come to her senses. Then she runs and gives me a tight hug. "Please don't let her die," she says so only I can hear.

Dread sours my mouth. That's a promise I cannot make.

> Exhausting an aspier's magic before they've had time to regenerate can destroy them.
>
> **Addendum:** Does not apply to the Imortalis and their bonds, as long as they remain with the same Aspieri.
>
> JOURNAL OF SILEAS RONIN, THE FIRST FOUNDER

twenty-three | viola

TUESDAY, NOVEMBER 23, 1939

Little Lake Albion is still tonight. The stars bleed diamonds in the sky. Are the Gods wishing us luck or sealing our fate?

The crisp air should feel familiar, but right now, it cuts my breath into pieces. I pull Lyria's jacket close. Every time the breeze brushes against my skin, I pretend it's Olivia. We stand not far from where her body lay cold against the dark cobbles that horrific morning.

"Beau and I will be waiting by the side door, so it's easier once you bring the bodies out." Victor breaks the silence as he turns to Sylas. We went over the plan at least five times while we were driving here.

Sylas ignores him, sheathing another four daggers into his harness. It's similar to the one he gave me, but where mine is a strong weave of Arkanimade fabric that should hopefully withstand a blade—or a claw—the material of his is hidden by at least a dozen daggers sheathed against his chest.

I take in every detail. How his black shirt hugs the muscles of his chest underneath, how his jaw could cut through glass, and how his eyes scrutinize every inch of our surroundings. Both his aspiers are awake and ready to engage. Out here, he's not the Sylas I've come to know. Something about him is different, deadlier.

"Once you regain your bodies, run to the car," Sylas commands Beau and Victor. "Railesza won't be able to heal all of you should you be injured."

"Let's get this done, so we can send the puppeteer to the ninth circle of the Underworld." Beau catches my eye and grins. For a treacherous moment, I feel like I belong here, with them. That I am part of this family. And I want so badly for it to be true.

The funeral home is pitch-black, the curtains pulled and the lights off. Like I thought, no one's here. This will be easy enough.

"It's empty. Victor, Beau, let's go straight to the cold room to get your bodies." I take the lead.

"No," Sylas replies, his voice menacingly low.

"No?" I question, whirling around.

He ignores me, giving directions to Beau instead. "Stand by the side door. The moment you come back to your body, get Viola and go straight to the car. If I'm not there soon after, drive away."

"I can't leave—"

"*Drive away.*" Sylas stresses each word, and Beau gives him a single nod.

I step in front of Sylas, and he barely spares me a glance. A momentary boldness takes over me, and my index finger digs into his chest. "No one's in, Archyr. You're wasting time and creating unnecessary commotion."

His head lowers, and his eyes bore into mine. They tell me I crossed a line. Slowly, I lower my finger. His silence cuts through my temerity, and I move. But his hands lower to my waist, scrunching both sides of my jacket. He pulls me into him, and my hands brace against his chest.

"You do not deviate from what was agreed upon, understood?" he says between clenched teeth. A storm brews in his eyes. Instead of taking shelter, I run straight to the eye.

"Plans change," I retort, flexing my fingers against his chest. My heart hammers against my own. I should've kept my mouth shut. But with him, that seems impossible.

"Corvi." He leans closer, his whisper a poisonous caress on my skin. "As long as you wear my House crest in the field, you do not talk back to me."

Right then and there, I unzip the jacket and shove it in his arms. Without a word, I get into my original position and tell myself once again that I'm doing all this for Olivia. For the first time, it feels like a lie.

The moment I press the door handle, the nape of my neck tingles with horror. The front door is never unlocked.

It's funny, how the people in town have this old saying that your life flashes before your eyes before you die. Because my life unravels with every step I take into Dearly Departed. This place used to be my second home; now I hug the walls that once provided me peace to escape death.

My ears reach for a semblance of a ghost, but nothing comes back. Even my cuff is ice cold. After the memories comes the regret. I wish I had listened to Olivia and worn my cuff sooner. Maybe then I could have dabbled in thread magic enough to save my life.

The main room is empty; the dim light of the moon pouring through the tall windows let in just enough for me to catch my bearings. Nothing has changed since last week. I allow myself a sigh. I was right. No one is here. The back door is right down the hallway; I should let them in.

But then, I hear it. The quiet snicker that steals my brief moment of respite.

"Resilience is admirable." I hear Mara's voice, but I don't see her.

I close my eyes, reaching for any semblance of color like I did in the catacombs, but I get nothing. She's not a ghost.

"Murder isn't." I peel away from the wall and step toward the reception desk. Only last week, I was scheduling funerals. I close my eyes; now isn't the time for nostalgia. The longer I can keep Mara occupied with me, the more time Sylas has to get the bodies out. If I make it out alive, I owe him a million apologies.

She scoffs. There's a quick shuffle but still no sign of her.

"Why Olivia?" I throw into the nothingness, although I already know the answer.

"You're a fool, Viola, if you think I don't know why you've come."

I remain silent. My presence has already sharpened the blade; I don't need to hand her the hilt as well.

"You're right." She sighs at my silence. "Poor darling Olivia. So tragic."

I bite my tongue. She's baiting me, just like I am her. "Death kills a mage's relic..." I whisper. "Why?"

Her laugh falters into pity. "Darling, when will you learn? You wear your heart on your sleeve for people who wouldn't spare you a glance."

A muted thud from the hallway toward the back room jerks my legs forward.

Sylas. He must have gotten the bodies out.

The cold room's metal door clangs against the wall. "Where are they?" Mara's voice bellows, but I still don't see her. "Where are the bodies?" Her breath crawls down my neck, like a rabid animal, thirsting for prey.

I whip around, and there she is. My former friend, the only person in Albion who gave me a home when mine was broken. Her eyes flash sickly green, reminding me that my friend is long gone, replaced by this twisted shell. My heart stutters. She lunges.

I duck, but she scoops me by the waist and shoves me against a wall.

Before she moves again, two daggers lodge in Mara's spine, and she roars, her features melting into something out of my nightmares. Her eyes are hollow, her nose gone, and her teeth are a serrated mess. She reeks of the sickly sharp stench of rot mixed with the copper tang of blood.

My eyes scan the back room, and Sylas crouches behind the kitchen table, a finger on his lips. He gestures to Mara. Raiku holds her legs in place, his fangs in her bones. She shakes him off like a pest, flinging the aspier against the nearest wall. Her head snaps back to me, and I gag. She cages me into a corner, and my eyes dart around for a way out. There is none, unless I push through her.

I *refuse* to die at the hands of my sister's killer. My magic is rooted in death. This is a funeral home with a cemetery in the back. There must be ghosts somewhere. I focus on anything out of the ordinary, but nothing happens. Gods, curse this forsaken magic. What is the use of this torture if it lets me die when I need it the most?

Mara collides with me, sending me flying to the floor with her on top of me. Pain blooms at the base of my neck. Right when I think she will strike me, she gently brushes one of her sharp claws from my temple to my jaw.

I hold my breath.

Gods, make it stop.

Up close, Mara looks like a grotesque piece of art at a gallery of horrors. She bares her serrated teeth, cocking her head. The claw is back again, this time going down the side of my neck. She takes her sweet time, like she's enjoying this.

I wince, readying for the inevitable tear of skin, but nothing comes.

My eyes flip open to find Sylas pulling Mara off me, slicing a dagger across her dark bony throat. She twists his hand, and the dagger falls to the floor.

"Run," Sylas yells. "Run now. Don't come back."

He doesn't need to tell me twice. I bolt across the room.

Stumbling out the back door, I catch my bearings on the railing, heart pounding in my throat. Victor's translucent face unclenches every muscle when he sees me. Beau hurries past him.

"You have to help him." My plea comes out as a raw scream. Sylas may be immortal, but Mara will find a way to torture him.

"Do you have what I asked?" Victor's eyebrows pull together. Beau glances at him, bewildered by his question, but Victor will need his relic if he wants to help.

"Here." I pull the silver laurel pendant out of my pocket. He and Beau asked if I could retrieve the spare relic from the Archyr safe right before we left. The pendant dangles at the end of a thin silver chain, occasionally catching the moonglow.

Behind the ghosts are the two metal stretchers holding their bodies. They are as fresh as the last time I saw them, not a wrinkle, not a single hair out of place, and not decomposing yet—Beau's venom must have been just enough. I stuff the relic in Victor's pocket, wishing on every star in the sky that stitching their bodies back is as simple as he explained on our way here.

"Are you certain about this?" Beau steps to my left.

My head bobs, but it's a lie. I am no longer certain about anything other than Sylas won't make it if they don't help him, and they can't help him as ghosts.

"Start by conjuring a single thread," Victor instructs.

Conjure threads? What is he talking about. "Victor, I can't learn magic in a minute. You said this was going to be simple."

He sighs. "It is. I mean, it should be. Year Ones can do it during their first week."

Wonderful. He's telling me I'm incapable now. "I don't know how to conjure threads."

"In the catacombs, when you threaded the voices to the river," he explains. "Same principle. Find the threads."

"There are no voices, and there is no river."

"Focus, Viola. All ghosts have threads." He paces back and forth, huffing occasionally, as if it's my fault he picked an untrained Mortemagi to do his bidding.

I can help. A sudden voice steals my breath. The light timbre of her tone reminds me of the woman from the catacombs, its texture soft and weightless. *I won't harm you,* she croons.

It *is* the ghost from Death Spire.

"Bloody saints," I mutter, closing my eyes and bracing myself for the floodgate of voices to open, but it doesn't. It's only hers.

"How?" I ask. "I can't see the threads."

Well, your eyes are closed.

Hilarious. I open my eyes, looking at Beau and Victor. There, I see them, the red and purple and silver threads. "I see them."

Good. Weave them with the bodies, but be wary: nothing comes for free.

I already know this will deplete my cuff's magic. Victor told me, and I agreed. After this, I will have no use for the cuff anyway. At least now, Nan's magic is bringing two people back to their families. It's what I know she would've done.

"I don't know how," I say.

"Viola." Beau gasps. "You've anchored to a ghost, haven't you."

My glare pins his mouth shut. I don't want to hear about what I should and shouldn't be doing. They threw me into the cave of death without a guide and expected me to come out its master.

May I?

"What will you do?"

Take over your body.

How kind of her to ask if she can possess me. "No."

A window breaks and my head jerks toward the funeral home. If Beau and Victor don't help Sylas, who knows what Mara will inflict upon him? He may be immortal, but I wouldn't wish the coldness of her sharp claws upon my worst enemy.

"Do it." I squeeze my eyes shut, bracing myself for what's to come. But instead, she laments, *All these centuries, and our downfall is still our heart.* I don't know what she means, but I need her to be less introspective and more active.

My ears ring. Victor's talking, but I hear nothing. I see Victor's broken smile and Beau's worried eyes, and I pray to the God of Death this isn't the last time I'm seeing them.

It happens in a blur. My eyes open again, and now Beau's and Victor's ghosts are gone. The bodies are still here, unmoving, still cold, and still very dead.

"You call this helping?" I yell at the ghost.

Leaning over Beau's chest, I listen for a heartbeat. One second, nothing. Two seconds, still nothing. Three seconds, my body warms, and my harness dampens. Frowning, I pull away, running my hand over my abdomen.

It comes away with red, sticky liquid.

My own blood.

> Resurrections are divided in two categories: simple and complex.
>
> Simple resurrections are a two-step process, requiring the materialized ghost and the body of the dead. **Note:** Bodies will come back as they are at the time of resurrection.
>
> Complex resurrections require human sacrifice.
>
> **ISOBEL CORVI**, *DEATH MAGIC, OR A LIFE OF SERVITUDE*, **CHAPTER 4**

twenty-four | sylas

TUESDAY, NOVEMBER 23, 1939

Mara cuts me faster than Railesza can heal me. Her hideous figure looks like a cross between a ghoul and a skeleton, with the strength of two elks. Haal, she reeks of death and unwashed clothes.

Now I understand why DOTS forbids this magic. I understand why the founders trapped Grimm in his relic, dooming his ghost to an eternity in limbo—this kind of power in the wrong hands would be the undoing of centuries of peace among Houses. That Faro's Cuff has been missing needs to be at the forefront of DOTS's investigations. The cuff was already powerful, and now it could be so much worse.

Raiku bites Mara for the twelfth time in vain. Fantastic. Aspier venom is useless on puppets. Her knifelike claws swipe, and I jerk away at just the right time to not lose an eye. It catches on my neck instead, peeling the skin. I throw a punch straight to her face, and she staggers backward.

"Why do you not die, weaver of serpents?" Mara hisses in an inhuman voice.

"Well," I scoff, "you hit like a toddler."

For that, she smacks me across the face so hard that I land on my side. I'm still reeling from the throw when the door opens. No. No. No. Viola shouldn't be back here. I told her to run.

But it's not her at all.

Victor walks through the door, spinning the spare relic from our safe. He is an even bigger idiot. I told him to hide for a reason—Railesza won't be able to heal him if Mara attacks. He is an Arkani, and Aspieri cannot heal different classes unless bonded to them.

"Remember me?" he taunts Mara.

Mara spins around. She croaks, "You're dead. I killed you myself."

"And what a piss-poor job it was," Victor drawls.

Mara forgets about me, zeroing in on him instead. He sidesteps her with ease. In a second, he's in front of her, his right hand waving across her face. In his left, the silver laurel relic glows. Mara stops and stares at him for a second.

He smirks, a quiet arrogance exuding from him.

I gasp when I realize what he's doing. His illusion magic is reaching through the puppet to confuse the puppeteer. Using illusions on a puppeteer is something I've only seen Firstline Arkani do, and not for long. Sure, he's a Grand Magus, but this particular magic requires a Mortemagi bond... because I know Victor's not a crossmage.

Victor's fingers twitch, and Mara's shoulders drop. "They're all dead. They don't have the relics we seek." It's not Mara speaking; it's the puppeteer speaking to someone else. Her words slap me with shock. Haal, there's more than one puppeteer, and they are looking for more relics.

Victor is good. No, he's excellent at his Arkani magic. He's managed to trick the puppeteer into speaking their thoughts in a puppet. In a single flick, he's brought answers we haven't found in a week.

"I must find the girl. I need the cuff." Mara drones in a slightly different accent this time, quieter, calmer. She tries to lift her arm and curses when she can't. She's fighting against Victor's magic and losing. After a few seconds, her limbs go still, her head dropping to her chest. Now is our time to leave.

"Beau?" I ask Victor as we rush through the back door onto the veranda. A low creak draws my attention to our left, but it's only the half-open metal gate of the cemetery swaying with the breeze.

"Beau's fine." He hesitates a moment too long. Why isn't he saying anything about Viola?

"Vi-Viola?" My head whips around, cursing the clouds shrouding the moon. I can't see them anywhere. My legs go still, my mind reaching for my worst nightmare: Viola dead.

Inside me, something breaks, every crack anchors deeper than the last.

"I need help," Beau yells from a few feet away, his voice laced with anguish. My legs propel me forward, and my brother is standing by a willow tree, Viola leaning against him, a hand on her abdomen. She's not dead. I breathe out, my steps slowing down. Not dead at all. She must have gotten injured when Mara threw her around in Dearly Departed.

Railesza hisses at me, giving me a disapproving stare before slithering off my arm toward Viola, sinking her fangs into her ankle the moment she reaches her.

"Sylas," Victor yells. "Relic's out of magic."

I turn to see Mara drag her feet out of the back door of Dearly Departed. Pieces of rotten flesh hang from her legs, and her arms are infested with black maggots crawling in and out of her ivory bones. From the veranda, Victor watches her in horror as she trudges past him, paying him no mind.

"The puppeteer controlling her is running out of magic." He nods at the decomposing body. As the words leave his mouth, Mara straightens, her eyes locked on me, but she doesn't move, and neither do we. Now that we're outside, my senses pick up on every sway of leaves. Poachers could be anywhere.

Raiku awakens, slithering up my finger, watching, waiting.

Muttering something under his breath, Victor draws up his sleeves. His borrowed relic hovers over the veins of his forearm.

"Stop," I yell. If the puppeteer is running out of magic, I can control Mara. Victor doesn't need to use the blood arts to create another diversion. At least, not yet.

"Beau," I say without looking at him. "Keep Railesza with you. I don't want you to become a deserted Aspieri."

"But . . ." he protests. Silver is gone, and he *knows* Aspieri cannot be without a relic for long, else they'll break covenant with Haal, the God of War, and he'll desert them.

"Heal Viola," I speak up, glancing at them over my shoulder. My brother's eyebrows shoot up, but he nods without saying a word. And I realize that this is the first time I haven't wished the bond away.

I turn my attention to Mara's frozen figure. This feels like a trap, like the puppeteer's waiting for us to let our guard down before they attack again.

"Can you fight, Victor?" I don't wait for his answer and throw him a dagger. He catches it by the blade as he approaches.

"I prefer to keep my hands clean, but there are exceptions," he says, stealing a glance at Beau. Victor Carver is an enigma, but right now, I have to trust him as we fight Mara.

Like I thought, it is a trap.

Mara lunges first. My knees buckle under her weight, but I don't drop. I shove her away from me. Victor swipes at her, yelping as a chunk of rotting flesh splatters on his pants.

Mara is on the ground, but her eyes aren't on us anymore. They leer at Viola with unbridled thirst. I don't have time to blink; she slides past me, diving straight for her. Beau pushes Viola aside, and Mara's claws cut across his shoulder. I grip her elbow, pulling her back. She flails, her long, skeletal hands still reaching toward Viola. I loop my arm around hers and jerk her away.

The upper half of Mara's body twists, and she drives her claws into my ribs. Haal, have mercy. It hurts.

Out of the corner of my eye, Beau urges Railesza toward me, but she doesn't move. At least someone around here is following orders. Mara kicks me in the abdomen, and my back clashes with the pavement before my head meets the ground. She straddles me, tilting her head as if she's trying to figure me out. Up close, her face is drooping, with large veins coming out of her eye sockets. Her eyeballs seem to be her only remaining human attribute, and they're now a deeper shade of green.

"I can handle her. The puppeteers can't be far," I shout to Victor, and he immediately sets off through the cemetery, quietly stalking into the woods.

Mara swipes at my neck, and the metallic smell of blood fills the air. My vision blurs, but regardless of how Raiek feels about me, I know the Imortalis won't let me die.

One after the other, three knives sink into Mara's neck. I look past her, and Beau readies a fourth. She removes them one by one and throws them back toward my brother with a wicked grin that crawls down my spine. I will my body to move, but it won't so much as twitch. Without Railesza to heal me, I'm as good as dead. The corners of my vision fade to black, and my eyes roll back.

When I come back to my senses, a tall male figure—a second puppet—drags Victor from the cemetery toward me. Haal, is he dead? The darkness takes me away. What good am I if I can't keep anyone alive? I don't deserve the Imortalis when all I do is push people to their deaths.

Light seeps through my eyelids again. Across the yard, Mara's long, sharp fingers pin Victor to a tree through his shoulder. He's alive. With his relic, coated in blood—his blood—he distracts her every few seconds, but his magic doesn't hold, and she punctuates every gap with a hit.

"Vi," Beau pleads, his voice faint. "Victor's going to die again. Aspieri cannot heal Arkani. Please cut the puppet's threads."

"I don't see the threads." Viola chokes. "I don't see them—"

I pass out again.

This time when I wake, Viola's legs are swinging, her hands trying to pry Mara's death grip from her neck. Behind them, Beau helps Victor toward the street. At the slightest movement, my neck hurts.

Will I have to watch everyone die by the hands of Mortemagi as I lie here, *useless*?

"Do not speak of Olivia." Viola's yell pierces through the chaos.

When my eyes find her again, her right palm is open, her fingers ebbing and flowing, like she's weaving invisible threads. Mara drops her abruptly, and Viola lands on her feet, scrambling away from the puppet.

"Something is tethering the threads," she calls out. "They're impossible to cut."

A moment later, Beau careens toward me, and Railesza half wraps around my arm, biting into my veins, healing me just enough to get up. I inhale, and my lungs fill with relief as I stagger to my feet, stumbling forward. My harness is empty, and Raiku doesn't respond when I call out to him. I scan the area, but my killer aspier is nowhere to be seen.

A dagger flies past me, landing straight between Mara's eyes. From the street, Victor falls to his knees, the other puppet lying still at his side. It looks deflated, empty. I only hope this means he's somehow found the second puppeteer.

Like a parasite who refuses to die, Mara pulls the dagger out and takes a step forward, aiming it toward me. If I can't fight, I can at least distract her with the little strength I have left. I close my eyes, bracing for the hit. It can't kill me, I remind myself.

Nothing comes. Or maybe it did, and I somehow died so fast I have no recollection of the moment.

A whimper forces my eyes open.

Viola is in front of me.

Her shoulders sag, and I catch her midfall, a dagger below her rib cage, so close to where I stabbed her days ago. This woman is out of her mind. Does she forget that I am immortal? My limbs refuse to move. I am a statue of confusion, anger, and guilt. She threw herself in front of me. She just tried to save *me*.

Mara spits, blood splattering in the air. She drags her limp leg forward. "Beau," I call out, and my brother wraps his arm around Viola's waist, holding her weight.

"Rai and I have her," my brother says.

I don't have time to reply when Mara darts toward me, her hands reaching straight for my neck. My arms slide between us, and I twist her hands away, kneeing her hard in the stomach. She recoils, the green of her eyes fading—the puppeteer is distancing themselves. Mara stumbles back to her feet, but I don't yield. I charge at her, and she drags me with her to the ground. This time, I have the upper hand. I throw punch after punch until my vision is hazy again, until I no longer know what is and what isn't. One moment, Beau is yelling, and the next, my body lies flat on the grass.

"Sylas," a voice calls.

Lifting my head, I see the silhouette of a man in the forest. Is this the God of Death? The hooded figure peels away from the tall evergreen trees and glides toward me. Is it over, then? Surely I must be dead. But then, Raiku slithers from the person's arm to mine.

Struggling to sit up, I take stock of the courtyard around Dearly Departed. Two Firstline Mortemagi are binding Mara and the other puppet by the street—they're both still, and both in an advanced state of decomposition now that the puppeteers have gone.

I squint to have a better view of the hooded man.

My question is immediately answered the moment the figure steps in front of me. He doesn't have to lower his hood; I would recognize the smell of burned sandalwood anywhere.

Overseer Paltro stands before me with the fury of a thousand gods.

> **Attention, Whisperers**: Anchored ghosts can and will possess you at length. See a nonmagi priest for help.
>
> **Tip**: Anchored ghosts cannot give out their names.
>
> Should the whisperer want to permanently keep or dismiss their anchored ghost, they must guess the correct name. However, if the mage guesses the wrong name, the anchor breaks, and the ghost is free to possess the mage. Be wary, ghosts are known tricksters.
>
> **Addendum**: Nonmagi priests are no longer taking expulsion requests.
>
> RULES & REGULATIONS OF GORHAIL, 2ND EDITION

twenty-five | viola

WEDNESDAY, NOVEMBER 24, 1939

If I hated magic before, I loathe it now.

Grasping the threads above Mara's shoulders felt like ripping my soul in two. The burning from my cuff carried through my veins; I thought it would set me on fire. And every time I tried to snap the threads, a sharp stab at my temples threatened to drill into my head.

Until the small voice of the woman from the catacombs spoke again. *Let me help*, she said. And I did. I don't remember a thing after that.

"Archyr, does prison mean nothing to you?" The overseer of the House of Poison stands over Sylas in the courtyard of Dearly Departed, winged by the shadow of the trees behind him. "Thank Haal your sister has more sense than you."

"Great." Sylas pushes himself up, dusting his palm against his tattered pants. His weapons harness is empty, and underneath, his shirt is ripped, dried blood caking at the exposed skin. Lyria saved our lives.

Beau and Victor stand side by side, awkwardly looking back and forth between Sylas and the overseer. They're both alive. I did it. I resurrected them... Well, the ghost did.

"Coming back from the dead doesn't bar you from expulsion from Gorhail, Mr. Carver," the overseer says without looking at Victor. Instead, his glare is trained on Beau. "Cardot, I'm rescinding your Grand Magus rank, effective immediately."

"Uncle—" Beau speaks up, but the overseer is no longer looking at him. His menacing blue eyes study me from head to toe. "And you..." His tone oozes with scorn. "A brand-new Mortemagi, so well versed in the blood arts. Only the Gods can spare you now."

The Gods know nothing of mercy. Why would they spare us when they were the ones who cursed us with magic?

"All four of you will answer to the Principal Grand Master immediately. I will be waiting in your car, Sylas, after we finish processing these puppets."

Paltro turns around and glances at the building. Quietly, his brown aspier slithers from his arm, through the grass, and into the back door. If he's hoping to find anyone else, he'll be disappointed. He walks toward the street, where two Firstline Mortemagi hold the sagging bodies of Mara and another man I now recognize as the Albion baker's husband. How could the Gods sit by as the monsters they created stole yet another innocent life?

Even if Firstline and DOTS investigate these two puppets, the truth remains that we are out of our depths—I overheard Victor say there were multiple puppeteers, and if we all nearly died to one, how will we survive against an army of them?

After tonight, I don't know that I can fulfill my promise to Olivia—I am not strong enough for this world; I don't have the grit to pursue a killer that hides behind other people's bodies.

"*You* started this." Sylas glares at Victor. "And now we have to sit in front of the Grand House because *she* used her wretched magic to help *you*." His mouth twists in contempt as he stalks over to where Victor stands.

She. He speaks of me with such disdain, like I *want* this magic, like I wouldn't scrape out every trace of it from my veins if I could. And now... I will be sentenced to death because of it. Maybe if I beg Priya and ask her to seal my magic, she will spare me from execution. It's my first infraction; I'll argue that I'm barely a mage. My foolish arrogance tricked me into believing I could make a difference, and I failed.

Beau levels his brother's glower. "Viola's magic is good when it brings me back, but wretched when we must answer for it." He shakes his head, briefly glancing at Victor. "Actions have consequences, Sylas; we all knew this, and we were all prepared for it. If Victor didn't *start this*, I wouldn't be here with you."

Victor's lips part in surprise, but he doesn't say a word.

Sylas holds his brother's stare for a second, then walks off toward the car, his fists balled at his sides. "Don't mind him." Beau gives me the smallest smile.

I don't think I'll ever be used to people speaking up for me. A treacherous feeling of belonging creeps into my heart, begging me to let it stay, but I tuck it away, squashing any hope blooming within me.

It starts to rain, a slow drizzle against the faint moonlight, a poetic mirror of my heart weeping at the thought of failing my sister. Sure, we caught the puppets, but we've also discovered a greater conspiracy. Even if I wanted to do something, I am powerless now, my fate in the hands of the Principal Grand Master.

I stand alone for a moment, taking in Dearly Departed behind me, Little Lake Albion across the street, and the stupid bench where I used to eat lunch with Mara every day. One week is all it took for me to become a stranger to this place, and with the raindrops trickles a sobering truth: Albion is not my home anymore, and neither is Gorhail.

Sylas's car is parked farther down the lake. Next to it, the overseer holds a clipboard, signing a few pages before leading the Firstline officers toward a second car a few feet down the road. I linger on the sidewalk a second longer. Once I cross this road and get into the car, my future solely rests in Priya's hands.

I step onto the road.

"Wait." Sylas's hoarse voice sets my heart alight when it should freeze over. His steps scrape against the pavement, hesitant.

Don't turn around. I do.

The raindrops run in rivulets down his face, washing away some of the blood and dirt. My breath falters, and a faint shiver ripples through me, trailing goose bumps along my skin. I don't know if it's the danger or the rain, but tonight Sylas is devastating. He watches me carefully, pausing at my neck. In a single step, he's in front of me, his hooded eyes darkening. "You're still bleeding."

I didn't even know I was bleeding.

He pulls a piece of cloth from his pocket and gently presses it to my neck. "Hold it there," he whispers. "I . . . Railesza is with Beau."

"It's fine." I replace his hand with mine, darting my eyes away. My traitorous cheeks flush. He is standing painfully close to me, the warmth of his body once again wrapping me with safety I *shouldn't* feel around him.

"Why did you jump in front of me?" he asks, and I forget how to breathe.

Instinct. I was certain Mara was going to kill him, and I couldn't leave Beau and Lyria without their brother. But if I'm honest, I don't *know* why I jumped in front of him. I just did.

"I am immortal." He points to Raiek. "You're not. Don't do anything this foolish again."

Don't do anything this foolish again. His words sober me up, and I let out a long breath. First, my magic is wretched, now my actions are foolish. I don't know why I stand here and let him riddle me with insults.

"There won't be a second time." With one final nod, I begin to cross the street. The fights, the magic, and the constant brush with death crash into me with a wave of exhaustion, and all I want to do is crawl into my bed in Albion and sleep. But instead, I'll have to talk my way out of death in Riverview.

"Don't do it," Sylas says behind me.

My legs obey him like he's their master. I stop and turn around, but this time he's not fooling me with his constant push and pull. "Do what, Sylas?"

"Don't get rid of your magic. It's all over your face."

"Why do you care? You hate Mortemagi."

He sucks in his lower lip, and my stupid, stupid eyes fall to his mouth. I quickly look back up, and he sighs in frustration. "Gorhail is where you belong. Despite how I feel about your magic, you deserve to study it."

I don't deserve anything. "I don't *want* this magic. This world has taken too much from me for me to want to be a part of it." I force a smile. Sylas has a way of drawing out my deepest fears and laying them bare. "Do you know what it's like to hate the very fiber of your being?"

To my surprise, he replies, "I do."

His eyes are distant, lost in a memory that wells them with tears. They are so raw, so human, like they contain a multitude of sorrows. The more I tell myself that his sorrows aren't mine to ease, the more I want to reach over to wipe away the tears before they fall.

"Vi." He doesn't break our gaze as he walks up to me, and my traitor heart leaps. Even drenched and covered in blood, Sylas still looks like he was blessed by the six Gods.

"I'm sorry," he whispers.

"I—" I pause, a lump in my throat. What do I even say to that?

"Come back to Gorhail." His brows are furrowed, his voice a plea that knots around my heart. And all I want to do is surrender.

"DOTS—" I remind him.

"I won't let them." He cuts me off.

My chest heaves, and my throat tightens. I should look away. I should leave.

I cannot.

The gray of his eyes leans to black in the low streetlight. Rain droplets glide along his long lashes as he searches my face, and I want so badly to lift my fingers to his face and brush them away.

"Please, stay." His voice breaks, and I let out a small gasp, but I don't reply.

For a moment too long, his words hang between us, full of promise that things could be different. And it's terrifying how every part of my body *wants* them to be different. But how long until this promise turns into poison?

When I take a while to answer, Sylas clears his throat. I immediately step back, my ears burning with embarrassment. There's a single truth between him and me: I am a Mortemagi. He's an Aspieri.

The drive to Priya's house in Riverview is quiet—the overseer didn't give us any explanation as to why we're heading to the Principal Grand Master's personal house, rather than to the Grand House at DOTS, but the sun also hasn't risen yet.

Sylas's leg fidgets against mine, and I place a hand on his knee, in reassurance or annoyance, or maybe a bit of both.

After what seemed like an hour, the car halts, and we get out in silence.

I look around, an ominous feeling crawling down my spine. I never expected my first time in Riverview to be for my judgment.

Something is deeply wrong about this place. The buildings are tall, streetlights line the pavement in nauseatingly even spaces, and even the slabs of concrete are precisely cut to maintain the symmetry. What's even more unnatural is that all the houses look alike, with the same black roofs, same white exterior, same white gate, and same small red mailbox. All ... except for the one in front of us.

This two-story house extends over two lots, with a garden that makes my own look like a child's playground. Under the shy glow of the streetlight, a row of blue flowers glints with pride. My eyes widen, and I blink hard. They're growing the rarest of all roses: the diamond blue. Nan would've lost her mind. If she were here, she would've knocked on their door and asked them a million questions about how they managed to grow such a temperamental species in Riverview, given that it shares Albion's weather.

Overseer Paltro unlocks the white gate, furtively glancing around. He moves across the garden like a fugitive, ushering the four of us forward. At the black oak door, he knocks twice, then thrice, then once more. A single lamp hangs to the right of the entrance, illuminating the worried wrinkles of the overseer's face.

The door opens, and my stomach drops.

Priya Parrish stands in front of us, wrapped in a thick, black shawl over a long black skirt, her eyebrows pulled into a scowl that makes the God of Death seem less scary.

Once we're all inside, she gingerly closes the door. "My aging parents are sleeping upstairs, so I will say this as calmly as possible." She rubs her temple and glares at the four of us, still huddled by the door. "What were you thinking? You have breached one fundamental law and at least two Gorhail rules."

"Neither Gorhail nor DOTS would have known we were gone if Lyria hadn't told Paltro."

"Mr. Archyr, I would zip my mouth if I were you. Had your sister not informed your uncle, you would've been arrested the moment you set foot back at Gorhail." Priya darts into a room on our left, grabbing a thick raincoat. "*What* would your explanation have been for two previously dead students walking around?"

Sylas's eyes flick to mine, then he lowers his head without saying a word. I've never seen him so submissive before. I hadn't considered the aftermath of Dearly Departed if we were caught, and now that I'm under Priya's terrifying stare, I realize just how reckless we've all been.

Priya studies me for a beat, then her calculating eyes shift to Overseer Paltro. "Thank you for reaching out to me before notifying the rest of the Grand House, Rodric." She hands him the raincoat. "As agreed upon, you *will* come with me to DOTS, and you *will* testify that you hired a rogue Mortemagi to resurrect Beau Cardot and Victor Carver."

Overseer Paltro gives her a curt nod. "I will say it's connected to the Grimm copycat investigation. Your orders or—"

"Mine." She takes one step toward Sylas, and he glances down at her, his brows furrowed. Her eyes scrutinize him for a moment, then in a menacingly low tone, she says, "I am only sparing you from prison because of your 'valuable contribution' to the Grimm task force."

Stepping away from Sylas, she sighs at Overseer Paltro, and something tells me there *is* no valuable contribution, and neither is there a Grimm task force. I wonder if they'll establish one now.

"Well, then." The overseer looks me up and down, then clasps his hands together, and I begin to unravel the power play between him and Priya. He seems to be using *me* as leverage to keep Sylas out of trouble. My gaze trails to Priya; she's going to great lengths for the Corvi cuff.

"Sylas, you're drafted to Firstline immediately," Overseer Paltro orders. "Riverview Division. You'll return to Gorhail this morning, pack your bags, and leave right away."

Sylas's head snaps to me, his worried gaze lingering a second too long. It moves something in me, because in that single second, I realize I'm not ready for him to leave Gorhail, and as one second stretches into the next, it becomes clearer that I don't want him to leave *me*.

"Uncle . . ." he starts, but Overseer Paltro's death stare shuts him up. We all stand in silence for a moment, the four of us huddled next to one another—Victor leaning against the entryway wall by the door, Sylas a statue between us, and Beau restless on my right.

"Cardot and Carver." Priya eyes them with a quiet menace. "Which one of you orchestrated this? A Mortemagi as green as Viola shouldn't even know about resurrections."

I drown out her words, because my attention is drawn to a photograph on the mantel. A younger Priya, an older couple whom I assume are her parents, and a woman shorter than Priya with shoulder-length black hair. I wonder if this was the sister she told me about on my first night at Gorhail, the one who was in the same year as my father.

"Miss Corvi," Priya says, jerking my attention back to the small foyer in which we stand. I freeze. "What in Death's name possessed you to carry out not one but two resurrections? And *how* did you do it?"

A ghost. Does she know I anchored to a ghost? Gods, save me from the madness about to descend upon me if she finds out.

"Er . . . I . . ." I scramble to find an excuse, but I don't even know *how* to lie about this.

But she's not even looking at me. She's inspecting every inch of Beau, pausing at his shoulders and narrowing her eyes. Slowly, her eyebrows raise, and her jaw falls open. "Dear God . . . you anchored to a ghost, haven't you, Viola?" She turns back to me.

I wince, unsure of what to say. Overseer Paltro lets out a strangled sound, and Priya brings her hand to her mouth, her eyes flaring with horror.

Well, now she definitely knows.

"The stitches are immaculate," she murmurs as she studies Victor this time. Then she shakes her head. "Well, I hope the cost of the resurrection was worth it to you."

Because I don't know when to keep my mouth shut, I mutter, "It's just magic." I haven't a clue why she's fussing about magic that can be replaced—I'll speak to a few ghosts, and the cuff will replenish. Then again, all she seems to care about is the cuff.

Priya's eyebrows pull into a confused frown. Slowly, her eyes wince, and her mouth parts in a quiet gasp. "By Death, you don't know."

Overseer Paltro shifts his weight next to her, his eyes trained on Victor. No one says a word, and the uncomfortable silence becomes suffocating the longer it drags.

"Mr. Carver, what did you tell her was the cost of resurrection?" Priya asks, her palm raised. "Because Mr. Cardot hasn't even had a chance to earn rank at the House of Death, so I doubt he even knew resurrections were possible."

"Magic." Victor clears his throat, and I turn my head to him. His back is flat against the wall, as if he's trying to crawl into it. The longer I stare, the more I realize something is deeply wrong. Victor won't meet my eyes.

"What is the true cost of resurrection, Grand Magus Carver?" Priya's fingers start to move, and Victor inches toward the front door. "It's useless trying to run."

She twists her wrist and slowly raises her hand. Behind Victor, a skeletal creature pushes itself out of the ground, blocking Victor's escape. It oozes darkness with the sickly sharp stench of death.

Not a puppet at all, but something that often haunted my nightmares after I'd read about them when I was younger: the undead.

Priya holds her palm open. "You need to tell her. What is the true cost of resurrection, Grand Magus Carver?"

Beau takes a step, but Overseer Paltro places a firm arm across his chest. Why is Priya using the blood arts against Victor? Although, she makes the rules, so I suppose she can bend them, too.

"Lifeblood." Victor speaks so quietly I almost miss it.

Sylas's eyes widen in horror; he looks back and forth between his brother and me, pausing on me to say something, then swallows his words instead. I look at Beau, and he's repeatedly shaking his head, as if he's trying to unhear the words Victor just spoke.

I did tell you nothing comes for free.

"What are you talking about?" I ask my anchored ghost. Everyone looks at me like I might break any moment. I wish they would stop.

Then Priya approaches me, her steps slow and cautious. Like the first time I met her, she gently takes my hands into hers and, with all the care in the world, murmurs, "Resurrection halves the life of a Mortemagi."

> Mortemagi relics refill magic in two ways.
> Every ghost led to the Underiver refills a conduit's relic.
> Every ghost spoken to refills a whisperer's relic.
>
> **YSENIA FARO, *DEATH MAGIC FOR BEGINNERS*, CHAPTER 10**

twenty-six | sylas

WEDNESDAY, NOVEMBER 24, 1939

Resurrection halves the life of a Mortemagi.

Parrish's words tear through my heart. Viola didn't know what she agreed to. Victor never gave her a choice; she was nothing but a pawn in his game. I look up to the ceiling, forcing myself not to curse out the Gods. I knew something was off about him, and I said nothing. I should have drilled him with questions, demanded he explain every part of his plan. Instead, I was too enthralled by the idea of having my brother back, and I unknowingly bled Viola's years dry.

"You knew..." I trail off, lowering my glare to Victor. His face twists into an expression I don't care enough to read. He briefly glances past me, at Beau, then his shoulders drop into a sigh. "I..."

Raiku uncoils himself. He perches on my hand, eyes locked on Victor, fangs out and ready to attack on my command. For a brief second, I consider making the call. Victor knows it, because he steps backward into Parrish's undead.

"Gods, what have we done?" Beau chokes out behind me, and I turn around. "I... I didn't know, Viola. I swear on my mother's grave. I... Can we reverse it?" My brother's eyes beg Parrish to say yes, but she rubs her thumb into her palm with force, her lips drawn into a straight line.

"If I die again, would she gain her lifeblood back?" Beau pleads.

"No." The sadness in Parrish's voice weighs the room with regret; even Paltro looks troubled. I can't bring myself to look at Viola. She cleaved her lifespan in four to bring my brother back to life.

"Viola." Victor speaks, and Raiku hisses. "I am sorry. You have to believe me. I really did need magic from the Corvi cuff to materialize us, and I *will* help you find answers about Olivia."

It's too late for apologies. His *help* won't give Viola her years back.

"It was her decision to make, not yours." My rage consumes me, and I see red. I take a step, but Railesza's hiss holds me back. Perched on Beau's hand, she studies Viola with interest. It's one thing to have an affinity for the Mortemagi she bonded to, but she guards Viola as her own.

Viola is still as she watches everything unfold around her. She hasn't said a single word since Parrish told her, and all I want is to take her away from this madness.

As Parrish and Paltro exchange words that I don't care to listen to, my eyes are glued to Viola. How will I leave for Firstline today? How will I leave *her*?

She runs a hand through her black hair and pulls away with a grimace. It's matted with blood. Even so, she's as beautiful as the rising sun on the sand dunes of the Farbon Desert. Her tongue flicks over her bottom lip, and for the first time, I find myself wondering how it would feel against my lips, if she would kiss me back at all. Her head tilts at me in confusion. I realize I'm staring, that I should probably stop. I gulp, suddenly conscious of my every move.

Pathetic. Too much has happened tonight, and my emotions are cloudy. I glare at Railesza; it must be that cursed bond. Having stupid thoughts at inconvenient times will get me in trouble.

"I'd like to leave." Viola's low voice quiets the room. The softness of it carries a silent hope, but the flare of her eyes cannot lie. She's afraid. Her chest rises and falls quicker than usual, and she slips on another one of her unreadable masks. Her calm is unnerving. I want her to be angry, to be so furious at this life she was thrown into, all because her sister wanted to play pretend mage.

Our gaze meets, and hers is empty, as if she's already accepted death as her fate. My chest tightens, my heart slamming against the walls I so carefully built. I don't want her to die soon. I don't want her to die at all.

"Viola." Parrish opens a drawer from the small console table behind her. She pulls out a stack of paper with the Grand House's letterhead. "From now on, I wouldn't use any magic other than ghost communication or listening to the dead's last wishes—bleeding any more years for the blood arts will kill you. As for your sanction for resurrection, dear child, I think you've been punished enough."

Viola's eyes are hollow when she nods. It doesn't matter that Parrish is sparing her from the Grand House's judgment; Viola already has one foot in the grave.

Parrish scribbles something on the sheet of paper, signs it, then hands it to her. "Take this to Dean Rhodes. She will arrange for expulsion of the anchored ghost."

Then she picks another sheet from the stack, scribbles something else, then signs it and gives it to Viola. "Congratulations, Magus Corvi. It's the least I can do, considering"—she pauses, throwing a disappointing glare at Victor—"your sacrifice."

It *is* the least she can do. Viola deserves at least her mastery of Death for her sacrifice, and if Parrish cared about her, she would've promoted her to High Magus instead of Magus. None of it matters anyway, no number of promotions will return her lifeblood.

Viola holds the two letters, her blank stare fixed ahead, and once again I want her to be angry. I want her to lash out at the absurdity of this situation. In one conversation, the Principal Grand Master of DOTS has wiped our slates clean—there will be no prison, no execution—but the cost is higher than I was prepared to pay. A week ago, I would've jumped at that Firstline assignment, but now I'm already trying to find my way out of it. And Viola . . . Haal, she cannot die.

"High Magus Archyr." Parrish clears her throat, and I turn my attention back to her. "Please take High Magus Cardot . . . and Magus Corvi back to Gorhail, after which you are to leave for the Riverview Division."

She tugs on her shawl and takes a deep breath. "Rodric, we'll walk to DOTS. It'll give you enough time to practice your lie—you hired a rogue Mortemagi to resurrect Cardot and Carver to investigate . . ." She trails off, waiting for Paltro to complete her sentence, as if he were a child. A strange sight, given Paltro is older than her.

"Grimm . . . on your behalf," Paltro finishes.

"Perfect." She gives me a pointed look, and for a blink, I see her sister, the Deathbringer, in her eyes. Sometimes I forget that the Deathbringer came from a crossmage family. It's easy to forget. Purists celebrate her as if she were a saint, and yet Parrish earns purist-led public protests every few months.

"Did you manage to find the body of a Mortemagi poacher with such short notice?"

"Of course," Overseer Paltro says. "It has been sent to Firstline headquarters, and readers are rearranging the last memories as we speak."

Parrish nods at Paltro in gratitude, then takes a step toward Victor. "Mr. Carver"—she moves her fingers, and the undead that stood behind Victor binds his hands with its own bony fingers—"pending sentencing by the Grand House for the murder of the rogue Mortemagi Rodric hired, you will be transferred to Riverview Prison for Highly Dangerous Individuals—"

By Haal, there is no rogue Mortemagi.

I look back and forth between Paltro and Parrish, and it takes me a moment to realize what they're doing. They've fabricated evidence to accuse Victor of murder so the three of us can walk away without repercussions.

Under normal circumstances, I would be livid, but right now, Victor can rot in a cell.

"No." Victor lunges forward, but the undead pulls him back. "Let me go. I can't go to prison. My mother—"

"Would be disappointed in how self-serving her son is," Parrish finishes with scorn.

Victor shakes his head, tears welling in his eyes. "You can't do this. She's alone. She has no one. They won't keep her at St. Fabian's if the bills aren't paid—" He's screaming now, raw and desperate. "Please, I'm begging you. Please, don't do this to my mother."

"You did this to her yourself," Beau says quietly, before wrapping his hand around Viola's and tugging her toward the front door. "Let's go."

With the same silence and resignation she's been simmering in for the last half hour, she lets my brother drag her forward. I reach for her other hand, and our fingers brush against each other's. But she doesn't stop. She is a shell of her former self, and all I want to do is breathe life back into her.

Right as I'm about to leave, Paltro's heavy hand grips my arm. "Son, I understand the obligations of your bond." He lifts his nose at Raiku. "But stay away from that Corvi girl. Nothing good comes from that family."

My head jerks backward. Paltro isn't drafting me to Firstline to cover for us; he's doing it to separate me from Viola.

Gorhail Institute is a murder of crows when we cross the main gate. Half the House of Death stands still, their black coats pulled tight, their eyes trained on our car. Above, the dark of the night gives way to the dancing blue and orange hues of the morning sun.

News travels fast, I suppose.

Lorne stands in the middle of the crowd, his face red. Overseer Delaney is at his side. They look like angry parents who have caught their children slipping into their house past curfew.

The moment the car comes to a halt, Lorne jerks the door open, dragging Viola out by the arm. His fingers dig into her skin as he pulls her farther. She stumbles.

Railesza's head snaps in her direction, uncoiling herself around Beau's arm. She hisses in frustration. Now that she's no longer with me, she cannot move at will—she has to wait for Beau's command.

"Viola, you're bleeding. What did they do to you?" Lorne squeezes her arm once more.

I'm already out of the car, Raiku's eyes locked on him.

Viola jerks away from him, losing her footing. I brace her fall, wrapping my arm around her waist. "Need I remind you about touching people against their will?" I ask. Raiku hisses at him, fangs out.

"Always with the threats, Archyr. If you never act upon them, they're worth as much as you. Nothing." Lorne bares his teeth. I don't care that I'm outnumbered by Mortemagi. If he touches her one more time, Raiku will pump him with so much venom he'll wish he was dead.

Viola gestures to the crowd of Mortemagi and raises her eyebrows in question. I shrug. If she thinks I care about us being seen together, I don't. Every time Lorne looks at her, I *want* him to know he'll have to contend with me. Bond aside, Viola brought my brother back to life, and I owe her the world.

Turning her eyes to Lorne, she lets out a long sigh, then speaks. "We found Olivia's killer."

Panic flits across Lorne's eyes, as if he's only now registering the possibility of Olivia's murder. He shakes his head in disbelief, his attention wholly turned to Viola. "Olivia was k-killed?"

"Corvi, Archyr—" Delaney barks. She breaks off from the crowd, hurrying toward us and Lorne.

With the haunting towers of the House of Death in the background, she looks like a wraith. Her eyes fall to my arm around Viola, and I pull her closer to me, holding Delaney's questioning gaze. She opens her mouth to say something but clamps it shut when a car door opens.

The moment she notices Beau, her eyes bulge out of their sockets. In typical Delaney fashion, she takes in a steadying breath and composes herself immediately, because Gods forbid anything catches her by surprise. "Cardot, you are . . . alive."

"Not by choice," Beau mumbles, and both Viola and I glare at him.

"Regardless," she snaps. "Corvi, report to my office immediately." Her head then tilts up to me. "Don't ever hold one of my Mortemagi hostage—"

A Magus Mortemagi taps on her shoulder, interrupting her threat. Her eyes widen, and her head snaps toward the institute. Without acknowledging Beau and me, Delaney directs everyone to the House of Death, dragging Viola with her.

As I watch her walk away, my mind screams that she doesn't belong with them. And if my heart feels like it's caving in only watching her walk to her House, how will I leave for Firstline later?

Hollow Tree's dining hall is alive this morning. For the first time in days, there's a semblance of normalcy. A couple of young Magus fight over honeyfig bread for breakfast. They only like it because it's new to them. By the Pine Festival in a month, they'll be sick of it.

"Someone snuck into the kitchens," Lyria teases me as she gestures to the honeyfig loaf I'm holding. She and Beau join me on the balcony overlooking Hollow Tree. After Lyria cried a river's worth of tears earlier this morning, they've been joined at the hip. She hasn't let him out of her sight for the last couple of hours.

"I still haven't forgiven you for snitching on us to Paltro," I say. If Lyria hears me, she doesn't show it; she carries on her observation of the dining floor.

"It's a bazaar down there. I had to fight my way for one muffin." She scrunches her nose. "Beau refuses to eat. I keep telling him that Viola didn't sacrifice herself so he could starve to death."

My sister is now at the stage of using humor to deal with tragedy—she did the same four months ago, when Dad died. Right after we came back and told her about Viola, she sat in silence for a while, then sobbed against Beau, and, after that, spent hours scattering her research on the floor of Founder's Room.

"I'm not hungry." Beau sighs through her glare, then raises his eyebrows at me. "Are you ready to leave?" He looks worse than he did when he was dead. Victor didn't only trick Viola. He tricked Beau, too, and knowing my brother, he won't rest until he somehow makes it up to her.

"Leave?" Lyria pokes her tongue against her cheek. She lets out a forceful exhale, glaring daggers at me. After watching her distress over Viola, I omitted that Paltro drafted me to Firstline. I was hoping Beau would fill her in.

"I've been drafted to Firstline," I say quietly. "I leave soon."

"Where did they station you?"

"Riverview Division," I reply.

Her lips pull into half a smile. I wish the joy was from relief, but Gryff is also stationed there, and now that I'll be joining him, Lyria has unlimited visitation hours.

"Good thing I have two brothers." Lyria wraps her arms around Beau's waist, resting her head against him. "I'm glad *you're* staying at Gorhail. This way, we can continue our lifedrain theory and find a way to give Viola her years back."

First was humor, now it's blind optimism. Perhaps I need to be like my sister. Her hope lies in her own achievements, and if anyone can pull Viola out of this mess, it has to be Lyria.

Beau's face falls. "Yeah, I'll be here for a while, too," he laments. "But I deserve it. Paltro demoted me back to High Magus, so I won't be able to help with lifedrain."

"What?" Lyria exclaims. "He can't do that. He—"

"I have to retest through the House of Poison in two years. At least this means he'll let me retrieve Briar from my father's vault." His head hangs low.

"Have you seen Viola?" I ask mindlessly, glancing over the dining floor again.

Beau shakes his head, and my sister clears her throat. "No, but Paltro's storming toward you like he's going to throw you over a cliff."

"Was I unclear when I told you to leave right away?" Paltro raises an eyebrow at my hands. I quickly tuck the honeyfig bread in the large inner pocket of my jacket.

"Follow me," Paltro barks.

I glance at my siblings, then at Railesza, mouthing a quick goodbye.

This is the first time since my father's death that I will be without my healing aspier. As if Beau can hear my concern, he says, "Take her. It doesn't feel right that I'm allowed to be here, practicing magic, while Viola will die if she uses hers."

"Your guilt won't bring her lifeblood back." I push his hand away. Selfishly, I don't want to lose him again. And he knows that an Aspieri cannot be without an aspier.

"Sylas," Paltro barks, and I fall into step with him as we climb down the stairs of Hollow Tree. He hands me a letter bearing the silver seal of Firstline. "This is your official draft letter, and your first case begins now. Another student was found dead on Gorhail grounds."

> Sylas, Riverview Division has located poacher cells in the nonmagi communities of Bale. I presume it's to deter Firstline from looking for them among nonmagi. We're inclined to believe they are preparing for a new Grimm, but we don't have clearance to investigate further. Firstline is under a strict oath of silence— DOTS wants to conclude investigations before causing hysteria.
>
> **LETTER FROM GRYFFIN DARRO, FIELD LEADER, RIVERVIEW DIVISION, FIRSTLINE, TO HM SYLAS ARCHYR, ~~PATROL LEADER, SECONDLINE~~ JUNIOR OFFICER, FIRSTLINE, NOVEMBER 1939**

twenty-seven | viola

WEDNESDAY, NOVEMBER 24, 1939

Half the lifeblood and half again. If I die tonight, it means I would have lived until at least eighty-eight. It's ironic, how the will to live rushes in when you're told you no longer have time. It was momentary, though, because now as I follow Lorne across yet another courtyard, I am as numb as on the frosty morning I found my dead sister by the lake. The tears won't come, the scream won't leave my lungs, and my heart beats out of sheer obligation.

I know two things to be true.

First, a Mortemagi puppeteer is in fact behind the killings. It could be anyone, even the ones I cross in Hollow Tree.

Second, Sylas Archyr clouds my mind in ways that make me question myself, because even with death at my door, I cannot shake the way he looked at me at Priya's house, nor the slight flex of his fingers when he pulled me closer in front of Delaney.

Soon after Delaney dragged all of us back into the House of Death, she ordered me to clean up and start lessons with Lorne before disappearing. To my dismay, Lorne insisted on following me "to keep me safe." He hovered outside my door as I showered, and the moment I was done, he urged me to go with him to collect some magical plants for today's lesson.

As we walk across a low bridge, I marvel at the beauty of Gorhail. The sky blends three hues of orange, with no cloud shrouding its magnificence. It's a rare sight around here amid the constant rain. The sun makes me think of Nan, of how she used to have her morning tea alone in the middle of her garden, like she was savoring each ray of sunlight.

"Viola." Lorne stops a few steps ahead of me. "You seem elsewhere. Is now not a good time to begin your lessons?"

Oh, Lorne. I buried my sister two days ago and found out that I was tricked by the ghost she told me to seek. Meanwhile, her killer is still at large, my stupid relic is still a target, a terrible conspiracy is afoot among poachers, and I am nowhere close to figuring out what happened to her and will likely die before I do. Now is the perfect time to begin lessons.

I say none of that.

"Congratulations." He gives me a sheepish smile. "On your promotion to Magus," he adds when I don't reply.

His praise sits on my chest like sour milk. There's no merit behind my promotion; it's not something I earned at all. "Grand Master Parrish gave it to me out of pity," I reply honestly.

It wasn't out of pity. The ghost speaks, and I let out a quiet gasp. I thought she was gone.

"You don't know that," I mutter.

"What was that?" Lorne cants his head. Of course he can't hear her. During our car ride back, Beau told me no one other than the anchored Mortemagi could hear or see their ghost. "I . . ."

As I prepare to spin another lie, I realize how exhausting this life is, and I think of my poor sister and how she must have struggled.

"I know you resurrected Cardot," Lorne says, his eyes boring into mine.

I blink a few times, my neck warms, and the tingling at the tips of my fingers grows more intense. He can't possibly know that. He wasn't there.

"I know about Carver, too," he adds.

I stop breathing.

"How?" The word escapes my mouth, like a gavel waiting for his answer to drop.

"Parrish sent an express courier to Dean Rhodes." He shrugs. "I overheard when he delivered the message. Don't worry, I won't tell."

But what does he *want*? People like him prey on information they can use as leverage, and sooner or later, he'll want something in return for his silence.

"I told you not to trust Aspieri." He leads me down another corridor that opens to a lush garden with several rounded, white-lattice gazebos and a marble pond in the middle. I am not prepared to hear a sermon about whom I should and shouldn't trust. Beau and Sylas didn't betray me. Victor did.

Lorne doesn't seem to understand that my continued silence means that I do not want to speak to him, and he sighs. "If it were up to me, I would've awarded you the High Magus title. Resurrection magic is an ancient art that very few Mortemagi have mastered. It takes decades."

Whether or not he meant this as an accusation, it still raises the hairs on my arms. I cannot risk his knowing the truth about my anchored ghost—more because I plan to keep her around than because I care about what he thinks, and something tells me he'll run straight to Delaney and lobby to have her expelled "to keep me safe."

"Victor instructed me." It's not entirely false.

"It's still impressive." He abruptly stops at the end of the corridor, turns around, and places his hands on my shoulders. I flinch.

"Have dinner with me, Viola."

And there it is. The ask for keeping quiet about my resurrection spectacle. I lower my eyes to where his thumb digs into my collarbone. Wasn't he in love with my sister two seconds ago?

"I'm not hungry," I say. I haven't eaten since yesterday.

"You'll be hungry by dinner." His lips curl into a wolfish smile. One that tells me he has me cornered, and there's no one to save me. "Besides, you'll need new allies at Gorhail, the *right* allies. Those snakes led your sister to her death, then they tricked you into cleaving your life to resurrect their serpent trash."

Beau isn't serpent trash.

I back up, taking him in. His moss-green eyes that are at once familiar and foreign, his predatory lips pulled upward, and his mouth that I want to punch. One moment it's Olivia, the love of my life, now it's *your sister*. Lorne is the only snake in this story.

He takes my silence as agreement and creeps closer. At the same time, I notice something in the pond behind him. I squint to get a better view.

It's not a thing at all, but a person.

"Someone's in there," I scream, pushing past Lorne. "Call the healers."

A young woman, not much older than me, floats at the edge of the pond. Her glassy blue eyes, red with tears, stare at the sky. Gods, the healers won't be able to do anything for her.

She's dead.

I lower to my knees, and the wetness of the grass seeps through the fabric of my pants. Priya said that listening to the last words of the dead was still possible, so I lean closer to her.

Pulling up the sleeves of my sweater, I reach in the water, the cold biting at my skin, until her bloated hand is in mine.

Time stops, and her eyes flip to cloudy white irises. I am prepared for the last piece of her story. *The serpent betrayed the sister's secret, leading her to her death.*

I withdraw my hand, wiping it against my sweater. Now more than ever, I long for Olivia. She'd have solved this riddle within seconds. My eyes travel over the woman's body, looking for any claw marks, but there are none. I lean in and notice a thin, clean-cut line across her neck, but no traces of blood.

"Viola! The overseers are on their way—they're already aware of the body. I suppose Secondline didn't section off the area," Lorne exclaims from behind me, but my mind is busy patching together the riddle.

A serpent. A sister. A death. The answer hovers at the tip of my tongue, but still, I sift through a million excuses, because it cannot be true.

The dead don't lie, my anchored ghost reminds me.

At the same time, footsteps hurry behind me. I rise to my feet and turn to see Rhodes, Overseer Delaney, and the overseer of House of Arcane emerge from the corridor. They don't seem alarmed at all; in fact, they're gesturing to the sun and the surroundings.

My anger coils at my fists. A young woman was killed, and they left her dead body to lie in the water for hours, for all I know. I hate this godforsaken place and the cruelty that lives within. Not far behind the overseers and Rhodes, Sylas walks besides Overseer Paltro, his eyes locked on to mine. Pressure builds in my chest until my heart begins to ache and my throat begins to close.

The serpent betrayed the sister's secret, leading her to her death.

Beware the serpent with one green eye. My sister's last words barrel into my head. She was telling me not to trust Sylas. And like a fool, I fell for his ruse.

> Alyria Parrish, Gorhail's Deathbringer, youngest
> Firstline chief in history, MISSING since early January.
> She was last seen patrolling Gorhail Woods. DOTS offers
> half a million gold coins upon her safe return.
>
> **THE DAILY MAGE, ISSUE 1917.34**

twenty-eight | sylas

WEDNESDAY, NOVEMBER 24, 1939

Paltro leads me to the Penbryn Gardens behind the House of Arcane. Nel Penbryn, one of the four founders of the House of Arcane, designed these gardens as a sanctuary for the winged insects of Gorhail Woods. Six gazebos enclose a marble fountain in the center, and each gazebo acts as a trellis to multiple bright varieties of flowers. On the rare occasions when it doesn't rain, colorful wildflies flap their thin wings, buzzing from flower to flower until they stop at one of the brass bird feeders. But today, the wildflies fly in circles far above the fountain.

"This is your first assignment on Firstline," Paltro commands as we approach Rhodes, the overseers of the Houses of Arcane and Death, Lorne... and Viola.

What is she doing here, and why is she looking at me with murder in her eyes? I don't have time to mull over the answer because everyone steps aside the moment we reach the fountain.

My knuckle flies between my teeth at the sight in front of me.

Fable Rowan's body floats in a pond of rust-brown water, her once yellow hair splayed around her head like a peacock's tail. Her razor-sharp eyes stare vacantly at the clouds above. It's a sorry sight. I don't *like* that she's dead, but I also don't care for Fable.

"Must we stay longer?" Lorne stifles a gag. He looks like he's about to spill the contents of his stomach on the ground. In his defense, it reeks of stale blood and the sourness of death.

Around Fable's neck is a clean cut across the throat. Nothing like—my eyes lower to her breastbone, where her Arkani dustmaker relic, an ornate silver pen, used to sit.

Now it's gone.

This is the third heirloom relic taken—fourth, if we count Olivia's fake one, the killer's only mistake. I remember Mara's comment at Dearly Departed, about how they were looking for more relics. How many more?

Different rituals have different requirements. And so far, they have one Aspieri relic, two Arkani relics, and we know they need Viola's Mortemagi relic. We need *The Founder's Book of Relics* now more than ever. I turn to Paltro to discuss my theory, but the slight flare of his eyes shuts my mouth.

"Why the hurry now, Magister Lawton?" Delaney asks. "Instead of running to us, you should have seen to it that this area was blocked off."

"Of course, Overseer." Lorne lowers his head. "But I was in the middle of a lesson with Magus Corvi when we happened upon the scene."

Lorne is teaching her? My left shoe would do a better job at teaching her death magic. Lorne knows nothing but a few party tricks. The only reason he's even a Magister is because he follows Delaney around like a wandering ghost. He is diligent, I'll give him that, but he folds so quickly in the face of any danger.

As I watch him step closer to Viola, my fists clench. Suspicious or not, I don't *want* him around my bonded mage, and Haal, she's been avoiding my gaze since I arrived.

"Overseer Paltro—" Delaney adjusts her glasses.

"High Magus Archyr, please begin your scene report," Paltro interrupts her. He gives me a nervous glance. So much for having faith in me. Then he turns his back to me, addressing Rhodes and the two overseers.

Lorne pulls Viola aside, and my legs jerk forward, but Raiku gently tightens around my wrist, reminding me that I shouldn't cause a scene that could get me thrown out of this investigation.

Pulling out a notepad and a pen from my jacket, I begin to draw the scene and scribble some words in between stolen glances. I need to make sure Lorne isn't encroaching on Viola's space.

"Should we send the students home?" Paltro asks quietly, drawing my attention to his conversation. I stop scribbling. Sending students home is the most divisive topic at Gorhail. The institute will never concede to not being able to offer the protection they promised at enrollment. They'd rather allow more students to die than admit failure.

"Overseer Paltro," Rhodes says. "We don't know that these murders are connected." The dean's thin lips lift ever so slightly, and her face flushes with a faint tinge of red. "This one happened within our walls, but the other ones were unfortunate poacher incidents—you've read the DOTS reports."

Paltro's eyebrows shoot up. "Dean Rhodes, pardon me, but it is too big a coincidence to have four student deaths so close together and not become suspicious. Have we considered that the murders could be a distraction from something else?" he tries. "Something... bigger."

"He has a point, Matilda," Delaney agrees. "It seems like we're dealing with a serial murderer. Missing relics, two young men killed by Mortemagi poachers, and two young women killed in a near-identical way." I never thought I would ever agree with Delaney, but here we are. She's making more sense than Rhodes.

"Are you saying that I'm failing to run my institution?" Rhodes smiles without her eyes, and Delaney pinches her lips together. "On that, classes should still resume today. It's high time we return to some normalcy within these walls, lest you and Rodric continue to fabricate more murder mysteries."

Both Paltro and Delaney try to argue, but I drown them out. "Vi—Magus Corvi," I call out. "May I have your witness account to report to Firstline?" I hate that my initial act as a Firstline officer is to misuse my rights to speak to her.

Lorne grabs her elbow, and Raiku hisses, nearly falling from my hand.

Delaney rolls her eyes and beckons Viola forward. At first, she doesn't move, but then Delaney huffs out, "Magus Corvi, for the love of Death, we don't have all day."

Viola still doesn't look at me as she drags her feet toward me, and a strange feeling stirs in my gut. I couldn't possibly have done anything to upset her; this is the first time I'm seeing her since we came back from Priya's house. Could she be sad that I'm leaving for Firstline?

Delaney clears her throat, and I look past Viola. "Magister Lawton will also be happy to give his account after Magus Corvi." Delaney pats Lorne on the back. He puffs out his chest like a peacock, reeking of self-importance. I don't intend to hear him out.

Viola follows me away from the crowd toward one of the gazebos, her fists balled at her sides. This can't be about me. Did Lorne do something to upset her? I tuck the notepad and pen back in my jacket and pull out the honeyfig bread.

"Are you—" I'm about to ask her if she's all right when she interrupts me.

"When did you find out that Olivia was a nonmagi?" The coldness of her voice takes me by surprise; it cracks through the wall I've built between us.

My eyes trail over to the pond, and I sigh.

Fable Rowan was a pain when she was alive. In death, she is worse. Using her last words to ruin my life is something only she would do. It wasn't even about her secret affair with Lorne; it was always about her blaming Dad for her mother's death.

"Viola—" I hold my breath, knowing the second the wall breaks, every carefully placed brick around my heart will break, too.

"Answer me." Her voice nooses around my neck; it's chilling and terrifyingly calm. Her eyebrows twitch, her lips quiver, and she searches my face for an answer I don't want to give.

"The night she died," I say, certain it will pull the noose.

I look her straight in the eyes. If this is the last time, I want to memorize every shade of brown, every flicker of red in her irises. I have never regretted trading a secret as much as I am right now, as I watch her complete the puzzle. Every piece she stitches chips away at her heart. And I can only watch as it shatters, alongside mine.

"You—" She chokes on her words, her eyes filled with sadness.

I want to close the distance between us. I want to hold her and wipe away her tears.

"You are the reason Ole left Gorhail that night." Her face tilts up, daring me to contradict her.

I want more than anything to tell her that none of it is true, that I did it out of despair to try to save my brother. The longer my silence lasts, the more her eyes well with sorrow. She thinks I'm responsible for her sister's death.

"I told Sierra she was a nonmagi." I reach for her, trying to explain, then stop halfway, letting her decide if she wants me to hold her. She looks down at my hand and shakes her head.

The tears are free-flowing now, down her cheeks, down her neck. She is breaking in front of me, because of me, and I cannot put her pieces back together. I suck in my cheeks and look up at the sky. Haal, I don't know how to fix this.

"It wasn't your truth to share," she breathes out, shaking her head. "I—I can't believe I trusted you. I can't believe I . . ." She frowns, tears still trickling down her cheeks. She looks down at my hands, then back up at me, sucking in her lower lip.

"Vi—" I press my hands into the honeyfig bread I got for her this morning.

The look in her eyes is worse than the first time I met her, when she actually thought I was a murderer. Now she looks at me with pain and contempt. She backs away, her voice breaking. "I hope you rot in the Underworld."

Lorne notices her moving away from me then and hastens his pace. Fantastic. He's just what we need.

"Viola, what happened?" He pulls her even farther away from me, and Raiku hisses. Lorne's eyes drop to my aspier, and he scoffs.

"We're late for our lessons," Viola replies without looking at me. She forces a smile, then beckons Lorne along. "Let's go."

> Resurrection is a complex ritual that requires a personal sacrifice from the Mortemagi. When his human lover died, Damas, the God of Luck and Treachery, begged the God of Death for a favor. In exchange for half of Damas's soul, Death brought her back as the first Mortemagi.
>
> **ISOBEL CORVI**, *DEATH MAGIC, OR A LIFE OF SERVITUDE*, **CHAPTER 2**

twenty-nine | viola

SATURDAY, NOVEMBER 27, 1939

My mood is as dark as the angry clouds outside. They remind me of Sylas's eyes, even when I should forget he exists.

I fiddle with my now-cold honeyfig bread, my ears reaching for any news of Firstline. It's been three days since Sylas left for Riverview, and I've seen neither Lyria nor Beau. We share one botany class at the House of Death, and they've skipped all three sessions.

Are they avoiding me because of Sylas? Then again, why should I care? What happens with them does not concern me anymore. Now that I am not safe anywhere, I might as well use my time at Gorhail to find more clues about the murderer.

"May I sit?" Sierra, the girl with golden-brown hair who bumped into me on my first day at Gorhail, approaches with a plate.

"It's a big table," I reply, looking down the length of the table that takes up the majority of the dining hall.

That was not very kind, says the ghost. She chooses the most random times to speak, surprisingly never when I'm by myself. I wonder if she fears that I will take up Priya's request of expelling her, which would be pointless. Why would I damn a ghost to wander around aimlessly when I don't have long to live anyway?

I don't mean to be rude, but I want to be alone. Breakfast is the only breathing time I have before Lorne takes up every second I'm not in class with his extra lessons. We only started three days ago, and I now know the full history of death magic, starting with the first Mortemagi.

"I owe you an apology." She slides her plate opposite where I sit. "I didn't know Olivia had a sister."

This stings. Hearing it over and over doesn't ease the hurt that Olivia erased me from her life. She didn't have to tell them our secret, but why did she not mention she had a sister at all? Was she ashamed of me?

"Oh." The word, feeble and raw, escapes my lips.

"Olivia was my best friend." She swirls a spoon in her steaming cup of tea, then gives me the smallest smile. I know who she is. I've heard all about her. Olivia used to tell me how Sierra would break curfew to help her study when they were at the academy.

"I'm sorry about Fable." It's the only thing I think to reply; I don't have any particular feelings toward her, not when she was the reason my sister walked to her death that fateful night. Still, Olivia told me they were all friends, and it's never easy losing friends.

Fable's death is an ominous indicator that danger is now within the walls of Gorhail, no matter how much Rhodes tries to deny it. And no matter how much I try to push back the thought, I *know* I could be next at any moment. Yet here we are, carrying on with lessons as usual, throwing nervous glances and smiles when we cross one another in the halls.

"Don't you think it's suspicious? Their deaths..." she trails off, looking both ways, as if she's afraid of someone overhearing.

"I do, but no one else seems concerned." I push my plate away.

"My mother used to say Gorhail only cares about producing Firstline officers, and DOTS measures their aptitude in how many poachers they kill." She sighs. "When my mother died, I told them I wanted an investigation. She was young, healthy... it didn't make sense. They denied me, of course, saying her heart gave out."

"I'm sorry about your mother." This feels too personal a conversation to have with someone I just met. But my sister cherished Sierra, so I listen in silence as she tells me how Firstline pauses any investigation that paints

DOTS in a bad light. After a short while, I ask, "Were you with Olivia on her last day?"

"I was." Sierra's eyes water, and I hate myself for asking. "Fable overheard when I told Olivia I knew her secret and wanted to help. They fought, and in a fit of rage, Fable spilled everything about how she was seeing Lorne behind Olivia's back. Olivia stormed out, and Fable followed her."

I clutch my neck.

"The next day, she was dead." She bites her lips, blinking a few times. "The irony is Fable had lied. She was enamored with Lorne, but he was only meeting her to buy dust recipes."

Nothing she can say about Lorne will redeem him to me. I sigh, thinking about how no one believed Victor. He didn't lie. Fable *was* the reason Olivia ran away to her death. And no one told Fable Olivia's secret. She overheard, and she still chose to threaten her; Sylas never said anything. Sure, he shared something he shouldn't have, even if I know in my heart that Sierra would never have used it against Olivia. But Fable did, and because of her, Olivia died that night.

"Thank you for telling me," I tell her sincerely. "Did you . . . did you notice anything odd about my sister in the days leading to her death?"

"No," she answers immediately before frantically looking both ways. What is she afraid of? "Find Victor Carver," she whispers. "He's been around her since she joined the academy. In the weeks leading to her death, they were meeting several times a week, and Olivia was always flustered after those meetings."

This doesn't help me. Victor is in prison, and he tricked me. But if he's hiding Olivia's secrets, I need to know. Visiting prison seems like an unsurmountable obstacle, with curfew and Lorne suffocating me with his presence. "How would I—"

"Beau will know where to get passes," she says. "Lyria told me about what you did for him and Victor, and after all you've given up, he can't refuse."

"I appreciate it."

"Let's have tea together one day," Sierra offers, her eyes crinkling when she smiles at me. For a heartbeat, I let myself believe that her kindness is true. But I know that all she sees when she looks at me is Olivia, and I will never fill her shoes.

"Should we reschedule?" Lorne pulls his hand away from the blackboard. We've been holed up in his office for hours now—it's so cramped there's barely any space to think. I sit at the only desk in the middle, facing the board. The rest of the walls are covered in bookcases filled with books about death magic. I shift my focus to what he's writing, and he's in the middle of drawing a dead bird. Gross.

"You are a fast learner, Viola, but it doesn't mean you don't have to pay attention," he says. He's teaching me so many of the theories I've already studied from Nan's books, and I wish he'd focus on showing me how to use my magic instead. Knowledge is great until monsters like Mara try to murder you. Instead, Lorne seems to think that we can bore the undead with facts.

My eyes drift to the single window overlooking Death Spire. From here, I see the top so clearly, the intricate metalwork of the railing and the lone bench.

I think of the ghost I anchored to. Did she jump? Was she pushed? Did Gorhail try to pin the blame on her, the victim, as they did with Olivia?

"Viola," Lorne snaps.

I jump. "Yes?"

"Why are you looking out the window?" he asks. "Death Spire is a bad omen. You already have one foot in the Underworld. Do you want to expedite your death?"

I glower at him. He's getting far too comfortable. "Do you think I want to die?"

The hard lines of his face soften into sympathy as he takes the seat next to mine. He glances at the door, then lowers his voice. "No, and I don't want you to die either." Then he turns a golden key into the third desk drawer, and, from a small hidden compartment, he pulls an old cloth-bound book with a muted blue raven embroidered on the front.

"What is this?"

His eyes meet mine, and I curse myself for thinking of how different they are from Sylas's eyes. Not only in color, but in the way they perceive me. Lorne looks at me like I'm an opportunity; Sylas looks at me like . . . I shouldn't be thinking about him.

"What if I told you, I could give you your years back . . ." He trails off, hesitant, waiting for any reaction from me.

"That's impossible," I say. Since I came back from Priya's house, I've scoured countless books from the library. They all said the same thing—resurrection is irreversible.

He smirks, and my skin tingles with fear. He doesn't have to say it. Of course, none of the books in the library would hold any information. He's talking about the blood arts—of magic so ancient and so morbid I refuse to even think about it. *This* is what should be a bad omen, not glancing at Death Spire.

"Today's lesson is about lifedrain." He flips the book open to a page with a dead bird, the same one he drew on the board. "Just like the blood arts drain lifeblood from the Mortemagi, they can also give it back through lifedrain."

I look at him in horror. Nothing about this sounds good, especially when a bird's lifeless body stares at me from his book. The drawing is so graphic, I can see the guts spilling out of its open stomach.

Lorne creeps closer to me, his long fingers reaching for my face, brushing my hair behind my ear. "I see potential in you, Viola. It would be a waste... to lose you." His voice is soft, enticing; it wraps around me like the tendrils of death.

Something tells me he doesn't speak of my potential as a student. "How?" I gulp, leaning into his darkness. As much as I despise Lorne, I don't want to die. At least not before I've solved my sister's murder.

"You see this bird?" He pulls away from me and taps on the book, then moves to the board. He sketches a bleeding human heart next to the existing bird. Then another bird. It reminds me of Lyria's research and the diagrams in Founder's Room, except she wasn't killing anything to heal Mortemagi. Here, Lorne's suggesting carving out hearts to take lifeblood back.

"The bird was how Rafael Grimm, the father of death magic, discovered lifedrain. He had a pet raven who died prematurely. At her funeral, he took the heart of a living raven and wove its threads into his dead raven. She went on to live longer than him."

He pauses, a shy smile on his lips. He speaks of Rafael Grimm so fondly, as one would a paternal figure. It's such a stark contrast to how alarmed everyone else seems to be about a second one coming around. I want to ask, but an odd feeling deep within tells me to stay quiet.

He must notice the questioning look on my face, because he continues, "Rafael Grimm was unfortunately terribly misguided." He shakes his head.

"He did unspeakable things in the name of magic, things that should never be forgiven nor forgotten. That being said, we can acknowledge his greatness as a scholar while condemning his actions."

My shoulders drop. For a moment, I thought he may have been one of his followers. "Of course," I reply. "Tell me more about lifedrain..."

"An animal can only give life back to another of the same kind," he explains with a nod. "When Mortemagi take a mage's heart, they absorb their remaining lifeblood—"

I gasp, questioning my hearing. Is he telling me to kill someone so I can live longer? "Lorne—"

His eyebrows lift at his name. He walks over and leans forward on my desk. I back up, terrified of the hunger in his eyes. "Not all lives are equal, Viola. I see raw power within you. With the right guidance, you could alter the fate of all Mortemagi in this world."

Suddenly, the room feels suffocating. The closer he gets, the more I feel like the walls are closing in on me. "No," I blurt out. "No. I refuse to kill anyone."

"I refuse to let you die and waste centuries of cultivated magic." He slams his hands on the desk, and I jump. My heart races, and I stare at him in disbelief. Why is everyone so obsessed with my magic?

"Poachers are murdering people senselessly. No one will miss their hearts, I assure you," he adds with the same fervor.

I stand, pressing my hands to my sides to hide that they're shaking. I need to leave.

"The choice isn't yours. It's mine," I say. Sylas's face flashes across my mind, but I shove it away.

"I'm sorry," he says. "I don't know what it is about you." He says something else under his breath, but I linger on his frustration. Why is he so concerned about whether I live or die? Maybe if he had shown Olivia the same concern, she wouldn't be gone.

Only a desk separates us. His eyes lower to mine, and I want to crawl out of my skin. "Viola, there's something I have to tell—"

He doesn't finish his sentence because there's a knock on the door. "What?" he barks.

The door opens, and Rhodes walks in, a smile on her face. The moment her eyes land on us and the board, her smile drops, and she glares at Lorne. I jerk away from the desk, nearly tripping over my chair.

"Magister Lawton is in the middle of a lifedrain lesson?" asks a familiar voice. My limbs relax, pure relief washing over me. I've never been happier to hear a voice in my life.

Lyria peeks into the room, winking at me. Behind her, Beau gives Lorne a blank stare. "I hope we're not too late to join." His smile doesn't reach his eyes.

"Dean Rhodes," Lorne stutters. "I believe it will be distracting for Viola to have a mage as talented as Grand Magus Archyr in the same class." He completely ignores Beau.

Dean Rhodes glares at him as if he were a disobedient child. "Their relic lifedrain research could change the fate of Firstline officers. I thought you'd be an excellent pairing, given your . . . natural interest." She gestures to the board, and Lorne's cheeks turn red.

"Let us hope this partnership completes Lilyana Ronin's Lifedrain Theory. It would serve us well to have something positive to show to DOTS," Rhodes tells Lyria and Beau before leaving.

Something tells me she doesn't care about the fate of Firstline officers, and she's hoping they make a breakthrough so no one questions her leadership.

"Lorne," Beau drawls. "I am so excited to learn from you."

"It's Magister Lawton." Lorne's upper lip twitches. "Don't get too comfortable, Beau."

"It's High Magus Archyr." Beau's jest is gone. He squares his shoulders, his lips drawn into a line. It reminds me of his brother, and the guilt that's been circling me since I spoke with Sierra finally chokes me.

"Lesson's over." Lorne snatches his book from the desk, burying it under his coat. He gives me a cold glance. "Self-study for the rest of the semester. You may find me in my office, should you need assistance."

Before he leaves, he turns to Lyria. "Overseer Delaney shared your most recent report with me, and the two equations weaving a healing aspier's venom into a cuff look very promising. With your help, Grand Magus Archyr, we may very well be at a turning point for Mortemagi."

Lyria's eyes light up, and she smiles at him. "Thank you, Magister."

"Lorne," he corrects her. "Feel free to drop by my office anytime to discuss."

With that, he leaves.

"Are you all right?" Lyria hugs me the moment the door closes. "I'm so sorry we didn't come sooner. Sylas told us to look out for you and not leave you alone with Lorne, but Paltro grounded Beau and stripped him of rank, and I had to make a million excuses about needing him to complete Mom's research so we could be assigned to the House of Death."

I nod, holding back tears. They are here for me. None of it was a facade; somewhere along the way, the lines blurred, and we did become friends.

WEDNESDAY, DECEMBER 1, 1939

The next four days are marked with two unsuccessful attempts in which I tried to seal my magic. The first had Overseer Delaney referring me to the institute's counselor, and the second had Dean Rhodes shutting her door in my face.

They don't seem to understand. If the murderer is indeed collecting relics for a ritual, sealing my magic solves a problem: no magic, no relic, no ritual.

Lyria thinks I'm losing my mind and we should focus on finding any hidden clues that we may have missed. Of course, there's nothing.

Ever since they rescued me from Lorne's lifedrain lesson, Lyria and Beau have been spending the majority of their time with me. When we're not in class, we scour books that Lyria gets from the library to research rituals. Beau has taken to randomly quizzing me on the history and rules of death magic, and surprisingly, between Olivia's homework and Nan's books, I've found I'm excellent at theory.

I wish things were going as smoothly with Lyria. It took me one whole day to learn to grip a fake dagger properly. Apparently, I have no proper fighting stance, and she says I flail like a fish out of the water when I'm under attack. She fails to consider that I've never had to worry about being murdered before.

Some nights after curfew, we slip into the Poisoned Stairwell, far enough to where I should hear the ghosts, but nothing happens. I think the anchored ghost keeps them away, but she's been silent since that exchange with Sierra in Hollow Tree.

In the mornings, I arrive early in Hollow Tree to grab the newest edition of *The Daily Mage* and read it while eating my breakfast. News of the murders are crumbs across the pages, with one tiny headline about Fable's death titled: "Are We Back to the Age of Grimm?"

Firstline takes up most of the front page and the five that follow. Somehow *The Daily Mage* feels the need to report that the Holm Division is getting a brand-new office in the South, and that the Premier Intelligence Division still holds the record for poacher kills. Sierra wasn't kidding; they do have a poacher kill count in the margins next to the Firstline unit names. So far, the Deathbringer holds the record of highest number of poachers killed in a week.

Poachers are terrible, but how can Firstline celebrate death as if it were a game? It makes sense why the Gorhail murders hold so little importance. To mages, death is part of their lives.

In the brief moments I forget that Sylas has the Imortalis, I catch myself wondering if he's hurt. Every passing day digs a bigger hole in my heart. Our last exchange was a burst of anger I wish I could erase.

Sitting on the ledge of the small window in my room, I run my hand over the shimmering glass. The faint glimmer of the setting sun caresses my fingers. I hope Sylas is making progress on the Grimm task force, because Beau, Lyria, and I have been sitting on the same information for a week now. Three dead relics, not including mine, one missing cuff, one missing book, and, more importantly, a bizarre sense of normalcy, as if the whole institute is under a trance.

My eyes land on the writing desk, now full of books, notebooks, and more homework than I had when I was at the nonmagi university. Homework makes me think of my sister, and my chest tightens... Gods, Olivia. What secrets were you keeping? Why couldn't you leave me a single clue? Or maybe she did, and I'm too blind to see it. We have yet to find the person who was paying Victor to help Olivia lie.

I unclasp my cuff, studying the delicate engraving. My mind flips through every book I've read from Nan's library. I wish she were still here to guide me through everything—and suddenly I realize that maybe she is. Maybe the answer lies in her library, in the old crate of books I haven't yet gone through.

I have to go to Albion.

There's a knock on the door, followed by hushed voices and two shushes. "Lorne refuses to elaborate about the blood arts at Gorhail," I overhear Lyria. "He knows so much, it's fascinating."

"Have you considered that it could be because they are forbidden?" Beau teases her.

I open the door. "I need to go to Albion," I say as I let them in.

"Why?" Lyria frowns as she walks in and takes a seat on my bed. Beau, on the other hand, greets me with a complicit smile, as his tall figure folds into the small chair by my writing desk.

"Because . . ." I pause, weighing my words. I need them to agree. "There may be books about relics in my nan's library."

Lyria's eyes light up. "Are you inviting us to the legendary Rhea Corvi's library?"

"You can borrow as many books as you want." I give her a tight nod. "And . . ." I pause, facing Beau. "I also need to speak to Victor."

He sighs, turning his attention to the mess on my desk. His mouth opens, as if to say something, but then he picks up a pen and nervously taps the back to the wood. Finally, he speaks. "Vi, that would—"

"Beau," I caution.

"Vi." He holds my gaze, and the tapping stops. We plunge into a brief silence until he breaks eye contact. "I'm not doing anything until we talk about Dearly Departed. You've been avoiding the conversation for the past four days, but it's killing *me*."

Gods, we're not doing this right now. My shoulders drop, and I lean against the dresser, crossing my arms, facing Lyria instead of him. I'm hoping she'll change the conversation, but she looks back and forth between Beau and me, and shakes her head.

"There's nothing to talk about," I murmur, sucking in my cheeks. I don't want to be reminded of my impending death. We have a murderer to find, we can't wallow on what we cannot change.

"Will you ever forgive me for taking your lifeblood?" His voice breaks, and my head snaps toward him. He looks down at the pen. I take a step forward, placing one hand on the desk and clenching the other at my side.

"Beau, look at me," I say, and he lifts his head up. "There's nothing to forgive." I stress every word.

Victor tricked me, not Beau. With how miserable Beau has been over the last few days, I know if he could trade his life for mine, he would do it in a heartbeat.

"I could have . . . I should have read more about resurrection before going along with it."

He should have. I don't react. Beau might have found out, but I don't need Lyria to know I anchored to a ghost.

"And so should I." I pause, watching him wrestle with my answer. Finally, he nods, and I smile. "Now that is settled, you can make it up to me."

His eyebrows shoot up in question, and I continue, "I need permission to leave Gorhail to go back to my house, and I need your help getting into the prison. Sierra told me Victor may have more information about Olivia's last days, and she also said you may have a way in?"

Delaney won't grant me permission to leave because she says it's too dangerous with a killer roaming about, waiting to murder me for my cuff. But I keep that detail to myself.

"I can help with the visit to Albion . . ." Lyria shifts, and the bed squeaks. "I'll request an official leave for research and say I need your help. Rhea Corvi's library is a reference; they won't deny me." She gets up and reaches over Beau, picking up today's issue of *The Daily Mage*. Then she lies back on the bed.

"Three pages of Grimm propaganda in the news today. Does *The Daily Mage* have nothing better to write about?" She frowns as she flips through the newspaper.

"Why is everyone so terrified of Grimm?" I walk over to my wardrobe, shuffling through wool sweaters, pausing at the one Sylas picked for me the night we left for the catacombs.

Beau clicks his tongue, and the chair scrapes against the wooden floor. "Grimm was the downfall of mages. He's responsible for two of our biggest problems today: purists and poachers. After his rise to power, purists argued that all crossmages would be corrupted. DOTS then passed the law that all crossmages were to seal one of their classes of magic."

Lyria hums in agreement. "Poachers were—are—his followers. They believe in his ideologies: magical freedom, free access to the blood arts regardless of the sacrifices it demands—a barbaric way of life. DOTS is right to control magic. Can you imagine the chaos that would ensue if we were free to practice lifeblood magic?"

A lot of people would certainly die. Still, with DOTS so quick to condemn people to their execution, why didn't it simply execute Grimm? "What did Grimm do that earned him his fate? Why trap him in a cuff as opposed to killing him?"

I turn around, and Beau and Lyria are looking at me like I've asked something sacrilegious. Lyria turns her head back to the newspaper, her voice lowering. "He murdered anyone who crossed him . . ."

Something tells me that wasn't the only reason. DOTS couldn't care less about murder—poachers murder mages every day, and mages do the same. As if she hears my thoughts, Lyria takes in a deep breath. "But I think . . . he was—still is—dangerous because of his influence. Poachers worshipped him, and to this day, they speak of him like a saint, if not a god."

It's been more than four hundred years, and DOTS not being able to control poachers despite its stringent rules is laughable. It's almost like they *want* poachers to exist so they can pass and maintain their nonsensical decrees.

After the usual disconcerting quietness that settles whenever Grimm is brought up, Beau says, "The founders didn't want to risk anyone being able to resurrect him." He scoffs. "Magic is always evolving, and I suppose their arrogance is catching up to them—neither the founders nor DOTS accounted for someone else to walk his path."

"Could the murders really be connected to this?" I speak my thoughts aloud. "And even if they are, why isn't Firstline doing anything about it?"

Lyria lets the newspaper drop on her face, and Beau lets out an audible groan. "Welcome to politics," they both say. Then Beau walks up to me, his eyebrows pulled in concern. I lift my head up to face him. He's an inch taller than Sylas. There I go thinking about Sylas again.

"I'll take you to Victor, but I need a favor after we're done. It's close to the prison . . ."

"Beau," Lyria exclaims, shooting upright. She seems to know what he's about to ask. "You've already been demoted once."

Beau waves her off. "After we see Victor, would you be able to come with me to the crypts in Riverview? I need to retrieve my father's aspier. Maybe your ghost . . ."

I'm not helping anyone, the ghost says, and I snort. *Besides, you'll die if I take over your body again.*

"No one asked for your help." I sigh. "You're barely there as is."

I'm resting.

"You're dead . . ." I say.

Even the dead need rest.

"Who are you . . ." Lyria's face blanches. "Viola, you anchored to a ghost? Haal, I told you—"

Damn the Gods. This is exactly what I was trying to avoid.

"Can we do this later?" Beau's side glare silences Lyria. "Paltro hasn't exactly authorized my release yet, but there's no rule against visiting my parents' vaults. I'll arrange for a prison visit, too, and we can leave as soon as that's set?"

Lyria stretches her arms. "I'll line up the Albion visit at the same time, so they aren't suspicious of Viola asking to visit Victor." Then she looks at me through her lashes. "You said I could borrow anything, right? No limits?" A smile pulls at her lips.

"No limits." I return her smile. "As long as we don't speak about my anchored ghost again. She's nice; she never talks," I jest.

I heard that.

"I know." I smile.

Do you wish for me to speak less?

"Speak as much or as little as you wish," I tell her softly, under Beau's and Lyria's confused stares. "See you both in Hollow Tree for breakfast?"

"As long as Beau doesn't sleep in again." Lyria laughs as she ushers him out of my room.

I smile, shutting the door behind them. That odd feeling of belonging creeps around me again, but this time, I let it stay, because I know Lyria and Beau aren't going anywhere.

A cool, crisp breeze caresses my cheek when I turn around. The smell of fresh linen envelops me, inviting me to my bed. Sleep doesn't take long to find me, and I dream of my sister. She is radiant in a field of tulips. Her white dress billows in the wind as she spins and spins. When her eyes meet mine, her smile falters. Red splatters across her dress, and her eyes turn bloody.

I scream, but no sound comes out.

Three loud knocks jolt me awake. It takes a second to catch my bearings. Someone raps quickly against the door. "Vi," Beau calls. Did I miss breakfast?

When I open the door, Beau wears the same haunted stare as Lyria. "Riverview Division was attacked in Gorhail Woods."

> Deathbringer believed to be dead. The Grand Master of Poison is offering a million gold coins for the safe return of Scar, the Deathbringer's aspier.
>
> *THE DAILY MAGE*, ISSUE 1939.258

thirty | sylas

WEDNESDAY, DECEMBER 1, 1939

The achingly sweet smell of roses made it a point to follow me through the three-day journey patrolling Gorhail Woods. Wren, our unit leader, has an awful habit of picking every rose she sees along our path because they are essential to some poison she uses to coat her daggers. To me, they are reminders of Viola.

"You're going to be transferred to a desk job," Gryff grunts as he stalks toward me. His white-blond hair is streaked with blood—not his, never his—and his left cheek is caked with dirt. We got into a scuffle with five poachers while responding to reports of a poacher cell in Gorhail Woods, and I was... distracted.

My first week on the Grimm task force was uneventful; Firstline has been throwing out every lead at the request of DOTS. Everyone is more afraid of propaganda than a potential copycat of the deadliest mage in history. During our downtime, Gryff and I have been digging into reports and pressing Firstline officers for information. It's been excruciatingly slow.

"Who's the girl anyway?" He throws me a rag soaked with alcohol.

"What girl?" I catch the rag, pressing it to my side, the cool sting a welcome feeling against the burning pain. Being on the field without Railesza is a nightmare; I don't die, but Haal, it hurts. I cannot wait for Beau to retrieve his aspier.

"Whoever has you moping like a lovesick bird." He stretches his arm, and Freya slithers the length of it, yawning as if she, too, is tired of my . . . moping.

"I am not moping," I retort. Viola was clear about not wanting to see me, and, by Haal's grace, so be it.

"Archyr, Darro, stop gossiping like old aunties," Wren snaps at us. She wears her hair like the Deathbringer, long and loose in the wind. How does it not bother her in the middle of fights? A poacher could easily strangle her with all that hair. "Tonight's our last night in Gorhail Woods. Then I'm splitting you up. Archyr, Riverview office for a week. Darro, up in Osneau."

I roll my eyes, and Gryff gives me a pointed look. We've only been in the same unit for a week, and now I have to sit behind a desk while he gets to enjoy all of Osneau's fine food. "Girls are distracting," he mutters.

"I'll be sure to mention that to Lyria." I grin.

"Jokes aside, you missed twelve throws in the last week." Gryff polishes his dagger with his shirt.

And I have five new cuts to show for it, including one the length of my left jaw that has yet to heal. "I've also killed as many poachers."

Poachers have been crawling the woods in search of magical animals and plants. Four days ago, they ransacked the Northern Greenhouse, leading to DOTS pulling all Secondline units from Gorhail Woods and sending us here instead.

Gryff gives me a look.

"Sorry," I add. He is right. My mind has been wandering the halls of Gorhail, wondering if Beau and Lyria are with Viola. Leaving her alone with Lorne circling her like a famished shark was out of the question. "It's the stupid bond," I mumble.

"Ah, the bond," Gryff drawls. "Everything makes sense now." By the way he's trying to hide his smile, Lyria must have told him about Viola.

Raiku stirs against my wrist. At the same time, Freya slithers to Gryff's hand, her head scanning the grounds. Around us, Firstliners straighten. Arkani get into position, manipulators with their knives and illusionists ready to weave any defense illusions we need. Mortemagi summon their undead in anticipation of any danger. Here, on the field, there is no division. Arkani, Mortemagi, Aspieri—we fight as one against poachers, whether we like it or not. Our survival depends on it.

"Do not attack," Wren says. "The illusionists are shrouding us."

Everything goes still. I can hear our breaths against the cold air, the slither of aspiers against our skin, and the single crack of a branch that lets all the demons loose.

The poachers come in threes. My eyes dart to Gryff. They are outnumbered. This should be an easy fight, so why is Wren telling us to stand down?

The poachers halt in front of us, a woman stepping forward. She stops inches from me. She cants her head, a wicked smile crawling on her bloodstained lips. Raiku tightens around my arm, and for a sliver of a second, I swear I feel Raiek move.

"Will you go down as fast as your brother?" The woman bares her teeth, and I see red. She's the one who killed Beau? My dagger unsheathes at once. Beau's killer stares straight at me, and all I want is for the knife to land between her eyes.

"Stand down, Archyr," Wren instructs quietly. "She's taunting you. She's projecting thoughts to your mind. We can't hear anything she's saying."

My wrist tightens around the hilt. It doesn't matter that they can't hear. This woman killed my brother.

"Archyr, do *not* move," Wren says, her tone measured, as if she doesn't want to disturb the poachers. "She's an Arkani Mortemagi crossmage, a reader-whisperer; look at her cuff and the key molded to it. She's fueling your rage to break the barrier."

"Unregistered crossmages are outlawed for a reason," mutters a Firstliner.

"Demoted for useless commentary," Wren clips. "Archyr, for the last time, she is toying with you. That's what they do."

"She killed my brother." I bite down.

Gryff tries to reason with me. "Beau is back now. Don't engage, Sylas. *We* aren't immortal."

He's right. They aren't immortal; we don't have Railesza; and there's only one healing Aspieri in this unit. I can't risk everyone's lives.

"What did you do when your father was begging for his life?" The poacher draws my attention back to her. "That's right, Sylas. You ran. Like a *coward*. And now you're hiding like one, too."

I don't think. I throw.

The next moments are utter chaos. Poachers swarm the unit. Wren barks out orders, but I ignore them. All I see is the woman with bloodstained lips running away into the woods. Raiku slithers from my arm. "Don't let her get away."

I stalk after her through the trees. The unit has half a decade more experience than I do on the field. They will be fine while I catch this monster who killed Dad and Beau.

Raiku stops. When I look up, the woman stands frozen in front of me, her head unnaturally bent forward. Her skin pales to gray, and in some areas, it begins to decompose, showing the ivory of her bone. And with it comes the agonizing stench of death.

No. *No.* It was a trick. How could I not see that she was a puppet?

Without second thought, I run back to my unit. Bodies drop, and what remains of our squad is swarmed by a row of skeletal creatures, oozing darkness, with the sickly sharp smell of death. The same creatures that killed Mom. The undead.

Are these undead ones our Mortemagi summoned, or are they the enemy's? I have my answer when one of them digs their claws into a Firstliner's torso. Blood pours down her body as the sharp fingers rip across her chest. I bite down on my tongue. Why aren't our Mortemagi snapping their threads? They are allowed to use the blood arts on the field for this very reason.

As I fight my way toward Gryff, Raiku bites as many poachers as he can. Some drop dead, and some are entirely unaffected. "There are too many puppets here," I yell to Gryff when I reach his side. "Why aren't the Mortemagi doing anything?"

"Because they're all dead," Gryff growls as his dagger tears through a poacher's shoulder.

I look around at the carnage, and my throat closes. So many bodies, and in the middle of the pile, right next to his Aspieri, the unit's only healing aspier snapped in half. Haal, this is barbaric.

Clutching my dagger, I'm unable to move, like the night Dad died. All this is because of me, because I didn't follow orders. Again.

"Stop standing there like a statue," Wren barks as she pushes a poacher off her. "Get their relics. Most of them have young children."

Her words wring my insides. They have children. These children will grow up alone, without one or both parents. What have I done?

Tucking my guilt away, I unclip a cuff from a dead woman perhaps a decade older than me. I don't know her name, but my hands are warm and crimson with her blood. Her abdomen is ripped, her legs bent in ways that shouldn't be possible, and she lies there, alone and lifeless. Because of me.

"Sylas." Gryff's muffled cry snaps me out of my circle of self-pity. His arms claw at the ground as he tries to pull himself toward me. Two poachers are on top of him, one slicing his arm with a knife.

"Raiku," I call out, but my aspier's already ahead of me. He loops around one of the poacher's necks until he's weak. I push him to the side, planting a dagger straight to his heart.

Gryff turns and strikes the other one, and Freya slithers to the poacher's throat, sinking her fangs in until his eyes are glassy and his breath stops. I reach for my friend's arm to pull him up, but when he stands, I notice the gash in his left leg. "Can you walk?" I ask.

He tries to take a step and stumbles. I catch him, wrapping a hand around his back. "We have to leave. You'll die without healing. Gorhail's not far from here."

"We can't leave the unit, Sylas." Gryff grunts in pain. "If we fall, we fall together."

"That's absurd, Darro." Wren grunts as she pushes a puppet off her, slicing off its head with her short blade. Her long hair is dripping with blood, and her face bears the claw marks of an undead. She looks like an avenging god with her weapon drawn. "It's not your time yet. Retreat. That's an order."

"But . . ." Gryff protests, but I pull him forward. I will drag him back to Gorhail if I have to. "I'm not letting you die."

As we move away, Wren struggles with the last poacher, a man who towers over her. He knocks the knife from her hand as Gryff stops and turns around. "Dagger," he says, but he's already slipped my dagger out of its sheath. He throws it, desperately.

But it's too late.

The poacher draws his own knife, slashing across Wren's neck to her collarbone. I nearly gag from the blood spraying everywhere. She drops her dagger, clutching her neck as her knees thump against the mud. We don't hear her scream, but the poacher lowers himself and snatches the knife relic around her neck, then takes off into the woods.

He didn't take any other relics, yet nearly all the relics in our unit were heirlooms. He came for Wren's. I have to stop this poacher; whoever he is working for is now one step closer to completing their collection. I jerk forward, forgetting that Gryff depends on me. He yowls in pain, and I move back, taking most of his weight again.

"Sorry," I say through gritted teeth, as the shadows of the trees swallow the poacher. "Sorry," I repeat, softer this time.

"Your recklessness..." Gryff sighs in pain, as we limp back to Gorhail. "You knew better. You were warned, yet you still gave in to your anger... Their blood is on your hands, Sy."

> The dead cannot be resurrected unless they were killed.
> The dead cannot be resurrected unless their body is present.
> Exceptions to the rule comprise: resurrection from entrapment.
>
> **YSENIA FARO**, *THE FOUNDER'S BOOK OF RELICS*, **CHAPTER 13**

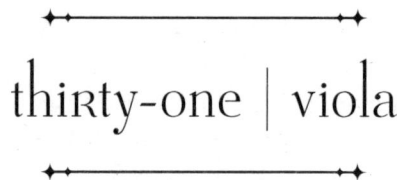

thirty-one | viola

THURSDAY, DECEMBER 2, 1939

My nails are painted with blood as I pace outside the infirmary. It took us half an hour to find which of the three Gorhail infirmaries they sent the Firstliners to, and now all we can do is wait.

My eyes fall on Azgar Fountain a few steps away from the round-roof building, where the statue of Helna Azgar winks at me with one hand holding a book and the other clutching her relic—a golden laurel leaf—behind her back. That same leaf later became part of the Arkani Coin when the four Houses merged into one in the name of unity. Maybe the Arkani were right all along—if mages weren't so busy with petty House rivalries, they could've worked together to find a solution against poachers. The Riverview Division officers wouldn't be dead or fighting for their lives right now.

For the third time, Beau touches my hand, prompting me to stop picking at my fingers. But I'm not the only one riddled with anxiety. Lyria sits on the steps, head hanging on her knees. She steals worried glances at Beau, jerks at the opening and closing of the door, and her usual optimism is gone.

I sit next to her, and she weaves her fingers through mine, her skin as cold as the morning frost. I glance down at our linked hands, and my throat knots.

I've told myself that Sylas cannot die about twenty times, yet I cannot help the pit of despair gnawing at my insides. He doesn't have Railesza anymore; he could be severely hurt. And what if they found a way to take Raiek off? My fist balls at my stomach, and I feel sick. The last time I spoke to Sylas, I told him to rot in the Underworld. Gods, if anything happens to him, I will never forgive my rotten tongue.

"We don't even know if they were part of this unit. They could be in Riverview." Beau kicks the pebbles in frustration, and Railesza hisses at him.

Boots slosh against the wet grass. I look up, and Overseer Paltro heads toward us, his face wearing a scathing look. When his eyes land on me, it's worse. "What are you doing here, Miss Corvi?"

"I..." I get up, flattening my coat. "I am..." I try again, but his threatening glare buries my tongue. Do I even have a right to be here? Sylas is *their* brother, and I've only known them for mere weeks.

"She's with us, Uncle," says Beau, while giving me a reassuring nod. "We told her to come."

The overseer doesn't spare him a glance. His eyebrows lift in question. "Miss Corvi, do you have family in Firstline?" He regards me from the bottom of his glasses, as if I am worthless. "Friends, perhaps?"

"I—" My face warms. No, I don't have family. Friends? Can I even call Sylas a friend?

"Then you have no business being here." His words are a final blow. My cheeks burn, my eyes sting, and my vision blurs from the hot tears. I begin to walk away, drowning out Beau's and Lyria's protests. The overseer is right. I don't belong here, not when I told Sylas to die the last time we spoke.

"Viola," Lyria calls out. "Wait."

"Sit down, Miss Archyr," the overseer snaps. "A Mortemagi killed your mother. It serves you well to remember that."

His harsh words seep into my heart, turning it to stone, and I sink in this poisonous reminder. Nothing will change that a Mortemagi killed their mother.

Nothing will change that I *am* a Mortemagi.

The hallway in the library is riddled with materialized ghosts. They gather in small groups, some talking about the weather and some about the poor selection of books in this century. As we walk by, my anchored ghost sighs.

"What?" I ask.

The dead complain more than the living.

"I suppose they lament the life they wish they had," I say honestly. A few translucent faces turn my way, and I hurry past them.

Materialized ghosts tend to think themselves above the rest of us normal ghosts. They forget they are dead, sometimes. And it helps not having to worry about conduits or expulsion.

"Is that something you worry about?" I ask. If she did worry about either, she must know that I would never expel her. She's the reason I was even able to bring Beau and Victor back; she is an excellent homework resource; and she feels more and more like a friend.

No. If you wanted to expel me, you would have a while ago.

I bite down a smile as I continue my walk.

Instead of going to my room to wallow about Sylas, I'm heading straight to the library, where I'm hoping the books might tell me more about heirloom relics. I didn't come to Gorhail to find friends or ... Sylas. I do not have much lifeblood left, and the killer might come after me any moment, so why would I spend my remaining time thinking about a man who probably hates me instead of focusing on uncovering the murderer?

Four hundred years, and Aspieri are still ever so pompous. The anchored ghost is probably talking about Overseer Paltro. *And they wonder why no one likes them.*

"Why are you so reclusive?" I ask the ghost as I push through the oak door of the library.

I don't like people. A pause. *When you live in solitude for so long, you get used to it.*

"Why did you anchor to me then?"

No answer.

Every step I take wraps me with the smell of old books. Rows and rows of bookshelves line the walls. In the middle are study desks, arranged next to one another, most empty. I suppose most people don't like to study at the crack of dawn—mages and nonmagi alike.

Gorhail's library is six stories tall, three times the size of our library back in Albion. When I was little, Nan used to take me there every Saturday, while Mother took Olivia to the playground. We'd always pick two books, and I'd read one to her every afternoon in her garden, and the other she'd read to me before bed at night.

"Hello," a soft, weary voice speaks.

I look around, and the welcome desk is empty. For a second, I think it's a ghost, but a chair scrapes against the wooden floor, and my eyes fall on an old lady, perhaps in her eighties. She stands, and I immediately reach forward to help her.

Laughing, she pats my hand twice. "You remind me of your mother."

"I do?" No one's ever told me that before, and I'm not sure it's a compliment, knowing my mother. But I'm not about to argue with this sweet old lady smiling at me. Did she meet Mother when she came to visit my father at Gorhail? Was she a different person then?

"I'm Zoya, the custodian of the library." She shakes my hand.

I smile, pressing my other hand over hers. Is this what Nan would've looked like today if she were still around? Would she have taken me to the library and taught me about magic? I would have loved to learn from her.

"I'm—"

"I know who you are, Viola." She gently lowers herself back into her seat. "How may I be of assistance today?"

"I am looking for books on relics."

She directs me to the third floor and makes me promise to visit often. If my life wasn't hanging by a thread, I would've honored that promise. Every day. I'd ask her to tell me about Nan when she was dean of Gorhail, for stories about Olivia from her time here, and even if she knew my father. Grief crawls around my heart again, every memory of all the people I've lost clutching it tighter.

The third floor opens to a large seating area. Empty, as expected. Zoya told me I'd find books on relics on the last three bookcases to my right, so I make my way down until I reach the very last bookcase. Built in the wall, it's narrowly stacked with books, and six shelves taller than me.

If you must know, I anchored to you because you listened to my song, the ghost finally answers.

I smile as I run my hands across the worn spines of the books. For the first time, I wonder if I made a mistake, running away from my magic. If it had been me instead of Olivia, would I have been able to defend myself?

A thick tome sits in the middle of the shelf, sandwiched between two brand-new editions of textbooks Lorne dumped in my room the other day. My hands wrap around the soft leather of the book, and I run my fingers over the gilded edges until they stop on the fabric bookmark. *Death*

Magic, or a Life of Servitude by Isobel Corvi opens on the title page, as if it wanted to be found.

Etched on the first page in beautiful cursive is a note from my ancestor. *Resurrection is a complex ritual that requires a personal sacrifice from the Mortemagi. When his human lover died, Damas, the God of Luck and Treachery, begged the God of Death for a favor. In exchange for half of Damas's soul, Death brought her back as the first Mortemagi,* the ghost reads aloud, and for a moment I forget that I cannot see her and look over my shoulder. *Pathetic story,* she adds.

"Who broke your heart?" I ask.

The state of the world.

I ignore her, letting the pages guide me to what the book wants me to know. There must be a way to connect the missing cuff and book to the heirloom relics. "You don't happen to know anything about relics, do you?"

I know a lot about relics, the ghost scoffs. I didn't mean my question as an offense.

"Why would someone collect heirloom relics?" I flip through pages and pages about the lifeblood and the cost of resurrection. Yet another reminder of my stupidity. If I had bothered to do my own research instead of hanging on to every one of Victor's false promises, I wouldn't be hanging on to life by a meager amount of lifeblood right now.

As awful as it sounds, my only consolation comes through the blotched ink in the margins, as if someone had been crying over the page. I *feel* the shattering realization of the mage through the shaky handwriting. I'm not the first mage who resurrected someone without knowing the consequences.

This book confirms that the only abilities that do not cost lifeblood are speaking to ghosts, listening to the dead's last words, and leading ghosts to the Underiver. If I so much as attempt to take over a puppet's threads like I did Mara's, I could die.

Does Gorhail no longer teach?

I roll my eyes. "I didn't . . . attend Gorhail."

Still, you're a Corvi. Yet you are nothing like your ancestor.

"I chose a life free of magic." I close the book, moving on to a different section.

The ghost laughs, then the soft timbre of her voice melts into sadness. *You never gave it a chance to begin with.*

The one time I gave it a chance, I cleaved my life in four. Don't mind me if I never want to have anything to do with it anymore. "Will you tell me about the heirlooms, or will you guilt me to my death?"

She sighs. *Heirlooms have many uses: personal collection, resurrection, entrapment, reforging. Perhaps even more uses now than when I was alive.*

Killing people for a personal collection of heirloom relics seems extreme, so does reforging. Who would reforge heirlooms from dead lines? Resurrection bears too high a cost for anyone in their right mind to sacrifice themselves. Still, I ask as I pick up another book, "What would resurrection with heirlooms entail?"

The usual Mortemagi recipe: a bloodline sacrifice, the heirloom relics, and more lifeblood than a person has. In short, it is improbable.

Improbable? I think it'd be impossible. This leaves me with entrapment, where souls are trapped into a relic so they can never become ghosts and never move on to the Underworld. "Entrapment..." As I muse aloud, the answer comes to me clear as day. It's not a copycat we should be worried about. The poachers are collecting everything to resurrect Grimm.

I slap the book shut. "What do you need to release a soul from entrapment?"

The blood that seals, and the relic.

I distinctly remember Beau saying two of the founders—Azgar and Telam—did not have any descendants, so there goes my theory. "I need your help," I finally concede. "Mages are being murdered, their heirlooms stolen. Faro's Cuff is missing, and *The Founder's Book of Relics* is also missing. How are all of these connected?"

For a moment, she goes quiet. *Are the lines being killed?* she asks.

I nod.

Dead lines, she mumbles, *tell no lies.* Then after a moment, her voice grows distant. *Killing lines is personal, Viola.*

> Tilda, perhaps consider upholding curfew. Gorhail students were at a bar in Riverview in the wee hours of the morning.
>
> **UNOFFICIAL LETTER FROM PRIYA PARRISH TO MATILDA RHODES, NOVEMBER 1939**

thirty-two | sylas

THURSDAY, DECEMBER 2, 1939

The atrocious dark green carpet leading to the library is as hideous as it was six years ago, the last time I set foot in here. Nothing about this place invites knowledge. From the black candles staggered on either side of the never-ending hallway to the wrought iron grill in front of the black double doors, it might as well be the path to the Underworld.

Gryff is recovering at the infirmary, and he refuses to speak to me. On Lyria's advice, I decided to leave him alone for a bit, but I don't blame him. As I was sitting there this morning, waiting to be treated, I learned that Wren was getting married in two weeks, and one of the dead Mortemagi had just had their first baby. Now someone's lost a wife and another a parent. All these lives stolen, because of my recklessness and blind rage. How many more will die because of me?

"Paltro is furious," Beau says, and my head whips to him. I had forgotten he was walking beside me. Railesza lifts her head in question. As much as I want to take her back, I can't until Beau gets his new aspier. "I overheard him saying you are mentally unfit for Firstline."

One moment, I am unfit for Gorhail; the next, I am unfit for Firstline. But I am somehow not unfit to wield one of the three most powerful relics. That's the problem with this administration. They only care about our magic, never us—we are only as valuable as our relics. The unit hasn't even been dead for a few hours, and they've already replaced them, while I wander around the halls of Gorhail with a slap on the wrist because Paltro likely pulled strings again. *This* is when the Grand House should push for an execution, but where is Viv Rowan with her pitchfork now? They had no problem sentencing me over murders I didn't commit, and now . . . I have to live with what I did.

"Sylas." Beau stops me, and I turn to face him. "Stop doing this," he pleads. "You're going back to your ways right after Dad died. You cannot do this to yourself . . . you cannot do this to us."

I shake my head. Beau doesn't understand what it's like to have so much blood on your hands that you're afraid your palms will never be rid of the red tinge. He doesn't understand the tightness in my chest that makes every breath a chore. He doesn't understand the guilt that sears my insides like the brand of death.

"Sy." He grips my shoulders, forcing me to meet his eyes. "Gryff told me what happened. Yes, you lost control . . . but those were whisperer-reader poachers. They could've manipulated anyone; you just happened to be the easiest to read. That's not your fault. We've lost so much . . ."

"No one else broke the line." Closing my eyes, I take a deep breath. I was under strict orders, and I broke the line out of my own free will. The poacher didn't force my legs forward. "I did," I say, and it will sit with me until the day I die.

"They spoke to no one but you," Beau says, trying again. "Gryff told us. So you don't know what anyone else would have done."

I don't reply, and we continue our walk in silence. After a brief moment, Beau breaks it. "Paltro and Rhodes were arguing outside his office." He lowers his voice. "Paltro mentioned your father's reports about Grimm, and Rhodes shut him down so fast."

"Paltro was alarmed when I told him the poachers left every other relic, except for Wren's, but Rhodes is in denial," I tell Beau. It's natural that Rhodes would dismiss anything that would ruin her image as Gorhail's most peaceful dean. So far, she's done nothing but cover up murders and dismiss any mention of a Grimm copycat. If Dad spent his last days investigating it, he must have been onto something. Maybe they could've even killed him for it.

"With Wren's relic, I am certain they are collecting one relic from each magic class. We just need to find the link between all of them," I explain. "It has to do with the families, but I don't know how they're all related."

"Victor's laurel, my aspier, Fable's pen, Wren's knife, and we know they want Vi's cuff. So what remains is a reader's key," Beau muses aloud as he pushes open the door.

The moment we walk through the doors of the library, wildberry incense wafts into my nostrils, taking me back to when Gryff and I were barely eighteen, being confined to the navy study desk in the middle of the main floor so the librarian could have eyes on us. In the far left, the wrought iron stairs we'd use to sneak to the higher floors stands frozen in time. In the back of the room, right in front of the shortest bookcase there, the broken floorboard under which we hid past exam books draws my attention. It's off center by a couple of degrees. I wonder what secrets it holds now.

We follow the light incense smoke to the custodian's desk. Zoya sits behind the newest issue of *The Daily Mage*, a steaming cup of tea in front of her.

"What tea smells so good today?" Beau reaches over to shake her hand. Zoya has been around since my parents were students at Gorhail. No one knows how old she is, but she has this sweet habit of personally welcoming every single person who walks into her library.

She presses against her desk to stand. I almost stop her, but I know how important it is for her to connect with each student.

"White peony rose, a nonmagi blend and as delicious as the name," she tells him.

Beau nods and clears his throat. "I need to access the faculty's section on the sixth floor. I no longer have the rank, but—"

"Oh, Beau, you probably know all the texts by heart anyway—off you go."

Then her wrinkled hands wrap around mine. "Your smile is as beautiful as your mother's. How can I help, Sylas?"

Her words take me by surprise. My throat thickens, and I can't answer. I squeeze her hands and blink away the tears that weaseled their way into my eyes. "I . . . I need all the books you have on relics."

"Third floor." Her eyes crinkle as she releases my hands. "Follow the signs."

Beau waits for me at the base of the stairs. "I'll pull as much history as I can on everyone who has been killed and their families. You gather as much relevant information on heirloom relics. We must find something."

"Have you seen Viola?" I ask Beau before he takes the stairs. I need to see her. To beg for forgiveness if I must, because at least she's alive to forgive. Everyone else is dead. More than anything, I *need* her, because no one else will understand the chaos threatening to rip apart my insides.

His face twists with a grimace. "She was with us this morning at the infirmary. Then Paltro told her she had no business being there."

Gods, Paltro. She gave up her own years to bring Beau back. She has every right to be anywhere she wants. And she's my . . . I shake my head. "I'll deal with it afterward."

Beau's eyebrows furrow, his face calculated. "Sy, how hard would it be to get authorization to visit a prisoner?"

I step back. I can't believe Beau is asking me to breach the rules again . . . after this morning. Even if I wanted to help, Paltro will probably rescind my Firstline appointment, so I'll have no clearance. "Why?" I ask instead of answering.

The corners of his lips pull up. "I need an audience with Victor Carver. His mother went to school with our parents, and he's the only one with access to her. That, and Viola wants to speak with him about Olivia."

I glare at my brother. Of course he had to mention Viola. Even if Paltro doesn't kick me out of Firstline, none of them will be allowed at the Riverview Prison. We'll have to leave right after curfew, forge passes, and risk Lyria and Beau being demoted further. I can't believe I'm considering his ask, but I suppose it would bring us closer to who is behind the murders. "I'll see what I can do. If we get caught—"

"We won't get caught." Beau snorts. "I'm not used to seeing this side of you."

"What side?"

"The cautious side."

I let out a dry laugh. What I don't tell him is that I'm not risking any of their lives or their ranks again; I refuse to have more blood on my hands, and especially not that of my siblings . . . and Viola.

"Go before I change my mind." Then I nod at Railesza. "Stop looking so miserable. You'll be back soon." She turns her head away from me, glancing at the third floor, as if she's telling me to leave already.

"Seriously?" I blink at her, but she coils back to sleep around Beau's arm as he heads to the sixth floor.

I climb the stairs by twos, breaking off at the third floor.

The study area is empty. Lyria always complains about how packed the library gets, that she has to ask for special authorization to study on the sixth floor. As hard as Rhodes is working to retain a semblance of normalcy within the institute, mages are afraid and mostly seem to be keeping to themselves. I follow the signs, crossing seven rows of shelves until I see the back wall, lined with shelves that are too tall for me to reach. It smells like old books and the sandalwood of Paltro's office.

A page flips, and my steps slow. A muffled voice asks a question, but no one answers. Around my wrist, Raiku's head perks. He throws me a cautious glance, and I lower my arm, letting him slither to the floor.

One second, there's no sound.

Two seconds, the book shuts.

Three seconds, he doesn't come back.

I turn right into one of the nooks, expecting to see a poacher. Or worse, the puppeteer. But Viola kneels on the ground, brushing her knuckles on Raiku's scaly head, and my aspier rubs against her hand like a house cat.

"Sylas..." she breathes as our eyes meet; my lungs empty, and my heart caves.

In her voice, I find peace.

> Priya, I am not responsible for what students choose to do in their free time. Those who have been breaking curfew have been dying, so unless you wish for me to punish ghosts, there is little I can do. There is, however, the matter of a relic collector murdering students. Parents are alarmed and requesting early leave. I'm awaiting directions from DOTS.
>
> **LETTER FROM DEAN MATILDA RHODES TO PGM PRIYA PARRISH, NOVEMBER 1939**

thirty-three | viola

THURSDAY, DECEMBER 2, 1939

I think I'm hallucinating.

Sylas is standing in front of me, a tempest raging in his eyes as he looks down at Raiku and me. I want to get up, go to him, and hold him, but I stop myself. It isn't my place. He and I, we are nothing.

"Why are you here?" I ask.

There's a slight flare in his eyes and a sudden tightness to his jaw. He leans against the wall of shelves, his arms crossed. "Same reason you're here, I suppose." His answer matches the coldness of my tone, but it's very real. He is a few steps away from me, alive, and my stupid heart picks up.

I scramble to my feet, and Raiku slithers back to him. My hands reach for a random book. I need to be holding something, need to be doing something. Anything. How do I face him after telling him to rot in the Underworld?

"Oh? And what is that?" My shaky voice is a traitor.

He chuckles. It's intoxicating.

"Viola." There's something about the way he says my name, the inflection in his tone, the silent command that compels me to pay attention. It lures a part of me that comes alive only when he's around. "Can we talk?"

My fingers drum on the spine of a book, and I turn around, my back against the shelves. He steps in front of me, and my breath hitches. It's hard to pretend he doesn't affect me, even harder to pretend there is nothing between us. His eyes drop to mine with a slight frown, and he tilts his head, his warm breath caressing my skin. I spent most of the morning shoving him out of my head, and I did not consider the possibility of seeing him again so soon. He sighs, and my cheeks flush and my throat tightens. He's too close.

"What"—I clear my throat—"what do you want?"

I shift my gaze to the three patches on the left of his Firstline uniform. One for his rank. One for his House. And two smaller ones for his healer and killer aspirers. None for the Imortalis; I suppose Raiek is glaring enough.

"To apologize," he says, his voice strained.

I lift my eyes to the smooth golden scales of Raiek, linger on the purple bruise on Sylas's bottom lip, and finally look him in the eyes again. My stomach drops. How much longer will I lie to myself?

"I'm sorry I drove Olivia away," he whispers, searching my eyes. By Death, I wish he would stop looking at me like my answer holds his fate.

"It wasn't your secret to share." My reply has no bite.

His apology should make me feel better, but it only drives the blade of guilt farther inside my heart—of course, he shouldn't have said anything to Sierra, but he didn't kill my sister. And I told him to rot in the Underworld. He doesn't need to apologize at all. I should be the one to apologize.

"I needed to be angry at someone. You didn't kill her. She . . . the cuff was already the target. I—" *I am sorry*, I want to say.

"Be angry at me. Be angry all you need." He takes my right hand, pressing it to his chest. "I needed Sierra's help. I was desperate—they were accusing Beau of killing Victor. I'm sorry, Vi. I'm so sorry."

I would've done the same in his position. "Sylas, I'm not angry." I place my other hand on his chest, studying the sharp lines of his face. A faint bruise is blooming under his left eye, and he has a new scar on his jaw. Against all the warnings in my head, I reach for his face, running my thumb along the length of his scar.

His throat bobs. My heart stops.

For a stolen moment, I am not a Mortemagi, and he isn't an Aspieri. We're just man and woman, locked in the possibilities of what could be.

In the distance, hurried steps clap the floor, breaking this fragile moment. I push away from Sylas. He frowns, but I ignore it. I think of Overseer Paltro's seething anger this morning. I shouldn't even be entertaining this. Sylas is a distraction I do not need. "The ghost told me—"

"Viola, I—"

We speak at the same time. I avert my eyes. "Go ahead."

"You first," he says.

"The ghost said heirlooms can be used for personal collection, resurrection, entrapment, and reforging," I explain.

Sylas bites his cheeks, mulling over the information. I don't stop there. I explain what she told me about resurrection and how she thinks the murders are personal because the lines are being killed. "At first, I thought poachers were collecting heirlooms to release Grimm, but it's not possible, is it? They would need the blood of all the people who sealed him."

He slides against the shelves and takes a seat on the wooden floor, watching as Raiku coils and uncoils around his wrist. "We know that Azgar and Telam didn't have any direct descendants, but have we considered that only one of them sealed him? Firstline has no lead on the copycat, and I have a hard time believing they're burying everything."

My hands fly to my mouth, thinking about what the ghost told me. This is entirely plausible, and if it is, we shouldn't be worried about a copycat at all, but Grimm himself.

"The ghost said *The blood that seals, and the relic* are needed to release him, which implies only one. Is there . . . could he . . . be back?"

He looks up at me, and a thatch of hair falls over his brow. I pull my hand closer to my chest, fighting the urge to reach for him again. "I'll scour reports, but if your ghost speaks true, then it's a possibility. What else did she say?"

I repeat what the ghost told me only moments ago, "Dead lines tell no lies. Killing lines is personal."

"Beau's looking into the link between the dead family lines on the sixth floor." He pauses, then looks away. "They . . . the poachers . . . they will come for your cuff, Viola. They have so many puppets. They are unlike anything I've ever fought against . . ."

This time, I'm the one who steps forward. I kneel in front of him, and his eyes find mine, the storm from earlier brewing anew. He sucks in his lower lip and gulps.

"Sylas," I barely manage, pressing my forehead against his. We're so close, I can smell the mint of his breath. "I'm not afraid," I tell him honestly, my voice barely a whisper. *I'm not afraid because I have you.* The words die in my throat.

"They're all dead because of me . . ." His voice is strained, his every breath cracking the invisible wall between us. Before I realize what I'm doing, my hands are around his neck and my fingers through his hair; he leans forward and buries his head into the crook of my neck. His shoulders shake against me, and I sit there quietly rubbing the back of his head. He doesn't have to say a word; the same guilt follows me around, hovering around my neck like a cleaver.

"I defied orders." He chokes up. "I . . . they were all dead. I could only save Gryff."

"Sylas," I whisper, holding him closer. It breaks something in me, knowing that he trusts me enough to take down his walls around me. "Don't do this to yourself. You don't know that things would've ended differently. We've all seen what they can do."

"It was different, Vi." He pulls away from me and leans back against the shelves, his eyes bloodshot and his ears red. He looks to the side, as if embarrassed he's sharing something so personal. "It was like they knew me; they knew my history, taunted me with personal things. I think . . . I think the puppeteer is someone we know."

We sit here for a moment, the silence charged with the unspoken understanding that something's changed between us.

Finally, I let out a heavy breath, lingering on his brooding face for a few seconds. "We're closer to solving this than we were two weeks ago." I rise to my feet, giving him my hand. He frowns at it, then tilts his head at me. "It's metaphorical, Archyr. I can't lift you up."

"Careful what you're offering, Corvi." He gets up on his own, then takes my hand. "I might not let go."

TUESDAY, DECEMBER 7, 1939

After our conversation in the library, I don't see Sylas for the next five days; his siblings tell me he went to their family house in Iserine. It turns out Paltro didn't kick him off Firstline. He was placed on bereavement leave for a week and has to see the institute's counselor three times a week for the next month. Beau has been in most of my classes, earning a few raised eyebrows from the Magisters. Between her own classes and her research, Lyria fills in anytime Beau's busy—Sylas apparently told them to be my shadow, and while I appreciate the sentiment, they shouldn't have to fit their regular lives around me.

Finally, yesterday, Rhodes walked in while we were having lunch in Hollow Tree, demanding I sign a form stating that I'm keeping my anchored ghost. Aside from being my friend, the ghost has been instrumental in our private investigation.

Since Fable's death, Firstline officers guard every courtyard of Gorhail, and one is stationed at the entrance of every House. Rhodes continues to reassure everyone during her assemblies, but deep down, we're all on the edge of a knife, waiting for the next murder. We've stopped receiving copies of *The Daily Mage* and now have to rely on hearsay to know what is going on outside of Gorhail.

Tonight, as we drive past the evenly spaced cypress trees of Riverview, I mull over Sylas's theory. That the poacher who murdered his unit in Gorhail Woods knew him.

"I shouldn't be here." Lyria clenches her counterfeit pass so tightly, I'm afraid it won't be usable by the time we reach Riverview Prison. I reach across the car's middle seat and squeeze her hand.

"Lyr, we'll be fine. Visiting Victor won't take long, and my parents' vault is near the entrance of the crypt, so it'll be quick. We'll be at Rhea Corvi's library in no time," Beau reassures her from the driver's seat.

"The last time you said we'd be fine, you died," Lyria clips, and he sighs. There's not much arguing with that.

Beau parks the car, and we get out in silence. I glance at the white square building in front of us. Sterile. That's the best word for Riverview. Albion and Gorhail have so much character compared to the boxy buildings and carefully manicured lawns in this town. Even their sidewalk is a series of perfectly cut concrete slabs.

"Sy's waiting at the entrance," Beau says, and I seek him out. He leans against the building, clad in his all-black Firstline uniform; he looks as deadly as he did the night we broke into Dearly Departed.

When he notices us, he pushes himself off and takes a few steps forward, waiting at the top of the stairs. I straighten my borrowed jacket;

Beau insisted that we all wear combat jackets in case we run into poachers, and I didn't have the heart to tell him that the jackets wouldn't matter. If we run into poachers tonight, we're dead.

"You look fine." Lyria stifles a smile as she loops her arm through mine.

The three of us cross the road and climb up the steps. Beau made us rehearse the script at least three times today: Beau is taking his sister—me—to see his boyfriend under the supervision of Sylas, whom Lyria is shadowing on duty.

Sylas glances at our locked arms and sighs. "Lyr, the officer on duty is thinking of earning his Grand Magus rank in death magic—distract him so he doesn't ask too many questions as they're visiting Victor. Our brother unfortunately has a very memorable face, and I doubt the fake passes will hold for long."

Beau winks at Sylas. "Just say I'm handsome."

"Beau," Lyria hisses, letting go of my arm and walking ahead. "Stop joking around. You're supposed to be sad."

As we watch his siblings walk in ahead of us, Sylas leans his head to the side. "Poison's red looks better on you than Death's blue."

Before I'm able to process his words, he files into the narrow door of the prison, following Lyria and Beau. I let out a shaky breath; now isn't the time to think about the meaning of his words.

The entrance opens to a rectangular room with a single raised desk in the back. Again, everything is white: the walls, the tiles, the desk. It's nauseating. The four of us step forward until we stand in front of the desk. An officer, dressed in black from head to toe, waves us over. He sticks out like a sore thumb. "Passes," he barks.

We hand them over in silence. He notices the slight shake of my hand, considers it for a moment, then his curious eyes land on me. "First time in a prison, miss?"

"Y-yes." I force a smile.

"Who are we here to see?" The man's eyes shift between my face and the pass. "A lover, perhaps?" Beside me, Sylas shifts his weight, and it takes all my might not to glower at him.

"Yes." Beau gently nudges me out of the way, inserting himself between Sylas and me. "We're here to see *my* lover. I want my sister to meet him in case he's placed on death row."

I glare at Beau. Someone whose boyfriend is on death row wouldn't wear the world's biggest smile. His face immediately drops into a solemn look.

The man grimaces, then looks at our passes again. "Weren't you the dead boy on the front page of *The Daily Mage*?"

So much for a distraction.

Beau throws his head back in laughter. "Pray tell, how would I have been able to drive a car here?"

The officer's look lingers for a second, before shifting to Sylas. "Division?"

"Riverview Division," Sylas replies. "My sister is shadowing me on orders from Paltro." He hands the officer Lyria's pass and a letter. "We're fine with waiting outside until they're finished. We have to escort them back to Gorhail."

The officer scribbles something down, then hands us the passes back. "Second door on the left, down the hallway, and another left. Prisoner is ready in a holding room; your visit was called in an hour ago."

Beau and I leave Sylas and Lyria chatting with the officer as we walk down the corridor and make our way to the holding room.

When we step in, I bite down a gasp.

Victor sits in the middle of the white room, at a lone white table, hands cuffed and feet bound. His head lifts at Beau. "Was this really necessary?"

Beau adjusts his collar but doesn't reply.

Firstline is still so cruel, my ghost comments.

I clear my throat. "Hi, Victor... er, I... I'm sorry about the restraints."

He cleaves your life in four, and you are offering sympathy. She's been a lot more vocal since our conversation in the library last Thursday, and right now, I wish she wasn't.

Victor nods, then lowers his head.

"Tell me about Olivia's last day." We don't have long, and I refuse to leave here without answers.

Victor looks up, considers me for a moment. "The last time I spoke to her was the night before I died. She mentioned she was going to leave Gorhail. Otherwise, business as usual."

My breath catches. She was trying to leave. Does that mean she was really considering coming to Osneau with me? Did the killer find out? "Who else knew?"

"Everyone. She wasn't distraught or anything. Lorne had planned a getaway for them to Wanora after her promotional exam. I think he was looking to move there for a research position at the local museum." Victor holds my gaze. He chews on his lower lip, then sighs. "I'm sorry, Viola. I really am."

Oh. Olivia wasn't going to leave for me; she was planning to leave with Lorne. Now her hesitation when I mentioned Osneau makes sense. I blink hard; I'm not crying here.

As I stand to the side, trying to quell the knot in my stomach, Beau takes the seat opposite Victor. He pulls a form from his jacket and lays it flat for Victor to see. "We think there's a link between the dead family lines and stolen relics. Most of these families went to school around the same time. The only person still alive is your—"

"Mom." Victor jerks his hands forward, but the chains hold him still. "Mom's been through enough. She doesn't even speak most days. Did anyone even tell her where I was?"

His eyes are red with anger or despair, I don't quite get a read. But my heart breaks all the same, watching him hang on to Beau's next words, and knowing that our ask will shatter him.

"Could we . . ." Beau tries, looking straight at Victor. "Could we take a reader to her?"

"No." Tears well in his eyes, and my heart drops at the agony in his voice. "You can't do that. No one's authorized to see her other than me. And . . . I haven't seen her in weeks. Please, Beau."

Beau holds Victor's gaze for a moment, then, without acknowledging him, coldly slides the form in front of him. "This is an authorization form. We'll make sure she's taken care of in case anything happens to you."

"Beau . . ." Victor pleads, slightly shaking his head. "Please don't do this."

The room begins to feel small, and I feel like an intruder. I clear my throat, and Beau glances at me, then sighs. "We don't have all night."

Victor looks at him a second longer, then nods.

"In case anything happens to me . . ." Victor mulls over Beau's words, lowering his head, tears dripping on his manacled wrists. "You've just confirmed they'll put me on death row for a crime I didn't commit. My *only* crime was misleading you, Viola, and I could beg for your forgiveness for eternity, but it wouldn't return your years."

I look down, remembering Priya charged him with the murder of a Mortemagi who doesn't exist.

In a way, he murdered you, the ghost comments. By Death, I wish she would stop.

"You don't get it. People like you and your siblings, and even you, Viola," he says through his tears. "What do you even have to worry about? The Archyrs could murder a room of people, and Paltro would erase all their charges. While I've had to fend for myself since I was a child."

Beau flinches but doesn't say a word. He cannot. Sylas was indirectly responsible for the death of a unit, and nothing happened to him.

"And you, Viola, the Corvi cuff is so valuable, they'd bend over to let you step on them."

I think of how Priya saved me from execution and how leadership at Gorhail kept quiet. Victor is right. This world is unfair, but we don't choose our blood; we can, however, choose to alter our legacy.

"I'll testify that there was no Mortemagi," I say, and Beau's head snaps toward me. "As long as you sign the form."

Your kindness is nauseating.

"Vi, you can't—" Beau protests. "I'm not letting you take the blame for the resurrection. They won't care that you barely have any years left. DOTS *will* execute you."

"Even if I were to live to a hundred, I'd only have three years left," I cut him off. "I'm as good as dead, Beau, but Victor has to live with his actions, and I think that's punishment enough."

Victor looks at me with gratitude. I wish he wouldn't; it isn't much, but I cannot stand here and watch him be put on death row because he loved his mother. We've all done desperate things for the people we love.

He scans the form, then he lifts his head at Beau. The disappointment in his eyes tugs at my heart. "I really thought you were different," he whispers. Then he pulls on the restraints, looking at Beau in question.

"Blood will suffice as an agreement."

"I'll sign." He holds Beau's stare. "On one condition . . ."

He's not in a position to make demands. I know she's only looking out for me, but Victor is so vulnerable right now that I wish she'd tuck her anger away momentarily.

Victor continues, "Tell my mother I'm away for research. And if something . . ." He inhales, regaining his composure. "If they end up executing me, don't tell her. She can't know I'm dead."

"I promise," Beau murmurs, then he draws his dagger. Ever so carefully, he pokes the tip of Victor's thumb, holding his hand a moment longer. Victor doesn't break eye contact with Beau as he presses his thumb to the authorization form.

My hands are clammy as we head to the door. Beau tucks the agreement in his jacket. Before we step out, he gives Victor one last look.

"What was that about?" I ask as we retrace our steps back to the front.

"I'm not as forgiving as you." Beau looks down. "Even if, sometimes, I wish I were."

When we come out to the front room, Lyria waits there alone. I wonder where the guard went. She sees us, and her face lights up. "He was trying to dig for old copies of *The Daily Mage* with your picture, Beau. Sylas offered to help him get out of prison duty. They're in the back room. Let's go before he's out and gets suspicious again. Sy will meet us at the cemetery."

Beau gives her a delayed nod, and she frowns. "Haal, you look frazzled. I'll drive."

Lyria drives two streets over from the prison and parks near a large lone mausoleum occupying a vast garden. Willow trees border the garden from the street. I expect to see more greenery and flowers, but the cold white stone building with a vaulted roof sits in the middle of the same unnatural manicured grass that's all over Riverview.

We step out of the car onto the wet grass. As we get closer to the structure, I pull my jacket closer; maybe it's just the drop in temperature or maybe it's my fear creeping up my spine, because I am suddenly deathly afraid of going in there. What if I'm stuck in ghost paralysis again?

I won't let you, my ghost reminds me. I nod in thanks, unable to form any words.

Beau steps in between the pillars and slides open the heavy door, and we walk in to find a large marble pedestal in the middle of the small, rectangular room. To my right and left are stairways, and toward the back of the room, two other stairways mirroring them.

"It's the registry," Lyria says as we pass the thick leatherbound book that sits on the pedestal. She takes the top right stairway and leads me down two flights that open to an endless maze of smaller marbled mausoleums.

If the burial chamber at Gorhail was extravagant, this place was forged by the Gods. It's huge, with its own path system and dustmaker-powered streetlamps. I stare in awe as I walk past the individual mausoleums lining the pathways in alphabetical order. All are marked by their House crest. It feels like we're in a small city, walking through the history of thousands of families.

Beau stops in front of a small white-and-gold mausoleum. "My parents are here," he says.

I remember Sylas told me most mages were buried in the crypts at Riverview. Beau runs his hand over the black plaque in the middle. Etched in gold is his last name: CARDOT.

He pats his coat, then turns to Lyria. "Do you have your dagger? I think I left mine back at the prison."

Lyria shakes her head. "Nyx can ..."

"What's the first rule of the field?" Sylas's voice echoes off the walls before I see his silhouette. Lyria mutters a curse under her breath. "What is it, Beau? Because you're a *regular* on the field now."

"Never step out without a dagger," Beau mumbles.

"Now, whose genius idea was it to forget all your weapons? It's after curfew. Do we think Riverview is immune to poachers?" Sylas scolds us as if we're a group of incapables. Incapable of making our own decisions, incapable of handling ourselves. The last one might hold some truth, but still, the condescension in his tone annoys me to no end.

Sylas hands Beau his dagger, then he cautiously approaches me, his eyes trailing the length of my body. "Did Victor help?"

"Nothing new." I shake my head. "We did get permission to bring a reader to his mother, but not before he aired out some frustrations about how we are privileged and never face consequences."

"Funny, coming from an Arkani." Sylas scoffs. "Our magic is our consequence. Death magic sacrifices the Mortemagi, and Aspieri are brainwashed to think that death is honorable during fights and somehow above survival. What consequences do *they* have for their magic? None. If they run out of magic, they refill it with dust, and they can make dust out of anything."

"I told him I'll testify that there was no Mortemagi," I blurt out, meeting his eyes.

"You can't do that." He echoes his brother's words.

"I only have two, maybe three more years left to live." A shiver crawls down my spine as I speak. Somehow, with Sylas in front of me, the words weigh heavier. I thought I had come to terms with dying, but the dread curling in my chest begs to differ.

"Viola..." Sylas's worried gaze stirs a low, warm feeling in my belly. I still don't know what to make of us: not quite friends, not quite more. I'm used to the cold, calculating, and volatile Sylas, not the calm, understanding, and concerned one.

"Ouch," Beau groans, drawing our attention. He hands the dagger back to Sylas and flattens his bloody palm on the crest to the right of the door. At first, it faintly lights up. Then it burns fiery red as the door opens with a high-pitched scrape.

"Wait here," Beau says. But Sylas is already following him into the darkness.

"He's not so bad, you know?" Lyria rests her head on my shoulder. "Losing Dad was tough for him." She blinks and a warm tear trickles down my arm. "He carries Dad's death as his personal failure. And now, a unit was killed, and Gryff is in recovery for weeks because of his actions..."

"What happened with your dad?" I ask. Then I realize I'm overstepping and immediately apologize. "You don't have to—"

"Sylas disobeyed orders and ran into poachers. They were outnumbered, he and Gryff. Dad let go of Raiek to save Sylas, and a poacher killed him so fast that Railesza couldn't heal him in time."

Gods. I bring my hand to my mouth, tears prickling at my eyes. I feel sorry for him, for all of us, for having to live through the loss of our parents, our family, and our friends. We were all children, robbed of our innocence too young.

"As I was saying..." She clears her throat. "He's not a bad person. You should give him a chance."

"He hates my magic," I murmur.

"Death magic killed Mom," she whispers. "But you aren't the worst of your magic. I'd argue you're the best of it."

I want to tell her that if I could scrape the magic from my veins, I would. What good has it brought me other than heartbreak and misery?

Before I can reply to her, Beau steps back out, his face beaming like the sun. Around his arm is a shiny emerald aspier.

Lyria's jaw drops. "Haal, she's even more stunning in person. No offense to you, Railesza," she calls back into the vault.

"Vi, this is Briar, my father's healing aspier," Beau introduces her.

Lyria reaches for the aspier, but Briar pulls back, cocking her head. Then, slowly, she rubs against Lyria's finger. "She's a healer like Railesza," Lyria says softly. Briar's scales are sharply woven along her slender body. Her emerald is lighter than Railesza's, and her eyes lean more yellow than green.

A moment later, Sylas joins us, brushing spiderwebs from his jacket, Railesza coiled around his left arm again. He tousles his raven-black hair, shuddering as he steps out of the crypt. "With all the money we sink into the Balish economy you'd *think* they'd clean these things."

"How many aspiers are there?" I ask.

Beau shrugs. "More than there are Aspieri, for certain. Our books say that in the beginning, Haal granted all Aspieri three aspiers. It's not until Gorhail was founded that the singular aspier became common practice. Then you have Sylas, who needs to be special."

"You ass." Sylas loops his arm around Beau's neck, ruffling his hair. Lyria pushes her way in the middle, wrapping her arms around both of them. I smile, watching them make their way through the paths, taking a different route than the stairs we came down.

My steps lag behind. The lavish decor of some of these mausoleums brings me pause; how important must the dead be for them to have a whole city in which to rest. Magic is so deeply rooted in family history—something that's forever lost to me.

As I cross over to another section, a dull, golden plaque glues me in place.

The Corvi name twinkles under the low light, our House crest above it. I look around, and my eyes fall on the statue of a raven standing on a short pillar to the right of the black marbled mausoleum. The raven's sapphire eyes burn into mine, daring me to take a step forward.

I do.

The raven blinks. Impossible. It's but a statue, guarding the bodies of the dead. My fingers caress the top of its head, running down the length of its beak, when something sharp pricks my finger, spilling blood in the small stone bowl that sits in front of it. The raven's eyes turn red, and the door scrapes open.

I hold my breath.

This could be a trap. Poachers could be waiting inside, ready to kill me and take my cuff. But my legs are ensorcelled, and the faint light coming from the inside lures me through the door.

An altar welcomes me with a single black candelabra in the middle. I run my hands along one of the three long, black candles, feeling the ridges of the melted wax. There is no dust; these candles seem to be new. My finger brushes across the altar, and it comes away with a thick layer of gray.

My suspicions ring true. Someone was here recently.

I glance over my shoulder. No one followed me in. I wonder if they even noticed my absence, but this place won't let me dwell for too long. The arched opening behind the altar invites me in, and I press my heels into the floor to mute my steps.

Several rows of vaults are laid out in the same fashion as the burial chamber. I approach one. Isobel Corvi, it reads. The next one: Percival Corvi. The next and the next are generations of Corvi I've never heard about. When I die, will I be buried here? Or will I be buried next to Olivia in Albion, even if we'll never be together in death?

I hold the thought, because the inscription on the last vault steals my breath. Rhea Visaya Corvi. Nan. I blink, and I am ten years old again, told I couldn't attend Nan's burial because only mages were allowed at mage burials. I had to say goodbye at the vigil, and Olivia was the only one allowed to watch her casket be placed into this vault.

Hesitantly, I brush the plaque with my finger. It's still bleeding, and red smears across the gold, filling in the cracks of her name. That's when I hear the quiet scrape of a boot against the marble.

My heart thumps, and I cling to the vault like Nan's ghost will crawl back from the Underworld to save me. I take comfort that if I do die, I'll die in my ancestor's resting place.

"Viola." Sylas's voice is breathy. There is no bite to it, only concern and . . . relief.

I whirl.

His eyebrows pull together as he runs his eyes all over my body, a new habit I've noticed since Dearly Departed, as if he's constantly making sure no part of me is hurt. No one's ever looked out for me like he does; no one's ever feared losing me before.

He comes closer, and the thump of his heart sets my own alight. Gods, he must have been worried if he hurried here. I lift my head to meet his eyes, swallowing hard. He's looking at me like nothing else matters, and

Gods, I want to run my hands through his soft hair. I want to hold his face and tell him to close the distance between us. And ancestors be damned, I want to kiss him.

His hand brushes my hair behind my ears, and he holds it there, cradling my head as his gaze trails from my eyes to my mouth. "Don't scare me like that again," he whispers.

The vault clicks open, startling us. He quickly lowers his hand, and I steal the briefest glance at his flushed cheeks while biting down a smile. Letting out a steadying breath, I return my attention to the vault in front of me, prying the door open with my fingers.

At first, I don't see anything, but Sylas brushes past me, Raiku perched on his hand, hissing violently. I watch helplessly as his face drains of color and his mouth falls open. Something from the vault rattled him, so much so that he's not saying anything.

Leaning in, I scan over Nan's belongings.

In the middle of her jewelry sits something I mistook for a choker countless times when I was a child rummaging through her jewelry drawer. Hidden in plain sight is a scaly, black metallic necklace.

But now I know it's not a necklace at all. It's an aspier.

> Let me tell you a story woven within the fabric of the castle.
> Two Houses at odds
> Two lovers with the Gods
> A buried tale
> A stolen veil
> A hidden snake
> A life at stake
>
> **SONGS FROM THE CATACOMBS**

thirty-four | sylas

TUESDAY, DECEMBER 7, 1939

The Deathbringer's aspier sits in the middle of Rhea Corvi's vault. Raiku is wound so tight around my wrist, my fingers are tingling. If the Deathbringer's aspier is here, it means that Dad was right, and she is dead. The real question is how did Rhea Corvi have an aspier belonging to one of the most powerful mages in the history of Draterra?

"This is Scar," I say softly, stepping next to Viola. "The Deathbringer's aspier." I would recognize Scar anywhere; she's exactly as our books described. Mesmerizing onyx imbricate scales wrap around a slender body.

As I move, Beau and Lyria join us, their steps faltering when their eyes land on Scar. Lyria's hand flies to her mouth, her eyes wide. She tugs on Beau's sleeve and gestures between Viola and me.

"Is she the Firstline officer who went missing years ago?" Viola asks, her voice empty.

"Yes," I answer. That Rhea Corvi has the Deathbringer's aspier can mean only one of two things: one, she killed the Deathbringer, which is preposterous, because Scar would've killed her before she could blink, or two, the Deathbringer willingly surrendered her aspier to her, for some inexplicable reason.

"The Deathbringer was a legend." Lyria fills in the silence. "You've seen her around. Her portrait is everywhere: by the entrance of the House of Poison, on the Chiefs of Firstline wall in the hallway next to Rhodes's office—"

"Parrish's house," I say, realizing that maybe Viola hasn't seen her portrait around Gorhail—she wouldn't have paid attention to the Chiefs of Firstline wall, and she isn't allowed in the House of Poison. "Straight black hair, brown skin, gold-brown eyes . . ." I trail off, studying Viola. My gaze shifts to Beau, then to Lyria, and we all come to the same realization. There's only one reason the Deathbringer would surrender her aspier.

The Deathbringer had a daughter.

Haal, it all makes sense now. Why she went into hiding and why she may have been killed. I don't know how I missed it. The resemblance was never to Rhea Corvi at all. She is a mirror of her mother with her nan's eyes. They have the same golden-brown skin, the same sparkle in their eyes when they smile. Haal, they have the same smile.

"Why does my nan have the Deathbringer's aspier in her vault?" Viola shakes her head. She takes a step backward, still shaking her head in disbelief, or maybe shock.

"Vi, you are—" Lyria tries, but Viola cuts her off by holding up her hand. A flash of betrayal passes over her face as she comes to the same realization that we have.

"It . . . it can't be. All this time, she knew, and she never bothered to tell me."

"No." I stop her. "Vi . . . no." I'm terrified to touch her, afraid that I might unleash an avalanche of repressed feelings. "We don't know your nan's reasons." I can't believe I'm defending Rhea Corvi. Then again, I'd probably defend poachers if it would help Viola.

Viola purses her lips and nods. When her eyes fall on Scar a second time, her breathing quickens and she staggers backward, clutching her chest. Without hesitation my hands wrap around her shoulders, and Railesza is already slithering down her forearm. Her knees buckle, and her body sags against me. I loop a hand around her waist, holding her up. "Vi?"

"I—" She gasps for air. "I— She lied to me."

I pull her into me, cradling her head against my chest as we stand there, one hand rubbing circles on the small of her back and the other stroking her hair.

"Breathe, Vi." I press my lips to her hair. Her body feels so small against mine, and I hold her as she falls apart in my arms. The world could end this precise moment, and I would spend every last of my remaining seconds putting together her broken pieces.

I don't know how long we remain like that. Lyria paces back and forth, occasionally huffing. And Beau stares at Scar, his face still in shock. Every few minutes, Railesza glances at me, and I don't know what to tell her. She's looking for something to heal, but she cannot heal heartbreak.

After a while, Viola stops crying. She gently pushes away from me, pressing her knuckles into her eyes. She returns to the open vault, her shoulders caved in. Deep down, I know that she's mourning more than this moment.

"What was her name?" Viola's chin wobbles. For a moment, I fear she's going to cry again, but she straightens up and lets out a slow exhale.

"Alyria." Lyria smiles at her namesake. "Alyria Parrish. Mom and the Deathbringer were lifelong friends. They met at the academy and were inseparable until Mom took a step back from Firstline when she was pregnant with me."

The moment my sister mentions Parrish, it occurs to me that Priya Parrish might have had her suspicions. Haal, it would explain her visceral reaction the first night I healed Viola, and how she had no trouble sacrificing Victor to save her. It's not the Corvi cuff she wanted; it has been Viola all along.

"You have the same name." Viola's gaze wanders into nothingness again. I want to erase the sorrow in the depths of her eyes, erase the pain straining her eyebrows, erase the hurt pulling down the corners of her mouth. But nothing I do will help.

Eventually, Viola's delicate fingers gingerly pick Scar up. I hold my breath, even if I already know what the outcome will be. If Scar awakens with her touch, her existence is in violation of the laws. Mortemagi-Aspieri crossmages are rare. Mainly because we usually can't stand each other, and aspiers are already notorious for rejecting secondary relics, let alone cuffs. The Mortemagi cuff draws too much magic from the aspiers for them to allow it. Even in the rare instances the aspiers allow it, Mortemagi usually don't survive long—they become drunk on sheer power, depleting their lifeblood for the blood arts.

Lyria presses her lips together. Beau frowns, tapping his foot. We all wait for Scar to do anything at all. For a moment, she doesn't, and I question if we were all wrong. But then, she uncoils into a long stretch and a yawn, exposing her sharp fangs. Haal, she wakes from a two-decade-long slumber.

When she opens her golden eyes, we know.

Her sharp face studies every one of us. It's odd, being judged by an aspier. Then her eyes settle on Raiku. He uncoils from my wrist and gives her a small bow. Only now does it make sense why Raiku was restless around Viola that first night. He must have recognized her blood, and he bit her to confirm it.

"Fascinating." Beau stares at Scar, half coiled in Viola's palm.

Fascinating? All I hear is that Viola will be dead the moment anyone finds out who she is. It's only a matter of time before DOTS's trackers pick up on Scar. I doubt DOTS will give her the option of magic sealing—they rarely do with Mortemagi crossmages, thanks to Grimm.

As if she read my mind, Scar's yellow eyes narrow at me, following my every move as I pace back and forth, trying to think of something, *anything*, to save Viola.

"She must have gone into hiding because you are a crossmage," Lyria muses as she studies Scar from a distance, her eyes lit with wonder.

"Hiding Scar will be impossible." Beau finally joins the conversation, voicing one of the thoughts racing through my head. "Everyone's looking for her."

"Maybe we don't have to hide her at all. She's been stuck in this tiny vault for so long," Viola says softly as she brushes her knuckles over Scar's head, but the aspier recoils and hisses at her cuff.

"Take off your cuff," I instruct.

Viola listens, sliding it into her jacket pocket. Only then does Scar slither along her forearm, coiling and uncoiling a few times as she finds her bearing. Finally, she lays her head in the crook between Viola's thumb and forefinger and nuzzles against her new Aspieri.

Watching her fiddle with Scar, I realize with a start that all this time, the bond I loathed so much never existed. Railesza is able to heal Viola because she is half Aspieri. And my feelings for her . . . all real.

WEDNESDAY, DECEMBER 8, 1939

Gorhail Woods used to be our favorite hiding spot growing up. When we joined Gorhail as children, Beau, Lyria, and I would often sneak into the woods on our own. We'd map out the muddy trails, become acquainted with the river flow, and feed the animals. Then we'd find the nearest clearing, and we'd sit and tell one another stories of Mom's and Beau's parents. Now, Gorhail Woods festers with the monsters that took them away from us.

"The sun will be up soon," Lyria says as we near the woods. "We don't have long, so I'm not coming in today, but Vi, I'm still going to hold you to the tour of Rhea Corvi's library." My sister glances at Viola from the driver's seat, and Viola returns her smile.

"I can go on my own," Viola whispers.

"Love the bravery, Corvi, but poachers are everywhere, and your cuff is a golden egg," I answer. She's out of her mind if she thinks I'm letting her go anywhere by herself. Poachers will kill her for her cuff, and DOTS will likely also kill her for Scar the moment they realize she's awake again. Bond or not, she's still my responsibility.

"Firstline is *everywhere* across Bale right now. Are you suggesting they're incompetent?" She lifts an eyebrow, looking at me intently, and Haal, why do her eyes keep slipping down to my mouth?

"That's exactly what I'm suggesting." Or that I don't trust anyone around her—other than my siblings. Tearing my gaze away from her, I focus on the road ahead.

Following Viola's directions, Lyria pulls up in front of a two-story house at the end of a cul-de-sac, the only one in the circle with a vaulted roof. "Be quick; we have less than an hour before we have to get back to Gorhail," my sister warns as she and Beau settle in to wait for us in the car.

Viola opens the front gate with a squeak and we walk up the steps, our boots crunching the dead leaves and slightly overgrown grass. To my left, rows and rows of dead rosebushes welcome me. Viola pauses at them and sighs. One day, when this nightmare is over, I'll take her to our home in Iserine. We have three gardens, each twice the size of this lot. I'd love to show her the flowers there.

Every corner of the front patio crawls with spiderwebs. Viola flips the switch next to the door, but the light doesn't turn on—that's the problem with nonmagi electricity; it is so inconsistent. She reaches under the torn cushion of a bench and retrieves a silver key. I hold in my surprise. Nonmagi have an interesting sense of security—anyone could get into their house with ease.

Viola unlocks the door and cracks it open. "Mother," she calls out, catching herself. "Ava—"

No one answers, probably because no one's here. After two more calls, she gives up and we step inside. This kitchen is the smallest I've ever seen, the dining table taking up most of the space. As we squeeze between the chairs and the sideboard, I make out several pictures of Olivia and none of Viola.

I follow her up two flights of stairs to the attic that houses Rhea Corvi's famed personal library. She presses on a switch, and an old chandelier lights the room softly. Piles of books sit in every corner, and old wooden crates are stacked on top of each other. Viola crosses to the far-most bookshelf. She runs a hand across the middle shelf, studying her fingers.

My eyes scan the room. Rugs are lifted, dressers uncovered, drawers half opened, and rows of shelves are missing books. "Someone's been here." Viola confirms my suspicions.

"We can't worry about that right now, look for any book on relics." She doesn't linger and, she runs through every book on the shelves, pauses to grab two letters from DOTS and tucks them into her jacket pocket, then moves on to the books on the floor. She opens a box, half closes it, before moving on to the next. She's gone through nearly every crate in the room and found nothing. Finally, she kneels next to a box bearing the embossed Gorhail logo. "These are . . . Olivia's belongings. They must have sent them back after she died."

She shuffles through the boxes, pulls out a book, holding it close to her chest, then tucks it inside her jacket pocket. When she notices me looking, she sighs. "Olivia's favorite collection of stories. Fairy tales."

I nod in silence and resume my search. I peek in one of the boxes. It's filled with all sorts of herbs and rare ingredients we use in classes. An open crate holds several textbooks we've used across our apprenticeship to Magus. Rhea Corvi didn't only hide Viola from DOTS, she gave her everything she needed to teach herself how to be a mage.

"There's a book missing," Viola grumbles as she empties the contents of Olivia's box on the floor. "Olivia came home the Monday before she died. She took a book with her, but I can't find it."

"What are you looking for?" I ask. "It'll go faster if I help."

"Ornate fabric cover, woven red, blue, and silver spine," she says.

I freeze. There's only one book in existence with a tricolor woven spine. *The Founder's Book of Relics.*

"This is not your home anymore," a voice snarls.

I whip around, Raiku on my hand. No one answered the door when we knocked, so I thought we were alone, but the woman who sat next to Viola at Olivia's funeral stands in the doorway. She pulls her frizzy braid over her shoulder, flattening her hair. When she notices Scar around Viola's forearm, her mouth twists in disgust. "I should have known you were the daughter of a who—"

"Do not—" I warn, but Viola shakes her head at me. Raiku's eyes are on Scar. She coils and uncoils around Viola's forearm, her eyes never leaving the woman's. One wrong move, and Scar will kill her.

The woman walks up to Viola, paying Scar or me no heed.

I take a step, but Viola steps between the woman and me, tucking her arm behind her back. Scar hisses in disapproval, and both Raiku and Railesza watch her carefully. This is the first time I'm afraid that an aspier won't heed their Aspieri's command. But to my surprise, Scar stays put.

"Olivia was only a couple of months old." The woman shakes her head like a madwoman. "The old crone came back with my dead husband and a bastard child. For ten years, I had to watch her raise you, love you more than she ever loved my Olivia. When she died, I wanted to throw you on the streets, but Olivia loved you so much, I let you stay . . . then she was killed because of you."

Viola's lower lip quivers, and it takes every muscle in my body to not move. I want to whisk her away, to tell her she doesn't have to suffer through the atrocities coming out of this woman's mouth, that she has a home. With us. With me.

"You can blame me all you want"—Viola holds her head high—"but I didn't kill her."

"I wish it had been you they killed," her so-called mother spews. Scar's tail lashes against Viola's arm, but she holds her in place. Raiku moves instead.

That's all I can take, and I don't want Raiku or Scar to slip and murder a nonmagi. I cross the room, my shoulder nudging Olivia's mom as I weave my fingers with Viola's, pulling her away from that vile woman. "Let's go home."

> Rodric, there is only so much pull I have within the Grand House concerning Sylas. Viv Rowan is asking for a reelection following the mismanagement of the Gorhail murders.
>
> **UNOFFICIAL LETTER FROM MAXIMUS PALTRO, GRAND MASTER OF POISON, DOTS, TO OVERSEER PALTRO, HEAD OF THE HOUSE OF POISON, GORHAIL, DECEMBER 1939**

thirty-five | viola

WEDNESDAY, DECEMBER 8, 1939

A part of me always knew my mother wasn't my mother, but the horrors she put me through don't sting any less. I am an Aspieri and a Mortemagi, daughter of a legend, granddaughter of another legend, and yet I know so little of the great magic I supposedly possess. In short, I am a waste of magic.

This morning we came back with enough time for me to drop Olivia's fairy-tale book on the study desk in Founder's Room and change into House of Death clothes before rushing to Delaney's class on ghost communication. I couldn't answer a single one of her questions, because I kept wondering whether Scar was all right—it felt cruel locking her up in Sylas's safe, but we didn't have a choice.

Now Lyria and I huddle around the low table in their living room, three empty cups of tea and two empty plates pushed to the side. Beau leans back on the sofa behind Lyria, raising the report he's reading above his face.

"If you think we are accomplished . . ." Lyria does this thing she always does when she's excited—her eyes widen, her lips break into a grin as if she's about to let you in on the biggest secret, and her legs can barely stay still. She grabs on to Beau's shirt and physically pulls him into our conversation.

His stack of paper drops onto his face, and he slides down next to his sister. "The Deathbringer was a Magus Principalis at sixteen, a Firstline chief at eighteen. She and Scar were the perfect pairing; she even has admirers among poachers. To this day, no one comes close to her."

Lyria has told me so many stories about the Deathbringer—my mother. After Delaney's class, she snuck me out to Fang's Nest to show me her portraits. In them, I saw a younger version of the woman from my dreams. I've been trying to find comfort in the fact that I knew her, even for a short time. That for me, she gave up everything—her highly decorated career, her future, and her life. Did she ask Nan to hide me because I was in danger? Because I know in my heart that the woman I've been dreaming about since I was a child would never let me go.

My eyes sting again, my vision hazy. I press my hands to my face to seize the tears. How do I stop crying over a life that was robbed from me? Nan could've told me stories of my mother. Instead, she let me believe I was hated because of a fatal flaw that made me different from Olivia. And she lied to me. I trusted her, and she lied.

"There's talk of Rhodes being dismissed," Beau says, bringing me back to the conversation. "With all the propaganda from *The Daily Mage*, mages are demanding to go home. Meanwhile, purists are fueling protests against Parrish for inaction about the Gorhail murders."

We all know it's because she's from a crossmage family, the ghost says. It's her first time speaking since the mausoleum last night. For a second, I wondered if she had forsaken me for being a crossmage.

With last night's events and now having to worry about Scar, I had briefly forgotten about the stolen relics and the potential return of Grimm.

"We now know that Olivia took *The Founder's Book of Relics* back to Gorhail the last time I saw her, but they didn't send it back with her belongings," I remind them. Sylas and I told them the moment we joined them in the car this morning, but by the time we started spinning theories, Gorhail was in front of us.

Lyria scrunches her nose. "We can assume that the person who killed her probably took the book. Did she say why she needed it?"

"Promotional exams." I sigh, wishing I'd asked more questions.

Beau drums his fingers on the table, his head lost in thought. After a moment of silence, he brings up what Sylas and I told them about Grimm. "Would the poachers need the book of relics to release Grimm from his cuff?"

Lyria and I exchange a worried glance. "I believe so," she says, but I quickly add, "None of it explains the dead lines and the stolen heirlooms." The more we talk about it, the more I wonder if the two are even connected. Maybe Olivia's taking the book was a mere coincidence, and Gorhail returned it to their library.

"Is Sylas still sleeping, Beau?" Lyria asks. "We could use him right now."

Three hours ago, Sylas walked in with a torn shirt and two new bruises. One below the right corner of his lips and a second one next to his left eye. He didn't say a word, didn't even look at us, and headed straight to Beau's room to sleep.

"I think so. Paltro came to see him when you were both at dinner, but he didn't answer." Beau glances toward his room door, then back at me. "Oh... I won't be in tonight; I may have found us a reader to take to Victor's mother in the morning, but they'll need some convincing."

"Beau, is it who I think it is?" Lyria exclaims, but he ignores her, and he's already halfway to the front door, jacket in hand.

"Anyway, Sy told you to move into his room, Vi. He's only here for a couple more days, until he goes back to Riverview."

I sigh. Because of my cuff, Sylas refuses to let me out of his sight. If not his, Beau's; and if not Beau's, Lyria's. And now that I have Scar, they all keep saying that I can't be away from her for more than a few hours. So I have unofficially moved into their rooms.

"Wait, I'll walk with you until the infirmary," Lyria calls out, rushing after her brother. "I still don't understand why you're set on torturing that poor woman. She went mad when her husband died," she says as they put on their boots by the door.

"That's the thing, sis." Beau taps her on the head. "One doesn't simply go mad when one's husband dies."

"Be back in a bit," Lyria shouts, and I wave at her.

"Good night, Vi," Beau says as he pulls the door closed behind them. "Oh, and if you see Sy, tell him Paltro wants to see him."

Sylas's room smells like mint and fire. I pause at the portrait of his family on the left wall of his bedroom, gently running my hand over the canvas. I don't see the happiness, I only glimpse the reminder that, at any moment, this world can take everything from us.

In the left corner of the room, nestled in a reading nook with three single-seat sofas, a candle flickers on a low table. Next to it is a book with a blank white cover. I pick it up and flip to the bookmarked page. Sylas was in the middle of a collection of field-leader reports from the last twenty years. Every page mentioning searches for the Deathbringer is marked, and he's been scribbling notes in the margin.

I lift my eyes to the hallway behind the seating area which links Sylas's room to Beau's through a door at the end. My legs begin to move, but I stop myself. Something clearly happened, and he wants to be alone. I hate how much I yearn for him when he's not around, how every little thing triggers a thought of him.

Glancing down at the report, I see that Sylas has been noting potential dates that the Deathbringer could've died. I turn the page, and it nicks my finger. "Bloody saints," I mutter as I set the book down and walk to the bathroom to wash away the faint trickle of blood.

But I'm not alone.

Sylas stands in front of the mirror, a towel loosely wrapped around his middle, sitting right above his hip bones. He tousles his wet hair, then rubs his hands over his face, pausing at the paling bruise on the corner of his lips. My mouth goes dry. I know I should leave right away, but my eyes linger on the flex of his back muscles and the countless white scars on his soft tawny skin. I want to kiss away every one of them.

An involuntary noise rises in my throat, and his eyes catch mine.

"Vi," he says tentatively.

"I'm so sorry." My hand reaches for the doorknob behind my back.

"Are you?" He lifts his eyebrows at me in the mirror, and I lower my head. My cheeks are burning, my body somehow shivering, and my throat flushes with a tangle of excuses that never make it out because, no, I am not sorry.

He turns away from the mirror, and my heart leaps with every slow step he takes toward me. He stops right in front of me, our bodies almost touching. My breaths are shallow, out of control, my chest rising and falling raggedly. Can he feel my heartbeat—how a single look from him makes me lose my inhibitions?

"I should have knocked." The first excuse bubbles out.

He lets out a throaty laugh that sinks into my bones. "You should have." His breath grazes the shell of my ear, and a shudder dances at the base of my neck. My lips part, but he's stolen all my words. If I could retrieve them, I'd tell him to undo me.

He leans closer, and I close my eyes. "We can't," I groan.

My stomach knots with agony. I would ruin him, like I ruined my mother. Maybe in another life, where being together wouldn't paint a red cross on our backs.

His eyes darken, kindling a fire low inside my belly. He doesn't say a word, just looks at me through his impossibly beautiful lashes, with a longing I can't ignore. In this moment I know I would break a thousand rules for him; I would go to war for him; I would follow him to the depths of the Underworld, if I must. Would he do the same for me?

"You hate my magic. You can't have one without the other," I whisper, a mild panic catching at the edge of my words. I stand in front of him, asking him to choose the magic he loathes for me.

Sylas cups my jaw with both hands, one of his thumbs lightly brushing across my lower lip, and Gods, I'm weak—my body yearns for his lips against mine, but I can't surrender to my desires. He studies my face, as if he's committing every minor detail to memory. I don't look away. I can't. I want the gray of his eyes to swallow me whole.

"I've never hated you, not for a single second, not even when your life was in my hands on that cold metal table the first time I saw you."

My foolish heart tugs. I cling to every word, because I want to believe there exists a world where we can be together. But reality is a cold plunge. He knows it, too. I don't have much lifeblood left, and Sylas will live forever. We were doomed before we could even begin.

He's lost too much. I cannot do this to him—give him another person to bury. "You're only here now because I'm half Aspieri."

A flicker of hurt crosses his eyes. "I've been here." His hands trace the length of my shoulders, leaving a trail of fire before settling at my waist. "I've been here since the first time I saw you confront Lorne in Hollow Tree, and then in the Poisoned Stairwell, and at your sister's funeral, and in the catacombs . . . I could go on, Viola."

He lowers his forehead to mine, the silence telling me everything he doesn't say. I close my eyes, breathing him in. The softness of mint and vanilla are an eternal reminder of how safe I feel with him. I press my palms against his bare chest, feeling the taut muscles under my fingers. He takes in a sharp inhale. He feels it, too. The undeniable electricity between us. But if I give in, even just this once, I could destroy him.

"We can't," I say with finality.

His burning gaze drags across my face, before he nods and gently pulls away. He needs to leave *now*, before I change my mind.

"You can have my room. If you need anything, I'll be next door." He slides past me, leaving before I can say another word.

That night, I toss and turn, haunted by Sylas's words. He has been my only constant at Gorhail, and I repaid him by doing what I've loathed all my life. I made a choice for him. How am I any better than Nan?

Shoving the covers aside, I swing my legs off the bed, not bothering with slippers. The door to Beau's room is at the end of the short hallway, behind Sylas's reading nook. I breathe out, cross the room, and walk down the hall. My heartbeat is the only sound I hear as I stand in the darkness, under the watchful eyes of their ancestors' portraits.

My insides are a mess of tucked-away feelings and agonized longing. Once I cross that door, it all becomes real. My hand hovers over the brass doorknob, and I'm torn between knocking and just walking in. Not for long, though, because I press down on the cold metal, settling the debate.

Beau's room is smaller than Sylas's. The forest-green walls lean to black in the night light. Even so, the wall of books with golden spines shimmers. I squint to get a better look of the bed.

It's empty.

I take a few steps forward, halting. Did Paltro send Sylas back out to Firstline?

"Viola." His husky voice washes me with cold relief.

I whirl, and there he is, sitting on a chaise near the small fireplace, setting down a book. He drags his gaze over my body, and I *feel* my cheeks burn. In fact, I'm certain they've caught fire.

"Nice shirt." He smirks.

I look down, remembering that I'm wearing one of his shirts as pajamas. I tug at the seams, as if that would turn the shirt into a floor-length dress, suddenly grateful for the low light so he can't see the panic on my face. "Thanks, I . . . will grab my own tomorrow."

"Can't sleep?" he asks.

I look at him, and my breath hitches. The soft glow of the fire brings out the warmth of his skin, and Gods, he is devastatingly handsome. The reflection of the flame in his gray eyes consumes me with want, and I take a step forward.

"I know you've been here all along," I say quietly. "But this"—I take another step, gesturing between him and me—"Paltro won't stand for it."

He straightens up. "What made you think I care about what Paltro thinks?"

"I might die any moment." Another step.

He lifts an eyebrow. "Does that mean you're to stop living out what remains?" The sharpness of his mouth is infuriating, so much so that I ache to seal it shut with my lips.

"You hate Mortemagi," I say, as a poor attempt to give him one last out.

He smiles on an abrupt exhale. "I don't hate you."

"Just once." I'm standing in front of him, the suppressed desire since we met pulsing beneath my skin. He tilts his head, eyes boring into mine, hungry and hopeful. I take in the painfully beautiful lines of his face, settle on the delicate curves of his lips, and the deep ache within me blooms into an insatiable need for him to touch me.

Reaching for my waist, he tugs me to him, the hunger in his eyes melting into quiet reverence. He looks at me like I am the answer to his every plea, like I am his salvation.

"Just once." His voice breaks, and I straddle his legs, settling in his lap.

My shirt lifts, and his fingers trail from my waist to my hips, pressing into my skin. His shallow breathing matches my own, hesitating yet demanding at once. It whispers *Are we really doing this* and *Please devour me* at the same time. His eyes drop to my mouth, and I bite my lower lip, raw anticipation coiling my insides.

"Viola," he moans, and I loop my hands around his neck, threading my fingers through his hair. It's so, so soft. My thumbs rub gentle circles on the back of his head and he leans forward, his nose brushing against mine. Our hearts thump in tandem, his hands firmly pressing into my thighs.

"What are you waiting for?" I groan against him, our lips almost touching.

"Your permission." He smirks, faintly brushing his lips against mine. It sends an electrifying jolt down my spine, and I arch into him. The next moment, my lips are closing on his. They are softer and warmer than I imagined. He tastes like mint and vanilla, like the first snow of Albion's winter.

Sylas kisses me like I'm the most fragile thing to exist. His lips take time to explore mine, his tongue tentatively teases mine, tangling it into a dance that unravels my core. And by Death, I would surrender to him, body and soul. He makes use of every inch of my mouth, kissing me like his life depends on it, like he's been waiting for this moment forever. Everything about him feels so right, I begin to panic.

It's not him I should have been worried about. It's the way he breathes life into my heart, the way my world begins and ends with him, the way time halts when we're together.

The moment he notices my slowed pace, he pulls away, our ragged breaths the only sound cutting through the silence. A frown settles between his eyebrows, and he drags his hands from my thighs to my waist. His eyes are all over my face, searching, questioning, making sure I want this. And I need him to know that I do, that in his arms I feel safe in a way I've never felt before.

I answer him by leaning forward and trailing kisses along his throat, up his neck, and right above the bruise in the corner of his lips. He lets out a gasp, and I take his lower lip between my teeth, tugging, teasing until he breaks. He meets me with hunger and despair this time, like if he lets go of me, I will vanish. I kiss him with the same fervor, every movement a silent demand for more. He meets my ask with more, more, and more until we're both out of breath. Still, we don't stop. I roll my hips against him, and something fierce, almost feral flashes across his eyes.

"Please," I murmur against his lips, and he claims my mouth again, his hands firmly pressing into my waist. Heat builds up in my lower belly, and I realize that there is nothing I wouldn't give him. Under his touch, I feel alive, invincible, like he knows exactly which pieces to take apart and which to put together. And it's terrifying. How my heart seems to want to beat only to the sound of his.

"Yes, but not here," he whispers, pulling away, our lips still brushing against each other's, and I let out an involuntary moan. "I will have you, Viola, but not here," he says as he moves me so I'm sitting sideways in his lap now.

I don't protest, the events of the day finally catching up to me. I settle my head in the crook of his neck, and he holds me so close, rubbing the small of my back as our hearts settle into a quiet rhythm. My eyelids feel heavy. I don't want to let go of him. "Sy," I mumble.

"Mm-hmm," he murmurs, pressing a kiss to the top of my head.

"Can I sleep here tonight?" I hold my breath. "Just tonight." I don't care what happens after this. Because this moment sealed my fate. I'm already over the cliff, whether he catches me or not.

"Sure." He smiles against my hair. "Just tonight."

"The Rise of Rafael Grimm: An Exploration of the Rise and Fall of One of the Greatest Mages Draterra Has Known"

THE DAILY MAGE, ISSUE 1939.291

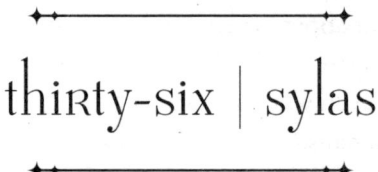

thirty-six | sylas

THURSDAY, DECEMBER 9, 1939

This morning, even though he's summoned me, I avoid Paltro like the plague. Maybe, by the time I inevitably run into him, I'll have perfected my lie.

Midday is nearly upon us, and I stare at the clock, once more wishing for time to run. Viola left for classes two hours ago with my sister, and I have half a mind to show up at the House of Death. Because now that the taste of her lips is forever seared on mine, any minute away from her feels like torture.

"Your death stares at the clock won't alter the fabric of time." Beau takes a sip of my tea, grimaces, then pushes it toward me. "This is gross. I can't believe you drink this willingly."

I sip on my tea, frowning. Nothing's wrong with it.

"What did you find?" I set my teacup down on the kitchen counter and shuffle through the papers scribbled with clues, dates, and timelines.

"I'll tell you, but first . . ." Beau leans forward, his eyes narrowing on the bruise on the side of my eye. "Where were you yesterday?"

My jaw clenches, and I debate walking away for a moment. I was hoping no one would ask about yesterday, but they'll find out eventually. I bring the cup to my lips, and nod. "DOTS requested reassessment for Firstline, because Viv Rowan filed a motion to dismiss me."

Beau's gaze clashes with mine. His face sours. "Haal, Sylas... how many?"

"Fourteen, in less than half a day." My gut wrenches when I think of DOTS's reassessment trial. They drove four other mages and me to a poacher cell on the border of Bale and Iserine and left us to fend for ourselves. Our assessment was to dismantle the cell without losing a single member of our small unit.

"Five of us against about twenty of them." I breathe out. Memories of ripped flesh and gouged eyes hurl up my stomach, memories that Viola's touch pushed away even when she wasn't aware.

"That's..." Beau pauses. "That's a lot..."

Even my brother can't bring himself to say the words. That's a lot of bodies—especially when I killed fourteen of them. Poacher or not, I am not the God of Death to take lives at the whim of DOTS. And even when later on, they told me half of those poachers were the ones responsible for the murder of my unit, I still felt deplorable. No amount of revenge brings back the dead—*I* would know this.

DOTS and Firstline thought retaliation was a way to redeem myself. Perhaps in their eyes, it was, but in mine, I had become the very enemies I hunted. In the end, how different are we from poachers if we all kill to further the dogma of the institutions we believe in?

Beau walks around the counter and throws his arms around me. "I'm sorry," he says. "Did they reassign you?"

"Premier Intelligence Division, headquarters," I reply. Being assigned to the same division as my father means nothing to me anymore. Three weeks ago, it would've been an honor; now it's just a reminder of my mistakes.

"What did you find?" I nod at the black pass with St. Fabian's logo, still hanging around his neck.

"Nothing we don't already know," he says uncomfortably.

"You went all the way to St. Fabian this morning, took a reader to our only lead, and came back with nothing." I love my brother's dedication, but I'm not in the mood for games. Viola's life—whatever is left of it—depends on how fast we work.

"I couldn't push it, Sy." He levels my gaze. "You should've seen Victor's mother. It's heartbreaking. She stares out a window all day. No reaction, no movement. The only time her eyes moved was when I told her Victor wasn't dead."

"Take another reader." I glare at him.

"I took one of the best."

"Sierra doesn't have the rank to untangle memories—"

"Grayson." Beau interrupts me, and my head snaps toward him. Grayson is Gryff's brother, and he is one of DOTS's primary readers, a memory detangler. If he couldn't read Mrs. Carver's memories, that avenue is a dead end.

"How did you get Gray—" I cut myself off, shaking my head. Beau and Grayson have had a *complicated* relationship, and I prefer to stay out of it, like I do with Lyria and Gryff. "Keep trying, please."

Beau gives me a tight smile. I'm not sure whether it's to thank me for not pushing my question or whether he's agreeing to try again with Mrs. Carver.

Sighing, I shuffle through the notes in front of me. "We know they want Viola's cuff, and I'm going to guess they're looking for a key. And from my encounter with the puppet in the woods, it's someone who knows us... or at least knows my history."

"The book..." Beau adds, and I scribble it down. "Olivia had *The Founder's Book of Relics*, but it was never returned to her house with her other belongings. It has to be someone from Gorhail."

As we throw theories back and forth, the door to the Poisoned Stairwell opens, and Lyria and Viola walk in laughing. My eyes momentarily drift to Viola as she sets her bag on the sofa. In two days, I leave for Firstline again, and that agonizing ache of being away from her knots my insides.

She looks up, smiles, and I forget the world.

"Please don't mind us." My sister inserts herself between Beau and me. I break our stare and return to the scattered pages. Viola joins me, and it takes everything in me to not pull her closer.

"You missed Beau's findings from the library the other day." Lyria taps a pen on the page. "Our parents and everyone who was killed attended the institute at the same time."

"That's hardly relevant, Lyr. Generations have walked these halls. So many other mages' parents have attended Gorhail at the same time."

"Maybe we're looking at it wrong. We still can't find a link between everyone who's died other than the fact that they were classmates." Viola plucks the page from underneath my hands, her eyebrows knotted in a frown. "The ghost did insist that we should be concerned about the lines being killed, so maybe we need to look at their deaths. What if it's something that started years ago? When did your parents die, Beau?" she asks, grabbing a pen.

"Right after my second birthday," he answers quietly. "March 1919."

"Sy and Lyr?"

"Mom was killed in December 1918." Lyria squeezes my hand.

Viola notes this down, too, then adds two more dates. "My father died at the beginning of 1919."

Lyria shifts over next to Viola. "We're getting somewhere. The Deathbringer went missing in early 1917. Could they all be connected?"

I slide off the chair, and step behind Viola, snaking my hand around her waist and leaning my chin on her shoulder. Her body melts into mine, this strange feeling of belonging twisting deep within me.

Beau and Lyria exchange a pointed look and a complicit smile, but they don't breathe a word.

"Fable's and Wren's parents break the pattern. I scoured the records, and their parents died in the last couple of years. I don't think it's related, unfortunately," I say quietly. It seems like their deaths were too spread out for there to be a connection.

Pulling away, I kiss the top of Viola's head and walk toward my room. "We have nothing, other than the likelihood of it being someone from Gorhail." The answer is within our grasp yet keeps sifting through our fingers like fine sand.

Out of nowhere, bells clang, jolting us from our conversation. There's a pause, before they clang again. Lyria rushes out the front door. She comes back moments later, a frown on her face. "Rhodes has called an emergency assembly."

Dean Rhodes stands on the balcony overlooking Hollow Tree, her usual red dress replaced by a somber black one, matching the uniforms of the faculty standing behind her. They've moved the dining tables, so we look like a colony of ants, stacked on top of one another.

Instead of being alarmed—as one should be about the first emergency assembly in over two decades—Hollow Tree is buzzing with theories about the murders. I swallow down my anger. Would they be this excitable if *their* family was targeted?

"Mages," Rhodes says, looking down at us.

The chatter only grows louder. Rhodes claps twice, but the urgent whispers from the new Magus in front of me are incessant. In reality, most of them are so young. They shouldn't have to worry about being killed in a place where they're supposed to be safe.

"Silence." The sharpness of her voice slashes through the noise. The younger mages freeze, lowering their heads in shame. Next to me, Lyria and Beau look nervous. A moment later, Viola joins us, her arms crossed, nodding at an empty space; I suppose it's her anchored ghost.

"Where were you?" I whisper without looking at her.

"Downstairs by your safe. I was checking in on Scar," she whispers, and Raiku gently hisses at her. In all the years I've had my aspier, he's never hissed at anyone *gently*. He slithers to my hand and nudges Viola's with his nose. I sigh. Even my aspiers are under her spell.

"As most of you are aware, poachers are attacking mages." She tries to sound indifferent, but her forced smile betrays the frailty of her outer nonchalance. "Per the request of DOTS, the school term is ending immediately, and all classes are canceled. A general Gorhail lockdown begins right away; you are not allowed outside of your respective Houses—should you require leaving Gorhail, please get approval from your overseers."

Gasps bounce off one another until they dwindle into an uncomfortable silence, as if they weren't just placing bets on who would be next. A couple of new Magus two rows ahead of me lock arms, fear dripping from the reassuring smiles they give each other.

"Sylas," Lyria hisses, but it's too late when I turn to her.

Lorne buzzes toward us like an angry wasp, his ridiculous cape-like coat billowing behind him. His eyes are locked on Viola, and I instinctively reach for her hand. But she doesn't take it.

"Paltro's looking straight at us from the balcony," she whispers between clenched teeth.

I want to tell her that she's wrong and kiss her in the middle of Hollow Tree without a care in the world. But she's right. I might not care about what Paltro thinks, but she's still a Mortemagi, and he won't let me hear the end of it.

She runs a hand through her loose hair; the waves cascade to just below her chest, conveniently covering the House of Poison crest on the left pocket. I should probably send Lyria to Viola's room to grab her some fresh clothes. Still, I fight back a smile. Lorne's about to lose it.

"Viola," Lorne barks as he stops in front of us. He appraises her from head to toe, his mouth twisting in disgust when his eyes land on the second Poison crest on the sleeve—Haal, she's wearing one of my old Secondline shirts. "You're in *his* shirt?"

Viola looks at me, looks down at her shirt, then looks at me again. "This shirt fits you?"

I bite down my laugh, but Beau isn't so gracious. He turns to the side, hiding the sound with a mockery of a cough that only antagonizes Lorne further.

"Report to Circle Three immediately. Lockdown has begun. And cover up that hideous serpent, for the love of Death," he sneers, his eyes fixed solely on Viola.

My fists clench, but my sister catches on before I can say anything. "Magister Lawton ... Lorne," she says hesitantly. "Would you grant me clearance to continue research on my lifedrain theory? Given the circumstances..."

Lorne's eyes shift to Lyria as he considers her request. "Of course, Grand Magus Archyr." He loses his bite, his face relaxing as he speaks to my sister. "We could use your brilliant mind to give our mages an advantage through these unprecedented times."

Unprecedented times. Funny how Lorne seems to forget that our ancestors lived through the Age of Grimm. And now he may be back.

"Please give me until this afternoon to get your request approved by Overseer Delaney," he tells Lyria, and my sister thanks him with a smile.

It's bizarre seeing him so docile, and my sister so civil with him. But Lorne has always respected Lyria for her work ethic, and while she thinks he is peculiar, she admits that he's perhaps one of the brightest Mortemagi at Gorhail.

"Let's go, Viola." He steps to the side, stretching his arm ahead. "I don't have all day."

Viola inhales abruptly and briefly glances at me before beaming at Lorne. "I have to stop by my room for a shirt," she says.

"Fine. I'll grant ten minutes because I cannot stand the sight of this atrocity." He shudders.

I wonder if he's still talking about the shirt, or about me.

As I watch Viola walk away with him, something stirs in the pit of my stomach, that same feeling of belonging, of home. There might not be a bond, but Viola's mine all the same.

"Horrible bond, isn't it?" Beau drawls, and Lyria stifles a chuckle.

I elbow him in the ribs, and he gives out a pained laugh.

Right before she steps out of Hollow Tree, Viola turns to me, and for the first time since Mom died, my heart comes alive. Her eyes hold every beginning, every middle, and every end of all the stories I ever want to tell.

"Sylas." Overseer Paltro touches my elbow, snapping me out of my reverie. Haal, why now? He beckons Beau, Lyria, and me to follow, and we fall into step with him as we head toward his office.

"Railesza is back where she belongs, I see," he muses, nodding to my forearm. "Beau, I cannot demote you further. Going to the crypt to retrieve your father's aspier without my authorization was... bold but foolish. So please compile the last twenty-five years of Hansel Archyr's field reports. I want them on my desk by Monday."

"Uncle," Beau groans.

"Lyria, sweet child, please report to the infirmary. Darro is getting discharged today, and he's been asking for you. Dismissed."

My siblings leave at the same time, Beau cursing and Lyria telling Beau he needs to get started on the reports immediately.

"Sylas, you have the most powerful aspier in existence. You've been assigned to one of the most prestigious divisions of Firstline, and you're well on your way to become Grand Master of this fine House one day. Yet you're throwing everything away because of this... woman," Paltro says as he leads me out of Hollow Tree. "Your parents would be so disappointed. A Mortemagi?"

I'm at a loss for words. He keeps reminding me, but I know in my heart that they would've *loved* Viola. And I've never said anything about wanting to become Grand Master. Was the whole Firstline reassignment his idea?

As the thought crosses my mind, he confirms it. "I'm pleased about your performance yesterday: fourteen kills. Viv Rowan had to throw away her case for dismissal. She was livid."

The words are stuck in my throat. I can't believe Paltro set this up just so I wouldn't be dismissed from Firstline, when I'd rather give up my patch than contribute to what I now know are senseless murders. I *know* that he's trying to be a good guardian, that he's trying to do what he thinks is best for Lyria, Beau, and me, but with every passing day I realize that this isn't the life I want. "I want to resign," I say.

Paltro stares at me. "You don't mean that, Sylas. Especially not when we're about to face one of the worst poacher uprisings since Grimm." Paltro's steps are heavy as we walk out of Hollow Tree. I wonder if now's a good time to tell him about what Viola's ghost said, or maybe he already knows, and he isn't sharing.

The air is warmer than usual today, a light drizzle grazing my face in the short walk to the sheltered stone hallway.

"What is our House motto, son?" He claps a gentle hand on my shoulder.

"Bound by loyalty," I reply like a parrot, and because I'm so used to adding Gorhail's motto at the end, I finish, "Resilient in purpose."

"Bound by loyalty," he repeats. "Our House has come a long way since Sileas Ronin etched those words onto the first stone, but our values, our commitment, our duty do not waver. It serves to remember that."

I gulp.

Paltro cannot possibly be questioning my loyalty, but what if he is... Will I have to betray Viola? Will I have to betray *him*?

"Scar has awoken," he says, as if it were a weather report. "I need you to find her."

> I'm afraid my end is near. All the secrets must come out. Let me begin with mine. I have done something terrible, something unforgivable—
>
> JOURNAL OF RHEA CORVI, FIRST AND LAST ENTRY, APRIL 1927

thirty-seven | viola

THURSDAY, DECEMBER 9, 1939

Lorne's hot breath scorches my neck. He walks so close to me, as if giving me any space would make me disappear. He ignores all my questions about rituals and relics, so I try asking about Gorhail's lockdown. "Are you worried the poachers might still be in here?"

"Huh?" He slows his steps, and I match them.

"The ones who killed Fable," I whisper, realizing how silly I sound. No poacher is around to hear me; we've passed by four Firstline officers on our way here, and I've watched all four of them not-so-subtly brush against students. All of them readers.

"Viola, you are too new to this world to understand the real dangers." He sighs. "We're safest within Gorhail walls."

I clamp my mouth shut. Fable was killed within the safety of said walls.

"Should I ask why you have a Poison shirt on?" he asks when I don't say anything.

No, you shouldn't, I want to say.

"Yesterday, I was studying with Lyria and fell asleep in her room." I impress myself with this lie, because it is plausible. "We had to report to assembly immediately, so I took her clothes."

"Of course." He heaves a sigh of . . . relief.

We turn into the hallway with the diamond-patterned rug, and I'm almost to my room when I abruptly stop, a question already slipping out. "Was Olivia planning to move to Wanora with you?" I ask.

Ever since Victor told me at the prison, the question has been burning at my lips. I need to know if she planned to leave with him.

"No, she mentioned there was somewhere else she needed to be, but she wouldn't say where." He lowers his head. "I wish I had insisted and left earlier. Perhaps she would have come then, and she would still be here now."

My chin quivers. Olivia was really going to leave with me to Osneau. I shake my head. The only thing I can do now is find her killer. And now that I'm back in my room, I can see if she may have hidden *The Founder's Book of Relics* somewhere here. I combed the room my very first night here, but maybe I missed something.

"I'll be out in ten." I unlock my door, but Lorne gives no sense that he will move away. He takes one step too close, and my heart plummets. Not again.

When I refuse to move, he grunts. "Be quick, Viola." He backs up. "I have business to attend to."

Once I'm in the room, I don't waste time. I turn over the drawers and run my hands inside to check for hidden compartments, but there's nothing there. If Olivia hid the book, it would still be in here. After digging through every drawer, I rush to the wardrobe, combing through every nook and cranny. Still nothing.

The door rattles, and a jolt zaps through me. Has it already been ten minutes? I pull on a House sweater without bothering to change the shirt. Two more knocks, and I jerk the door open.

No one's there.

I step in the hallway, peek to the left and then to the right. Shaking my head, I turn around, but a forearm laces around my neck. It drags me back with so much force, I only manage to slip my palms in front of my neck to prevent it from crushing my windpipe. My nails dig into the pale flesh, but it doesn't budge. So I do the only thing I can think of and bite down hard. The acrid taste of rotten flesh takes over my mouth. My bite should have drawn blood, but it doesn't.

The person recoils, cursing.

Panicked, I whirl.

Mara cradles her arm against her stomach. Bloody saints, I thought Firstline had her locked up.

Something's changed about her since the attack at Dearly Departed. Her edges are sharper, her posture straighter, and she's not rotting away anymore. This defies everything I've learned about puppets, unless... the magic controlling her is also changing her appearance.

I could scream and try to alert someone, but I will be dead before anyone comes. Or I could run, but Mara is faster than me. The only remaining option will drive me to death at best, madness at worst, but at least it will be on my own terms.

I bolt to the Poisoned Stairwell. My hands are practiced now, and the notch clicks open immediately. Mara lunges for me, and I step into the darkness in the nick of time, closing the door on her. She bangs on the door with the force of a rabid animal, but it will hold. At least that's what I tell myself.

My chest heaves, and I lean forward, steadying myself on the railing, and try to catch my breath. Saints, I wish I had traded the cuff for Scar, but all I have is the cold metal wrapped around my arm.

"Where do I go?" I ask the ghost, hoping she's returned. She'd mentioned she would try to find out more about the sudden lockdown earlier, and she never came back.

No answer.

The door cracks behind me. Mara will break it open any moment. I leap forward, desperate, my heart thumping with terror. "Please, tell me where to go."

Thank Death, I hear her voice again.

Straight, take three flights of stairs down, then take the long hallway to your left.

I follow like I am the epitome of piety, and she is my God. We stop in front of an entrance to another stairway. *Up.* Looking at the winding stairs that seem to lead to the skies, I hesitate. I know where I am.

What if she's trying to trick me?

She's closing in. But she won't be able to get in here. The magic keeps puppets out.

My life teeters between certain death and a likely death. So I climb. I climb until my thighs burn, until my shins threaten to split down the middle, until I can no longer walk and have to crawl up the steps. Until I reach a landing with a single, arched, wooden, black door with four square windows. I stumble on the last step, falling flat on the ground, tears blazing in my eyes. The sinister feeling from the first night Mara attacked me by surprise clutches my neck, and for the first time since then, the acrid smell of death wafts around me. Gods, I might die tonight.

Get up, Viola. The ghost is insistent. *I didn't put myself through this for you to give up now.*

What is she talking about? She's a ghost. Nothing will happen to her. "You're a ghost. So what if you walked through a few walls?"

I don't hear her for a little. Then she lets out a quiet sigh. *When I died, my memories were sealed to this cursed place. The moment I walked in, they all came back.*

Gods, she chose to relive her horrifying death to help me. Gathering strength from her words, I push myself up, my limbs aching with every step I take toward the door. I push it open, and a gasp flows out of my lips.

Clouds roll off the highest peak of Mount Chazal, and blue-eared hawks circle some of the tall, flat trees on the top. The tallest waterfall in Draterra twinkles as the water cascades down the ridges of the mountain into the thick clouds. I was mistaken to think Sylas's room had the most beautiful view in all of Gorhail. We're up so high that I feel like I'm in the skies. The hawks move to the sound of the waves crashing on the cliffs in their own choreographed dance.

I sit on the bench, allowing myself to calm down. Mara can't get to me here. I have to trust in the magic and trust in the ghost. She's never led me astray before . . . but what if . . . My chest heaves again, and I grip the sides of the bench.

I didn't bring you here to kill you.

It does nothing, my breaths are haphazard gulps of air, and my ears ring with paralyzing fear.

If I wanted to, you'd have already been dead in the catacombs. Remember . . . I can possess you at length, make you forget yourself . . . I drown out the rest of her words, reaching forward to the railing to prevent myself from getting sick. The stretch helps, and tension eases in my shoulders, and slowly, my heart returns to its regular pace.

When I finally calm down, my eyes narrow at the intricate railing. It's a mesh of ravens, roses, and bones carved in a beautiful pattern in the cold metal.

You freed me from the catacombs after four centuries. It's time you know who I am.

"What is your name?" I ask, like a fool. Ghosts can't give their names to whisperers. They can only confirm it. If I get it wrong, she can possess me forever, but I know she won't.

This used to be my favorite place.

"You said you died here?"

There's a note of sadness in her hum, but no regret. *My lover was a prophet, a whisperer extraordinaire with reader magic. Spirits would tell him of the future. It was a gift until it became a curse.*

My breath hitches, caught in the elegance of how she strings her words up here. Something's changed within her, like a deep sorrow took root the moment she came back to Death Spire. I don't dare speak, afraid that if I do, she will stop telling me her story.

I loved someone who was in love with himself. I never stood a chance. He wanted the world to see the greatness of our magic, but as you witnessed, our magic comes at a great cost. He began to sacrifice innocent lives. In a vision of the future, he saw them—the world of mages—shunning us Mortemagi, burning us, throwing us behind bars, executing us.

Dread fills my bones, because I can see mages doing this. There is so much prejudice, so much unfounded hatred across the classes. Purists would have no trouble executing crossmages, and Aspieri would sooner be rid of Mortemagi if they could.

I tried to stop him. I tried. I told him I couldn't love someone whose lust for power ran so deep, that I wouldn't stand by someone who chose to kill people over helping them see our differences.

She pauses. Her heart bleeds out through her voice, as I sit there, helpless, listening to a story from centuries ago. I remember Lyria telling me this is how poachers came about. Mages who rebelled against DOTS, who sided with the powerful Mortemagi who wanted magical freedom, freedom that would come at the expense of innocents. Perhaps death magic isn't meant to be practiced at all, other than our base magic as whisperers and conduits, helping the dead find their resting place. Perhaps, the Gods made a mistake in giving us the power to control what's left of the dead.

He was wrong. His arrogance wouldn't let him see reason. What he saw of the future was the aftermath of his abuse of power. The spirits were warning him of a world where Mortemagi and crossmages would be feared by all. But the fear existed only because of him.

The truth is in front of me. Rafael Grimm.

I came up here on my final night. I wanted to see the stars one last time, to beg for forgiveness from the Gods who gave us a piece of themselves so we could make our world a little like theirs. In exchange for my cuff, I begged them to take my life and return all the innocence lost. But it wasn't the Gods who answered. It was my lover. He pushed me, and the moment the rocks claimed my last breath, he doomed us all with the cuff I foolishly left behind.*

My face is wet with tears I didn't realize were flowing. The pain blooming in my chest for this woman I do not know, for all these people I never knew, for all of us who live in the shadow of Grimm, knocks me to my knees. And I let it swallow me whole, crying until I run out of tears.

I know who she is. I know her as well as I know my own name. Ysenia Faro, the Sixth Founder of Gorhail. "Ysenia."

She hums quietly.

"What happened to him after you . . . ?" Died? Disappeared? Were imprisoned in the catacombs? All of these feel wrong. He robbed us of the greatest Mortemagi. She authored and hand-illustrated nearly all of our earliest texts.

He amassed a following, convincing anyone who would listen that mages were blessed by the Gods and that restricting our magic was only to the benefit of DOTS. He harbored, encouraged, and trained an army of crossmages to fight against our own. He did unspeakable things in the name of magical freedom. Sileas Ronin, the founder of the House of Poison, trapped his soul in his—my—relic, and the price he paid for it was dear. The Gods allowed me mercy. Right after I died, they made it so I—my ghost—couldn't see him or hear him. With that came the condition that I can never cross the Underiver. But he's long gone now, while I'm trapped here for eternity.

Ysenia traded freedom for an eternity trapped in the catacombs to be away from this evil man. "Entrapment . . . someone released him, didn't they?" I ask.

She hums in confirmation. *Two decades ago, a young mage released him.*

Dear Gods, we were wrong to assume Grimm couldn't come back. Sylas and I were correct in our theory that the history books didn't record the events correctly. The cuff has been missing for over twenty years. But . . . if a mage released Grimm's trapped soul, he's either a wandering ghost, or he's anchored to someone. If we go by poacher movements and *The Daily Mage*'s propaganda, it's easy to guess which he is.

Then again, the book I was reading in the library, Isobel Corvi's *Death Magic, or a Life of Servitude*, had a passage on complex resurrections. They don't require a body, only a human sacrifice to resurrect someone. The pieces are slowly falling into place. Grimm could be trying to resurrect himself.

A shudder rips through me, and I pause at my thought, at the implications that Grimm has had two decades to prepare an uprising, and Firstline continues to bury leads.

Given all his power, it would make sense why he needs so many human sacrifices. That would also account for the missing cuff and perhaps the missing book. Still, something doesn't quite add up. Why us and why heirloom relics?

"What was his name?" I know my question drives a knife through her, but I still want to hear her confirm it. She doesn't answer me at first. In fact, she doesn't answer me for a while, until I see the moon creeping from behind the mountain.

Rafe, she finally says. *Rafael Grimm.*

I was right.

"I think you may have helped me solve the murders, at least partially," I tell her. "And you must know, even before you anchored to me, your books helped me navigate my magic when I had no one to turn to."

A smile, or at least I think I hear her smile. *You are a direct descendant of Isobel Corvi, the reason Mortemagi even have a right to education after Grimm's catastrophe. You don't need a book.*

"I am only a whisperer," I say.

Only a whisperer. She laughs. *You're judging yourself against inexperience. You cannot compare magic you've been honing since you were a child to the burst of magic you must learn to control with a newly acquired relic. These things take time.*

"And if I don't have time..."

Then you have choices. You can either give up your magic and live out the rest of your years. Or you can lifedrain those who seek to do you harm.

"I don't want to be like Grimm," I say, remembering what Lorne taught me about the bird. "I don't want to trade people's lives for mine."

Oh, Viola. You are a Mortemagi. Thread magic comes with great sacrifice, but it also comes with raw beauty. It is what makes us, us. Besides, if someone is out to kill you, I would hope you don't spare them.

As she tells me more about our magic, I can't help but think of how long Grimm has been back, and how he could be anyone among us.

> Attn: Editor in Chief, *The Daily Mage*
> Report to DOTS headquarters immediately.
> **LETTER FROM DOTS TO *THE DAILY MAGE* OFFICE, DECEMBER 1939**

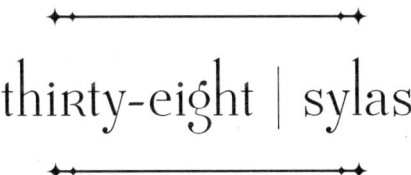

thirty-eight | sylas

THURSDAY, DECEMBER 9, 1939

Paltro's office basks in the evergreen scent of pine and the crispness of late-afternoon snowfall. It's also freezing cold, and the flimsy House shirt does little to keep away the sting of frost on my skin.

The brown cushioned armchair wraps me in a welcomed warmth when I settle in. Looking at the trinkets and books lining the multiple-wall shelves in front of me, I realize that Paltro's office is a map of his travels. There's something from each of the Ten Provinces and so many photographs. Only then does it occur to me that these aren't books at all, but photo albums. I've been in and out of here since he joined Gorhail months ago, right after Dad's death, and this is the first time I'm noticing that Paltro is a hoarder of memories.

Boots dust against the doormat, anchoring me to the reality that awaits me. My leg won't stop fidgeting, and Railesza keeps glaring at me to stop. I am nervous. I don't know how to lie to Paltro. I cannot. Dad trusted him with the three of us, and he's never wavered.

"Scar has awoken," he says again as he lays a black briefcase across his desk. He immediately reaches for a small tin—a new silver one—and scoops out two heaping teaspoons of leaves into the teapot. "The Deathbringer is alive."

Or dead. And she has a daughter whose magic is forbidden by the laws we refuse to challenge.

He gives me a pointed look, waiting for me to correct him. We fall into an uncomfortable silence, interrupted by the gradual bubbling of the teapot. I feel exactly like the tea, like I've been dropped in boiling water. My clothes feel too tight, my skin burns, and my chest constricts. I get up, catching my breath in small increments.

"Oh, sit down, Sylas." He rolls his eyes. "You are as good a liar as your father was. I know Alyria is dead, and you've confirmed that you know the whereabouts of her child."

I stare at him, unblinking.

"Tea?" he asks, and I shake my head.

"Please, it's a special blend Sierra brought from Aurignan," he insists, but I don't want tea right now. I want to leave.

"No," I manage, and he sighs, giving me a look. I wasn't expecting my refusal of drinking tea to affect him so much; and I almost consider asking him to pour me a cup. But he unbuckles the briefcase, laying it flat across his desk. He moves several papers around, a few photographs here and there. I recognize the neat calligraphy of my father's handwriting.

"What do you know of—"

I drown him out because my eyes lock on to a photograph of a group of people in front of Helna Azgar's statue. They are all in Gorhail uniforms, some of them looking at one another with love; some of them in mid-laughter. I gingerly pluck up the photograph, bringing it closer. Mom and Dad are in there; so are Beau's parents, the Deathbringer, and an almost identical version of Victor. In this photo, they look younger than us, so full of hopes, dreams, and life. Now most of them are dead.

Between the Deathbringer and my mom stands a short girl with black hair cropped to her ears. They lean on each of her shoulders, and smile to the camera. Her eyes, and especially her smile, remind me of someone, but who that is escapes me.

"Uncle." I don't look away from the picture, afraid that if I do, I'll stop piecing together the clues we've amassed. "Who are these people?"

He peers over my shoulder, adjusting his glasses. "I haven't seen this photograph in more than twenty years." He lets out a long exhale. "From left to right, Eloise Beauchamps, Lily Ronin, Willow LaCroix, Aly Parrish, Elena Carver, Yasmin Darro, Alis Ducas, Faal Rowan, Benoit Cardot, Victor Carver Sr., Petyr Quince, Han Archyr, and Tobias Corvi."

My mind is working faster than I can speak. I need to get out of here.

Beau's findings weren't absurd at all, and Viola's words swirl in my mind: the killings were personal. Nearly everyone in this picture is dead, save for Gryff's mom, Aunt Yas; Elena Carver; and the LaCroix girl.

"Sylas?" Paltro calls my name, but I don't reply. Most of our parents are dead, and now the killer is coming for who remains of their bloodlines. Still, I cannot grasp how it's linked to Grimm and the missing cuff and book.

"Can I take this photograph?" One of my boots is already out the door when Paltro stops me.

"Sylas, I am not finished. We have much to discuss about your father's investigations."

I pocket the photo anyway. Paltro continues, "Han was investigating your mother's lifedrain research shortly before his death. I have scoured his notes to no avail. Could we look over them together, and perhaps take a reader to Zoya?"

What would the library custodian know about Dad? That she's nice and greets people every day doesn't mean people will tell her their every secret. More than anything, I want to find out more about my parents, but they are already dead. Viola isn't. My choice is clear.

"Son, you look unwell. Have some tea, please..."

I run a hand over my face. I'll have to tell him sooner or later.

"We know the killer is collecting a set of relics and is killing mage lines," I blurt out, dragging the photograph out of my pocket to Paltro's face. And suddenly it all clicks together. "I think... the killer needed *The Founder's Book of Relics*, the heirlooms, and the dead lines for a ritual. They have an aspier, a laurel, a pen, a knife. We know they want the Corvi cuff, and what remains is—"

"A key. Rituals usually require one of each relic." Paltro looks at me cautiously.

"Viola..." I clear my throat, looking away. "Viola's anchored ghost said the killings were personal." I pause, blowing out a heavy breath. "Everyone in this photograph is dead, Uncle. Save for Aunt Yas, Victor's mom, and this girl—Willow." I tap the girl between Mom and the Deathbringer.

Paltro takes the picture from my hands, shaking his head. "Yasmin left Gorhail shortly after this picture was taken. Sadly, Willow died a few years later, not long after your mother. Her death was tragic, a spell gone wrong—all of them were involved, and some say that's why Elena went mad. It's the reason interclass magic is forbidden unless you acquire the proper rank."

"Did Willow have any children?" I ask. Because this may lead us to the next victim . . . or maybe to the murderer.

"No." He reaches for a pen and a stack of letters. "Her father, Noa LaCroix, tragically passed away during her first year at the institute, and her sole living relative is her mother, Overseer Delaney."

The moment he says her name, my limbs freeze. The pen slides out of Paltro's hand, clattering onto the desk, and we stare at each other, the air tight with panic and shock. I don't have to ask; I already know we share the same thought. They'll need two more relics for their ritual, and if we are to go by this picture, the only two relics that remain are Sierra's key and Viola's cuff.

"Check on Sierra, and I'll go find Viola," I say as I rush to the door. The next moment, he's scribbling on multiple sheets of paper, and I am bolting onto the wet grass with the picture in my hand.

Overseer Delaney knows more than she's letting on. And I would bet my life that she's trying to resurrect her daughter.

As I run, all I can think of is how Viola is alone in her death lair.

"Have you seen Magus Corvi?" I ask a scrawny Magus Mortemagi when I reach Hollow Tree. The boy's face pales, his eyes darting to my aspiers. He shakes his head vigorously, scurrying away toward the buffet soon after. One would think I am the murderer around here. Railesza hisses at me to calm down.

I look around and see a few mages eating an early dinner under the watchful eyes of Secondline officers. Two of them bark at a group of boys to finish their meals so they can return to their respective Houses. Gorhail feels more like a prison than usual. With Secondline reduced to sitters, they're grasping at any avenue to exert their dominance. Pathetic.

I glance toward the entrance to the House of Death. Three Firstline officers stand in front of it, the red glow of the hallway behind them making it look like they're guarding the doors to the Underworld.

Screw this lockdown—there's no way they will let me into their forsaken House right now, and I won't be able to sneak in with Firstline guarding every entrance. So much for being promoted to the highest Firstline Division—I can't even pull rank to be let in the House of Death.

Still, I have to try. I hope Firstline isn't also guarding the Poisoned Stairwell. As I rush back to the House of Poison, images of Viola dying cross my mind. I shove them away; I will not rest until I know she is safe and away from Delaney. And as much as I hate Lorne, his overbearingness may prove useful for once. He is likely hovering over Viola like the ghosts he corrals, and Delaney wouldn't dare kill a Magister in the middle of Gorhail. Would she?

When I cross through Fang's Nest, I speak to no one. Two Grand Magus try to stop me to talk about the importance of Aspieri staying behind to protect Gorhail. I don't care. If they knew better, they would be far from this place right now.

I step into Founder's Room, slamming the door shut behind me. I walk across the living room and head straight for the Poisoned Stairwell, pulling on the door. It doesn't budge. "Fuck." My fist slams on the wooden panel, but it doesn't even shake.

Pacing back and forth, I weigh my options. The main entrance is barred, my only access to the Poisoned Stairwell is locked, and I have to assume that they've locked all the others, too. Haal, make yourself useful for once. I slam on the panel a second time, and Raiku startles awake and hisses at me.

"Sylas," Beau calls out as he walks out of his room. "What's wrong?"

I look at him, a lump in my throat. I shouldn't be here right now. I should be tearing down the doors of the House of Death. "Viola..."

He glances at the angry mark on my fist. "If you break into the House of Death, Firstline will take you away... you know it as well as I do."

Lyria opens her door moments later. She takes one look at me, and her hands twist together. "They still haven't approved my clearance," she says, shaking her head.

"Sylas, what's going on?" Beau demands as he strides toward me.

"Our theory, your findings about the families, Viola's theory..." I speak every word that comes to my mind. "I don't think this was about Grimm at all. The killer used Grimm's return and Faro's Cuff to throw us off." I pause, catching my breath. "Delaney is behind all this. She's trying to resurrect her daughter with the relics."

Lyria glares at me like I've said something sacrilegious. "Sylas, you're ridiculous." She laughs, fixing a stack of books on the nearest shelf right outside her bedroom door. "Delaney would never do that. She has her quirks, but she bleeds for Gorhail." She shakes her head. "Besides, her daughter has been dead for over twenty years. If she required the relics to resurrect her, she could've killed everyone while they were children."

Beau's eyes meet mine, a frown knotting them. "Not if she didn't know she needed the relics," he says, slowly turning to face our sister.

Lyria's face goes through the five stages of grief in mere seconds. My naive sister thinks that the rules are written in our favor and those who maintain them do so with honor. In an ideal world, she would be right. As I watch her face fall at the realization that someone she respects so much betrayed the order and structure she stands for, I feel like *I* failed her.

"*The Founder's Book* . . ." she lets out, clasping her mouth.

"The last time Olivia went back to Albion—three weeks ago—she retrieved *The Founder's Book of Relics* from her grandmother's library," I remind them. "The heirloom thefts and murders started around that time. The first one was Victor, then Beau, then Olivia . . ."

"Gods," she utters. "Delaney probably *told* Olivia to get the book . . . Viola . . . Sylas, Viola is at the House of Death."

My stomach roils with agony, as if I haven't replayed the first night I met Viola a thousand times over in my head. She could be dead right now, and I wouldn't know. I have no way of getting to her. The moment the thought crosses my mind, I let out a curse.

Beau's head whips to me, and he approaches, laying a hand on my shoulder. "Listen, Sy. I *hate* Lorne, but I guarantee you he won't leave her alone. And the House of Death is stacked with Firstline officers, because they're already suspecting a Mortemagi."

That Beau's mind went straight to where mine went earlier eases me a little. I have to believe that Viola is safe, and once Lyria receives her clearance pass, she'll be with her. As if my sister hears my thoughts, she says, "The second I receive my pass, I'll run . . . Now, tell us everything."

After a moment, I nod in gratitude and walk over to the coffee table by the fireplace. I kneel, pulling the photograph out of my pocket. If we have to wait, I might as well walk them through our findings. Beau and Lyria join me, kneeling opposite me. My brother opens the drawer under the table and retrieves two pens and blank pages. He starts scribbling down the dead family lines: Cardot, Carver, Quince, Rowan.

"Corvi, because we know they are after Viola's relic. Sierra, because Aunt Yas was gone before Willow died, and Mom died before Willow," I tell him.

Beau breathes out a curse. "All this time, we're worrying about Faro's Cuff being missing, and it was right here, under our noses, at Gorhail. I wish I could say we were blind, but I would never have thought—"

The Poisoned Stairwell door jerks open, startling the three of us. I scramble to my feet, thinking it's Viola and she's found a way to me instead. But Paltro walks in, a small pouch in his hands.

"Uncle," Lyria exclaims. He returns her greeting with less enthusiasm than usual. Something is wrong, I see it in the slight twitch of his lips, the flare of his nostrils, the purse of his lips. He lingers on every one of us, before settling on me.

"Is Sierra—" I ask, realizing he can get in and out of the Poisoned Stairwell. Thank Haal, I have a way to Viola. I move, but Paltro's words stop me.

"Rest assured, Miss Ducas had her magic sealed and left her relic behind. She's now in Riverview. I was patrolling the stairwell and thought to drop some tea off." His eyes move to my hands. "You have to trust that we're doing our job, Sylas."

"Sierra sealed her magic?" I ask.

"It was the only way to kill her line without killing her—you know that."

I know that, just like I know that magic, once sealed, never comes back. She'll live out her days as a nonmagi, never fulfilling her dream of being a reader at DOTS, all because of Delaney and her bloodlust. All because she was forced to trade her magic for her life.

I close the distance to where Paltro stands. I feel sorry for my friend, but she'll live. I can't say the same for Viola if I don't get to her in time. Now that I have a way into the Poisoned Stairwell, I *need* to go to her.

"Here you go." Paltro hands me the pouch and blocks the door. "It should help with all the stress."

I snatch the pouch out of his hands. "What is this?"

"Memories Zoya was willing to offer." He inhales. "About your parents."

Paltro doesn't care about my *stress* at all. My parents are already dead; their memories will remain whether I look at them now or in ten years.

Haal, Viola is dying, and Paltro wants to force memories down my throat through tea. I huff out a frustrated breath, but he continues, "Zoya is one of our most precious assets at Gorhail. She harbors the memories of every student who has ever crossed the library, unless they remember to block them out before they step in."

So *this* is why she insists on greeting every one of us. It isn't endearing at all. It's a violation of our minds. Haal, everything is wrong with this institute.

"Not now, Uncle." I return the pouch to Paltro. No memory that Zoya has for me will ease the sheer panic that I may never see Viola again. The longer he keeps me here, the higher the likelihood that Delaney's got her claws on her.

"Viola . . ." Lyria steps forward, Beau right behind her. "Uncle, Viola is at the House of Death, and Delaney is there, too . . . Please let Sylas through."

Paltro regards me with disappointment. Maybe if he knew who Viola was, he would be more inclined to help her. Everything unsaid piles at my throat, and I look at my uncle with a silent plea.

"It's her," I confess. "She's the Deathbringer's daughter."

"Ah," he says, without a hint of surprise. Did he already know? "A word of advice, if I may?" Paltro blows out a breath. Whether I want to hear it or not, Paltro has the key to the Poisoned Stairwell, and he'll hold me hostage until he's said what he wants.

"Aspieri-Mortemagi crossmages are volatile. They rarely survive to tell their story. I would advise Viola to seal her Aspieri magic and return Scar to DOTS," he says calmly.

Now my impatience bleeds into anger. All this talk about loyalty, but when it comes to Viola, she must seal away her magic.

"It won't change that she's one of us." I hold his disapproving stare. Viola, a half Aspieri, daughter of the Deathbringer, might die, and he's more concerned with getting Scar back. "Bound by loyalty, Uncle."

"Mortemagi know little of loyalty, Sylas."

"She's different," I plead, slowly realizing that Paltro is just as much a purist as those he condemns. Just because he isn't prejudiced against Arkani crossmages doesn't mean he doesn't share purist ideologies. "She sacrificed her own life to bring Beau back."

"Would she have done so had she known the cost?" Paltro taunts. I look away, hating the seed of doubt he's sowing in my mind.

Beau's stare bores into my eyes for a few seconds, and I realize I'm an idiot for even doubting that she would. Without looking away from me, Beau answers, "She would."

Paltro sighs, shaking his head. "Not even Parrish would be able to sway DOTS's decision when it comes to an Aspieri-Mortemagi cross-mage, not even if she's the Deathbringer's daughter." He walks back to the Poisoned Stairwell. "Rhodes can take her to Gorhail's magic sealer. It's for the best."

"Do not tell Rhodes." Viola isn't just any Mortemagi. She is the daughter of a Draterran legend. Above all, she is *my* Mortemagi, and I will fight so she can tell her story.

"Son." Paltro holds my eyes for a moment, one hand on the stairwell door. "Young love is ephemeral. Your House is permanent."

It was fine when I had to "bond" with a Mortemagi to keep my aspier, but now it's my House over the Mortemagi *they* shoved onto me. "Uncle, please..."

But Paltro leaves my plea hanging and pulls the door closed behind him.

I release a painful breath. My only way to Viola is gone, and my heart feels like it's caving in. I don't know how I'm supposed to just... wait and have faith in a system that routinely fails us.

"She's one of us, Sy," my sister says, drawing my attention as she grabs her coat from the entryway. "Aspieri or not, she's been one of us for a while now, and we fight for our own. I'll go to the House of Death, under the guise of looking for my clearance pass."

"And I"—Beau joins her by the door, glancing at the clock—"will sneak out through the woods to see if I can convince Grayson to read Victor's mom."

I don't say anything, my tongue still paralyzed by worry. The last time we decided to take things into our own hands, Beau died. He lifts his head and immediately narrows his eyes. "Sy... look behind you. I didn't hear... I think... Paltro left the door unlocked."

I whirl around without thinking twice and reach for the handle. It clicks, and the door opens. I linger for a few seconds, caught between Paltro's bitter words and the fact that he did leave the door unlocked. Even in his hostility, he's still bound by loyalty.

"Go," my siblings yell at the same time. My feet propel me into the dark.

And for the first time in my life, I pray to the God of Death.

> Founder Ysenia Faro's Cuff was buried in the vault below my statue in the courtyard of the House of Poison, the sole access granted to my chosen bloodline, given that my blood sealed Grimm in. As we agreed, amend the books and declare that the five of us sealed Rafael in the cuff. We cannot risk anyone releasing him. This tragedy is further proof that Mortemagi need to be driven out of existence. How long until another Rafael emerges?
>
> **LETTER FROM SILEAS RONIN TO THE FOUNDERS, 1511**

thirty-nine | viola

THURSDAY, DECEMBER 9, 1939

The Poisoned Stairwell crawls with ghosts when we climb down from the tower, but none of them bother me because of Ysenia. I cannot hear them, but they announce their presence with frosty caresses and biting goose bumps. She leads me back to the House of Death, reassuring me several times that Mara is gone. I pull the hidden door open, stepping into the empty hallway. As I push it closed, Overseer Delaney greets me with a murderous glare.

"Miss Corvi."

The weight of my name hovers over my head like a boulder, threatening to crush me. I press my back against the tapestry, counting my breaths. Overseer Delaney's glare pins me with dread—she just watched me walk out of the Poisoned Stairwell. I've not only violated lockdown but also probably curfew. But I must tell her about Mara coming back, about Rafael Grimm, and about how he's trying to resurrect himself.

"To your room," she orders, and I scurry forward, my nerves swallowing all I wanted to say.

The key shakes as I try to fit it into the lock. Delaney's huff of impatience over my shoulder isn't helping. When I fail a second time, she snatches the key from my hand, opens the door, and shoves me inside. The dresser catches my stumble, and she walks in behind me, eyes scanning every corner.

I understand that rules are important for Delaney, but using brute force simply because I broke them seems excessive. Even for her.

"Your grandmother used to be dean of this fine institution," she begins. Oh no. Here comes the speech of disappointment, about how I do not live up to her reputation, about how I am a waste of magic. "She is remembered as one of the greatest deans that Gorhail has ever seen. Do you know why?"

"No." I shake my head, fiddling with the hem of my shirt. I never knew Nan as a dean. To me, she was a grandmother, like any other. We would bake, we would plant flowers, and she would read me stories at bedtime. She made my life in Albion bearable, and her lying to me about who I am doesn't change that she loved me.

Overseer Delaney retrieves a rolled issue of *The Daily Mage* from under her coat. The edges are torn, the pages yellow. Her long, wrinkly fingers unfold it to a picture of Nan. Her black hair is pulled into a tight bun, her round silver glasses sit lightly on her rounded nose, and her thin lips are drawn into a line. I don't know this version of Nan. Mine has loosely braided gray hair, the kindest eyes, and creases around her lips from smiling too much. The headline gives me pause:

"Gorhail Matriarch Thwarts a Second Catastrophe"

The date on the paper is 1919, twenty years ago.

Delaney's sneer drops into a mockery. "Saint Corvi. She saved the world." She folds the paper in four and places it on the dresser. Something about her demeanor makes me step back.

"Do you know *how* she saved the world?" She draws out every word. I return a blank stare, and she slaps her hand on the dresser.

I flinch.

"She killed my daughter." Delaney cants her head, her stare hollow. Confusion and dread knot tighter in my stomach. I didn't even know she *had* a daughter, but this woman isn't thinking straight. Nan didn't kill anyone. She was a liar, but she wasn't a killer.

My eyes dart around for an escape, but there's only one door, and she stands in my way.

"W-why?" I ask. I don't know if I'm buying time or trying to make sense of her accusations.

She shifts her weight, and her chest rises and falls with annoyance. As she shoves the newspaper across the dresser, my eyes catch on the headline again. And suddenly, my mind is untangling everything I've been told today. Twenty years ago, Nan stopped a catastrophe. And earlier, Ysenia told me about the mage who released Rafael Grimm's soul.

Twenty years ago.

Gods. I look up at Delaney's ominous smile. That mage must have been her daughter.

"Because . . . my Willow brought back our true founder, the heart and soul of death magic." She confirms my thoughts just as I make the connection. "No longer are we going to live under the thumbs of those who seek to control us."

My heart sinks as I realize what this means. The dead lines, the stolen relics . . . Delaney is behind the murders. How could I have been so blind? *She* killed Olivia.

"It was you," I whisper. I have to get out of here. My eyes cast toward the door, hoping, *praying* Lyria, Beau, or even Lorne comes by.

"Oh, your little friends won't come," Delaney scoffs. "Friendship is meaningless at Gorhail. Willow released Rafael Grimm, tethering his soul to hers. When Rhea found out, she didn't even give me a chance to reason with my daughter. No . . ." She pauses, glancing at the photograph of Nan on the newspaper. "Your dearest grandmother fragmented Willow's soul across six relics. Do *you* know who trapped my beautiful child?"

When I don't answer, she continues, "Her own friends, Viola. I will never forget their names. Rhea Corvi, who was a second mother to her; Peter Quince, who loved her once; Victor Carver Sr., who was like a brother to her; Faal Rowan and Sara Ducas, both of whom grew up with her; and the last one was a surprise—Eloise Beauchamps, Gorhail's darling, not a mean bone in her body, they'd all said."

My belly twists. Realization cascades through me like a cold shower; I would never have pieced it together on my own. Delaney is collecting the six relics that trapped her daughter's soul so she can release her ghost. The dead lines, the blood that seals, the six heirloom relics. But Nan would never inflict this pain upon anyone without reason. I have to believe that. The alternative would break me.

"I-I don't..." I inch closer to the door with every word. My heart beats in my throat, the same acrid smell of death circling me, telling me my end is fast approaching. If she's telling me all of this, she doesn't intend to let me live. But I *need* to live. Sylas needs to know that Delaney is the mastermind, that Rafael Grimm is back, and that Delaney was behind the murders.

Delaney beams, victory pulling the corners of her lips. It's sickening. "Go ahead, open the door," she coos.

I don't wait. But I wish I had.

The sharp stench of sweat, blood, and decay fills my nostrils. Mara stands there, and despite the smell, she's looking like her old self, my boss and friend. I wonder if they continue to use Mara as a puppet to fool me into these narrow moments of oblivion. Her shoulders slouch forward, and she looks at me with a blank stare.

Sweat beads on the nape of my neck. My heart slams against my rib cage, begging me to run. But I have nowhere to go. I am trapped between the puppet and its master. I expect Mara to swing at me or shove me backward, but the blow never comes.

Delaney seems to be playing at something, biding her time. I will probably die here, but before I do, I have to find out as much as I can so that maybe a reader can extract my memories and Firstline can catch her. I start with the most puzzling question. Why now? "How long have you known Nan had *The Founder's Book of Relics*?"

"I had my suspicions." The saccharine timbre of her voice doesn't dull the sharpness of what comes next. "Your idiot sister casually offered the information Rhea died guarding, said her sister wrote about some of the most beautiful books that were recently unboxed from her nan's belongings."

My heart sinks, and tears fill my eyes. It was *my* fault.

"You tricked her." I straighten, edging closer to Mara, knowing very well that any moment she could snap my head into two. Even knowing that this is a losing fight, I cannot give up.

"She was by far the easiest kill," Delaney says. "Didn't even put up a fight."

Rage bubbles inside of me. I've wanted so badly to face Olivia's killer and ask them why. Yet I stand in the same room as Delaney, guilt carving out a bigger hole in my chest the more she speaks. She died because of me, because of my forsaken magic, because of that stupid cuff, because of the stupid book I unboxed after a decade of its collecting dust in a crate.

"Olivia was a liar, albeit an excellent one. Twelve years, no suspicions, and all that time we thought her magic was weak because of her nonmagi parent," she continues in my silence.

I press my hands to my sides. Nothing I say will bring Olivia back.

"At least her death wasn't in vain, because it brought us *you*. Hidden in plain sight. The heir to the final piece I need to reunite with my daughter."

Mara's face is inches from mine now, and she's still immobile. Maybe if I keep Delaney talking, I'll be able to make a run for Circle Three. Lorne should be in his office.

"Viola, sweet Viola." She pushes off the dresser, her wrinkled lips curling into a crooked grin. "You've only been here weeks, and look at you. Two resurrections, one solved serial murder case, sadly at your expense. You could give me your cuff willingly . . . seal your magic, alter your memories, and walk away."

"I would never—"

"But you won't, and for what . . . your little Aspieri lover?"

"He's not my—" I roll my eyes at the absurdity of my thoughts. She's about to kill me, and here I am with a growing concern about what Sylas and I are. A concern I will not address unless I survive.

I bolt.

One moment, I'm slipping past Mara, running down the diamond-checkered hallway. The next, her claws dig into my arms, and I fall. She drags me across the carpet, slamming me against the wall.

My head lolls forward, my vision growing hazy. My tongue fills with the copper tang of blood, and I want to throw up. Mara's long, sharp fingers pull my hair backward, dragging my face in front of hers. "Pitiful legacy."

Get up, Viola. You have to make it to the Poisoned Stairwell, Ysenia urges.

Mara raises her arm. Before I can comprehend what's happening, a dull pain crawls along my spine, exploding right above my tailbone. I try to kick my legs, but they barely move. Gods, I have no fight in me.

Viola, you cannot die now. Try to take over her— No, I don't know how much lifeblood you have left.

My magic mocks me. It only wants to watch me die.

Delaney's laugh forces my eyes open. She crouches next to me, peering into my soul, as if she's trying to find Nan there to claim victory over her. "There, there, my dear. Give me your cuff, and I'll let you live."

"No," I force out, knowing she can kill me, take the cuff, and walk away without anyone knowing it was her. But a nagging feeling tells me she would've killed me sooner if she wanted to. My mind reaches to when we fought Mara off at Dearly Departed, how Sylas and Victor mentioned there was more than one puppeteer. No. If I'm still alive right now, it means that she—or they—need me for something. "I won't."

"Very well." She shrugs, rising to her feet.

I let out a slow exhale, trying to steady my pain, but Gods, it hurts.

Delaney flicks her palm forward, and Mara is in front of me again, crouching where Delaney was only seconds ago. Mara wraps her long, bony fingers around my right wrist. Painfully, she drags my own hand to my torn sweater, and with her free hand, forces my fingers to click open the cuff. I try to fight, but I am so . . . so weak, my eyes struggling to stay open.

Mara collects the cuff as it falls off and promptly hands it to Delaney, who holds it up like a trophy. The brass catches a stray ray of light, blinding her. I seize her distraction and drag myself forward. My arms scrape against the carpet as I try to crawl my way to the Poisoned Stairwell. I must get out of here.

"You are smart, Viola, yet so naive. It's a pity—" The ringing in my ears drowns her words, and the edges of my vision pull me into the shadows. When I force my eyes open again, Delaney is at the end of the hallway, and Mara stands a few feet away from me.

She's leaving. Soon, she'll be too far away to control her puppet. Now is my chance. Digging one elbow into the carpet, I only move a few more inches before something strikes me across the head.

Mara's bony shins are in front of my face. Instead of ivory, her skin is ashen gray. She eyes me with a newfound interest. Her right leg shuffles forward. I will die here if I don't fight.

There is no escape, no one to save me. In a poor attempt at self-preservation, I loop my hand around Mara's disgusting leg, the cold, moist flesh sticking to my skin. I pull as hard as I can. She loses her balance, falling against the wall.

In a moment of delusion, I tell myself that I can crawl the few steps to the Poisoned Stairwell. I will make it. For my sister. For my friends. For all the people yet to die. For Sylas.

Pushing one knee forward, I crawl.

A low, guttural laugh stops me in my tracks.

It's over.

Mara crouches in front of me. She lifts my chin with her bony finger until the pain in my neck stretches into my spine. Something's different about her; her eyes are lighter, menacing.

"Go." She releases me. Is she playing with me? "Go, Viola." Her voice isn't her own. It's foreign. It's dangerous. It chills me to my bones. "You will bleed to death in minutes, and I want him to watch you die."

By the time I make it to the door, my pants are thick, warm, and sticky with blood. My breathing wanes. Maybe my last moments give me the strength, or maybe Death has mercy on me, but the door clicks open on my first try.

I crawl inside, welcoming the coolness of the floor on my chest. The feeling is brief, because the next moment, I topple down the stairs until I no longer know if the stars I see are real or Death welcoming me home.

> Tilda, effective immediately, you are dismissed from your position as dean of Gorhail. You will be reassigned to the Grimm task force, reporting to Overseer Paltro.
>
> **LETTER FROM PGM PARRISH TO DEAN MATILDA RHODES, DECEMBER 1939**

forty | sylas

THURSDAY, DECEMBER 9, 1939

The Poisoned Stairwell is toying with me.

I've been in here for what feels like hours, and the corridors bleed into one another. The lights seem broken, and I have to rely on their faintest glow to make out my path. Even my aspiers are confused. Raiku hisses at Railesza, and she turns her head away from him, eyes focused ahead as we walk. But Raiku's restlessness stirs a sense of unease within me. What does he know that I don't?

Railesza's head jerks to the left toward a dark, narrow hallway with deep red walls and three faint basket lights floating at the top. I follow her lead, every step heavy with a cursed possibility. Soon after, she lets her body drop to the ground, slithering away faster than I can run. Raiku tightens himself around my wrist, his fangs out.

At the end of the hallway, I notice the silhouette of a body.

One step forward, and I curse myself for wishing this is anyone but Viola.

My second step splits my soul in two.

Viola lies face up on the floor, her beautiful hair matted with blood, her eyes swollen and closed. I search for the slightest movement in her chest. It remains still. I glance at her arm and can almost see the ivory of her bone through the gash that's still oozing blood. A few inches above, her cuff is gone.

No. She can't be... I refuse to think about the word.

Railesza violently hisses at me before wrapping herself around Viola's neck, as if she's chastising me for even considering the possibility of her dying.

I still don't move, paralyzed by a fear that slowly seeped into my veins until its tendrils wrapped around my heart. The fear of losing her.

Raiku nudges me with his nose, and I lower myself to the ground. My fingers are cold, shaking, and my heart beats in my ears. It's so loud that it's all I can hear.

My movement is almost mechanical; I gather Viola against me, resting her head on my knees. Her body's still warm. As I brush her hair away from her face, Railesza continues to heal her, but Viola doesn't respond.

It's over. I'm too late. She's dead.

It cannot be.

Raiku glances at me in question, then at Railesza, but she doesn't look worried at all; in fact, she switches between veins methodically. There's no frantic movement, nothing like when she was trying to heal Dad or Beau. It almost seems like when it comes to Viola, Railesza heals with certainty.

The seconds bleed one into the next, and I don't know if we're here for a minute or an hour, but Viola's eyelids flicker, and my breath hitches.

I blink hard, peering at her eyes in case I've gone mad. Placing two fingers at her wrist, her pulse beats against my touch, slowly at first, then faster.

She's alive. If the God of Death had a name, I would worship him to eternity.

Viola groans in agony, and I pull her closer, placing a soft kiss on her forehead. She's alive. I breathe out. And she's with me.

"Not real," she mumbles.

"Shhh—" I whisper. "I have you, Vi. I'll always have you."

"The cuff." She forces the word out. "Not real..."

The sound of Viola's shaky breathing haunts me until I cross the threshold of Founder's Room with her in my arms. Railesza latches on to her arm, and I thank the Gods for Beau's defiance to Paltro in retrieving his own aspier earlier. If he still had Railesza, Viola would've been dead. My chest constricts again. She's not dead. That's all that matters. Finally, her breathing eases into a steadiness that releases my lungs.

"Lyria," I call out. No answer. "Beau?" Nothing. I begin to panic. It's night, and they've been gone for a while now. Lyria should've been back from the House of Death, and Beau should've returned from meeting up with Grayson.

Once more, Raiku hisses at me, and I carry Viola to my bedroom. The door welcomes me with an eerie creak. I head straight to the bathroom, and Raiku slithers to the bathtub, pulling the tap. The steam is a warm welcome to the knotted muscles in my back while I wait.

After a minute, the gentle sound of lapping water stirs Viola awake.

Her eyes flare, but when she notices it's me holding her, her body sags in my arms and she lets out a painfully slow exhale. With all the care in the world, I set her down on the counter between the double sinks. She places both hands at her sides to brace herself and eases herself away from me.

"I changed the cuffs," she says.

"When? How?" I ask as I stare at her, taking in all the new bruises on her face and neck. Haal, she's alive. I can't believe she's alive.

"When I went to see Scar in your safe downstairs, I swapped my cuff with one of the spare ones you keep." She pauses. "I just ... I had a horrible feeling about the lockdown. Delaney has the wrong cuff."

It takes me a moment, my mind still reeling from almost losing her. *Delaney has the wrong cuff.* I blink. Delaney will come back for her. Haal, I hate that my first thought goes there, because Viola is a genius for swapping the cuffs. But this time, I'm not leaving her out of my sight—Paltro, Firstline, and DOTS be damned. No one is touching her.

"You're brilliant." I clasp her hands between mine, placing a kiss on the tip of her fingers, and she sighs, shaking her head.

"She killed all of them, Sylas. To think all this started because of the stupid *Founder's Book* ... if I hadn't unpacked it—"

"Shhh." I step between her legs, pressing my forehead against hers, my hands on either side of her on the counter. I'm not letting her wallow in self-pity again. Delaney's bloodlust wasn't her fault. "She's been set on revenge for decades now. No one saw it coming. I didn't realize it was her until this morning in Paltro's office."

"It doesn't matter," she whispers, and I pull back. Her head is lowered again; she's wrestling with guilt that shouldn't be hers. I wish she could see herself through my eyes, wish she could see how she makes me whole. She's the calm to my storm, the ember to my fire, the life to my heart.

"Can you manage—" I glance at the bathtub then back to her. "Or do you need help . . . I can . . ."

"I can manage." Her cheeks flush, but she doesn't look at me.

As I prepare to turn away, she calls my name. "Sylas." She pauses. "My arms hurt when I lift them. Can you cut the shirt?"

I suck in a breath. I'm blinking at her like she's speaking a language I cannot comprehend. Without a word, I unsheathe my dagger and grip it tightly to mask the slight shake of my hand. I help her off the counter, willing my breath to steady.

"Turn around," I mumble. It'll be easier if she's not looking at me.

Viola's soft gaze meets mine, then falls to my lips. She lingers for a moment before giving me her back. Her hair is still stiff with blood when I brush it over her shoulder. Inch by inch, I peel the shirt away from her skin. Gathering the cold, wet cloth in my hand, I make a single vertical cut and tear the rest.

The fabric drops, and I gasp.

Her back is a canvas of old and new scars. Mindlessly, my fingers trace along the longest one from her shoulder blade to her waist. I don't need to ask. I know each of these scars like the back of my hand. Because I healed the wounds, every single one of them.

"How bad is it?"

"It's bad."

"Sylas . . ." She turns to me, and I stop breathing.

My mouth goes dry, and I forget my words, forget my own name. My gaze trails from the sharpness of her collarbone to the curves of her breasts. The warmth blooming at the nape of my neck spreads to my cheeks. And my heart races, every beat awakening an ache deep within me.

I step back. This is a line I cannot cross. Not here. Not now, when our emotions are heightened by the fragility of life. "I . . . I have to find Beau."

I leave before she has time to answer.

"Does Viola need anything?" Lyria asks as I walk into Founder's Room. "I . . . I figured she was here from the blood trail." She's collecting stray sheets of paper from the coffee table and shoving them into her bag. I glance at the clock. It's eight in the evening, and Gorhail is on lockdown, so why does it look like my sister's about to head out again?

I run a hand over my face, shaking my head, a futile attempt to clear the thoughts of Viola. *What has become of me? Paltro says young love is ephemeral, but there's nothing transitory about the sheer terror I felt when I thought she was dead.*

"Where are you going?" I ask.

"Got my clearance pass," she says. "I'll be holed up in the library the whole night. Lorne gave me some insights as I was collecting my pass—I have two equations wrong, and I'm approaching lifedrain from the wrong angle, but I'm *so* close, Sy, I can feel it."

"Don't overwork yourself, Lyr, please."

She waves me off, then raises her eyebrows. "Beau won't be back tonight... so you can use his room."

When I frown in question, she replies, "Yes... with Gray. Gryff sent me an express courier an hour ago."

"Haal..." Beau and Grayson have had a tumultuous relationship that ended in their not speaking for over a year. Family gatherings were impossible, and they even avoided each other at Dad's funeral five months ago. "I wonder what changed."

"Gryff and I are staying out of it."

"So am I."

She shakes her head and smiles, then picks up a book from the coffee table, and I recognize it as the one Viola took from her house in Albion; Olivia's favorite book of fairy tales. "I found this on the study desk and figured Viola would want it closer."

My sister sits on the sofa, sets the book at her side, and pats the empty seat next to her. I walk over with a sigh, sinking into the softness of the velvet. Lyria leans her head against my arm like she used to do in the early days after Mom's death. "Mom would've loved her. They'd probably spend hours in the garden together."

"You think?"

She hums quietly. It's all in the words she doesn't say, the quiet permission to lean into these feelings that have become my reason to breathe. "Tomorrow isn't promised, Sy," she murmurs.

I nod against her head. We sit in silence, the soft crackling fire fooling us into a moment of normalcy. Then Lyria stands and picks up her bag. "If I solve Mom's theory—as much as I hate to admit it, with Lorne's help—Viola might have her years back." She smiles. It's ripe with promises of a future I would die for. I know not to hope in our world, but tonight I will.

"What would I do without you?"

"Not much, I'm afraid." She winks, then she's out the door.

The hot water scalds my skin, pooling at my feet in a dark, red puddle, but it does nothing to quell my fears. Once Delaney realizes she has the wrong cuff, she *will* come back for Viola. Even if she sealed her death magic—that's hardly an option because I would *never* let her seal her magic, but even if she did—Delaney's lust for revenge would still hunt her down. I let out a heavy exhale. Fear is a dangerous thing. It's all-encompassing, suffocating, and demanding all at once.

I turn off the water, dry myself, and pull the first pair of pajama pants I find in Beau's drawers. Coincidentally, they are mine. Actually, most of the clothes in this drawer are mine. I make a mental note to gift my brother a whole new wardrobe for the Pine Festival.

The night is quiet, the stars twinkling low in the sky. It's treacherous, how close they appear, like the calm that reigns over Gorhail right now. As I stare at the sky, my sister's words swirl at the forefront of my mind. She's right. Tomorrow isn't promised.

I turn on my heels, and head straight toward the inner door linking my and Beau's rooms. My fist hovers over the wooden panel, but I don't knock. I lower my hand; I can't do this. I can't feed into the delusion of a happy ending and rope Viola along. Huffing out a long sigh, I prepare to turn around, but a soft click stops me.

"Sylas." Viola stands in the doorway wearing one of my shirts, which falls to her upper thigh. My eyes trail the length of her legs, up the curve of her hips, and the dip in her waist. Around her arm, Scar rests peacefully, like she's always belonged there.

My throat knots, and I nod a second too long.

Viola's tongue runs over her bottom lip, and . . . I *really* cannot be here right now.

"I," she says, and I become a statue. Her voice is like a siren's song, luring me to her. I'm fighting every muscle in my body not to press my hands into her waist and devour every inch of her full lips.

"It's late, Viola." My voice comes out low and hoarse. I don't know if I'm trying to convince her or myself. Her gaze meets mine, and I can no longer think straight.

"How do you bond?" she asks.

Did I mishear?

"How do Aspieri bond?" she repeats, the sharp edges of her voice demanding an answer.

Walk away. Walk away, my head screams at me.

"May I . . ." I swallow hard. My tongue needs to be ripped out. "May I come in?"

Idiot.

"It's your room—you don't need my permission." She leads me through the short hallway, under the glares of my ancestors. *Fool*, their portraits seem to say. *You cannot be considering bonding the Imortalis to a Mortemagi.*

I wait by my reading nook as Viola walks to the nightstand. The dark fabric of my shirt sways against her skin when she bends to retrieve her cuff. She must have gotten her relics back from the safe while I was in the shower.

Like a guest in my own room, I settle in the chair facing away from her, reaching for the nearest book from the coffee table. I flip to a random page, burying my face into it. I'm afraid to meet her eyes, afraid that if I take one more look at her lips, I will never leave.

"It's upside down." She gestures at the book, a smile playing on her gorgeous lips. She sits in the chair closest to me, her cuff in her right hand. My eyes fall to her exposed thighs, and I avert them immediately.

"Different mages bond differently," I begin as I slide the book onto the low glass table. I ramble about how Arkani bond with tattoos, Mortemagi with intent, and Aspieri with their relic's venom. I don't leave a moment for questions, and I move on to how interclass bonding is a combination of both.

"I'm not asking for a history lesson, Sylas. How do *we* bond?"

I sink farther in my chair, wishing it would swallow me. She wants to bond with *me*. She is part Mortemagi. Bonding with me lets her pull magic from all three of my aspiers, from Raiek. Perhaps it'd let her live longer. If it does, the moment she masters her magic, the world will be at her mercy. But now, instead of running away, I want to be at her side. What does that say about me—about my loyalty to my House?

"Uh—"

She doesn't say a word, doesn't break our gaze, as she moves off her chair and steps in front of me. Leaning forward, her long black hair cascades over my chest. Haal, I want to tangle my hand through her hair and pull her to my lips. I blink the thought away.

Viola brings her forearm next to mine, her cuff clasped in her other hand as it holds on to the arm of the chair for balance. Her face is only inches away from me; if I wanted to, I could reach for her and kiss her into oblivion. But I don't. Instead, my eyes trail over her knitted eyebrows while she murmurs something to Scar.

"Why do you want to bond?" The words catch in my throat.

"A bond is the only way Scar won't have to choose a new Aspieri when I . . ." She purses her lips, her eyes watering. "I read that not all aspiers choose new Aspieri; some choose death. I don't want that for her. And so my ghost won't become a wandering ghost. She told me . . ."

Haal, she's so selfless. She cares more about the fate of an aspier who refuses to accept her cuff and a ghost who anchored to her. She's given up so much of herself for all of us. She brought my brother back without asking for anything in return, and still, no matter how much I tried to push her away, she held her ground.

"Are they the only reasons?" I don't know why I ask. Mage bonds are sacred. Firstline mages bond strategically, in order to benefit from magic different from theirs, but most mages bond to honor it, to place the life of the other mage above theirs. They're more than a promise; they're a lifelong commitment, one that doesn't break until both mages die.

The Gods must be laughing, because only three weeks ago, the prospect of bonding with her was my worst nightmare, and now . . . I would carve her name into my rib cage.

"No." She gulps, lifting her eyes to me. "Not the only reasons."

"Viola . . . you're asking me to bond the Imortalis, a healing aspier, and a killing aspier," I say softly. "Bonds are a commitment that you'll always value the mage's life over yours."

She lets out an abrupt exhale, her eyes not leaving mine. "I was thrown into your life, and you've never once wavered. You fight harder for my choices than your own. You gave me a home when mine was shattered. You are my voice when I'm afraid to speak. You saved me in more ways than one. I look for you in the dark, and you find me with your eyes closed. Gods, I've only known you for a few weeks, but . . . you're etched in me, Sylas, woven into the fabric of my soul. I don't have many years left in this life . . . and I want them to be yours."

"Are you saying wh-what I think you're saying?" I stumble on my words.

"Yes."

Mom, forgive me, I am in love with a Mortemagi.

My heart thumps at the admission. It's useless fighting my feelings for her; I love her above my name, above my House, above my aspiers, above my life, and above my God.

"Because I don't want just this life . . . I want all of them," I admit, nudging Raiku awake. He sleepily uncoils himself halfway, wrapping his other half around Viola's wrist. His fangs hover over her vein.

"You can have this life . . ." Viola replies, "and the next." Scar half coils herself around my wrist, her golden eyes drilling into me. *A Mortemagi, you, too?* She seems to judge me.

"And as many as you want after that," she adds so quietly. Then, she clips her cuff to the same arm Scar is on. Her aspier's eyes snap to the cuff, but Raiku hisses at her once, and she turns her head toward him again.

"Are you sure?" I search her eyes for a sliver of hesitation, but she doesn't waver. Her beautiful mouth moves. "Yes, of course, yes. Sorry, I never asked if you wanted to . . ." she says. "I don't know what death magic you'll inherit. Are *you* sure?"

Our eyes lock. I lick my lips. I've seen mages bond before, and it was nothing like this. Between the stolen glances and the promises, this feels intimate. *Yes, I am sure.* As sure as I am that my heart is no longer mine.

Raiku bites her, and her eyes flare.

"Does this answer you?" I ask.

Her lips part in a gasp, and Scar bites my wrist. I'm overcome by warmth that I realize is coming from her cuff, followed by liquid ice seeping into my veins, taking over my heart. Is this it? Death's embrace?

After a few seconds, our aspiers return to us, and Viola unclasps her cuff again and sets it on the table behind her.

"I should . . . I should probably sleep." Her whisper drags me back to the reality of us. Her face inches away from mine, her warm breath on my cheeks. I've bonded with a half Mortemagi, giving her the reins of the founder's aspier, without knowing what kind of death magic will bleed into my veins. More importantly, I've bonded with a woman I am so hopelessly in love with, and the tragedy of it all is that she doesn't have many tomorrows left, while I have all of them. Maybe I should get up, walk away, live my life and let her live hers, save us the heartbreak. But there is no me without her.

Her fingers brush against my arm as she turns away. Against my resolve, I grab her wrist.

> Aspieri-Mortemagi double bonding is one
> of the most dangerous bonds.
>
> Mortemagi are fed so much magic; they often use
> too much, in turn depleting their lifeblood.
>
> Aspieri break their sacred bond with Haal, the
> God of War, placing them at the mercy of the God
> of Death. When they cross into the Underworld,
> they will never be at rest with their kin.
>
> **YSENIA FARO, *ON BONDS AND INTERCLASS MAGIC*, CHAPTER 27**

forty-one | viola

THURSDAY, DECEMBER 9, 1939

Sylas unravels parts of me I never knew were knotted. His fingers on my skin burn me with all-consuming, incapacitating desire. I look down at his hand and sigh. His thumb rubs slow, lazy circles on my inner wrist. "Tell me to leave."

Faint light from the stars outside spills through the tall windows, basking Sylas in an ethereal glow that makes me question whether he is human. I should do what he asks. Tell him to leave, keep him away from the inevitable heartbreak of my death. But looking at him, sitting on the edge of the chair, the light casting shadows on the lean muscles of his chest, I allow myself to be selfish.

"I don't want you to leave," I breathe out.

With a groan, he tugs me forward, and I brace a knee to the right of his legs. His gaze darkens, and he trails a finger up my thigh, sliding his hand underneath my shirt. Maybe it's the constant threat of death, or maybe it's just pure, unbridled lust, but I want him to rip it off.

He helps my other knee up, so I'm caging him with my body. My shirt rides up farther, and my bare skin sits against the soft linen of his pants—I should have asked Lyria to grab me some new clothes. When he realizes, his eyes flare with a primal need, his fingers digging deeper into my waist.

I hold his face, brushing my thumbs over his cheekbones. I never want to forget the flecks of amber in his gray eyes nor how they look at me, like he is my disciple and I am his God.

Not just this life, he'd said. All of them.

All of them . . . My breaths are shallow, my pulse rising. I am in love with him. By Death, I am in love with him. It almost feels painful to admit, because we are a tragedy, like the Gods let me taste the sweet nectar of life before lacing it with poison.

"Are you sure?" His unfairly beautiful mouth parts.

"I've never been surer of anything." I bury my hands in his hair, and he kisses down my neck. I need him to give in. I need him to take the whole of me, make me forget that my days are numbered. I *need* him.

"Viola, I will stop whenever you want . . ."

"Don't stop," I whisper, my heart thrumming at the rhythm of his kisses on my neck, the insatiable hunger in my lower belly only intensifying.

His hands slide up my chest, caressing the sides of my breasts. His smooth palm on my skin lights a fire inside me, threatening to ravage everything in its path. He takes his time, exploring my body with his hands, his thumbs grazing over my nipples as his lips kiss my throat, my neck, my collarbone.

"Viola," he groans against my throat. Pressing my hands on his chest, I move against him. His hands go still and a pained sigh leaves his lips. If this is a battle of wills, I've just won.

He slams his mouth against mine, breathing life into me, and my body shudders with pleasure. Our kiss is full of hopeless surrender, of whispered apologies and unspoken vows. His lips take mine, tugging, teasing, biting. It's nothing like I've experienced before. It screams *Don't leave me* and *This is our last time* at once. We're a tangle of tongues and lips, ragged breaths and quiet moans. I can taste the sharpness of mint, the softness of the vanilla; above all, I can taste how easy it will be for him to destroy me.

He glides his hands between my thighs, meeting my eyes with a question. I kiss him again, nodding against his lips. His fingers move against me, slow and gentle against the throbbing, then ever so carefully, he slides a finger in, curling it as his thumb rolls over my most sensitive spot. Heat flushes across my chest, and I don't know who I am anymore. He smiles as he finds his rhythm, steady and urgent, soft and demanding.

My heart is racing, my body coiled with a mix of euphoria and despair. I wanted him to make me forget, but Gods, he's ruining me, his touch burning away the ones before him, permanently etching himself on my soul. I bury my head in the crook of his neck in complete surrender, but his fingers slow.

The next moment, he is standing, lifting me with him, his solid grip on my thighs. My legs wrap around his waist, and I press my body against him, agonizing over how long it takes to walk to his bed. He kisses me the whole way there, as if a moment away from my lips would kill him. I think it would kill me.

He settles me in bed, my legs still wrapped tight around his waist, and he brings his mouth back to mine, his tongue parting my lips with delicate purpose. I don't want to wait anymore; I need him all over me. I slow down my kisses and arch my hips against him, and he growls against my mouth. "We can stop . . ."

My ragged breaths hold my tongue. He is thinking about stopping, when I'm thinking about him inside me.

"Say the word . . ." He bites my earlobe, trails kisses along my jaw, my neck, pausing right above my collarbone. "Viola, talk to me," he grunts, rising over me, his arms caging me in.

"Sylas." His name is a breath I cannot hold, not when he's worshipping every inch of my body and making me feel things I never knew I could feel. "Please."

His gaze climbs from my lips to my eyes, and he swallows, searching my face for hesitation he won't find. I want him more than I've ever wanted before. He lets out a long, ragged sigh, and I smirk.

"May I?" He straightens, leaning against the side of the bed, and tugs on my shirt.

Pushing myself up on my elbows, he helps me slide the fabric over my arms and neck. My chest rises and falls, my breath uneven. I am naked in front of him, my soul bare, trusting him with the most vulnerable parts of me.

"Gods, you're beautiful." He takes in a sharp breath, his cheeks blushing. His hand gently nudges my legs off him. "You're breathtaking," he murmurs as he bends, kissing between my breasts, his palms cupping them, his fingers gently squeezing my nipples. Pleasure ripples through me, and I let out a silent gasp.

"You're everything," he whispers as his mouth moves lower. He kisses above my belly button, then lower and lower. He pulls back, and I bite down a moan.

"Don't even think about stopping right now..."

He lets out a low chuckle. Gods, he's infuriatingly beautiful, and he's entirely mine. He stretches his arm. His aspiers uncoil to stillness before he places them on the nightstand. He reaches for Scar, and she does the same. Then his ravenous eyes are back on me.

Without looking away, he kneels in front of me. My breath hitches, and my hands freeze at my sides. Slowly, he parts my knees, kissing right above the bone. "Above my name," he whispers, then another kiss a little higher. "Above my House." Another kiss in the middle of my inner thigh. "Above my aspiers."

I gasp, but he doesn't stop, and kisses me again, so, so close.

"Above my life." His breath grazes my delicate skin, and I shudder... from both his admission and the ache his lips lit within me. My heart drums against my chest, and I know that if he stops touching me right now, it will give out.

Right before he reaches the sensitive spot between my legs, his eyes meet mine, and he smirks. "Above my God." Fuck. His head dips, and he kisses me there.

A desperate moan escapes my lips, but he doesn't rush. Every flick of his tongue sends my body close to the edge, ready to explode, but he recoils, teasing me, testing my self-control. My fingers curl into the soft bedding, and I lose myself further in the quiet demand of his mouth.

"Sylas." I'm breathless, caught in the ecstasy of the moment.

His fingers dig into my hips, and he quickens his pace. There's an urgency in the movement of his lips now, a purpose to every curl of his tongue. He kisses me with more intensity, and pleasure builds and builds until it crests through me. My body shivers, my legs freeze and then go limp.

Sylas trails kisses along my stomach as he moves back up. He pauses in the middle of my sternum, then moves right. I hold my breath. His tongue runs over one nipple, and I cry out in sheer despair of him. He swallows my cry with a kiss, and the taste of me on his lips sends me into a frenzy.

He pushes himself up, bracing his arms on the sides of my head as he searches my eyes for something. I think he finds it because he smiles.

Heat pulses between my thighs, and I run my hands down the lean muscles of his back, settling at his waist. My hands fiddle with the strings of his pants. His breath hitches—I know how he feels, because I feel it, too. The raw anticipation and the fear, the quiet reminder of everything the bond changed between us.

"Let me." I thread my fingers through his hair, and lock his lips in another kiss, pushing the soft linen down with my feet.

"Vi?" My name is a prayer on his lips, a silent plea that I am eager to answer. I arch my hips into him and loop my legs around his waist. He holds himself up with one hand, and the other laces with mine. He lowers my hand until my fingers wrap around the length of him.

I gasp. "I . . . I'm not on—"

He pauses, his shallow breath fanning my cheeks. "Aspier venom acts as contraceptive."

I don't look away, and I guide him inside me. A small frown knots his eyebrows. He searches my eyes for approval as he pushes himself in, inch by inch. And every time, I surrender. My heart is no longer mine; it beats in tandem with his. Pure, unbridled pleasure coils at my abdomen, begging for release.

I hook my legs tighter, giving him a gentle push. His pupils widen, and he lets out a low, achy groan in submission. "Is this . . . are you . . ." He swallows hard.

"Yes," I breathe.

The first thrust is bliss, the second one makes me question my name, and the third one unwinds a feral need for more. More this, more him, more us. He moves against me so gently, keeping himself propped with a hand so I don't feel his weight. But right now, I don't need care. I need him to send me over the edge. Again and again and again.

"Do your worst, Archyr." I grin, running my hands through his soft hair.

He raises his eyebrows. "Careful what you ask for, Corvi."

Then he's kissing me again, his body moving with the kiss. The rhythm of his thrusts takes me so close to release and brings me down almost immediately. By his smirk, I know he's taking his time to completely ruin me. His free hand palms my breast, pulling and pinching, as he works me to madness. My nails dig into his back, begging for mercy.

"Please." The word comes out in a strangled moan.

He laughs and kisses below my ear, moving at a steady pace. I tighten my legs around his waist, and he picks me up, turns us around, and lies down so I'm on top of him. He holds my waist and works me up and down until I'm screaming out his name. I've never felt anything like this. Euphoria. He's breaking me and putting me back together again. Gods, now that I've had a taste of him, how do I exist without him?

I frown when his movements slow, but I don't protest. Catching my breath, I fold on top of him, our bodies pressed together.

"Tired?" His fingers trail up and down my spine, and it ignites a second wave of crushing desire within me.

"Never of you . . ." I kiss his neck, suckling on the most sensitive part, right above where Raiek sits. His grip on me grows firmer, his moves are deeper, slower. My lips drag to his jaw, kissing the length of his scar.

"You're made for me." He sighs.

The surging desire crashes low in my belly. I am a mess in his arms, my body shuddering with a release bigger than my previous one. He gives me a few seconds to catch my breath, then he's moving again, pressing deeper inside me, thrusting like it's his life's purpose. And I want *more*.

And he gives me more. He flips me around again, his strong body wrapped around me. I close my eyes, lost in the warmth of his lips all over me. "You should've warned me," he says, breathless. His hips shift, thrusting hard again, making me forget how to speak.

I hum in question, my mind too cloudy to string words together. He smiles, and my heart dips. "That you're divine, Viola." He kisses the corner of my mouth. "I don't think I'll ever let you go."

My body tightens, the ache between my legs bursting into a quivering moan. He watches me as I catch my breath slowly, chest rising and falling. My fingers brush away the stray strand of black hair from his forehead, and now more than ever, I wish for eternity with him.

"I did promise you all my lives." I roll my hips against him. His pupils flare, and something dark flashes across his eyes. His hands grip my waist, pulling me into him. Once, twice, and then one last time. His body shivers as he lowers himself onto me. He presses a final kiss to my lips. Then he rolls over to my side.

My head rests against his chest, against his racing heart, and I smile. If I could carry anything to the Underworld, it would be this feeling. Forever.

"Did you mean it when you promised me all your lives?" He kisses my temple, his knuckles brushing up and down my arm.

"Mm-hmm," I murmur, sleep already pulling at my eyelids. I could get used to this, the safety of his arms, the soft caress of his breath, and the steady beat of his heart.

"Good." He pulls the quilted blanket on top of us, holding me closer. I don't know if I imagine the next words, but I swear he says, "I promise you all of mine, too."

> Priya, Viola is Alyria's daughter. Be warned that a Corvi relic even accidentally pulling magic from an aspier as powerful as Scar will kill her. I come to you in earnest—she must seal her Aspieri magic and return Scar to DOTS.
>
> **LETTER FROM OVERSEER RODRIC PALTRO TO PGM PRIYA PARRISH, DECEMBER 1939**

forty-two | sylas

FRIDAY, DECEMBER 10, 1939

I wake to an empty bed. Was last night a dream? I run my hand over the sheets. Still warm. Slowly, I come around. The shower is running. Viola is here. Viola is safe.

Not bothering to cover up, I make my way to the bathroom. She stands, her eyes closed, water running down her tangled hair, down her back, down her legs. I don't think twice, and I walk in.

"Something doesn't make sense," she muses, washing the soap out of her hair. "If Willow brought back Rafael Grimm all these years ago, where is he?"

"Grimm?" I ask mindlessly. Why is she talking about Grimm when all I can think about is the arch of her body against mine and how much I want to press her against the cold marble of the shower. "Grimm is gone, Vi. Willow might have released his ghost, but he could've been picked up by a conduit or even became a wandering ghost. I don't think he's involved," I tell her, trailing my finger along the curve of her hip.

"Ysenia mentioned Willow released him, and Delaney confirmed it." She doesn't acknowledge my hand, washing the minty soap off her body.

I pull my hand away. Maybe last night was the only one she was willing to give and today is a whole other story. *Sylas, you idiot.*

"Why'd you stop?" Viola glances at me over her shoulder.

"I thought..."

"Stop thinking."

I wrap my hands around her waist, pulling her into me. She laces one hand with mine, throwing the other one around my neck. The water runs over both of us. I kiss along her shoulder to her neck, pressing my body into hers.

"Sylas," she breathes out. My name belongs to her and only her.

"Sylas," a different voice yells. Three loud bangs pull us apart. Viola frowns at the door, then reaches for a towel, handing me a second one.

"Sylas." Beau's voice is urgent, in my room.

"Sorry." I kiss Viola, making quick work of the towel around my waist. I wonder if this is a glimpse into our lives together, always having to borrow time, always running to put out fires.

"Sylas, for Haal's sake." Beau raps on the door with an unusual impatience.

"What, Beau?" I shut the bathroom door behind me, stalking to my wardrobe with my brother tailing me. "Give me a minute."

"I'll wait for you outside," he grumbles, walking out into the living room.

Raiku slithers up my leg, settling in his usual position around my wrist. Railesza takes her sweet time. By the time she coils around my forearm, I'm already dressed in uniform.

"Mrs. Carver..." Beau hesitates the moment I step out of my room, handing me two of my daggers as we walk past the sofas and cross over to the kitchen counter.

"What did you find?"

"Grayson brought a second reader, and they were able to detangle some of Mrs. Carver's memories. They were so hazy; the second reader said someone's tried to reframe them multiple times. It's what has messed with her mind so much, the poor woman." Beau pours us two cups of tea, and I look between him and the teacup in surprise. "But I did learn one important thing... Willow LaCroix was trying to resurrect your mother with Faro's Cuff."

"What?" My head jerks toward him. That's impossible. How would she have gotten Faro's Cuff? Unless... unless Mom gave her the cuff before she died. At that time, she was the only one who'd have been able to, but why would Mom give Willow Faro's Cuff when she knew how dangerous it was?

"Where's Lyria?" I ask without waiting for him to answer. This could have been part of Mom's lifedrain theory research, and only my sister will know how to make sense of it all.

"She briefly came back and left for the library again this morning." Beau shrugs. "Willow was unsuccessful because your mother's ghost had already crossed into the Underiver," he finishes.

My thoughts are a jumble of theories, trying to piece together every single clue we have. Behind us, my bedroom door softly clicks, and Viola joins us in the kitchen, dressed in Lyria's clothes again. Scar perches on her finger, her eyes drilling the Corvi cuff in Viola's other hand; I'm still in disbelief that she let us bond with the cuff yesterday.

Beau slides a teacup toward her and catches her up on Victor's mom, and she's already grabbing a pen and the page with all our theories. As I watch her with my brother, my heart swells. That's it about Viola, she completes us.

"My nan fragmented pieces of Willow's soul across six relics—her friends' relics—and Delaney is collecting them to resurrect her." Viola brings her arm next to mine, and Scar slithers from her forearm to mine, crawling over Railesza. My healing aspier wakes up with an angry hiss, then Scar slithers to the other arm and settles above Raiku, resting her head close to his. Seeing our aspiers together somehow makes the bond... tangible.

Viola clicks her cuff around her arm. "Delaney admitted to the killings. I'm certain she killed Beau's parents, you"—she looks awkwardly at Beau—"then Ysenia said Willow released Rafael Grimm and Delaney confirmed it, but that's not all... When Willow released Grimm, his soul probably tethered to her body, like an anchored ghost. Don't ask how I know, but someone as terrifying as Grimm wouldn't simply become a wandering ghost."

At the mention of his name, the air shifts. If there's one thing we can all rally behind, it's that Grimm needs to be dead. Dead dead. Not trapped, not imprisoned, not a wandering ghost, just dead.

I glance up at Beau, repeating Viola's ghost's words. "The blood that seals... what if Willow released Grimm while using the cuff to resurrect Mom? It's the only way they would've gotten the blood of our ancestor."

But Beau isn't listening to me. He gapes at Viola. "You anchored to Ysenia Faro, the sixth founder of Gorhail?"

"Yes, but that's not important right now." Viola takes a sip from her cup, and sighs. "My question remains, where is Grimm if he's been back for over two decades? Surely, *someone* would've said or noticed something that would have given him away by now. Although I suppose . . . Maybe there's some truth to all the *Daily Mage* propaganda—"

Stairwell door. I hear a woman's voice, faint, quiet.

Viola turns around at the same time I do, but my legs are already moving, with her and Beau close behind. I jerk open the door, and Lyria falls to the floor, eyes glassy, her body halfway between the Poisoned Stairwell and Founder's Room.

"Sylas . . ."

I don't hear what Viola says. My ears are ringing, my vision darkening at the sides, and heat flushing up my neck. Railesza is already around Lyria's arm, fangs in her veins, but she doesn't look injured. I kneel in front of my sister, my fingers feeling for a pulse. It's steady. So why is she lying on the floor, her eyes wide open toward the ceiling?

"She's alive," I say. Thank Haal, but what's wrong with her? I need to take her to the infirmary.

Nyx hisses, drawing my eyes to a second body behind her. In the middle of that body's chest, I notice Lyria's dagger, blood pooling where the blade meets the flesh. "There's someone else."

"Sylas, don't move," Beau warns, but it's already too late.

Puppet. I hear the voice clear as day now, youthful, firm, with a low rasp. Ysenia.

Right as Ysenia says the word, the body—a woman—sits up, the darkness of the Poisoned Stairwell enveloping her with eeriness. Lyria's dagger still extends from her chest; my sister must have killed her just before she fainted. I don't recognize the woman who is turning into a puppet before our eyes, but from the tattoo on her neck, she's a poacher. My hands are on my dagger, Raiku and Scar both alert, but the woman doesn't move any closer.

"Take this as a warning. I only seek what was taken away from me."

Haal, this is Delaney coming back for Viola's cuff.

"What did you do to Lyria?" Viola asks as she steps closer to me.

"She fought till the very end, Lyria. What a beautiful name," the puppet scoffs, lifting her head toward Viola. The sinister depth in her voice grazes over my skin like a razor. Her eyes morph from brown to green—the same green as all the puppets we faced. "Believe it or not, I couldn't bring myself to kill her after the poacher failed. Her brilliant mind knew too much, like someone I knew centuries ago . . . alas, now it's gone."

Gods, oh Gods. Even as I think the worst, I refuse to acknowledge it.

"Grimm." The words escape Viola's lips so quietly. "Is it . . . did you hear that?"

No. Ysenia's voice comes through again.

Viola lets out a gasp, and the puppet holds Viola's stare, then the poacher's neck snaps and her body thuds on the floor.

When I reach over to gather Lyria, my hand brushes against the poacher's. It all happens in a fraction of a second. The complete chill of my skin. Time around me stopping, and the poacher's fingers digging in my wrist. *Only when the maiden and the crone die at the hands of the usurper will he be free.*

I jerk my arm away, the ice-cold press of her fingers permeating through my body. The furious rise and fall of my chest gradually settle, and I stare at the void with shaky breaths, reeling from the last few seconds. It's unmistakable, that feeling of complete emptiness and total surrender to Death.

Viola's whisperer magic now flows through my veins.

"What did she say?" Viola asks, her hand rubbing my back.

"Only when the maiden and the crone die at the hands of the usurper will he be free," I repeat, my eyes still on my sister's limp body. "I . . . I have to . . ."

My throat is dry. I glance from Lyria, to Viola, to Beau. I don't know what I have to do. "Gryff . . . someone needs . . ."

"Bring her in," Viola says, and I lift my sister in my arms. She's warm, and she's still breathing, so why is she staring into nothingness?

Unable to think for myself, I do as she says and take Lyria to her room. As I lay her down in her bed, her eyes blink. For a moment, hope strings me along. "Lyria, can you hear me?"

No answer.

"Lyr, please . . . do anything." Beau sobs next to me, kneeling on the floor beside Lyria's bed. But her eyes don't even flutter. She stares at the ceiling, her chest rising and falling, but it's useless.

"Sy," Beau says through tears. "Sy, she... Mrs. Carver..." He doesn't finish his sentence.

It takes me a moment. Then blood rushes to my ears. My eyes go in and out of focus, and all the air leaves my lungs. I try to open my mouth three times to tell him no. No, it cannot be. Not Lyria. She cannot be mindtrapped like Victor's mom, living like a shell of herself for the rest of her life. We don't know the extent of the damage on her memories; we don't know if she can see or hear us.

Impossible. Lyria would've accounted for this; she'd have found a solution to this already; it's probably in her notes. "Where are her notes?" My voice breaks as I fall to the ground next to Beau. "Where the fuck are her notes?" I yell.

"Sy," Viola tries, her soft hands gathering my head against her. I lean against the warmth of her abdomen and try to catch my breath. Grief and I should be well acquainted by now. So why does it feel like I'm drowning in quicksand, mourning a sister who's still alive?

"They will send her to St. Fabian's, Sylas. She can't go there... she..." Beau leans his head on her bed. "She'll end up like Mrs. Carver."

I *know* what DOTS will do to her. It won't try to fix her. It'll shove her in a room, make sure she's fed, and dismiss her like she's dead. My sister, one of the most brilliant minds of our generation, doesn't deserve this. And it's all because of me. Deep down I knew her research would lead her to the same fate as Mom, and I didn't stop her.

"I should never have let her go to that forsaken House!"

"Sylas." Beau turns to me and grips my shoulder, pulling me away from Viola. "We're not going through this again. Lyria wouldn't want you to drown in guilt. She's not dead; we don't know the extent of the damage. We can fix this."

"Delaney..."

"Not Delaney..." Viola trails off as she steps away from us. "Grimm."

As she says the name, Beau and I stop in our tracks. We both get up, turn to her.

"Ysenia cannot hear him nor see him. And he cannot hear her nor see her. She didn't hear what the puppet said. It was him."

Viola was right. Grimm must have infiltrated Gorhail's walls. I have to get to Paltro.

My fingers reach for Nyx, coiled asleep around Lyria's arm. I run my knuckles along her scales. Aspiers know us better than we know ourselves. If she hasn't left Lyria, there's still hope. As long as my sister's still in there, she will fight this.

"I'll send an express courier to Gryff and Grayson," Beau says.

I take one last look at my sister, her big brown eyes—Mom's eyes—looking up. *How could you let this happen again?* they seem to ask. They seem to want me to bury myself in my guilt until it chokes me out of reason. But this time, I steel myself. Lyria is alive, and if Grimm freely wanders the halls of Gorhail, it's not just my sister who'll need saving.

Viola squeezes my hand. "Go," she says. "We'll take care of her."

So I do.

Death magic is terrifying—the way it opens a line between the living and the dead. Sitting on a bench outside of Fang's Nest, I spend a few moments listening to the slightest noise and any stray whispers, wondering if Lyria will join me. I think I'm going mad, but anything is better than having to face Paltro with the news.

Finally, I stand.

The powdery snow cushions the crunch of my combat boots as I march uphill to Paltro's office. The wind picks up, and my head jerks around, looking for my sister each time. But it's just the wind, and she's not dead.

The grounds of Gorhail exude a quiet hostility that tells us it no longer wants us here. The clouds refuse to let the sun peek—even the trees weep about it, snow weighing down their branches.

I have half a mind to turn around and let Beau tell Paltro instead. But I can't burden him with that. It is my responsibility, just like it was my responsibility to watch after her, and I failed.

Fresh snow dusts the steps, and Paltro's office lights are on. I push the door open, and he straightens in his chair. It takes him a second before he scrambles up and meets me by the door.

"Come in, son."

He wraps his steady arms around me, and I let myself cry. I cry for the mother who was stolen from me, for the father who died saving me, for the brother who was killed because of me, and for the sister who sacrificed her sanity to save someone I love.

> Dear Viola, every day I have to lie to you, it kills me. I hope these letters find you one day so you can understand why I did what I did.
>
> **UNSENT LETTER FROM OLIVIA CORVI TO VIOLA CORVI, FEBRUARY 1931**

forty-three | viola

FRIDAY, DECEMBER 10, 1939

Lyria lies flat on her bed, her long black hair neatly splayed on her chest. She looks like she's dead, but her chest rises and falls steadily, and Nyx checks on her every few minutes.

Beau and I take turns by her side, going through theories about Grimm and Delaney with her in the off chance that she can hear us. Founder's Room is empty without Lyria's bright eyes, her excitement over the littlest things, and her optimism through our darkest days. Right now, we could use all of it.

"They won't be able to come in here," Beau reminds me for the twelfth time. "Founder's Room has ancient magic dating back to Sileas Ronin. It works like our aspiers, so if the Aspieri don't willingly let you in . . . we're safest here."

I nod, then sigh at Ysenia, bringing up the same question I've asked repeatedly since Sylas left. "Are you sure that I can't rearrange Lyria's mind?"

Yes, unless you're somehow also a reader, she replies every time. This time, though, she adds, *You should probably have bonded with a reader Arkani instead of . . . the petulant serpent.*

I sigh, ignoring her purist comment. She adds, *Before you accuse me of being a purist, did it really have to be the descendant of Sileas Ronin? Any other Aspieri would've been fine.*

"Ysenia, Grimm is back, and Delaney will still try to murder me. Could we talk about your dislike of the Ronins later?"

She doesn't reply to me.

After a short while, when it is clear Lyria is stable, Beau joins me on the sofa by the fireplace. We sit in silence; every now and then, his eyes glance toward Lyria's room. "I keep expecting her to get up."

I nod. Words don't come easily anymore. Lyria didn't have anything to do with heirloom relics, Delaney's revenge, or Grimm. Why her?

I lean back against the couch, and my hand catches on something hard. In the corner of the sofa is Olivia's book of dark fairy tales. I had forgotten where it went after we came from Albion. I had wanted to read Lyria a few tales; now I don't know if she would even be able to hear them.

My hands close around the book, Olivia's DOTS letters extending from the top edge, their golden seal glowing under the muted fire. "Did Gorhail send you these letters?" Beau asks.

I frown. "No, these are letters DOTS sent my sister . . ." I pull them out, studying the address carefully this time. It reads Olivia's name and our address in Albion. I blink . . . this is Olivia's handwriting.

"Golden seals are from Gorhail, Vi," he says. "Official DOTS correspondence bears a red seal."

Why would Olivia send herself self-addressed letters? Before I answer my question, I slide my finger under the lip of one and tear it open. "Ouch." The paper cuts my skin, and blood smears on the envelope, some over the letter inside. I hand it over to Beau as I put pressure on the paper cut.

Beau winces. "Sorry, do you need a bandage?" he asks. "I'd offer my aspier, but Briar has been a bit reclusive lately."

I shake my head and gesture for him to continue. He pulls the letter out, his eyebrows knitting together as he unfolds it. "Viola, you have to see this."

He hands me the letter as the words slowly appear, one after the other, like magic.

"Dear Vi," it reads. "*These two letters are enchanted. My friend, Sierra, made me this sparkly pink dust that makes words disappear. Victor, my other friend, enchanted it so it could only be opened by you and your blood. Morbid, I know. But there is a second letter with instructions, should I leave before I have the chance to speak to you.*"

Leave? To go where? I reach for the second envelope, tearing it open. The moment my finger slides across the side, words appear.

"*Dear Vi,*" I read. My heart slams against my chest. Reading Olivia's words weeks after she died... I can't even be happy. Because all I'm thinking about is how I will never see her again, and if we don't manage to save Lyria, how I will handle losing a second sister.

The letter continues. "*If you're reading this right now, I must have already left—I can't tell you where, Vi. But I am safe and away from this lie I can no longer keep up with.*"

My eyes fill with tears. No, Ole. You're dead.

"*Remember my favorite book about dark fairy tales?*" I read further. "*Between every two pages is an extra page. Sierra handstitched them together and enchanted it all so it looks like it's part of the story. Blood smeared on every other page should open my journal through all my years at Gorhail. I wrote it addressed as letters to you. I'm sorry I won't get to say goodbye, but I promise we'll meet again.*"

"Give me your dagger," I say to Beau, but he just tilts his head at me. "Your dagger, now."

He pulls it out, and I snatch it from his hands and make a straight cut along the length of my index finger. Then I flip to the first page of Olivia's book of fairy tales. Before my eyes, the letters change into new words.

The first pages detail her life at Gorhail Institute, her favorite food, her favorite classes, mundane things that she found fascinating, like Arkani-made pens that never ran out of ink, or Arkani-enchanted fabric that stretches. Toward the middle of the book, my eyes catch on a familiar name.

"*There's a new Magister. Lorne. I fell in love so fast. I know I'm not supposed to, but he is everything I've ever dreamed of. Maybe one day, after graduation, you'll meet him.*"

The next pages detail more of her recent life at Gorhail. I read them with a pinch in my heart. Her happiness radiates through the page, through her outings with her friends, her new classes, her frequent visits to the Penbryn Gardens. How could Delaney rob her of that? How could she rob me of her?

Then the next page makes me stop.

"*Viola.*" She used my name; she never used my full name. I sit up, holding the letter tight. "*I wanted to tell you in person today, but I didn't want to risk Mom hearing. It breaks my heart that you think I'd choose Gorhail over you, and I think it's time you know the truth. Right before her death, Nan told me to hide your magic, to take your place at Gorhail to keep you safe and hidden from a world that would inevitably kill you. I believed her. It killed Dad, after all. So I went, and I've never spoken about you, never told anyone I had a sister. I tried. I've worked so hard, Vi. I've sent you two self-addressed letters; I thought I was going to leave, go far away to the Isles of Carac in the North. But after our conversation today, I think I'm ready to come back. I'll go to Osneau with you and maybe start a bakery."*

My hands are shaking. She wrote this the Monday I last saw her. I don't know that I am reading her words right, so I flip to the next page and watch as my blood smears across the parchment and the letters jumble into the right order.

"Viola. Victor died this morning. I have a horrible feeling. Yesterday, Overseer Delaney told me to retrieve a book about relics from Nan's library—the one you just unboxed last week. She's always asking to borrow books from Nan, and they're usually regular textbooks. But this one was different. I read it cover to cover. I tore three pages about resurrection and relic merging out before I handed it over to her. No one should have that much power."

Every single word I read drives a knife farther through my heart, and every apology twists it. My sister, my beautiful sister, sacrificed herself to keep me safe, because Nan *sent* her to this forsaken place.

Anger surges through me, and I grip the book. I do not doubt that Nan would have done the same to me had Olivia been the mage and I the nonmagi. What happened to telling me I was the most precious thing to her? Was she talking about me? Or was she talking about the cuff she knew I would inherit? Now that I know about Willow's entrapment, I know it wasn't me she was trying to keep safe. It was her stupid cuff, one of the six relics she'd used to trap Grimm. The cuff Olivia died for. The cuff Delaney and Grimm will kill me for. It has always been about the magic in the end. How could her love of magic be greater than her love for us?

I flip through the last three pages of the book, meticulously stitched with the rest. By now, the pages and my hand are a bloody mess. Still, I read the words ever so carefully. My conversation with Ysenia resurges. "This details how to carry out resurrections, simple and complex, and how to break tethers."

Beau shifts closer. "You were right . . . about Grimm being tethered to Willow."

The poacher's riddle is as clear as day in my mind. "Only when the maiden and the crone die at the hands of the usurper will he be free." Sliding the book to Beau, I explain, "Grimm needs to sacrifice Delaney to resurrect Willow. Ysenia?"

Correct.

Her word encourages me further. "And then he needs to kill Willow to break the tether." I pause, waiting for Ysenia's confirmation. *Also correct.*

Maybe Nan did have a good reason to hide the cuff—Delaney only wants to bring back her daughter, but Grimm lurks in the shadows, waiting for her to do his dirty work before pouncing.

"Delaney wouldn't stand for that. She didn't damn herself to the tenth circle of the Underworld to allow her daughter to be killed again." Beau studies the page.

"What if she doesn't know?" I wonder aloud.

Ysenia scoffs. *Mortemagi have a habit of sacrificing their own in pursuit of... power.*

Sylas would've loved to hear the Founder of the House of Death lay our sins bare. After what Nan did to Olivia, it wouldn't surprise me if Delaney was on board for everything.

"Ysenia, didn't you say complex resurrections were impossible?"

Improbable.

"What happens when he breaks the tether to Willow?" I reach for the book in Beau's hands. The second page is covered in notes. Some I recognize as Nan's handwriting, some Olivia's, and some foreign. Delaney was wrong about one thing: Willow never released Grimm on purpose. Nan's notes confirm that she brought him back while trying to carry out a resurrection, and this resulted in his soul tethering to hers when it escaped. He needs to kill her to be free.

He regains true form, the full extent of his whisperer magic and his reader magic. I pray you don't see that day, Viola. The ages of Grimm were dark, if I am to go by the ghosts of the catacombs.

"If we live through this, we owe Olivia everything." I get up, reaching for a thick jacket. I refuse to sit and do nothing. I won't let Olivia's sacrifice go in vain, won't let Lyria lie half dead when all she was trying to do was find a way to save me. "Does Grimm know about this?"

Grimm, yes. Delaney, I doubt it. Although, when I wrote about it in The Founder's Book of Relics, *it was a working theory. Of course, I never tested* it. *If he's waited this long, he may very well have. He's not someone who strikes without thought.*

There is a tiny chance that Grimm has never done this before. I laugh at my hopelessness. If we can prevent Delaney from resurrecting Willow, we can keep Grimm from regaining his true form. "How do we stop him?"

We cannot stop him. But we can weaken him. Ysenia goes silent for a moment.

"Tell me."

Viola, it would require an immense sacrifice.

"Tell me . . . please."

I'll have to take over your body, throw your cuff to Delaney, and let her carry out Willow's resurrection. Then, when Grimm sacrifices Willow and begins regaining his true form, I'll take Faro's Cuff. Other than him, I'm the only one who can unclip it. We won't have long, only between the time the host dies and Grimm is born anew. But if I take over your body . . .

"I die."

My heart stutters. Even if I know it's inevitable, I don't *want* to die. I let out a sharp exhale as I turn to Beau, my chin quivering. I don't want to die. I don't want to leave them. I don't want to leave Sylas.

"Vi." Beau's voice trembles as he finally realizes what I'm talking about. "Olivia gave up her life to keep you hidden. Don't do this."

But there is no other way. Ysenia is the only one who can stop Grimm from coming back with a relic so powerful it could break apart our world. This is bigger than us now, bigger than my life.

"Viola, please. DOTS has to be aware of both Delaney's crimes and Grimm's return by now—Sylas would've told Paltro. Firstline can use Sierra's relic as bait; other than yours, Grimm still needs hers to complete the set. There are other ways. Viola, please don't do this . . . Let DOTS do its job for once."

"Do its job . . ." I laugh, an empty, barren laugh like all of DOTS's and Gorhail's promises. "If DOTS and even Gorhail did their jobs, Lyria wouldn't be trapped in her own body! Olivia would still be alive. Our parents would still be alive. I wouldn't be a prisoner to magic I cannot use." As the words tumble out of my mouth, I wish I could take them back. Beau doesn't deserve my frustration. "They don't care about any of us, Beau. We're all disposable to them. If we don't do anything, we'll doom everyone else to a terrible fate."

"Leave then, Viola. Seal your magic and start a new life with however many years you have left," he says, voice cracking, a hot tear rolling down his cheek onto my arm. "But don't throw away Olivia's sacrifice."

A few weeks ago, before Olivia's death, I would've jumped at his words, given up my magic, and run away without sparing a glance back at this twisted, horrid world. But this is my one chance to change the story, to give back all that was given to me. More people can't die because of these monsters. "What is a life if I'm always running from something?"

> Death fell in love with the first Mortemagi. After centuries in the Underworld, he let her go back to the living world. He waited and waited for her, until years after her second death.
>
> She never came back.
>
> **LUCIA KAN,** *TALES FROM THE UNDERWORLD,* **PASSAGE 6**

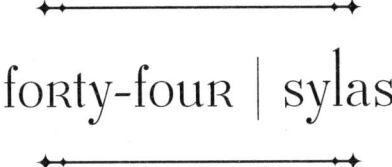

forty-four | sylas

FRIDAY, DECEMBER 10, 1939

"Rafael Grimm mindtrapped Lyria."

For a moment, Paltro sits still, his eyes lingering on my forearm, where Scar coils herself above Raiku. Then he leans back in his chair and drags his accusatory stare up my face. "Why was Lyria outside of the House of Poison when Gorhail is on lockdown?"

"She . . ." I hesitate. He's going to blame Viola, I can see it in his eyes. Still, I don't lie. Despite how Paltro feels about Viola, I refuse to hide my feelings for her to quell Paltro's concerns. "She was in the library, trying to complete Mom's lifedrain theory to give Viola her lifeblood back."

Mom's research is cursed; she died in the middle of it, and perhaps because of it, and now it's doomed Lyria, too.

"This woman again." Paltro lifts his nose at the mention of Viola. "And now your sister is as good as dead because of her. At least you had the good sense to get Scar back." His eyes fall on Viola's aspier.

I retract my arm. Scar is Viola's—I only have her because she refuses to be worn with Vi's cuff—not mine and certainly not DOTS's. My fists clench on my knees. Viola didn't harm Lyria. If he's going to try to spin my sister's predicament, I will leave. "Grimm"—I stress the name—"is back.

He mindtrapped Lyria, and, as you already know, Delaney is a murderer. You should focus on that instead of trying to pin this on Viola."

He looks at me for a long moment. "Very well." His kettle whistles, and he pours the scalding-hot water into a small white teapot, then adds two heaping teaspoons of tea. Pulling two teacups from his drawer, he slides one toward me.

"I don't want tea." The only thirst I have is for Grimm's body to be ripped apart so even the Underworld can't piece his ghost together.

"Son," Paltro says, his eyes moist. My gut twists, my throat thick with uncertainty. His tone echoes so much sadness. Perhaps he needs this, my joining him for tea. Lyria was close to a daughter to him. So after a pause, I nod. He gently pours the steaming liquid for both of us, then brings one cup to his lips.

I do the same.

One moment, I am sitting in Paltro's office. The next, I am standing outside it, in the height of summer.

Lyria... no, that's *Mom*. She stands outside of Paltro's office, except it's not the office I know. This one has freshly painted black walls, matching the rest of Gorhail. She clutches a small box against her chest and casts furtive glances over her shoulder.

This isn't real, I realize. I'm in Mom's memory. Paltro tricked me into drinking the tea he brought to Founder's Room yesterday, the one Sierra extracted from Zoya.

Mom hurries forward, and I follow her across a greener courtyard with pink and purple flowering trees instead of the sheltered stone hallway we now have, through a different Fang's Nest, and out into an unchanged Hollow Tree. She waves at a girl with short black hair. Willow. They leave through a door that leads to the Poisoned Stairwell, and she hands Willow the box. Willow opens it, and Ysenia Faro's Cuff sits inside. Willow hugs Mom, thanking her, telling her she'll finally be able to pull enough magic to resurrect her father.

Oh, Mom, how could you have been so foolish? Our ancestor locked up the cuff for a reason.

Then the frame cuts to the catacombs, and I'm already moving. Mom zips through the dark, her hands palming the limestone like it's a familiar map. Raiku is around her forearm.

Haal, Raiku was Mom's aspier.

Everything makes sense now, why Dad brought him to me instead of taking me to a relicsmith like he did with Lyria, and why the name was scribbled in Mom's journal.

Mom keeps throwing worried glances over her shoulder. Then she disappears into the burial chamber. When she walks out, Raiek is around her neck, and Raiku is gone.

Everything goes dark for a moment, and I find myself in a different memory. It's not as linear as the other ones. The frame jumps around, as if the magic is trying to hem memories together.

Mom comes back in frame, her eyes darting around. She reaches for her dagger. Then a voice speaks. "Magus Principalis Ronin. Where is she?"

Mom spits, "Even if I knew, I would never tell you."

My heart clenches, and my eyes sting. I haven't heard her voice in so long—I had forgotten the soft timbre of it. That same voice once told me endless stories before I slept. She never refused, even as I asked for more and her eyes began to close with exhaustion.

"Don't make me pull it out of you," the voice replies. I don't recognize it. It's weary, with a low hoarseness that doesn't match the severity of the tone. "I know Alyria is alive."

Mom stutters, clenching her dagger. Lyria has the same frozen look when she's lying. Mom knows where the Deathbringer is. "I haven't seen Aly in years."

"My patience has limits, Ronin," the voice threatens, sharpening its edges.

"I hope you can push those limits . . ." Mom replies, and I want to tell her to take her words back, not to provoke whoever that horrible voice belongs to. But it's too late.

Three bony creatures push up from the ground, their sharp skeletal hands upturning the stones. I grip my dagger, even though there's nothing I can do. They stand tall, their hollow eyes pointed toward her. From here, they seem like they'd fall from a push, but the magic that powers them is wicked, unforgiving. They lurch toward Mom, but she is nimble. She stabs several of them in a row, her blade landing straight into the back of their necks. "I was the Deathbringer's second, Dean; are you sure you want to test me?"

Dean. Who was the dean when Mom was in school?

The answer strikes me just as Rhea Corvi comes into view. She's unmissable—gray hair pulled into a tight bun, face painted with annoyance, the same face that colors her later portraits in the halls of Gorhail.

"Ronin," she snaps. "I know that Alyria has a child."

"How?" Mom's face sobers with the realization that she's confirmed Rhea Corvi's guess. Her face falls. "You're a bitch," she says.

"I am clever," Rhea Corvi scoffs. "The child is a crossmage with Corvi magic and Scar. I must find her before DOTS learns of her."

"Enough," Mom lashes out. "You hate crossmages. You've sent every single one to their execution, and you'd do the same to the child. Admit it, you're furious they tainted your perfect purist bloodline."

"My legacy will not be a crossmage," Rhea Corvi shouts as she raises five more undead behind Mom, who shakes her head, readying her dagger. Then the faint lights flicker, and Rhea's head snaps to the side before she disappears, leaving Mom in the middle of a dozen undead.

I want to tell her to run back to the burial chamber to get Raiku. In fact, I think I am screaming at her to get Raiku. But of course she doesn't hear me. She's dead.

Mom fights three undead, killing them one after the other. The other one approaches her in the back, claws drawn, ready to stab her. I scream, but someone else shields her, taking the claws in the center of his chest.

Dad.

"Han, no!" she screams and drops to her knees, catching him as he falls. I feel her pain as though it is my own. My mother grabs on to my father, rolling him onto his back. "You weren't supposed to be here." She's not even looking as she throws daggers at two more approaching undead. They both screech and turn to ash. "Han, wake up, for the love of Haal." She presses her forehead against his. "I came down here for Raiek, to help Willow with our lifedrain theory. Nothing would've happened to me. I'm immortal with him."

Raiek slithers from her neck to my father's then, and the moment Raiek settles at his collarbone, Dad wakes, shoving Mom away from another undead.

I know how this story ends. I've known it my whole life. I don't know why I'm watching them, hopeful that she sidesteps, that she makes it, that I get to go home and hug her. But instead of staying behind Dad, she whirls, throwing a dagger at the undead, right as another one digs its claws straight into her heart.

My own heart shatters all over again. I had always known how she died, but watching the life slowly fade from her eyes as Dad lowers her to the ground, his hands covered in her blood, breaks me. "Tell them stories about me, Han. Remind them that it isn't our magic that makes us, but we—" She goes limp in Dad's arms.

I blink, realizing I've been watching a blend of Mom's and Dad's memories, and I'm back in Paltro's office, out of breath, tears streaming down my face. My heart is pounding against my chest, and my limbs are frozen in place.

Rhea Corvi killed my mother.

Viola. Does she know? Is that why she's helped us so much? Was any of it real, or was it her guilt pushing her forward? The weight of betrayal threatens to crush my windpipe. Her grandmother killed my mother, because of her mother, because of . . . her.

No. This can't be it. I reach for the cup and gulp down the rest.

I don't know whose memory I land in this time, but it's the same hazy picture, as if multiple memories have been stitched together.

I'm in the middle of a forest with tall red tree trunks and low black bushes that I don't recognize. We're not in Gorhail Woods. We're in an unfamiliar clearing, and looking at the white deer grazing on the black leaves, I think we're somewhere in the province of Aurignan. In the middle of the clearing stands a small yellow house with a wraparound veranda.

A little girl plays with the Deathbringer, who beams as she picks her up, whirling her around, hugging her, making her laugh. Out here, she isn't the Deathbringer from our textbooks; she's just a mother spending time with her daughter.

A branch cracks, and Alyria sets Viola down.

In a second, she morphs from a loving mother to the legendary mage I know. Scar is perched on her left hand, and the right holds Viola against her leg. A slow shuffle of leaves later, and she lowers her guard.

"Tobias," she exclaims. "How did you—"

"Why did you leave, Aly?" His voice breaks. When he comes into the frame, I don't question who he is. Tobias Corvi. Viola's father.

"I couldn't do that to her." She tucks Viola behind her. "She's a crossmage, Tobias."

"Gods, she looks like you." He kneels, placing his arms on his knees.

At first, Viola hesitates, but soon, she runs to him, giggling. He holds her for what seems like hours.

"I know." The Deathbringer softens, but she doesn't lower Scar. "But she has your eyes."

"The whole world is looking for you, Aly," he says softly. "Come home. We'll seal her death magic if we need to, but please come home."

"She has a right to both classes of magic." Alyria approaches them with caution. Slowly, she kneels in front of him, her hand reaching for his face. "How did you find us? Did Lily tell you?"

"Willow." He chokes up at the name. Gods, she doesn't know.

"Lily . . . and Willow, they . . ." he trails. "Lily was killed in the catacombs, likely by poachers. Willow tried to resurrect her, but she released Grimm from Faro's Cuff instead. My mother sealed her soul across six relics. Everything is falling apart. Han is inconsolable . . . the children ask for their mother every day . . ."

"No." Her hands clasp her mouth, and she shakes her head as tears fill her eyes. "No, Tobias. No."

Her shoulders shake as she sobs; the air is charged with a raw heartbreak that makes *me* want to reach for them. With his free arm, Tobias reaches for her, and she leans against his shoulder, staining his shirt with her tears. Viola plays with her mother's hair, unaware of all the tragedy around her. My heart shatters at the sight of what could have been for Viola. She deserves this family, not the repugnant excuse of a life she was forced into.

Right when I think the memory is over, a quiet shuffle draws my attention. My hand hovers over the hilt of my dagger, forgetting once more that I stand here, a prisoner of the past, unable to change anything.

Scar's golden eyes narrow. She slithers down the Deathbringer's arm, fangs out, ready to strike.

"Mom." Tobias kisses Viola's head before handing her over to Alyria. Stepping in front of them in defense, he opens his palm. "What are you doing here?"

"Give me the child," says Rhea Corvi. "I promise to keep her safe. You do not understand what's at stake."

Alyria hugs Viola tighter, shielding her from her grandmother. "I've kept her safe and hidden for two years, Rhea. I don't need help, especially not from a purist."

Tobias's fingers move. "Leave, Mother."

"You do not understand." Rhea splays her fingers. Around her, an army of undead takes root. "That child is the only way to prevent our world from falling into darkness."

That child. Viola isn't an object. Her small hands clutch her mother's neck, her big brown eyes widening at the undead.

Run, I want to yell. Rhea Corvi hasn't come to negotiate.

"Gods, save them," I plead in vain to the Gods that stood by, watching this wretched woman steal everything from Viola.

"I love you, Aly." Tobias throws one last look over his shoulder, pausing on his daughter. "Maybe in another life . . ." he says, his eyes holding years of regret. Then he turns back toward his mother, his sadness replaced by the same fierce determination I see in Viola's eyes.

Then they're gone.

My gut wrings in worry. I know this is Viola's memory, and it isn't finished yet.

Now Viola sits alone in the hollow of a tree trunk. She wraps her hand around her knees, her eyes pressing together at the slightest sound. Haal, she's just a baby.

The frame moves, and Alyria stabs Tobias straight in the abdomen. He doesn't flinch. He pulls out the knife, and there's no blood. It takes me a moment to realize that this isn't Tobias at all, not anymore. Rhea Corvi stands in the back, watching them with interest.

My stomach turns. Suddenly, I'm gasping for air. In the moment I did not see, she killed her own son and used him as a puppet to fight the mother of his child.

But the Deathbringer earns her name. Scar drops the undead faster than Rhea Corvi can summon them, and Alyria is relentless. She lands punches and stabs, and the puppet of Tobias doesn't graze a single hair.

Rhea plays a dangerous game. Every time Alyria goes for a hit, she inches closer to Viola. But Alyria is faster. She stabs puppet Tobias in the neck and lunges for Rhea, throwing her to the ground and knocking her unconscious. Instead of getting up, Alyria's body is still, over Rhea's.

Maybe I'm foolish, but a part of me hopes the Deathbringer escaped, that she really did go into hiding all these years, plotting how to get her daughter back.

"Mama," Viola screams, but it's too late.

Alyria's white dress blooms red, the tip of an undead's claw protruding from her back. Scar slithers over, hissing as she looks back and forth between Alyria and Viola. The aspier is torn between staying with her Aspieri and bonding with her legacy. But Viola's too young to bond.

"The time will come, Scar." Alyria's words weaken. Scar approaches her, gently rubbing her head against Alyria's cheek. Haal, have mercy on the Deathbringer's aspier. She gives her a final nod, a final look, before coiling herself into a stillness that would last twenty years.

"Mama," Viola cries again.

Alyria drags herself off Rhea's unconscious body. The crimson of her blood stains the grass as she crawls to her daughter. Huffing out labored breaths, she digs her elbows into the ground, pushing her body forward until she reaches Viola. But now, she can't lift herself up, can't give her a final hug. Viola throws her arms around her neck, and with one final push, Alyria drags her arm over her.

"Being your mother is the greatest honor of my life," Alyria croaks, the light leaving her eyes.

"Sylas." Paltro is shaking me. But all I see is Viola's arms around her dead mother's neck. She was raised by her parents' murderer, who still failed at hiding her. The cuff she wears killed my mother and both of her own parents.

She can't possibly know any of this, and now... I'll have to tell her.

"Snap out of it, Sylas," Paltro urges. He taps me on the cheeks.

The cluttered office comes into focus again, and the faint smell of mint assaults my nose. I open my eyes and wish I hadn't. My face is wet with tears.

"We don't have the luxury of grieving, son." Paltro wipes his eyes. "Sierra's dead relic was stolen. Bring me Viola's cuff before it falls into Delaney's hands."

My heart is fighting between what I know to be true and what I have been taught to believe. Viola isn't like Rhea or Delaney. She is *my* Viola. But her cuff killed my mother. That despicable relic is the only remaining obstacle for Delaney to resurrect her daughter.

"Willow released Grimm," I say.

"Yes, Tobias confirmed it in the memory." Paltro pulls down his map with the red crosses, the same one I saw here weeks ago. "I believe that

Grimm is tethered to Willow, but we don't know where he is. We don't know what he looks like. Your father was investigating when he died. The red crosses are all the places we think he's been."

Dad. Another person Grimm probably took from me.

Paltro breathes in. "Get me that forsaken cuff, Sylas, so we can put an end to this. Without the cuff, Delaney can't bring Willow back, and Grimm won't be able to regain his body."

"Of course, Uncle." I leave his office with the promise of putting an end to twenty years of murders because of revenge. Viola will understand. She has to. But am I ready to forgive that her cuff killed Mom?

> Aurelia, your thirst for revenge reminds me of what it's like to be a Mortemagi. What if I told you there was a way to bring back your daughter? All you need is *The Founder's Book of Relics*. Bring it to me, and I will grant you eternity.
>
> **LETTER FROM [REDACTED] TO AURELIA DELANEY, JULY 1937**

forty-five | viola

FRIDAY, DECEMBER 10, 1939

"Sylas." I open the door of Founder's Room to let him in. "Beau's accompanying Lyria to St. Fabian's in Riverview. They won't let her stay at the infirmary—"

He doesn't give me a second. He wraps his arms around me, pulling me closer to him. I relax in the warmth his body provides, and he lowers his head until our foreheads meet.

Time stills.

His every breath plays the strings of my heart like a fiddle. For a second, I think he's going to kiss me, and I wish he would. I wish he would make me forget the horrors that await us. I wish we could go back to when our biggest problem was each other.

Pulling away, he stares at me for a second and lets out a slow exhale.

"Come with me." He drags me past the kitchen and Lyria's room, through the living room, past his bedroom, and behind the study area and Beau's room to the large balcony outside.

In the daylight, the magnificent range of Mount Chazal stands in all her glory. With the clouds gone, we can see its long waterfall cascade like silk into the sea. Three spitfire hawks fly in a circle, their screech piercing through the distance. Gorhail is so beautiful. One day, if Death allows, I wish to explore Mount Chazal and collect these tiny moments of nature's perfection.

"Did you know your grandmother killed my mother?" He lets go of me, flexing his fingers.

For a moment, I don't speak. Because I don't know what to say. His words are so ugly in contrast to the beauty that's in front of us. Of course Nan didn't kill his mother. She was wrong for not telling me about my mother and sending Olivia to Gorhail to hide me, but now I know she had her reasons. If Lyria's predicament is a small glimpse into what Grimm's magic can do, Nan was right to hide the cuff.

"Why would—"

"I saw it." Accusation laces his words with venom. He finally looks at me, but I don't recognize the Sylas I know. This one glowers at me like I've betrayed him, like I'm withholding truths that I'm unaware of.

"Sylas," I start.

"Viola." He stops me, and takes a sharp inhale. "Rhea Corvi didn't just murder my mother. She killed your mother and father, too."

"Enough." I back away from him. His venom holds no truth. Is he spewing these lies to make me go away? Did Beau tell him of my plans to stand as bait?

He lifts his right forearm, and Scar slithers along, glaring at my cuff and hissing at it violently. It's one thing to reject me, but must the traitor aspier so vehemently remind me of how she hates this side of me?

"It's no surprise Scar refuses to have anything to do with you while you wear this." His mouth curls at the cuff in disgust. "This cuff was used to kill her Aspieri, your mother."

Scar's head bobs.

The air around me grows thicker. I struggle to swallow, struggle to breathe. My head is spinning. Nan would never kill Dad. She mourned him every single day, kept him alive through every single story she told us about him, through every one of his favorite meals she made. Why would she hurt so much for someone she murdered?

"You're wrong."

"Viola, you are my reason to breathe. Fuck, I'm in love with you." Sylas cups my face, the gentleness of his fingers a stark contrast to the anger in his tear-filled eyes. "I have no reason to lie to you."

One breath. He's in love with me. Two breaths. Nan sent Olivia to her death to protect me. Three breaths. Was it to protect me, or my magic, or the cuff she knew I would inherit? The cuff that helped seal Willow away so Grimm couldn't regain his magic.

I hold his stare for a moment, notice the tears pooling in his eyes. Gods, I love him, too, I love him like I've never loved anyone before, like I'll never love anyone after him, but I can't stand here and let him slander Nan.

"It could have been poachers." The excuse spills out of my lips, a poor attempt to quell my racing thoughts.

Sylas's mouth draws into a line.

Nan knowingly sacrificed Olivia, so the harrowing possibility of her murdering our parents for the same cause rings true. Gods, have mercy.

"We know there are Mortemagi poachers." I offer yet another feeble attempt to defend her. I don't know why. Maybe I owe it to the person I thought she was, to the years when she was the only one who kept me safe.

"My mother died because she was protecting *you*." His voice breaks as he drops his hands to his sides. Tears stream down his cheeks, and I want to reach out to him. He is fighting against himself . . . over me, over whether I am worth the pain of the constant reminder of his mother's death.

"Nan isn't a murderer." I gently push him away. "Maybe someone lied to you."

"Vi, I saw a collection of memories from my parents, your nan, and you. A reader's magic is always true."

"Paltro has a million reasons—"

"Vi," he says, his voice softer, his eyes drilling into mine. And right then, I realize this is the end of us. He will never let go of his prejudice of Mortemagi, and I will never apologize enough for the sins of my kin.

"*I* have no reason to lie," he says, and it breaks me.

"Yes, you do," I retort, my chin wobbling. "You hate death magic. You'd latch on to any excuse for me to rid that part of myself." As the words leave my mouth, I wish I could take them back. Sylas bonded with me, inherited my magic, which I now claim he despises. But words, once sharpened, can only cut.

"Is that what you think of me?" He backs up toward the door, shaking his head. "That I am telling you all of this because I hate death magic? That I have some ulterior motive for you to destroy a part of yourself?"

I don't know what I think. My mind is a collection of broken memories and the sudden revelation that my life is a lie. He's telling me I was brought up by my parents' murderer, who sent my sister to her death and killed the mother of the man I love.

"Gods, Viola." He looks out to the skies, balling his fists.

My throat lumps with unspoken words. I am terrified that if I utter anything at all, I will unleash a river of rage. My head tells me that Sylas is telling the truth, but my sanity begs for a different story.

"Nan loved me." I am trying to convince myself. My insides are numb. A knife could cut through my heart right now, and I would feel nothing at all.

"Did she?" His eyes flinch. At the same time, Railesza and Raiku awaken. They both look back and forth between Sylas and me. "Is it out of love that she killed your father? Your mother? Then sent your sister to her death?"

I say nothing.

"Your grandmother reported the highest number of unregistered crossmages to DOTS in the history of Gorhail." He shifts his weight, and his aspiers won't even look at me anymore, not even Railesza. "Corvis are notorious purists. Why else would your mother, one of the deadliest mages to ever exist, give up her life to hide you?"

The reminder that I am the reason our world lost the Deathbringer slashes through my insides. If my existence is the cause of so much death and misery, then my choice is clear. The only thing I can do is to stop Grimm from regaining his full magic.

"My mother died protecting you." Something inexplicable flashes across his eyes. At first, I think it's anger, but it's the slow realization that this will always hang between us, keeping me at the mercy of his forgiveness.

"What do you want me to do, Sylas?" I bite, hoping it drives him away. The sooner this is done, the sooner I won't have to worry about his stopping me. "Apologize? For other people's choices?"

"Vi." He runs a hand across his face, blowing out a steadying breath. "Just give me your cuff, and let's put an end to this. Paltro—"

"That's what this is about?" I step back until my body presses against the concrete parapet surrounding the balcony. "Paltro hates me. He's probably made up a mountain of lies so you stay away from me. Why should I give you my cuff?" What I don't say is that I need the cuff to stop Grimm.

"If anything, do it for Lyria," he pleads. "She... the night before... she went to the library to figure out how to return your lifeblood."

My heart sinks. I would give up my life if I could return Lyria's mind.

"So you're using Lyria to manipulate me now?" As I speak the words, I want to throw up. I love Lyria like my own sister. "I'm not giving you my cuff, Sylas."

Sylas takes a step forward, then stops himself, his expression morphing from disappointment to anger. "Paltro was right. Mortemagi know nothing of loyalty." He shakes his head. "If you don't care enough to sacrifice one stupid relic, don't bother visiting my sister at St. Fabian's. In fact, don't bother seeing any of us again. I was wrong about you; in the end, you're just another corrupt Mortemagi."

"Grow up, Sylas," I force out, hoping my words push him further away. As his eyes flare at me in surprise, my insides fracture. "Life isn't black or white. Maybe if you stopped trying to fit everything that goes against your beliefs into a box, you'd not have so much blood on your hands."

I feel sick, but I need to be certain that he won't come for me.

Without acknowledging the poison I just spewed, Sylas takes one last look at me, turns, and walks back into Founder's Room with Scar still wrapped around his arm. I look out over the twisted beauty of this place, praying that crushing my own heart will be worth it.

"It's true, isn't it?" I climb the stairs of the Poisoned Stairwell without an aspier.

Ysenia is quiet for a short while. Then she sighs. *I'm sorry. I asked around. You need to understand her choices. I've known Grimm, Viola. I've seen all he can do. Rhea placed her duty toward the people first. Although, I don't agree with her actions—she could have explained the situation to the Deathbringer instead of murdering her and your father.*

Sylas was telling me the truth, and I made him believe he was selfish and threw his vulnerability in his face. I hope that someday he understands why I did what I did, even if he never forgives me for it. If I hadn't driven him away, he would've tried to stop me. Of course, none of it will change the ugly words spoken today.

Footsteps echo behind me.

Bloody saints, I wish Sylas had left me alone long enough for me to wallow in self-pity about losing the greatest love I've known, to grieve a life I could have had, to further bury the pain of Nan being a murderer. I'm not ready to talk things through, and I am certainly not ready for him to talk me out of stopping Grimm.

Viola, Ysenia screams.

I sidestep Delaney's hit by a second, nearly tripping on the stairs.

"Clever girl, foolish heart," Delaney says, regaining her footing. I don't wait for her to summon Gods-know-what, and I bolt. Ysenia guides me to the House of Death. Delaney won't risk being seen in public. By now, Paltro must have notified Firstline, and everyone must be looking for her.

I find the door to my hallway with ease. Damn the Gods, it's empty. I run across until I reach Circle Three. Empty. Where are all the students?

In the far corner, light filters out of Lorne's office. I jerk open the door and bless the Gods.

"Lorne," I scream. Never in my life could I have thought I'd be happy to see him. "Delaney . . . she . . . help me." I stumble into his arms, and he catches me effortlessly, pressing me against his chest.

"I will most certainly help you, darling."

Then everything goes black.

Announcement: Dispatch Firstline along all borders. No one leaves any province until we've apprehended Grimm and Aurelia Delaney. Kill poachers on sight. Lock up all crossmages—sealed or unsealed.

RODRIC PALTRO, NEWLY APPOINTED CHIEF OF FIRSTLINE

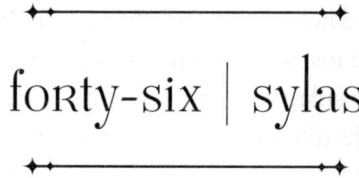

forty-six | sylas

SATURDAY, DECEMBER 11, 1939

The woman I love is the reason my mother was killed. *She didn't choose her fate*, I tell myself for the tenth time today. Of course she was in denial and lashed out at me. I broke the tapestry of her life and expected her to weave everything back together with the snap of my fingers.

I come to terms with a single truth: I am an idiot who could've handled things better.

"I cannot tell if you're sad about Lyria or sad that Viola isn't here yet," Beau whispers in a poor attempt at a joke as we stand outside of St. Fabian's Ward for Altered Minds, the white two-story building that looks like a coal factory with the sheer number of black uniforms going in and out to visit Lyria. So many people. Except Viola.

"Shut up," I tell Beau between clenched teeth. I haven't told him about the memories Paltro showed me yet, and I wish he would stop reminding me of what an asshole I am.

At the same time, Lorne walks out of the building. He notices us, sighs, then approaches us with slouched shoulders and sunken eyes, pausing a couple of steps away.

"Thank you for coming," Beau and I say at the same time, our tones clipped.

"Lyria doesn't deserve this." He shakes Beau's hand, then mine, holding the handshake a second too long. His gaze trails past us, landing on St. Fabian's brass name plaque. He blinks a couple of times, the beginning of a tear forming at his inner lid.

Beau and I exchange an uncomfortable glance. I cannot decide whether this is part of his usual theatrics; he's not known Lyria for long.

"I've recommended her for an honorary Magus Principalis promotion. I cannot believe we've lost such a brilliant mind."

Beau tenses at my side. We haven't *lost* her, but he's not the first to be talking about Lyria like she's dead—even Paltro commented on his disbelief that Lyria was *gone*.

"Thanks."

Lorne nods and walks down the steps toward his car. Perhaps he thought it was a nice gesture, but what's Lyria going to do with a promotion when she can't even function?

A moment later, Gryff steps out the front door, his Firstline uniform traded for a House shirt and black trousers. Whoever stands before us is a morose version of our friend, like he's the one who died instead of Lyria's mind. He rubs his eyes, the dark circles more apparent in the daylight. "Grayson says they're assigning her a private room, and they've commissioned some of DOTS's best readers to untangle her memories."

"It's the least they can do," I reply, considering that Lyria's mindtrap was irrefutable proof that Grimm has infiltrated Gorhail. News caught on like wildfire, and by the evening, even the Common Ministry of Draterra was aware and pressuring DOTS to come clean about the real reason behind the Gorhail murders.

"Come with me," Gryff says. Beau and I follow him inside the ward. It's as sterile as Riverview Prison, terrifyingly white. I hate it. Hate that my sister has to spend her days staring at white walls or out a window facing a frozen lake and dead trees. But we had no choice; our home in Iserine is too dangerous, and Gorhail is now a minefield of Firstline officers who are quick to throw any remotely suspicious mage in prison.

Grayson reassured us that he would personally oversee her treatment, and as our guardian, Paltro signed off on her admission because one of DOTS's readers deemed both Beau and me as too emotional to make rational decisions. He wasn't wrong. Beau has fought with two healers and three readers since yesterday. And between learning about my mother's killer and watching my sister's unblinking eyes, I cannot stop thinking about Viola. I called her a corrupt Mortemagi, when all she's ever done is prove that Mortemagi can be good. If she hadn't refused to hand over her stupid cuff, it wouldn't have gotten as ugly as this. She was angry; I'm certain she didn't mean her words. Maybe after we leave Riverview, I can apologize and convince her to surrender the Corvi cuff and get her own.

"I've resigned from Firstline," says Gryff, pulling me back to the present. My jaw falls open. Firstline has been his dream since we were five years old; it was his reason to live and breathe, much to my sister's chagrin.

"Someone's finally seeing reason . . ." Beau drawls, and I glare at him.

"Why?" I frown.

Gryff runs his fingers along the large glass window separating us from Lyria. "Without her, everything is worthless." He lowers his head. "I always thought I had more time."

I swallow a lump as I think about my sister's words: Tomorrow isn't promised.

"She's not dead, Gryff." I glance at Lyria, sitting in a wheelchair, hands in her lap, eyes empty, facing that stupid frozen lake. My chest hurts. Everyone's right; she might as well be dead. I chew on my lower lip. Without Lyria, life seems bleak, but Paltro's words hold my tears. I can't grieve now. Grimm mindtrapped Lyria because she was too close to the truth. I can't give in. She wouldn't want us to wallow; she would want us to find him . . . and she would want me to apologize to Viola.

"Sy." Beau pulls me aside. Mages have dwindled in number, a few still hovering around Lyria, setting books and cakes on her dresser. I don't know why they keep bringing her gifts. She cannot read, cannot speak, cannot eat other than what comes through these Arkani-made tubes in her arms.

"Viola wouldn't miss Lyria's first visiting day." Beau leans forward, looking past the crowd that just walked down the steps. Their presence makes the air stuffier. I know they come in support, but I wish they would leave and act like a five-century-old murderous mage is about to turn our world upside down.

"I told her not to come," I mutter.

"You . . . what?" Beau jerks away from me. "You barred her from visiting our sister? Our sister who lost her mind while trying to save her?"

I was wrong, but instead of admitting that, I lash out. "Rhea Corvi started this whole thing; if she hadn't killed Mom to find Viola because of her obsession with her untainted line, Willow wouldn't have released Grimm by trying to resurrect her. Rhea wouldn't have had to fragment Willow's soul into six relics, damning six families to Delaney's revenge. And Rhea wouldn't have had to murder the Deathbringer for Viola because she was the cuff's sole heir and needed to be hidden away. Your parents would still be alive . . . and so would everyone else."

Gryff's head snaps toward us, and Beau's eyes twitch; I shouldn't have told him in this way, but he deserves to know who caused his parents' deaths. Briar uncoils from around his forearm and rests her head on the back of his palm. Her eyes narrow at me, then lower to Scar, but the aspier looks away.

"Viola . . ." Beau takes in a sharp breath, his eyes drilling into me, his fists curling at his sides. "Thank Haal Lyria cannot watch your prejudice blind you yet again. You're blaming Viola for something entirely out of her control."

"That's not it." I exhale, releasing yesterday's frustrations. "When I told her to give me the cuff, she refused. Maybe you're blinded because she brought you back from the dead, but Mortemagi are all the same in the end; it's their magic over everyone else."

"You're a fucking idiot," Beau huffs out, stepping away from me. "You've no idea what she's prepared to give up for us."

What is he talking about? She made it clear. She chose her vicious grandmother over *me*. She chose her cuff over *me* . . . Haal, Beau is right. I *am* an idiot. It was never about her murderous lineage; I'm angry because I thought she'd trust me enough to believe me.

Sylas.

A soft breeze grazes against my skin, raising the hairs on my neck. We're inside St. Fabian's, and there are no open windows or doors around us. Dread coils in the pit of my stomach. I look around, but no one seems to have called my name. Haal . . . something is wrong.

Sylas, please. We don't have much time.

Ysenia's grave tone fills me with guilt when I should be moving. Beau and Gryff frown at me in question, and I gulp, my lungs drowning from the realization that Viola is in danger.

"Sy." Gryff hesitates. "Is everything—" I don't hear him over the deafening sound of my own heart. *Where is she*, I want to ask, but my lips don't move.

Hurry, Sylas. Delaney is holding her in the Eastern Greenhouse.

I don't wait for her to speak again—I bolt.

As I speed down the stairs, through the reception area, and out the door to my car, I pray to all six Gods that I make it in time. Because I'll never forgive myself for this. I let my prejudice consume me, and I may lose Viola because of it.

The rivers are quiet, the birds absent, and the snow slushed into low piles under the trees. The orange hues of the afternoon sun give way to the mesmerizing silver of the moon, not quite her time but still announcing her presence. My boots slosh in the melted snow, drawing the attention of a white owl, a rarity in Gorhail Woods. Maybe it's a sign that I'm getting closer to the Eastern Greenhouse.

"Scar, please find her." She drops to the ground, slithering ahead. A moment later, she stops, her golden eyes fixed on a narrow muddy path. She hisses once, twice, then starts moving at lightning speed. I follow her across two ponds, through an abandoned courtyard, past a thick stone pathway, through a small gazebo, and along paths I never knew existed before. I run past a wild doe, and she freezes. This part of Gorhail isn't even on our maps; no wonder my presence is confusing the wild animals.

Scar leads me farther east into the woods, closer to the border between Gorhail and Albion, to a cottage with a small greenhouse attached to the side. The low waterfall of Albion creek masks the sound of my footsteps. Scar pauses, hissing at Raiku and Railesza.

My aspiers listen. Then the three of them disperse toward the cottage, moving silently through fallen leaves and piles of snow.

Right in front of the main door, two poachers stand, lost in quiet conversation with each other. I squint, trying to make out their class of magic. One of them shifts, her pendant catching the porch light. An Arkani; this shouldn't be a hard kill, but the other one is still out of sight. If they have poachers guarding the door, there must be more around the perimeter and even inside.

I look around, and there are no trees to shroud me, nothing to hide behind. If I want to get close, I'll have to crawl to the back door, preferably somewhere the poachers don't notice me.

A deep sense of unease stirs through me. It tells me to turn around and run for help. But I'm already flat on the ground; I'm not leaving Viola alone again.

Crawling through the wet grass is colder than I anticipated. The poachers should've noticed me by now, but they're too busy talking about whether they'll be assigned positions when Grimm takes over. From their obnoxiously loud conversation, I gather one of them is a reader and the other a dustmaker. It makes no sense to have the two noncombative Arkani classes as guards.

I crouch onto the flaky wooden side steps of the cottage, right below a broken window, wiping grass and mud from my shirt and waiting for one of my aspiers to signal me to move forward. The poachers are now debating why Viola is still alive.

I huff, and they quiet.

Haal. I hold my breath, pressing my back to the wooden planks.

Footsteps clap against the wood, and my heart races. Killing them will be easy, but if I cause a commotion out here, Delaney might kill Viola before I can get to her.

"I don't feel so well," one of the poachers says.

"Here, sit on the steps," the other replies, and the wood creaks, then stops. A moment later, I hear a soft thump, a gasp, and another muted thump. Then Raiku slithers around the corner, his head held high. I nod at him, breathing out a sigh of relief.

Beau and Gryff are on the way, Ysenia says.

Once I'm certain the poachers are dead and there are no other guards around, I peer into the broken side window, looking for Scar and Railesza. But it's not my aspiers I see.

In the middle of the room, Viola is bound to a chair, her eyes heavy with defiance as she raises her head at . . . Lorne.

> For one century, Death asked every soul that crossed into the Underworld about the first Mortemagi. But no one knew her, as if she were erased from history.
>
> LUCIA KAN, *TALES FROM THE UNDERWORLD*, PASSAGE 8

forty-seven | viola

SATURDAY, DECEMBER 11, 1939

If I am to die young, let it be somewhere beautiful. Not in this filthy place that stinks like rotten wood and blood. I force my eyes open, and they shut immediately, blinded by the sun. Or perhaps it's a light. My throat is scratchy, my mouth feels like it's filled with sand, and my head is splitting in two.

"Darling Viola, finally awake..."

That voice. I would recognize that wicked, silvery voice anywhere.

Lorne.

Gods, I should have known. He was praising Grimm. What was I thinking?

"I don't need her alive. I don't know why you insist on letting her live," says another voice. Overseer Delaney. It has the same rasp, the same stress at the end of her words.

My eyes are fighting a battle to stay closed, but I push through. I want to look at Lorne when I tell him to eat a dead rat.

"You should've killed her like her sister," Delaney scoffs.

Lorne killed Olivia? Impossible. Delaney told me... she never told me *she* killed Olivia. I jerk my hands apart, but they lock against something rough behind my back. My stomach churns, threatening to spill over myself. If they kill me and take my cuff before we find Grimm and Ysenia takes over my body...

I bite my lips, forcing my mind to stop spiraling. And I do the only thing within my control. I breathe.

One. Two. There must be a misunderstanding. Lorne is overbearing, but he loved Olivia. He *has* to have loved Olivia. He was devastated at her funeral; no one pretends like that.

Three. Four. She wrote about him. She was in love with him. She was an excellent judge of character, and I have to trust her judgment. He wouldn't do that to her.

Five. Six. My eyes peel open, and the single, bright bulb in the middle of the room assaults me. I blink hard. Where am I?

There are desks, large stained glass windows that look hundreds of years old, torn curtains, broken chairs, a door in the back to the left behind Delaney and Lorne, stairs in the right corner, and another door to my right. It reeks of stale wood and decaying leaves, of old blood and tears.

How long have I been here? I try to gather my wits. If they bothered to shackle me instead of killing me, they must want something from me. Did Grimm tell them to hold me?

"Why not just kill me and end this?" My hoarse voice catches me off guard.

Lorne scoffs, shaking his head, and Delaney places *The Founder's Book of Relics* on the desk behind her. "Sweet child, ignorance is bliss. Rhea's relic is wasted on you. All that magic, all that *power*, in a foolish girl who wasted her lifeblood over what?"

"If you wanted the relic, why did you kill Olivia?" I already know the answer, but I need to stall until Ysenia comes back and Grimm appears.

Delaney's lips twitch, and her jaw clenches. She lifts her nose, nostrils flaring at my question. I've wounded her pride. She didn't know Olivia's relic was a fake until they killed her.

"It was an accident." Lorne steps in front of me, and I want to crawl into myself. "Olivia did slip on that boardwalk, and I don't know how to swim," he says coolly, as if Olivia's death was a minor, unfortunate event. "I liked your sister, Viola. Maybe I didn't love her, but I did like her. I was going to ask to borrow her cuff that night... alas..."

I want to punch Olivia's name out of his lips. He doesn't deserve the privilege of having known her, of having had a modicum of her love.

Lorne looks at me expectantly, and I nearly spit in his face, but I'm too weak for that, and retaliation might muddle my and Ysenia's plan. Sure, I wasn't planning on waking up shackled to a chair, but the idea was always for them to take me in as bait.

"I don't want the cuff." The words tumble out of my lips like the river of lies I'm preparing to unleash. Anything to buy me time. "I never wanted my magic—"

As I speak, I realize how much has changed. It started off that way, but knowing how many people died so I could exist, it would be a stain on their memory. Along with the heartbreak, this magic brought me friends; it brought me a home. And now, I have to leave them all behind: Beau, Lyria, Sylas, the aspiers.

Lorne cocks his head, a light frown pulling his eyebrows together. Gone is the overbearing Magister, reeking of desperation. Now, his moss-green eyes look at me with precision, as if he's searching my face for a long-lost answer. "Our hearing and sight of the dead are a gift. Our corpse control, a weapon. Centuries of magic cultivated in a single relic, the most powerful relic after the Founder's. And what do you make of it all?"

I press my lips together in defiance. Gods, give me the strength to punch him square in the mouth. Instead, I laugh. Nothing is funny, but I'm hoping my laughter is distracting enough to keep him from hearing the soft scrape of rope as I try to loosen my bindings.

He watches me with interest. "Do you, darling Viola, know the history of our people?" His voice is the same, but the inflection of his tone sounds ancient. "Do you think Gorhail is a sanctuary for us?"

No, of course not. If Gorhail had no trouble harboring scum like Lorne and Delaney, it doesn't care for *any* student, not just Mortemagi. Gorhail's sanctity has been desecrated since the moment it decided to heed DOTS guidelines and cover up the murders as regular poacher attacks.

"No!" he exclaims. I jump, and his voice lowers to a hiss. "No, it's a prison. Gorhail keeps us under control. It watches our every move. It uses *our* magic to further *its* purpose."

"Isn't that all institutions?" I need to keep him talking, long enough so I can work my wrists out of this binding.

"Yes!" he exclaims, his face lighting up with a sinister grin, as though I've just said something profound. "Grimm was the only one with the right idea, and look at what they did to him. We deserve the freedom to practice magic at will. We deserve both the good and the ugly. After all, it is how we learn."

"But you can't kill innocent people in the name of magical freedom." I hold his gaze as he approaches; it chokes me with doubt. DOTS cares about no one but its own ideologies. Despite all the stability it provides, DOTS sends people to their deaths with no remorse and an inflated sense of duty—poacher kill counts are barbaric. But Grimm is volatile; he kills on a whim. Even at its height, DOTS still folds to the law. Grimm, on the other hand, makes his own law.

"Magic has no master, my darling." He runs a long finger along the edge of my face, stopping at my chin. "If even the God of Death bowed away from the magic he bestowed upon us, what makes DOTS think it can control us?" He jerks my jaw up in one quick motion.

I bite my scream.

"It doesn't seek control . . ." I don't finish my thought, because even I know it does.

Lorne gives me a knowing look, and Delaney laughs under her breath.

"Do you know how much magic it takes to resurrect someone? How much expertise?" His voice drops to a thorny caress. He pulls back, stretching like a cat.

"A lot," I rasp, a faint copper tang filling my mouth. The inner lining of my throat is on fire. He doesn't know about Ysenia. He thinks I resurrected Victor and Beau by myself.

Lorne frowns, kissing his teeth. He glances at Delaney and sighs. "I haven't seen magic this raw in years, and you want to kill her?"

"I—" Delaney begins.

"Quiet." Lorne drags his stare back to me, and I swallow, flinching as my saliva scrapes against my throat. I wonder why Delaney listens to him, how he seems to be in control here. "Now tell me, Viola. How did you manage to stitch two bodies together with no training?"

"Victor and Lyria helped me through it," I say, my heart tearing through my throat. If he finds out that I'm anchored to a ghost—worse, that I'm anchored to one of the founders of Gorhail—who knows what he'll do?

"Yet it was your lifeblood they used, my darling." He reaches for my face again, brushing my hair away.

I wince.

The chill of his touch digs into my soul, freezing me in place. When our eyes meet, his flash with chagrin. I frown, taken aback by the emotion. He rubs his thumb over my left temple. "Your little friends' treachery cost you so much," he says. "The other Houses are always ready to bury us, yet they have no qualms using us when they want their dead back."

"They didn't trick me." The words come out on their own, but they're untrue. Victor did trick me. He had his reasons, but he didn't hesitate to sacrifice my life for his . . . and Beau's. In the end, Sylas was right; most people are driven by selfishness.

"You're extraordinary, Viola Corvi," he murmurs, studying my face for a pause. "It's a pity you chose the enemy."

"The enemy?" I scoff, snapping away from his touch. "No one but you is murdering people, Lorne."

"Darling . . ." He kneels in front of me, brings his fingers around my chin, and jerks it toward him so I have no choice but to look at him. "You remind me of a girl I once loved. A girl with hair as red as fire and eyes as black as coal. A Mortemagi who defied me to save the world, the same world who was ready to sacrifice her for my downfall. Do you know what it's like to watch your heart shatter against the cliffs?"

I gasp.

"A necessary sacrifice," he whines. "I mourn her to this day, the only woman I've ever loved and the only one I will ever love."

Ysenia.

Young Ysenia, who laments her death in the catacombs. Sweet Ysenia, who cannot move on to the Underworld because of him. Brilliant Ysenia, whose life was cut short because he saw her as a weakness.

Gods have mercy.

Lorne is Rafael Grimm.

"Grimm," I utter. A cold smile stretches across his lips, and I gulp. Rafael Grimm stands in front of me; he has been close to me the entire time I've been at Gorhail.

"I prefer Rafe, if you don't mind." He sighs, his face still so close to mine. "Grimm is so . . . grim."

"You could've killed me and taken the cuff so many times . . ." My throat thickens with the realization that I am only alive because he *wants* me alive, like a mouse he's toying with before he claws my guts open. *What does he want then?*

"At first, I was going to." He finally drops my face and walks away, his hands clasped behind his back. I don't wait, and my wrists are back at work trying to slip out of this stubborn rope. The sooner I'm free, the sooner we can take Faro's Cuff away from Grimm. Gods, this isn't a good time for Ysenia to have disappeared.

He stops a few steps away from Delaney, who stares at him with murder in her eyes.

"But then, you grew on me. I've tried to keep you out, Viola. Tried to stay away, but not anymore," he says, turning around again. My wrists stop moving. "I see your potential for greatness. You weave magic so skillfully. I've seen your work on Beau. The stitches are seamless; you practice like you've been doing this for centuries."

Ysenia's work. I remain silent.

"Oh, darling." Grimm's lips twist into an apologetic smile. "You and I—together, we could've started a new dawn for Mortemagi. But you had to ruin it all because of a stale serpent."

"You're lying." My head lolls, the weight of his admissions too heavy for me to bear. He waxes poetic, but his words are laced with poison. He killed Ysenia with a cold heart and no soul. If he didn't hesitate for one second to sacrifice the only woman he loved, what will he do to me? "You'll still kill me for the Corvi cuff."

Behind him, Delaney clasps her hands together. "I assure you, Rafe, that my Willow is a spectacular mage. Kill her, and let's proceed with the resurrection."

"Overseer," I try, desperate to create a wedge between them. "He cannot resurrect your daughter without killing you. I've read the missing pages of *The Founder's Book of Relics*. He's plotting something—"

"Enough." She looks at me in disgust. "You don't know Rafe like I do." Delaney bows her head to Grimm, as if she's apologizing for my accusation.

My wrists are almost free. "He will kill you. He will kill your daughter. The only one he seeks to resurrect is himself," I blurt, freeing my hands. Now all I need is Ysenia. Gods, where is she?

Delaney narrows her eyes at me, and I see it. The flash of doubt. She's questioning his motives. For a second, I wonder if I can convince her. If she refuses to go through with resurrecting her daughter, Grimm will remain trapped in Lorne's body, his magic limited to that of the poor mage—Lorne—he possessed.

"Instead of worrying about us, Miss Corvi," she scoffs, "worry about yourself. Where's your little Aspieri now?"

My Aspieri. The word is comical. Sylas isn't mine at all. He hates my magic; he hates that I wear a relic that killed his mother; he hates me enough to have let me walk straight to my death. Still, my heart stutters at the thought of him. Gods, please, keep him away from this circus of maniacs.

"He won't come." My eyes blur, and a single tear rolls down my cheek. I hope he doesn't come.

"Darling." Grimm smiles apologetically out of Lorne's face. "Take it from me. Love makes you weak. It takes away your defenses. If there's a single thing to learn before your inevitable death, it's that the House of Poison thinks of no one but their own."

Then, I feel it, cold at first, but the moment she coils around my wrist, she warms. The scales are familiar as they rub against my skin. Railesza slithers the length of my forearm and the moment her fangs sink into my vein, I catch a second wind.

"You're right." I cough. "Aspieri only care about their own."

"See, Aurelia," he drawls, without looking at her. "She's coming around. She has the makings of a Mortemagi as powerful as my Ysenia."

Keep her name out of your mouth, I want to shout, but I press my lips together and shake my head. "I'm not joining you, Grimm," I say quietly.

He tilts his head, holding my gaze for a moment. Then he presses his fingers together one by one. "If you aren't willing to join me, I am afraid, darling Viola, that we have a problem."

He opens his palm, the veins in his right forearm flexing, black against his pale skin. At his command, sharp, bony fingers emerge from the floor, chipping through the wooden floorboard. The bones press on the ground, and a dark skull pushes through, stretching its neck, and screeches like a newborn babe. As the undead rises, the unmistakable sharp scent of death assaults me.

I recoil.

Right when I think the undead is about to come for me, Grimm turns and walks over to the stairs in the right corner of the room, the skeletal figure following closely behind him.

The moment he's gone, I lurch out of the chair toward the door, but Delaney stops me with one arm and throws me back.

"Did you think we'd never find you?" she scoffs. "After your little trick with the fake cuff, I can't wait for him to kill you."

She whistles, and Mara emerges from the darkness below the stairs Lorne just took. Her face is a memory of what it once was; her skin is ashen gray, her eyes now bright blue, and her teeth serrated. She moves like a rabid animal, salivating at the sight of me.

"Take her to the greenhouse," she snaps at Mara. Then she turns on her heels.

If she's giving Mara verbal instructions, it means there's another puppeteer controlling her. Gods, it has to be, because this is the first time Mara's had blue eyes. Now that I think about it, the previous times her eyes were the green of Delaney's or the moss shade of Lorne's.

Mara—the other puppeteer—hesitates. My foolish heart thinks the puppeteer will have mercy on me, that they will save me. I don't break Mara's stare as she bends toward me, clinging to this futile hope that maybe she'll reconsider.

For a moment, I think she does. Her features relax, her head tilts, but the next second, a wicked grin stretches along her lips and her claws come out.

> Sylas, I dream of your mother often these days, as if she's trying to tell me something. Some might say I simply miss her, but I know our world far too well: my end is near.
>
> You are enough, son. You've always been enough.
>
> **LETTER FROM HANSEL ARCHYR TO SYLAS ARCHYR, JUNE 1939**

forty-eight | sylas

SATURDAY, DECEMBER 11, 1939

Mara's claws wrap around Viola's arms, and I move.

Ysenia pleads with me to wait for reinforcements. I consider it. Even with the Imortalis, two killer aspiers, and a healing aspier, I am no match for the sheer number of undead Delaney and Lorne can summon and the poachers they must have inside the cottage. But as I watch Mara drag Viola through a small door into the greenhouse, I know time is our enemy.

Damn waiting for help. If I wait, I lose her.

Delaney is upstairs, Ysenia says.

I hug the walls of the cottage, and Raiku and Scar join me, slithering ahead and making sure there are no poachers around—it is odd how few of them I've encountered. Are Delaney and Lorne so arrogant to think they don't need reinforcements?

My only solace is that Railesza is with Viola.

Lit by a string of lights running down the center, the white greenhouse is full of plants, dead and alive, crawling on the glass. I fiddle with the white metal hook, and it comes apart easily. I pause. All this feels ... almost too easy.

Still upstairs. They are arguing. The poacher controlling Mara is threatening Delaney. Get Viola and get out.

Where is Lorne? I want to ask, but Ysenia is right. I need to get to Viola.

The overgrown bushes make it hard for me to move forward, but my dagger cuts some of the vines, creating a path. In front of me, Viola sits on the first steps of a white metal staircase, her hands bound to the rails.

My heart leaps at the sight of her.

Sometime in third year, I read a fable about the God of Death kneeling before the other Gods, begging for mortality in exchange for the love of his life. I thought it to be foolish then, but now I understand it.

"How long do I have?"

Ysenia doesn't reply.

It doesn't matter anyway; I'm too far in now. And if anything happens, Raiku sits at the door between the cottage and the greenhouse, and Scar is perched on a branch above him. They will slow anyone down.

Viola's head jerks up at me, her eyes melting in relief. "You came?"

"This life and the next, Viola." I slash through the bindings around her wrist, annoyed that my dagger doesn't cut faster. "I am so, so sorry. I'm an idiot." I work her feet free and pull her up against me. My heart finally calms; it's finally home.

"Lorne—" she says.

"I know," I murmur, brushing her hair away, holding her face like it's the last time I'll ever see her. She looks at me with renewed hope, and in her eyes, I find my truth. I am so desperately in love with her.

"Your heart is my home, Viola. Without you, my soul has no anchor. I love you, and I will love you. I hope you'll forgive my outburst. I was so wrong..." I blurt out.

"Sylas..."

"Shh..." I snake my arms around her waist, tipping her closer to me. Then I kiss her, without thinking of the chaos moments away from swallowing us whole. She tastes like fire, like salt and wildberries. She tastes like hope, like the future I want to fight for.

"Can you walk?" I ask as I pull away.

The poacher dismembered Mara. Delaney killed the poacher. Hurry. You can reconcile later.

"Yes," Viola answers.

We don't have long before Delaney comes down, but the door is only a few steps away. The aspiers slither back, Raiku and Scar coiling around my arms. And Railesza lifts her eyes at me from Viola's arm. I nod at her to stay with Viola. She can heal her if anyone attacks.

We step out of the greenhouse and hurry across the clearing. All the while I glance at the cottage, at the silent windows that seem to mock me. The moment we cross into the woods, my shoulders tense. No poacher, no Delaney, and no Lorne—it's almost like they wanted me to find Viola, wanted to let her go...

"Sylas." Viola urges us forward. Once we blend into the tall trees, we'll have more chance of escape. Maybe letting us go was their plan all along, but at least now, Viola is with me, and I can keep her safe. Gryff and Beau are on the way, and I'm certain they've alerted Paltro.

As we're about to take a left to a path that'll lead us closer to Junction Bridge, a slow clap takes over the silence.

Viola's hand tightens in mine, and we turn around.

"I liked her drive, your sister." Lorne slowly peels away from the cottage, bringing his arms behind his back while walking toward us. Behind him, an undead trails. "She would've made a fine Mortemagi. Brilliant till the very end, how she connected the dots from my teachings to her research."

Why is he talking about Lyria?

Viola squeezes my hand, wrapping her other hand around my arm and pulling me backward. "Sy, don't fall into his trap."

"When she confronted me, I offered her the opportunity to join me." Lorne lets out a longer sigh. "Aspieri and their loyalty. Did you know, there isn't a single Aspieri within my army. She would've been the first. A pioneer."

I offered her the opportunity to join me... I don't hear Lorne's mumbling past that. I let go of Viola's hand, Raiku already primed to attack.

"Lorne mindtrapped Lyria," I say aloud as my mind catches up with the events of the last few days.

"Lorne is Grimm," Viola croaks. "I was trying to tell you—Sylas, don't be reckless. He has Faro's cuff. He's immortal."

"So am I." Scar slithers ahead as I march toward Lorne. If I have to die to kill him, I will.

"So easily provoked." Lorne—no, *Grimm*—tips his head back, laughing. "Killing is so messy, and I don't like to get my hands dirty."

Another undead emerges from the ground, spitting dirt as it rises, but

Raiku's already at its neck, fangs in the top of its spine. It crumples to dust in front of Grimm. His eyes flare, then he scoffs, raising three more. "I can do this all day."

"So can I." I close in on him, throwing the first punch.

Grimm is surprisingly nimble. He moves to the side and spins behind me. His lanky arm wraps around my throat, pulling me back. I slide my hand behind his arm and push forward, whirling to come face-to-face with him. The sneer he wears reeks of overconfidence, then twists into something evil.

He lunges for my neck. I kick him. Raiku bites his leg, and Scar wraps herself around his neck. None of it works. Grimm is relentless. He throws punch after punch to my jaw, my shoulder, my temple. Palming my pants for a dagger, I find it just before his fist reaches my eye.

I stab straight into his neck. He won't die, but the quick loss of blood will slow him down. He staggers, and I shove him to the ground, whirling around to check on Viola.

As I turn, Delaney walks up to her out of nowhere, grabbing her by the hair. Viola spins and pushes Delaney away, and the vile woman loses her grip on Vi's hair. It doesn't last long, because she closes her hands around Viola's arm and drags her forward.

This is why everything felt so easy. They planned this. They could have killed Viola at any point. That she is still alive means that Grimm is playing a different game.

Behind you.

I duck and roll away, in time to avoid an undead's claws from impaling my chest, and land in the dirt. Behind the skeleton, Grimm summons two more, and they crawl toward me, quicker than bones have any right to be.

"You remind me of your ancestor. Smug and stupid."

I ignore him, spinning my dagger, ready to tear into the skeletons, but these undead don't attack. I try to kick them away, but they are too fast: they grab my arms and hold them down, pinning me to the ground. I struggle against their grip, but it's like pushing against a rock.

Grimm steps over me, sharpening a golden blade against his cuff—Faro's Cuff. "Do you want to know how he died, Sylas? Your ancestor?"

I jerk my head away, try to pull myself up, but his minions of death are too strong. To my side, Raiku and Scar fight an incessant stream of undead that Grimm summoned; for every few they turn to dust, more keep emerging from the soil.

"Let me kill her." Delaney throws Viola to the ground, and I lurch forward suddenly, breaking free from the undeads' hold for a moment, only to be slapped back down by Grimm. "Her cuff is all we need." Delaney clutches a pack of relics to her chest.

"Do not touch her," Grimm snaps. "Not yet. I want Viola to watch." Grimm smiles as he brings the knife close to my neck. The cold of the blade brushes against my skin; I don't move. He lowers his head to my ear. "I will tell you how he died, Sylas. He was beheaded while his children watched, but Gorhail never taught you this, did they? He tried to drive Mortemagi to extinction, and he paid the price."

"That's not—" I stop.

Every mage knows the story, but I know it best because it's the story of my ancestor, Fia Ronin.

Poachers beheaded Sileas Ronin in his own home in front of his wife and children. They stabbed his oldest daughter, Fia, only seven at the time, and he passed the Imortalis to her to save her life, placing himself at the mercy of the poacher's blade. And when Raiek went to the girl, her mother threw herself onto the poachers to give her children enough time to run. But her younger brothers were too slow; they didn't even make it across the threshold of their house before Mortemagi poachers dismembered them. All in the name of Grimm.

He pulls away from my face, one hand gripping my collar and the other holding his golden dagger to my throat. "Hating us is in your blood. You can lie to yourself, Sylas, but she will always be a Mortemagi. Her veins will always pulse with her line's bloodshed."

My gaze trails to Viola, who fights against one of Grimm's undead. Grimm could kill me right now, and I would claw my way out of the Underworld for her. I would defy every one of the six Gods for her.

Our eyes meet, and I understand why our bonds are sacred. It's not even about love; it's about surrender.

I let out a dry laugh. "She's *my* Mortemagi, that's the diff—"

I *feel* the first slice of the blade.

"Stop," Viola screams, reaching for her cuff. "I'll give you the cuff. Just stop."

"Don't." I choke up, and Grimm's dagger halts, my warm blood clashing with the cold metal. If she gives them the cuff, they'll kill her. "Olivia died to protect you, and Lyria lost her mind trying to save you. I am immortal, Vi. Don't do this."

She reconsiders at my words. Tears stream down her cheeks, and she turns to Delaney again. "If Grimm cared about resurrecting Willow, why hasn't he killed me and taken the cuff? He's playing a game, Overseer, and you're just a pawn."

Viola is right. It's all been too easy, too convenient. He is playing a game, and he wants something more than Viola's cuff. Perhaps more than his own resurrection.

Delaney's eyes narrow at Grimm in suspicion, and she clutches the pack of relics even tighter.

"I have been nothing but loyal and true these last two years, Aurelia. I brought you the book, the only one in existence." His tone mellows, but his hold on me doesn't. "You know me, Aurelia. Everything I do is to protect our right to magic."

"Three pages are missing, Overseer." Viola scrambles backward, her head tilted at Delaney. "He's lying to you. The puppet he sent after Lyria . . . her last words were—"

Grimm drives his dagger straight through my heart. A flash of agony sears through my chest, into my very bones.

Viola shrieks.

"He won't die, darling, but I promise he will *feel* everything." He draws the blade out, and stabs again, and I wail as the metal twists into my flesh. It's torture. My breaths are shaky, and I try to steady them. Haal, I can survive this. My ancestor suffered a worse fate.

"What do you see in him?" Another stab, but this time the pain numbs itself.

Viola catches my gaze, and her eyes flick to the side. A flash of green slithers past me, then up my leg.

"He abandoned you," Grimm tries again. "He loathes our magic. He will never love you." He forces the words through gritted teeth, equal parts despair and frustration, like an unrequited lover begging for scraps.

Railesza's fangs sink into my thigh, relief washing over me.

"Grimm, your archaic mind games won't work." The waning pain emboldens my words. "Vi, I love you because of your magic, because of all the good you've done with it." My confession is a prayer to the six Gods, a plea to forgive my prejudice, a promise to change.

Viola's gaze shifts from Delaney to me, and she smiles, tears twinkling in her eyes.

"All my lives, Sylas," she says, before facing Delaney again. Why does this feel like goodbye?

"Only when the maiden and the crone die at the hands of the usurper will he be free," Viola recites. "The dead do not lie, Overseer. It's the single fundamental truth of death magic."

Grimm mutters a curse and shoves me backward. He stalks toward Delaney, but she clutches the pack of relics tighter and backtracks as fast as she can, her face warring between confusion and realization. Viola got through to her.

Our escape window narrows by the second. If we want to make it out, we have to move now.

Ready. I hear Ysenia, and Viola meets my gaze again with one last smile. This *is* goodbye. Whatever she's planning to do, I wish she wouldn't do it.

"Don't blame yourself," she mouths as I stagger to my feet.

"Ysenia," Viola shouts. "Now."

I struggle to keep up. Viola unclips and throws her cuff at Delaney, and she catches it and shoves it into her bag.

"What are you doing?" Grimm roars at Viola, his eyes darkening with fury.

With a single flick of his hand, two undeads emerge behind Delaney, closing in on her at rapid speed. She slows down, palms out, raising her own undead to fight his, and they succeed. But for every one she defeats, Grimm raises two more. I take a step forward to help her but immediately retract. Murderers don't deserve mercy.

"This is a lost battle, Aurelia. You'll deplete your lifeblood. Surrender," Grimm orders.

Delaney runs.

She only makes it three steps. She stumbles right as she's about to leave the clearing, at the edge of the forest not too far ahead, falling on all fours, the contents of her pack spilling out. All six relics that she brutally murdered mages for: Beau's Silver, Victor's laurel, Fable's pen, Wren's knife, Sierra's key, and Viola's cuff. It's ironic, how the relics she killed for are now her downfall. She screams in frustration and tries to reach for them, but Grimm steps on her hand.

Now's our chance. I move, reaching Viola in two strides. I tug on her arm, but she doesn't move. "Vi, let's go."

She stands still, palms open, her head facing straight ahead. I wait for her to snap out of her death magic like she always does, but it never comes. This can't be ghost paralysis; she's anchored to Ysenia.

"Viola." I step in front of her, reaching for her face. Haal, it's too late. I am too late. Her eyes are no longer the soft brown that sets my heart alight. They are pitch-black.

"Aurelia, dear Aurelia. What a disappointment." Grimm kisses his teeth, dragging my attention back to him and Delaney.

I wrap my hand around Viola's; hers is as cold as the magic that flowed through my veins the night we bonded. I don't have a clue what she and Ysenia are doing, but I'm not leaving her.

"Sacrifice is at the root of our magic." Grimm draws his golden blade.

Delaney holds her face up, prepared to meet death. She knows it's over. She stands no chance against a five-century-old mastermind. Then again, do any of us?

"Willow deserves peace. Don't let her die again," she begs as she looks at me. "Forgive m—"

In one fluid motion, Grimm slides the blade across Delaney's throat, and blood sprays over the relics in front of her. He doesn't waste any time, and his palms are up, black veins creeping along his forearm to his fingertips that ooze darkness toward the ground.

"Run, Sylas," Viola purrs, but it's not her voice. It's Ysenia's. It's so strange hearing it come out of Viola's mouth. "It's what she wanted."

"I'm not leaving her," I mutter, watching Grimm's eyes cloud over. His fingers splay out, and the relics hover in midair over Delaney's body. The ground undulates like angry waves right before a storm, threading mud over her still-bleeding corpse. Grimm closes his palms, and the relics drop with force, shoving the overseer deeper into the ground. He kneels, brings his fists together, and the ground swallows the relics and Delaney whole.

One moment, it's eerily quiet. The next, a gradual scream pierces through.

Grass clippings and clover leaves swirl low on the ground, and a young woman about our age materializes, translucent at first, then entirely human. She runs her hands through her short black hair, feels her arms, and pats down her body. When she lowers her head at Grimm, still kneeling in the mud, her catlike eyes flare in horror.

I remember her from the photograph in Paltro's office. Willow. Delaney's daughter.

Don't speak. Don't move. Trust Viola. I hope Viola knows what she's doing, because if Grimm kills Willow, he will break the tether and regain his full form.

Willow whirls around, and Grimm is on his feet. Before she can even take a step, he plunges his dagger into her back, pulling her into him. Her pupils widen, then her eyes tear up. She doesn't have to speak for me to understand the regret her tears carry.

All these deaths, senseless and in vain, because in the end, he's coming back. None of us could stop him, no matter how many died trying.

Grimm lowers his head in the crook of her neck, bringing his lips to her ear. "All these years, exiled in limbo . . . for nothing." He twists the blade, and Willow's eyes fade; her limp body drops at his feet. His shoulders cave in, like he's now letting out a two-decade-long sigh. He laughs to himself as he steps over her.

"It's always sad to lose one of our own. After all, you are *all* my children, some misguided, but still all mine. I bleed when you bleed. Rest now," he says in a prayer over Willow's body. How strange it is to see him mourning someone he's just ruthlessly killed. What kind of sick, twisted monster are we dealing with?

Slowly, he turns toward us. At first, I don't notice it, but slowly, Lorne's soft features morph into sharper, more dangerous lines.

At his feet, the ground pulses, dirt curling over his shoes, until it wraps around his ankles. At first, I think it's part of his transformation, but then the soil dissipates, and two skeletal hands grab at his legs, and behind him four more emerge from the ground.

Next to me, Viola's fingers ebb and flow with the movement of the skeletal hands. Grimm jerks his leg forward impatiently, but the undead root him in place. He whips his head in Viola's direction and seems to recognize something in those deep, inky eyes. "It's you . . ."

Grimm twists his right palm, and the undead fall to dust. He straightens himself up, canting his head toward Viola, a half smile grazing his lips. "You've always been too soft for this world, Ysenia."

As he speaks, his hair darkens from Lorne's blond to black, and the moss green of his eyes deepens to the green of the forest, and soon his features are nothing like Lorne's. They are strong, angular, exuding godhood. All three aspiers lock their eyes on him. What do they see that I don't?

"Overconfidence is a fool's favorite attribute, Rafael." Viola—Ysenia—laughs.

Grimm's smile fades. He tries to move, but dark tendrils of death emerge like whips from the dirt, snaking around his every limb, around his neck. A skeletal hand rips the sleeve of his shirt, clicks open his golden cuff—Faro's Cuff—and drags it straight back through the ground.

I sigh at the irony. Lorne was wearing Faro's Cuff all this time, and we never knew. And now, the cuff's rightful owner has claimed it back.

"No," Grimm roars, the tendrils dissipating into dust. He drops to his knees. "No." His hands feel the ground around him; his fingers claw at the dirt, upturning the soil only to find rocks and twigs.

Viola's knees buckle, and I wrap a hand around her waist, holding her against me as I lower us to the soft grass. Ysenia's possession must have depleted her energy.

"Vi." My thumb brushes over her cheek.

It's cold.

"Vi." Her eyes are sealed, her chest unmoving.

Panic catches in my throat as I lower my fingers to her neck. No pulse. No. Please, Gods. No.

Viola's mortality impales me. This isn't happening. She's not dead; she's survived worse than this. I've saved her before. I can do it again.

Railesza bites into vein after vein, so much so that Viola's arms are littered with fang marks. Venom takes time to work, I remind myself.

Soon after, Railesza pauses. It must be working; my aspier wouldn't just stop. But she lifts her head at me, holding my stare for a moment, and I realize that she's asking for permission . . . to stop.

I return a singular nod, and she stills, coiling herself at Viola's heart. Scar leaps off my arm, violently hissing at Railesza, but my healing aspier doesn't move.

A stillness settles around me. Gryff and Beau should've been here by now, but there's no one. Even Grimm has disappeared.

It's over.

I cradle Viola's head against my chest, my heart slamming against my rib cage. Brushing her hair away from her forehead, I linger on her face. She looks calm, content, and I want more than anything to disrupt her peace. She can't leave me here; she can't leave me alone. We've only just begun.

Without her, life has no meaning, no purpose.

We deserve more time.

Tears drop onto her cheeks, and for a moment I think they're hers... but they're mine. Her warmth is slowly dissipating, so I hold her closer to give her some of my own warmth. I shake my head. This cannot be the end. Maybe Briar and Railesza can try again. Maybe one of DOTS's healers can bring her back. Maybe Parrish can resurrect her. Maybe... Maybe...

As I catch my breath, a deep ache blooms within my chest. It gnaws at my heart, splitting it into pieces from within, and I know I'll never be whole again.

The love of my life is gone.

I bury my head against her hair, whispering a million apologies.

"I should never have left," I cry.

"I should never have left.

"I should never have left."

> **Attention:** Grand House
>
> Lyria Archyr's mind is fragmented in the same pattern as Elena Carver's. Authorization requested for an Arkani-Aspieri crossmage to consult on their cases. Treat with highest priority, as their memories may clue us in on Grimm's motivations.
>
> **GRAYSON DARRO, MAGUS PRINCIPALIS, PRINCIPAL READER, ST. FABIAN'S WARD FOR ALTERED MINDS**

forty-nine | viola

SATURDAY, DECEMBER 11, 1939

> **Attention**: Grayson Darro, M.P. Principal Reader,
> St. Fabian's Ward for Altered Minds
>
> Crossmages are in violation of Decree 15258.
>
> **Authorization**: Denied.
>
> Use of unregistered/underground crossmages will strip you of rank and position. Fines begin at 100,000 gold coins, and penalty is a maximum of five years in prison.
>
> **VIV ROWAN, THIRD GRAND MASTER OF ARCANE**

fifty | sylas

SATURDAY, DECEMBER 11, 1939

"Archyr, you're smothering me."

I think I'm dreaming, that I passed out from the heartbreak. Or better, that I'm dead, and this is the afterlife. Because there is no other reason Viola would be talking to me.

Lifting my head, I run my knuckles over her cheek. Her skin is so cold, covered in angry bruises. I must have heard her ghost speak—did she really just use her last words to tell me to let go of her?—because her eyes are still shut, her lips dry and still. I sigh, placing a kiss on her forehead.

When I pull back, Viola's eyelids peel open, and she draws in the sharpest breath. I blink at her in horror, thinking Grimm's risen her as a puppet.

Looking around, I realize we're alone. Is this a trick of the Gods?

Then I see it.

Around her neck sits the golden aspier. For the first time since he saved my life, Raiek opens his eyes.

> The days without you are long, the nights impossible.
> I made a mistake letting you go to a world where
> they hate you because of the magic I gave you.
>
> Come back. Come back, and the Underworld is yours.
>
> **LETTER FROM THE GOD OF DEATH TO YSENIA FARO,
> THE FIRST MORTEMAGI**

fifty-one | viola

SATURDAY, DECEMBER 11, 1939

Sylas holds my face between his rough hands, pressing his forehead against mine. I place my palm against his racing heart. Finally, his breathing steadies.

"Corvi, if you ever do that again, I will drag you back from the Underworld and kill you myself."

"I'd haunt you," I whisper.

He wraps me tighter in the safety of his arms, and my heart beats to the sound of his. *We're home,* it seems to say. And I agree. Sylas *is* my home.

"I should never have left you," he says softly, pulling back to look at me. "I'm sorry—"

"Sylas." I push away from him, my eyes narrowing at his bare neck. "Where is Raiek?"

His gaze flicks to my collarbone, but he doesn't answer me. I scramble to a sitting position, clutching my chest as I look down.

The Imortalis loops around my neck, his head resting at the start of my left shoulder, and his tail stopping at the top of my breastbone. His golden scales glow under the bright light of the full moon.

"Take him back," I utter.

Does Sylas even remember how to be mortal? He had had Raiek for only five months, but I doubt he'll shake the recklessness that the Imortalis brought him.

"Raiek is yours." He helps me up.

He can't possibly mean that. The Imortalis is his ancestor's aspier, and I . . . I stop my spiral. He saved me, like his mother saved his father, like his father saved him. He sacrificed his immortality for *me*.

"What happens if I take him off?" I ask.

When he doesn't reply, I step in front of him, lifting my head, forcing him to look at me. Gods, his face is a mess, temple bloody, cheekbone swollen, lips busted. His eyes darken, a frown worrying at his eyebrows as his eyes trail down the length of my body. Even after giving me the Imortalis, he's still making sure I'm okay. And Gods, I am in love with him.

I reach for his cheek, hesitating. He catches my hand, presses a kiss to my fingers, and whispers, "I don't want to find out."

"But—" I protest.

"Vi." He lowers my hand, his voice firmer than before. "With Raiek, you are invincible; his magic grants you unlimited lifeblood. And now that Grimm no longer has Faro's Cuff, we may have a chance against him."

His eyes search mine for hope, but I don't know what to give him. I hate this magic too much to cultivate it. I've always hated it. It cost me my parents, Olivia, and Lyria; and now it might cost me the man I love.

"The magic wasn't me," I say. "It was Ysenia." I look around. "Where's Grimm?"

As I speak his name, a tall man in his late twenties, with dark hair and eyes as deep as the forest surrounding us, walks toward us from the cottage. He looks at me, and I'm paralyzed. Death doesn't scare me as much as the man fiddling with a brass cuff as he stops a few feet away from us. It's neither mine nor Ysenia's, so he must've gotten it from one of the poachers in the cottage.

"I knew you were different, darling Viola." Grimm spreads his arms wide. "I've always known. Crossmages are, after all, the backbone of our world." His eyes fall to Raiek. "Do you know the things we could do together with the Imortalis?"

"The only thing we'll do together is ensure your death, Grimm," I reply. Without Faro's Cuff, he is no longer immortal. If we strike fast, he can die.

Before we can even order the aspiers, Scar slithers to the ground. Raiku uncoils but doesn't follow her. Instead, he narrows his eyes at Grimm, then hisses at Sylas.

Grimm curls his fingers, and a skeletal hand rises from the ground, grabbing Scar, pinning her in place. Raiku hisses but still doesn't move.

Grimm laughs. "I am a reader-whisperer, darling. Nothing you do will ever surprise me."

I scoff. He didn't see Ysenia coming—Lorne's magic was probably not strong enough—but I'm not about to antagonize him. Sylas is no longer immortal, and I don't have a cuff to use my death magic.

"A fool, after all." He flicks his wrist, and Scar flies across the clearing, past us, and lands against a tree. Then his eyes trail to Sylas, and a slow, sinister cackle trickles from his mouth. "When I left her for dead outside her room, I thought you'd give her the aspier then."

My throat bobs. *This* is why he didn't kill me. He never wanted me dead, because he *knew* Sylas would come for me. He *knew* he would save me with Raiek.

"Sylas, run." My words come out as cold as my insides.

"I'm not going anywhere, Vi." He laces his fingers through mine, his grip tight with apologies and promises. I glance at him, and he returns my gaze with conviction. Gods, I love him, but if he doesn't leave, he *will* die.

"Let me ask you, darling Viola," Grimm drawls, a sneer on his face. His calculating eyes shift from Sylas to me. A glint of victory flashes across his face. He reeks of arrogance. "Do you want to watch when he dies?"

I won't let him die.

Sylas's grip on my hand loosens, but I hold it in place; he's no longer immortal. I can't risk his being reckless right now. Scar slithers to my side, her golden eyes trained on Grimm. She hisses once, then buries herself into the ground, slithering ahead.

"Your bravery means nothing when you're untrained." Grimm raises his hand, his fingers manipulating invisible threads. "Swear loyalty to me, and I will teach you greatness."

"Magic has no master, Grimm." I repeat his own words. "It swears no loyalty." I take a step forward as Scar's head emerges an inch from his ankle.

"Stall," Sylas says, barely above a whisper. "Beau and Gryff should be here soon. Probably Firstline, too."

Grimm laughs, both his hands weaving an invisible thread now. I blink at Scar, and she strikes. He curses, reaching for her, but my aspier is fast; she slips through his grip, slithering toward the forest.

"Bold choice," he mutters through clenched teeth. "But not without consequence."

He waves his hand, and a single undead emerges in front of us. It lunges forward, and I throw myself in front of Sylas, shielding him with my body. The long, bony claws slice clean through my rib cage, the frozen graze of death searing my skin with ice. I wince, bracing myself for the agonizing pain I'm so familiar with, but it never comes. Instead, Sylas's arm is around my abdomen, Railesza half coiled around his forearm, her fangs in my veins.

"I can take it," I whisper. I'll take every hit, every claw of death if it means keeping him safe.

Behind me, Sylas lets out the faintest groan.

I turn around just in time for him to fall forward, my knees buckling under the weight of his body. I wrap an arm around him to lower him to the ground, resting his head on my lap. When I pull my hand away, it shakes, slick with warm, sticky blood. Sylas's blood.

"No," I say so quietly. "No . . . Sy . . ."

Railesza's fangs sink into the veins of his neck, her body gently coiled where Raiek used to be. Grimm is saying something, but I can't look away from Sylas's closed eyes, his waning breaths, on Railesza's fury as she switches veins. He's not dead; she will heal him like she's healed me so many times before.

"Please don't leave me." I hold his face, placing a gentle kiss to his lips, and his eyelids flicker, a strained moan escaping his mouth. His eyes open, and I stroke his hair, begging the Gods to spare him.

"I'll never leave you," he murmurs. "I love you." Then he fades again.

Death be my witness, I love this man through this life, through all my lives.

"Let him go, Viola," croons Grimm, and I lift my head up to face him. Across the clearing, he stands alone, hands clasped as he looks at us with glee.

Sylas coughs once, and I hold him closer. Blood is trickling down his jaw, and his breaths are now shallow, his lips turning blue. He cannot die. Railesza won't let him. *I* won't let him. Gods, take everything, but I beg you, don't take him from me.

"Your love for him is pathetic," Grimm mocks, his palms upturned at his sides.

"What do you even know about love, Grimm? When you sacrificed yours in pursuit of power that will never find you?" I say through gritted teeth. "Your name breeds fear across Draterra; you know nothing of love."

He shakes his head, a slow smile creeping across his wicked lips. "Love is a necessary sacrifice, darling Viola."

He closes his fingers, and three claws pierce through Sylas's chest from the ground.

I don't hear myself scream, but I am certain that I do.

Time moves so slowly, yet so fast. One of Grimm's undead drags me away from Sylas, slamming me against a tree a few feet back. The unmistakable sound of my bones breaking fills the air, but I drag myself forward, crawling toward Sylas.

Seconds later, a second undead grabs Railesza and, despite her struggles, cages her to the ground within its claws. Sylas *will* die without her healing. I fight back, kicking and reaching for him, but it's futile. The undead digs its claws into my ankles, nailing me to the ground. I howl in pain, tears stinging my eyes. Railesza's questioning gaze meets mine as she tries to slip out of the cage of bones, but we're trapped.

And Sylas is dying.

"Ysenia, promise you won't leave him alone," I plead, hoping she hears me even if I cannot hear her. I am a Mortemagi. Even if he dies, I will bring him back.

"Nauseating," Grimm scoffs. He lowers his arms, his fingers weaving anew. Dirt, grass, and rocks swirl around Sylas, and soft tendrils wrap around him.

Gods, Grimm is trying to turn him into a puppet.

"Stop," I scream, and he pauses, tilts his head at me.

I realize too late what he's doing.

Without breaking our stare his hands part, and in a single motion, the earth swallows Sylas whole. "You cannot resurrect what you cannot reach."

My mind is empty.

I want to scream, but my lungs give out. I feel like my heart will, too.

"He was but a distraction, darling Viola. Soon, you will learn. They will never accept you for who you are. Not the Aspieri, not the Mortemagi, not Gorhail, not DOTS, no one but me." Grimm clasps his hands together, and the undead pulls its claws out of my ankles, returning to the ground without resistance.

My body is numb, and I stare at the empty patch of dirt where Sylas was. He can't be gone. He can't . . . He was just here. It's impossible. Magic can't do this. Did he bury Sylas alive? Gods. I can't breathe, can't think.

"Darling," Grimm continues, the corner of his mouth pulling into a frightening smile. "They don't like what they cannot control, and *you* are now a weapon fueled by anger so deep it almost terrifies me. Almost." Then he laughs as he turns toward the woods, to the right of the cottage. "When you are ready, look for me in the darkest hour."

I watch him walk away, my heart blazing with rage. Right there, I make myself a promise. I will kill him, even if it kills me, even if it brings this entire world down.

As the trees swallow Grimm, poachers peel away from the barks one by one and follow him into the darkness, leaving me alone in the middle of the forest with two aspiers that aren't mine and one that hates me. A few seconds later, the stupid trees begin to hum again, a melancholic melody that I want to stifle.

My eyes sting, and my lungs strain with every breath.

Sylas is gone.

Railesza slowly approaches me. She coils around my arm and bites my wrist in silence. Soon after, Scar slithers back from the woods. She glances at me, then at Railesza. I extend my arm, and she carefully coils around, laying her head next to Railesza's.

I look up, expecting Raiku to come back any moment. But the grass doesn't move. I feel the ground around me, in case one of the undead buried him by accident. When I don't find him, I drag my body to where the earth is overturned, where Sylas lay only moments ago.

The soil is still wet with his blood; how can he be gone?

Dirt cakes under my fingernails as I dig and dig and dig. I dig until my tongue goes dry and my breath wanes. I dig until my fingers are raw and the world around me fades. I dig until the hole is deep enough to bury me completely.

Sylas died, and I never told him I loved him.

Hands reach out for me, but I shrug them off. I will stay in the grave until Death claims me, too.

"Vi." Beau's soft voice carries over to me.

I wish he hadn't come at all. Why is he here when Sylas is already dead? I want to turn around and yell at him. If only he'd followed Sylas here... if he hadn't been late... if... if... If I'm honest, I cannot face him with Sylas's blood imprinted on my palms.

"Stop," he whispers on a sob.

The warmth of his body grazes my skin when he sits next to me. I don't utter a word. I want him to go away; maybe if heartbreak won't take me, the cold will.

After a moment, he wraps me in a hug and pulls me to my feet. I push at him, but his hands hold steady, until I fall apart against his chest, wailing like a child.

"He's gone." I gasp between sobs.

"We . . . we don't know that," he says, stroking my hair as my tears spill uncontrollably. Behind him, a quiet shuffle of grass grows louder. I pull back.

A tall man with silver hair, about our age, takes a careful step toward us. He looks around, then asks, "Where's his body?"

I shake my head, unable to string words together. The man slips past Beau and me until he's in the middle of the clearing. He kneels and feels the soil. "This is our fault . . ."

"Don't," Beau warns. "Don't start. Guilt is a slippery slope, Gryff."

Gryff. How do I tell him his best friend was killed because of me, because he gave me this stupid relic when he was not even supposed to be here? Because, even in his last moments, Sylas put me first.

"We were too late . . ." Gryff's voice breaks. "We shouldn't have gone to alert Paltro."

"What happened, Vi?" Beau's tone softens as he gently pulls me out of the shallow grave. He searches my face for answers that I'm not ready to give. I wonder if he hears my heart breaking, if he hears my soul shattering with every gulp of air I force in.

As he eyes me expectantly, all I can think about is that only yesterday we were having tea together in their kitchen, and now Sylas will never drink tea again. But it's not even about tea. It's that Sylas and I ended before we could even begin.

"I never told him I loved him," I sob, and Beau wraps his arms around me again.

"He knew." Beau nods against my head, warm tears trickling onto my scalp. "He knew, Vi."

Gryff stifles a sob. We stand there for a few minutes, Beau's arms around me, Gryff unable to hold back tears, and me cursing every breath I take. The silence builds and builds until it cracks with a passing gust of wind.

I gently push away from Beau.

"I'm not letting you go until you can stand on your own." He loosens his grip on me, and I nod. "I'm... I'll be all right." I want to die, I should've said instead.

Pulling away, I wipe my eyes with the backs of my hands and steady myself with a deep breath.

"This isn't how I wanted to meet you." Gryff sighs at me, his lower lids red and heavy with grief. "Sylas loved..." He doesn't finish his thought.

Boots thump against the wet grass, and the three of us break apart, aspiers alert. But it's only Overseer Paltro. He rushes toward us, like a stray deer, his craggy face strained. When he notices me, his steps slow. His eyes fall on the golden aspier around my neck, then on Scar and Railesza coiled next to each other around my left forearm.

"Where is Sylas?" he barks.

We don't say a word, and suddenly I'm back in my kitchen, listening to the sheriff tell us that Olivia is dead. The same feeling weighs my tongue down; that maybe if we don't say it aloud, it means it isn't real.

"Miss Corvi, report to DOTS immediately for the murder of Sylas Archyr and the theft of three aspiers." He doesn't even look at me.

I'll gladly report to DOTS if they sentence me to immediate death and are somehow able to kill me with the Imortalis.

I move forward, but Gryff steps in front of me, and Beau places a protective arm around my shoulders.

"Uncle." Beau glares at Paltro. "Sylas is dead because no one took the reports of a potential Grimm copycat seriously. Gorhail, Firstline, and DOTS were busy burying the murders and blaming them on random poacher attacks. Until you took over days ago, they were still trying to convince everyone that a Grimm copycat was just propaganda. But we know now that Grimm himself is back, and *he* killed Sylas. You can't possibly be pinning the blame on Viola."

Paltro considers me for a moment, his round glasses low on his nose. Then his eyes fall on Raiek again, and his lips pull up in disdain. "Rules are rules, Beau, and as chief of Firstline, it is my duty to report her to DOTS."

"You can't—" Beau says, but Paltro interrupts him.

"Your blind loyalty should be to your House, not to a Mortemagi crossmage who killed your brother and sent your sister into an irreversible mindtrap," he spits.

Around Beau's arm, Briar stirs, her eyes locked on Paltro. Then Scar slithers up the length of my arm, glides over Raiek, and settles with her head next to my cheek. She hisses at Paltro, and he lifts his nose at her.

"What will you do, Chief? Throw her in prison to appease public unrest while the real murderer roams free?" Gryff shifts his weight, his cool blue aspier slithering around his neck. "Because that's what the administration does; it spends more resources on maintaining status quo than facing the truth of its failure to keep us safe."

"Perhaps she didn't kill Sylas, but that doesn't explain why she has two of his aspiers." Paltro lets go of his own aspier, and the serpent pauses at my boots before slithering to where Sylas died.

"They're bonded," Beau blurts out. Did Sylas tell him?

"One-way bonds hardly count," Paltro scoffs. "It won't stand in court."

"They're double bonded," Gryff adds. "We witnessed it: Beau, Lyria, and I. Our bonds are above the law—you know that. Our aspiers speak for us when we cannot, and the Imortalis has *chosen*, and it isn't within our right to question the first aspier."

Of course, they weren't there. They're lying... for me.

"I'm sure you and Beau won't have any trouble testifying under a reader's touch then." Paltro's nostrils flare, and he folds his arms behind his back. After a brief pause, he looks at Gryff. "Unsealed crossmages still face execution, Mr. Darro."

Gryff's arm tenses, but Beau reaches for his shoulder. At the same time, a figure rushes toward us. My tears cloud who it is. The closer she gets, the more clearly I can make out the crown braid that sits tight on her head. She shoves past Paltro, past Gryff and Beau, and takes me in her arms, and the moment she says my name, I crumble.

The air fills with the piercing sound of my own sobs. I don't stop. I can't. I don't want to be roped into the politics of DOTS. I just want Sylas back.

"Report to DOTS within the hour." Paltro turns around and begins walking, leaving us behind.

"Rodric," Priya calls after him. "Do not start an internal feud when Grimm walks free around the Ten Provinces."

"As far as I know, Priya," he replies, not bothering to stop, "Miss Corvi is an Aspieri-Mortemagi crossmage, last seen with my nephew. He is now dead, and she has two of his aspiers and the Deathbringer's aspier, none of which belong to her."

There's so much venom in his words. I want to tell him to take all of them. The aspiers, the magic, my life.

Sylas is gone, and there's nothing left for me.

> Sylas, I love you.
> I never told you.
> I love you. I love you. I love you.
>
> **LOST LETTER FROM VIOLA CORVI TO SYLAS ARCHYR**
> **(D. DECEMBER 11, 1939)**

fifty-two | viola

TWO WEEKS LATER
SATURDAY, DECEMBER 25, 1939

No matter how many times I flip the mattress, it feels like I'm lying on a bed of rocks. So I slide down to the cold, white marble floor, where I've slept for most of the last two weeks. The cell is depressingly white, down to the metal bars that lock me in. I'm surprised they were merciful enough to hold me somewhere with a tiny window and an in-room sink and latrine.

Paltro was relentless, filing charge after charge, channeling the anger and pain of Sylas's death through every new accusation he made that night. Hours after I stepped into the Grand House, I walked out, my clothes still soaked in Sylas's blood, straight into Riverview Prison for Highly Dangerous Individuals, where they handed me a blue jumpsuit that scratches against my skin like sandpaper. They can't execute me because of Raiek, so every mode of torture has become acceptable.

"Prisoner sixty-three," my new guard calls, and I rise to my feet. She stops in front of my cell, fiddles with one of the bars, and finally clicks open the lock. She's a manipulator Arkani who failed her Firstline assessment three times, I've learned since yesterday. She has a beautiful name,

Aria Lan. "You must be the most visited prisoner in the history of Riverview Prison. What are you in for?"

The familiarity of her tone gives me pause.

"Every offense in the rule book," I deadpan as I walk out, following her. She was assigned to me only two days ago, and she's the only one who doesn't handcuff my feet and hands while leading me to the visitor's room. She's also the only one who talks to me; the other guards shove me around instead of using words.

"We have a couple of minutes," she quips as we walk down the corridor between the full prison cells.

"One count of murder, one count of endangerment, three counts of theft, one count of stolen identity, and one count of existence, I suppose," I muse. "And whatever else the chief of Firstline feels like adding at the next hearing."

"Existence—" She chuckles.

"I was cursed to be born a crossmage." I cut her off, and she leaves me be.

When we walk past Victor's cell—four cells down from mine—I glance inside. He straightens, less surprised now than when he was the first few times our eyes met when I walked by. His mouth parts when he notices my new guard, then he nods at me and I nod back, a silent acknowledgment of our unfair predicaments while a mass murderer walks free, amassing an army of mages to take over Draterra. I understand his anger now. Maybe that's exactly what they deserve.

Officer Lan leads me down a flight of stairs, and we take a left turn, stopping at the third door on the right. Behind us, a cleaner dumps a bucket of soapy water on the floor and frantically gets to mopping. Riverview's obsession with upkeeping their white floors and walls is outlandish.

"I'll be out here when you're done." She unlocks the door, and I step in, taking a seat at the lone table in the middle of the room.

The other door opens, and Priya walks in, Gan in tow. Gan. My mother's mother. My grandmother. They visit every day without fail, sometimes with my grandfather, eyes full of hope, smiles filled with warmth, and food that keeps me sane.

Gan sits, lifting her rattan-woven lunch basket to the table. She pulls out a plate full of toast, freshly made jam, and clotted cream, then sets the basket on the floor. Yesterday, she held my hand and told me she was proud of me. I didn't even say thank you. I don't deserve their patience. I don't deserve their love.

Priya takes the empty seat next to her and slides the plate toward me. "Eat."

She doesn't have to tell me twice; the moment my tongue tastes the sweetness of the jam, tears fill my eyes. This is much better than the soggy grains and burned bread the prison serves us once a day.

"Beau and Gryff testified yesterday, so the theft charges have been dropped," Priya tells me.

If the charges have been dropped, they must have lied under a reader's touch. She lowers her head and adds, "Paltro is now accusing you of collusion with Grimm. Your hearing is at four in the afternoon tomorrow. He . . . he has poachers ready to testify against you, and you'll be sent to solitary again, this time in the Farbon Desert. It's brutal out there, and I won't be able to help."

The piece of toast slips through my fingers, and I gape at her. Paltro will really stop at nothing until he tortures me by every means possible; first was solitary, which Priya got me out of; then it was no food for three days, which was ridiculous; and now, it'll be whatever other horrible punishment they come up with.

Grimm's words play in my mind like a broken symphony: *They will never accept you for who you are.*

But I cannot give up, not until I rip out Grimm's heart with my bare hands so he can *feel* what he did to me when he killed Sylas.

"A whole world stretches between today and tomorrow, my dear." Gan smiles sweetly, her statement oiling the cogwheels in my head with quiet hope. "Death magic and poison magic are your birthright. No one can take that away from you."

She reaches for my free hand, Scar uncoiling around her forearm. My aspier nuzzles her head against the back of my hand, and I sigh, grateful that she was returned to her family and that Railesza was allowed to go to Beau, instead of them both rotting in a vault, waiting for my sentencing. It's been two weeks, and we still haven't found Raiku.

My skin pricks. Two beads of blood form at my wrist. I jerk my hand back, and in my haste, the plate clangs to the floor, shattering into pieces.

Priya doesn't waste time, and she's on the floor within seconds, picking up the broken porcelain. "Follow the voice," she whispers, placing her hand on my knee as she stares at me.

At the same time, the doors open, and three guards storm in—the woman from earlier and two others who've done night rounds before. "Visiting hour is over. PGM, you of all people know not to have contact with the prisoner."

"Take sixty-three back to her cell, Officer Lan," one of the guards barks at her.

Officer Lan grips my arm, dragging me through the door Priya and Gan came through. She hurries her steps down a long corridor, and I recognize it from the time we visited Victor.

"Vi," she says, looking over her shoulder. "I don't know what Parrish told you, but if we don't leave now, they'll send you to the Farbon Desert Solitary Prison for five years."

Parrish said to follow the voice. Did she mean... "Beau?" I ask, as he takes me through a second hallway. I knew something was off with the new guard's overt friendliness. I should've known for certain when Victor lingered on us earlier; he only looks at Beau that way.

"Took you long enough," he clips. "Don't ask. Illusions, and yes, Officer Lan gave her consent."

"Where are we going—"

"Out." He pushes through a wooden door, and we come face-to-face with the floor warden.

Beau's grip on me tightens, and he mutters a curse.

The man, at least six foot-five, looks down at us, his brows furrowed, his dark eyes dubious. "The cells are in the opposite direction," he drawls. Even if we were to make a run for it, he'd catch us in two strides.

I stand still, looking straight ahead.

Lan—Beau—gestures behind us. "Ground floor is covered in suds. I'm taking her through the other wing."

"Unshackled?" The warden's eyes fall to my loose hands, and Beau immediately pulls handcuffs from his pockets. He steps in front of me, and I lift my wrists. As he fastens the handcuffs, he leans in, and ever so silently says, "Fourth bar."

He pulls back and shoves me forward. "Warden, make yourself useful instead of standing here, questioning command. Take her back to her cell."

The warden grabs the back of my collar, dragging me forward. When I hear the door close behind us, I realize that my only chance at an escape is gone.

The lights go off for the night, and I sit against the wall, contemplating the last couple of months. I run a hand over Raiek's cool scales; only a few hours now until I walk to a fate worse than death.

The faint ray of moonlight trickles through the small window above the sink onto the bars of the cell. Something glimmers, and I press my eyes together. When I open them again, the glimmer is still there.

Pushing myself up, I tiptoe to the gate, softly running my hand along every bar until I reach the fourth one from the lock. My fingers catch on something cold. As I feel around, an open cuff slowly materializes.

My breath hitches.

I gingerly loop it free, walk backward, and slide down to the floor, my back facing the door in case a guard walks past. Turning the cuff over, I study the intricate details—roses, aspiers, a teacup, and honeyfig bread are hidden among the vines, and Scar's scales wrap around the borders.

My throat thickens. Someone had this made for me. As I turn over the cuff, I notice a faint engraving on the inside. *This life and the next*, it says, and I gasp.

Sylas.

My tears are hot against my cheeks, the repressed grief of the past two weeks bubbling over.

I unzip my jumpsuit, tug the left sleeve to the side, and bring the relic to my bare arm. Gan is right. Death magic and poison magic are my birthright, and with this cuff, Sylas will be in every strand of magic I weave.

The moment the relic clips around my arm, I feel . . . alive. Like a missing part of me has come together at last.

Finally, a sharp musical voice whispers, and my heart stops. I look around, holding on to a broken string of hope that Ysenia has returned. But it's not her. The voice chuckles. *Let me show you the way to the Underworld.*

THE END

> **HAVE YOU SEEN RAFAEL GRIMM?**
> DOTS offers 10 million coins for capture.
> **Note:** No recent photo is available. **Age:** 500+ years old.
> **Characteristics:** Highly dangerous, chameleon, manipulative, tall.
> *THE DAILY MAGE*, ISSUE 1939.334

epilogue | sylas

I always thought that I would have a poetic death, killed by the aspier supposed to grant me immortality. Or, perhaps, at the hands of Overseer Paltro for disobeying orders. But not as poetic as giving up my life to save Viola. Now I finally understand Raiek—he moves only for love. Mom to Dad, Dad to me, and me to Viola.

As I stand in the middle of a dome-shaped room, waiting for a short lady dressed in a bright pink suit to process my case, I lament my fate. How am I expected to sit in the Underworld without my only reason to exist?

The smell of burned roses wafts into my nostrils, and I sneeze. I approach the counter in the room, and the woman turns up her nose.

"Do you smell that?" she hisses. "*Someone* is trying to escape."

My face must betray my confusion, because she rolls her eyes. "The smell of burned roses is an alarm for when souls are trying to escape from the ten circles." She gestures toward the ten doors to my right. "Do they teach you nothing up there?"

Jumping off her chair, she opens every one of the ten black doors, slamming them shut one right after the other. Any harder and the brass plaques will fall off. Frowning, she spins and reaches for one of the two identical silver doors on the opposite side. "These," she explains without being prompted, "are where the Conduit Master ferries ghosts along the Underiver to the Underworld."

"Why am I here?" I follow her.

"You're right. You shouldn't be here; you should be on the other side, where Fenn processes ghosts." The short lady pauses at the second silver door, considering me with a long, exasperated sigh. "You arrived with your body, so we have to confirm your status with the Conduit Master."

"Is that common?"

She scrunches her nose. "Not as common as you think, but more common than we would like." She gestures to the domed space. "Otherwise, we wouldn't have a whole processing room dedicated to mishaps."

Yesterday, I was the wielder of the most powerful aspier in the world, and today I'm a mishap. "How long will the Conduit Master be?" I press. "I've been waiting a while."

The woman adjusts her glasses. "Could be five minutes, could be five centuries. Time isn't real in the Underworld."

She huffs out a breath and jerks open the silver door.

"The Conduit Master is dead," a young female voice says. I recognize her before she even walks through the door. Her fiery red hair cascades down her back in angry waves. Her eyes, black as the raven, find the lady in the pink suit. She smiles. "Lucia, you redecorated."

Lucia drops her jaw so quickly I worry it's permanently damaged. "You're back," she gasps. "You're back."

"Not for long, sweet Lucia." Ysenia takes her into her arms. "I'm only here to guide Sylas back. He was an anomaly, as you've noticed."

"My queen, you know the rules." Lucia takes her hand, her eyebrows knitting together. "No one leaves the Underworld unless they speak to Death himself."

"Just Ysenia," Ysenia corrects her. "We've known each other for so long, can't you make an exception? For me?"

She holds Lucia's hand, her eyes boring into the other woman's, waiting for an answer. I suddenly remember the fables we read at the academy, and I understand why Ysenia doesn't want to speak to the God of Death. If I had abandoned Death for centuries, I, too, would avoid him.

"Ysenia, only he decides the fates in the Underworld."

"Very well," Ysenia says, sucking in her cheeks. "Where is he?"

I clear my throat. "You don't have to—"

Ysenia's eyes zero in on me. Against the black walls, she looks like a raging flame threatening to ravage everything in her path. "My Mortemagi will die a premature death should you be forever stuck here."

Her Mortemagi. Did the fumes from the burned roses go to Ysenia's head? Because I'm certain Viola is *my* Mortemagi.

"Why are you here?" I ask, looking around. This feels too mundane for the Underworld. I don't know what I was expecting, burning gates or drowning skeletons... but definitely not a room that might as well have been one of DOTS's offices.

Her tone sharpens. "I had to come down here to babysit, at the request of *my* Mortemagi."

"She did not—" I retort.

Her eyes snap up at me, the unsettling black of her irises pinning my mouth shut. If the fables hold any truth, Ysenia wouldn't have come back to the Underworld if she didn't have a good reason.

"Ysenia." Lucia offers her an oval, red-stoned ring. "Death hasn't been seen in centuries. A century or so after you left, he locked himself away."

Could this explain why Mortemagi have grown more unhinged over the years? Abandoned by their God. Forced to navigate the world without guidance? Could this be how Grimm took over so easily?

Ysenia studies the ring in her palm, then closes her hand over it. She thanks Lucia and sets her jaw, taking in a sharp breath. She doesn't want to be here any more than I do.

"Here." Lucia guides Ysenia to a short hallway that leads to a small room tucked behind her tall counter.

"Come, Sylas." Ysenia beckons me over, and I follow behind.

Two mirrors hang on opposite walls of the short hallway, neither of them showing my reflection. I pause in horror, but then realize—of *course*—the dead don't have reflections.

Right ahead, Ysenia stands in front of an ornate red door. The closer I get, I notice that the paint moves like blood flowing through tiny veins. "Is this..."

"Blood? Yes," Lucia answers behind us. "The Underworld runs on the lifeblood mages sacrifice. You wouldn't know that, of course. Haal's subjects know nothing of sacrifice."

"*All* we know is sacrifice," I retort.

"Enough," Ysenia snaps. She runs her knuckles over a brass raven affixed to the right wall. It reminds me of the one outside the Corvi crypt in Riverview. She places the ring in a small, rounded dish underneath the raven's break, and the door opens.

She plucks the ring, considers it for a moment, then shoves it onto her ring finger. Lucia gasps, but she doesn't dare speak. I don't either.

"Death's residence is at the end of the Underworld. I don't know how long it will take, and you may be lost forever. But if we succeed, we'll convince Death to send you back up. Do you agree to these terms?" Ysenia drones.

No. I stare at her blankly. I cannot be lost forever. Now that I know I'm an anomaly, I have to find my way back to Viola. Not even Death will keep us apart.

"Let's go," she says. Has she lost her mind? I haven't agreed.

Before she takes the first step into this pit of darkness, Ysenia's gaze cuts to me, sharp and accusatory. "If anything happens to Viola while I'm gone, I will create a new circle of the Underworld and see to it that you relive your worst fears for eternity."

I gulp.

Watching Ysenia threaten *me* over Viola tells me all I need to know. If she loves Viola as fiercely as I do, we're going to get out of here.

"Lead the way."

As I prepare to potentially lose my soul to the depths of the Underworld, something stirs in my pocket.

For a moment, I think it's a trick of wicked ghosts I have yet to meet. I dig through, and a cool, scaled body wraps around my wrist. I pull my hand out, and Raiku winks at me.

"Do you love her?" Ysenia asks, without looking back.

"I died for her." Even if I had known this love would seal my coffin, I'd have fallen in love with her a thousand times over.

"Good." She takes the first step. "Because that's a lot of lives promised."

THE REAL END

Acknowledgments

If you'll allow me for a sentence or five, I'd like to begin by thanking me. This book was written in the stolen 5–10 minutes between dinner prep, in the pickup line, after bedtime until the wee hours of the morning. It taught me patience, resilience, and to let go of my crippling perfectionism. I am incredibly proud of myself for pushing through, and, dear reader, I hope that when the world says no, the biggest "yes" comes from yourself.

My deepest gratitude to Juliet Mushens, secret weapon, human treasure. Your steadfast belief in me and this book changed my life. Thank you for answering my 7 trillion questions, for solving all my problems with a single call, for all the reassurance when I feel like the world is on fire, for having my back in this roller coaster of an industry, and for the endless hilarious memes. My pen is so sure only because of your guidance, and for that I remain eternally grateful.

To my super team at Mushens Entertainment (Emma, Alba, Catriona), for your tireless work in getting this book to foreign markets, your kindness, and support. To my champion across the pond: Ginger Clark, for holding my hand through meetings, being incredibly kind, and always making sure my needs are met.

My dream team, my editors, Charlotte Trumble and Elizabeth Hitti. I've said from the start that I couldn't have thought of better people to work with on *Deathbringer* and I was right. This book is only as strong as it is thanks to your stellar vision and deep love of the world and the characters. Charlotte, your love and enthusiasm for this book from the very first call carried through every note you gave; the world is only as sharp as it is thanks to you. Elizabeth, I believe you finding this book was fate. You pull out emotion from scenes like a magician, and your love for this story makes it shine so much brighter. Thank you for always going along with my crazy what-ifs! To both, it's an absolute privilege to work with you and my forever appreciation for taking a chance on me.

My teams at Simon & Schuster UK: Katherine, who has been incredible on all fronts, Sarah, Solstice's marketing genius to whom I owe my eternal thanks for one of the best debut campaigns I've seen, and Atria Books: Nora Reichard, Annette Pagliaro Sweeney, Sierra Swanson, Aleaha Reneé, Vanessa Ioannidi, Lauren Castner, and Leora Bernstein, thank you endlessly for your continuous enthusiasm for *Deathbringer* and for all that you do behind the scenes. It means the world to me!

My cover designers: thank you to Kelli McAdams for giving me the dramatic and glamorous US cover of my dreams. Micaela Alcaino, to have your golden hands illustrate my jaw-dropping UK cover is a dream come true.

Saf, extraordinary human with a golden heart, would I even be an author without you? A paragraph in an acknowledgement section will never be enough to express my gratitude for all you are and all you do, but I'll try. Thank you for reading every single story I've ever put to paper and always cheering me on, for holding my hand and telling me to carry on every time I've wanted to stop. For yelling at me to query when I was terrified, for reminding me to never count myself out, for being the best soundboard, the best cheerleader, and for being the sister I've always wanted. I adore you, thank you.

My dearest husband, love of all my lives, where do I even begin? Thank you for believing in me when I don't believe in myself. For not batting an eye when I said I wanted to "give this writing thing a shot." For being my biggest role model and inspiration. For always keeping me on task. For handling drop-off, pickup, chores, and dinner just so I have extra hours to work. For grabbing my favorite pastries and making me the best coffee in the world every morning. For loving me through all the chaos. I love you. I don't know if any of this would've been possible without your tireless support.

And to my precious child, the light of my life, everything I do is for you. Your "have a good work" and the "of course you did it, Mum" keep me going ... I hope one day you look back and you're proud.

To Mama and Papa, my grandparents who raised me, I would be nothing without you. I am deeply grateful for your unconditional love and support, but especially for teaching me that nothing is unreachable. Thank you for the endless hours of childcare on weekends so I could squeeze in a few writing sessions. I'm so lucky to have you.

To Di, Dany, Vanya, and Dyan, for your endless love and support, all the jokes, all the laughter, and all the food adventures we've been on and have yet to go on. For always being here through the highs and the lows.

To my parents, for teaching me the value of education, for fostering my love of reading, and for the biggest gift of a debt-free uni education. To my brother, please let me steal some of your special editions.

To my ancestors, not a day goes by without me thinking about how brave you must have been to have left your home and started a new life in the middle of nowhere. I hope you look down with pride because we've only come so far thanks to your courage.

My best friend, Anusha—I don't know that I would've continued to write this story if you hadn't asked for more. You celebrate my wins louder than I do; and you ground me when publishing is wild. You and Avi have become family, and your love and encouragement mean the world to me. You still owe me lemon cake!

My dearest Christine and Michael (and Ethan and Reed), thank you always for being the best found family. Can't wait to eat around the world and have more girly drinks (lol!) again!

Thank you to Amélie and Francesca, for all the late-night pep talks, for all the industry insights, all the laughs, and for a friendship I hold very dear. I look forward to our retreats!

To Hannah Brohm, thank you for letting me barge into your DMs in full panic mode about plot points that refuse to make sense. Grateful that this journey brought us together.

Nabz, for your contagious joy in shouting about this book to everyone and for being such a ray of sunshine, thank you. Special mention to Salima, Cerise, and Heaven, who never fail to spread the word about *Deathbringer* on socials. My dearest Kenza, for always going along with my crazy ideas and bringing my characters to life. It's a privilege to work with you, and an honor to call you my friend.

The Creative Cottage, what an honor to be part of the most supportive writing community. My forever love to Kristin (for keeping me stocked on coffee from across the world), Mallory (can you believe this is a real book?), Carrie, Cassie, Cassy, Catherine, Chelsea, Elle, Elora, Erynne, Jess, Kayla D., Kayla H., Leslie, Molly, McKell, Naomi, Syn, and Val.

Bori and Mikayla, thank you for commiserating about publishing with me—our chats bring me so much joy! Bar, thank you for letting me blab endlessly about everything, for your friendship, and for loving this little book as much as you do! To Courtney, Suzanna, and Sydney, my first writing friends, I carry a piece of you through everything I write.

The *Deathbringer* Street Team—I am in awe of your creativity and brilliance. You have quickly become some of my favorite people. May we have a million more Mondays to complain about! Thank you for taking a chance on me and being so loud about the book! And also, for all the pet pictures!

To Anissa and the Fairyloot team, I will never cease to thank you for championing *Deathbringer*, bringing it to so many readers, and making my dreams of having my own FL edition come true.

To my friends and family, from Mauritius through England to North America, thank you, thank you, thank you for your love and support, always. To my dishwasher, my rice cooker, and my Instant Pot—you're the real MVPs of this writing journey!

To you, dear reader, thank you for giving this debut author a chance, it will forever mean the world to me.

Lastly, to Viola and Sylas, thank you for taking me on this wild journey.

About the Author

Sonia Tagliareni is a fantasy author who's always looking for the next best cup of tea. The first story she wrote was a murder mystery for French class at thirteen, and rumor has it the murderer outsmarted her but also left her with a deep love of storytelling. Born and raised in Mauritius, she moved to the United States in her late teens before deciding she prefers to hop around the world. If she's not glued to her laptop, you can find her dragging her husband and son to high tea. Visit SoniaTagliareni.com for more information.